# SNIPER'S KISS

SECURITIES INTERNATIONAL BOOK 1

E.M. SHUE

Cover Design by Anna Crosswell of Cover Couture
Editing by Nadine Winningham
Ebook Formatting by Vivian Freeman
www.authoremshue.com
P.O. Box
Chugiak, AK 99567

# DEDICATION

*To the man that taught me to sing You Are My Sunshine, to fish and helped me catch my first King Salmon, I love you. Thank you for teaching me a love of reading.*

*To the two men that didn't have to love me like they did but still chose too. I miss you every day and you taught me what true unconditional love was. Heaven received some truly magical angels when you left us.*

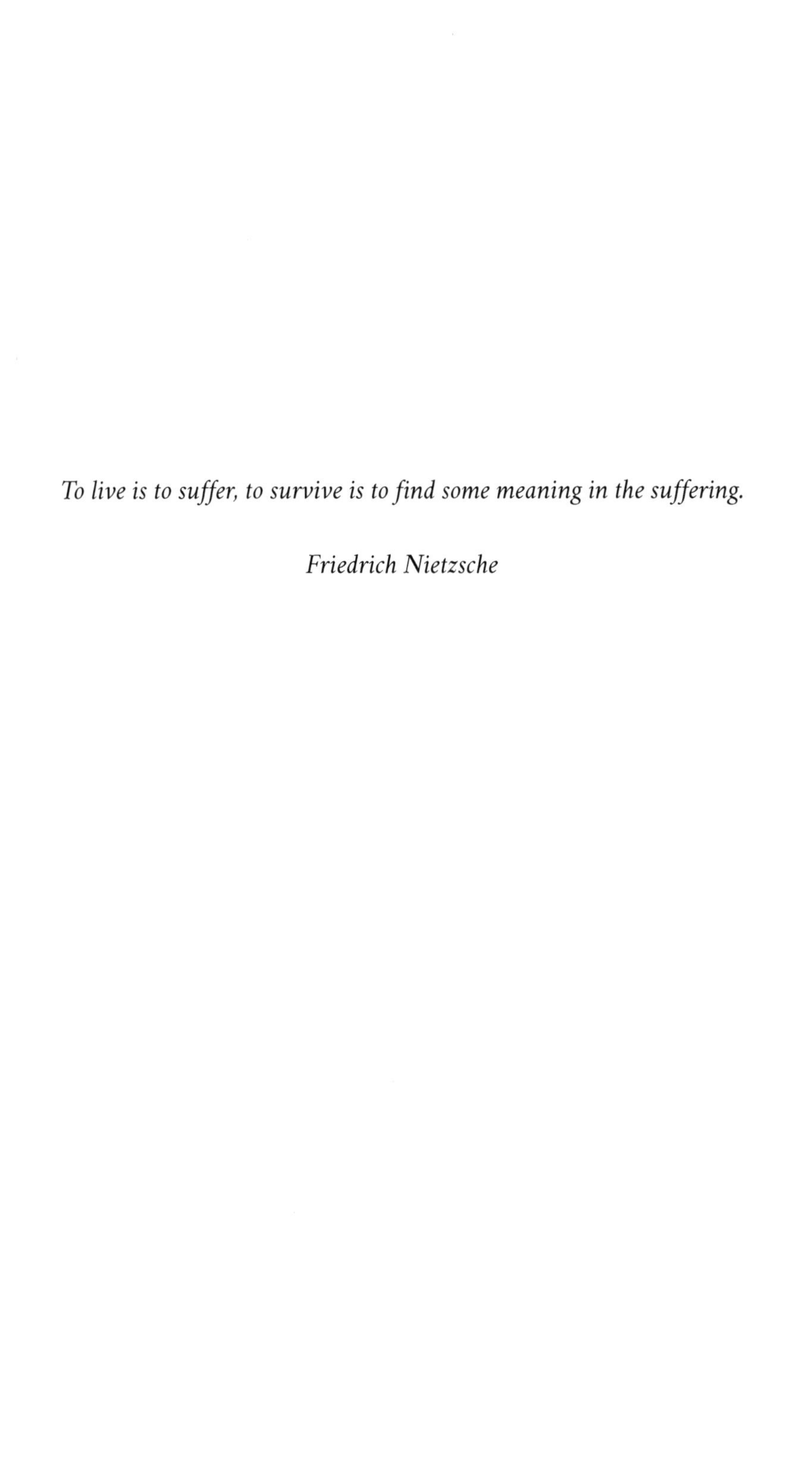

*To live is to suffer, to survive is to find some meaning in the suffering.*

*Friedrich Nietzsche*

# CHAPTER ONE

## MAYA

WASHINGTON, D.C.

"Entry teams are lined up. Team One is primary, you've got the front. Team Two, you're secondary, take the rear. No side doors. By the books, everyone, no showboating. Do you hear me, Sierra and Echo One? I will bench you both if there is a problem."

I listen as the captain continues to brief us. My hands start to sweat in my gloves as the anticipation builds. This was my first call with the Emergency Response Team; I've waited not only the last few grueling weeks for this, but since the day *they* left me. I need to get my head into the game. I calm my breathing, and press my gloved hand into my watch face pressed against the inside of my wrist.

My partner moves next to me and I look over at him. Only our eyes are visible through all our gear, but I see his hazel eyes focused on me, see his determination. I nod my head and sync my breathing with his. He and I have been a team for years now, mostly off the job, but he helps center me when I'm unfocused.

The squeal of tires draws the team's attention, some swinging around and taking aim. A large man jumps from an SUV, pushes past the barriers and right up to the captain. I attempt to ignore him and watch the building in the distance that all my focus needs to be on. I can barely make out the hostages through the glass windows. I turn to look at the monitor with a feed from a camera we hijacked from the bank across the street. I can see the hostages lined up preventing us from breaching or shooting. The hostage-taker is standing in the middle of the room, his gun flailing around.

The transport arrives to take us to where we will stage, and the four of us jog to it. Sierra and Echo, as the primaries, will be dropped at the first and closest location. Derek and I get the further but back up position. I jump onto the running board of the transport and grab the rail above my head, my body jerks as it takes off. The weight of my gun strapped to my back comforts me.

I brace for the stop, waiting as the brakes lock up. Team One jumps off and Sierra One leers at me.

"Hey, girly, don't puke on your first gig." His remark makes me want to punch him.

Derek's gloved hand hits my shoulder and I know what he's trying to say. The transport takes off again and stops about five hundred yards from where Team One was dropped. We jump off and run into the building, bypassing security and head for the stairwell.

"Let's go, sexy," Derek says as his long legs eat up the steps.

My five-seven, long-legged frame is used to running with gear, so I'm only a step or two behind him. My breathing is controlled and I push the adrenaline overload from earlier into keeping pace and maintaining control. We make the rooftop and push through the door, my sidearm in my hand while Derek has his M4 out. We clear the roof in a pie formation, each of us checking a quadrant. Then we make for the edge of the roof and start setting up.

"Team Two, are you set?" comes across the comm.

"This is Victor, Team Two, we are on the roof and setting up now," Derek informs the captain as I lie down prone to my rifle and start getting ready for the measurements necessary.

Through the airwaves, we can hear the captain talking to someone with a strong British accent, and I then remember the man that ran up as we were getting ready to leave.

"Okay, sexy, how about the Brit that's arguing with Captain?"

"Six hundred yards."

"Pick the next."

"Door to convention center, seven hundred yards. Transport, five hundred yards."

We continue with our data sheet for the shot and I know in my gut that I won't shoot from this distance. Oh hell, who am I kidding? If Carl has his way I'll never shoot. I wasn't supposed to make this team or become the secondary sniper. Derek and I have only been on the force for two years. We were personally asked to join the team, we didn't have to apply. It's not because I'm a woman and they had to fulfill some bureaucratic quota. It's because I'm that good. This is all I've ever wanted to do.

~

"ALL TEAMS, prepare. We will be going hot in fifteen."

I pull back from the scope and drop my head to the roof, my helmet and gear keeps me from smacking my face.

"Hey, Maya, you got this. Don't let the douche talk you out of it. You've always been a better shot than him." Derek's hand lands on my shoulder and I tense. "Calm down. Focus. Breathe. Accept." He recites the mantra and I lift my head to smile. Of course the balaclava and gear cover it but his eyes twinkle in return.

"Team One, what is your status?"

No answer comes and I know that they are doing their own thing again. Radio silence continues and I return to my scope. I line up with the building entrance and wait for the command. I've got this. I know I can shoot from this distance.

"This is Echo, Team One, we went offline for a moment and are now ready."

"You mean to tell me you can't even control your own teams! It's time to call in the real marksmen instead of the cowboys. I have an associate in there. Thank goodness I got the high value out of there," a deep voice comes across the captain's radio.

"Sir, I've asked you several times to step behind the line. My team has it..."

As the captain yells at the interloper, I watch through my scope as the hostage-taker emerges slouched behind a hostage. It's not a clear shot. At this distance I can't hear what is being said, but the gun is further pressed into the hostage's neck. The front entry team falls back to protect the hostage.

I focus through the scope and take a look at the hostage. He's about five-ten, with dark hair and an olive complexion. My gut twists and I see Abba in my eyes.

*Focus! Focus, Maya. This is why you do this.*

"No clean shot," Sierra says through the comms.

I look again.

"I have a shot but it will be close," I say on a choke. Clearing my throat, I try again. "Captain, I have a tight shot."

"Sierra, how about you?"

"Negative, sir. I don't know what she sees, but she's wrong. There is no clean shot."

That's twice he's identified me as a female over the comms, and everyone is silent, waiting for the hammer to drop.

"Sierra, Team One, please remember your radio protocols."

"Captain, Bravo has no shot!" he grits out.

I can hear his teeth clenching over the comms, and I wait and hope.

The hostage-taker hits the hostage in the side of the face with the gun. My vision blurs and I'm taken back. The anger, the pain, and the distance all swell. I will kill him.

"Captain, this is Victor, Team Two, Bravo has a shot," Derek says in frustration.

"Team One, disengage. Bravo, you are now Sierra, Team Two. Prepare."

"Yes, sir." I control my breathing. Three big breaths and I let it all out, then I squeeze the trigger and watch.

DUNCAN

I turn as I hear the order given and watch the hostage-taker's head explode in a fine pink mist of blood and brain matter.

"Who the bloody hell took that shot?" I yell at the captain.

"My sniper!"

That was an impossible shot for a military trained marksman. I don't know at what distance she was, but I do know it was a lass. When I pulled up earlier to offer my assistance, I saw the smaller person with the group but I never would have pegged her as a woman.

The ERT entry team clears the area and I watch as Raul walks out among the hostages and right up to me. The hostages are being checked over. Emergency personnel are treating the one that was held at gunpoint, his shoulder was nicked by the sniper's bullet.

After about twenty minutes the team's transport pulls up. They tried to push me back behind the barriers again but because of Raul I got to stay close by. I can't get close enough to the officers, so I watch from our SUV.

"Sierra and Echo, Team Two, head back to the precinct to give your reports, then you're off for the mandatory twenty-four hours. Bravo and Victor, Team One, reports and then my office. I want to know why you changed your position." The captain demands.

"Hey, Williams, drinks at Murphy's later? Bring Aaron." One of the team members asks the tall figure with the woman as they prepare to load up into another transport.

I want to see what she looks like. I want to ask her about the shot. Something keeps me fixated on her. She turns and I see her eyes instantly focus on me. My body tingles and I'm instantly hard. I know it's been a while, but I can't even see this woman's body.

"Hey, Aaron, awesome shot." Another team member thumps her on the back and her eyes soften behind the balaclava. "What was that, like seven hundred yards?"

"Something like that." Her voice is muffled.

I make the decision then and turn to find a cab, leaving the SUV for Raul.

"See you back at the hotel, Raul." I sprint off toward the perimeter, not waiting for his response.

~

AN HOUR and a half later I'm about to change my mind when the loud pipes of a Harley draws my attention to the parking lot as a sleek, black V-Rod motorcycle pulls up. The rider swings off the bike and I watch, my eyes bulging with each reveal.

She removes the white helmet with a candy skull on it, pulls her hair free from a band, and long auburn locks fall to mid-back. A shapely arse and long legs are encased in a type of Kevlar riding jeans with cowboy boots. She unzips the leather jacket and turns as I continue to watch. She's in a white t-shirt, her breasts begging to fill my hands. Her expressive forest-green eyes are fringed by a long bang and dark eye lashes. She has pale skin with freckles across her nose and no make-up covering her beauty.

She nods as she walks by me and I almost miss my chance.

"Excuse me, ma'am, can I talk to you about the shot you took tonight?" I ask, not thinking about how it sounds.

Her back stiffens and she steps back on her right foot. Her stance tells me she's trained.

"I'm sorry. I work for a security company that was at the gala tonight. One of my men was in the convention center. I saw the shot you took. It was amazing. Can I buy you a drink?"

"Someone died and a man was hurt, so, no, it wasn't that amazing. Now, excuse me." She pushes past me with a huff and I grab her arm. The electric shock of touching her almost has me pulling back but I want to feel more of her.

"Please. One drink?"

"Let her go. Now! She isn't interested and never will be." A deep voice says from behind me. I turn to see a cheeky bastard walking up. He is in all leather gear too, so he must have been riding. He is shorter than me and I know I could take him, but I drop her arm and step back. I look over to see another motorcycle parked next to hers.

"I was just asking the lass if she would like a drink."

"Take off, she doesn't drink with anyone." He pushes past her into me.

"Look, tosser, I didn't know she was spoken for." I step back and he closes the distance again. She reaches out and grabs his arm, pulling him back.

"I'm not spoken for, now stop, both of you." Her voice rises slightly.

"I apologize, have a good evening," I tilt my head to her and smell the jasmine and vanilla scent of her. Stepping back, I watch as his arm goes around her shoulder. I hail a cab and wish I met her first as she's clearly taken.

As the cab pulls away, I watch her with the guy. They talk and she ends up jumping on her motorcycle and leaving without going into the bar. Her motorcycle sails past, weaving in and out of traffic. I want to follow her but know that would make matters worse. I don't want to be with just anyone. I want to finally find my one. I want to know that person is worth it. I want to settle down. Something about her sets my blood on fire. I discreetly adjust myself as I think of her under me, or us on that bike.

MAYA

I slide my bike in-between traffic, passing the cab he got in. I want to turn and get a look into those eyes again. My body still feels like I touched a live wire. I can't do this. I speed off, slipping into my parking garage with a deep sigh.

Home. My sanctuary.

As I ride the elevator up to my penthouse condo, I lean back against the back wall, the evening rolling through my head.

Carl is no longer Sierra. I am now. That means I'm the primary sniper for the team. I will still be Team Two, but by the end of summer, I will be Team One Sierra. This is a huge step for me. The smile on my face falls when I think of my encounter with Carl after I showered.

Carl yelled at me for taking the shot, and his position. He said it was my fault he was suspended. I found out from Derek that he was actually suspended for leaving his original location for a spot with less visual. The second spot didn't take into account if the hostage-taker stepped out of the building just as he had.

Carl and I used to date back in college and I never wanted to compete against him because I knew he wouldn't be able to handle me being a better shot than him. He's a male chauvinist who believes women shouldn't be cops. My luck landed us in the same department and then on the same team. D.C. was my home before my life went to hell, and he knew that. Maybe he knew I would come back here and was hoping to get back together. So not happening.

My superiors knew how good I was. With all my extra training, they just wanted to keep me with Metro PD instead of jumping over to Secret Service like I was thinking. I do every extra training at Quantico that I can.

The elevator pings, letting me know I've reached my floor, and I step out and walk to my door. Habit has me checking all the shadowy areas and confirming I'm alone before I put in my code to enter my space. I grab the remote for the blinds and open the shades. The view of D.C. at night are the only lights I need for my mood.

I'm restless tonight; my whole body is on fire. I grab the remote from the counter as I pass and click on the sound system. Skillet's *Monster* blares through the speakers. I quickly change and then jump onto my treadmill. I run while staring out the windows, looking down at the city that used to mean so much to me. When they were alive this was home. Now it is where I work and just exist.

Out of nowhere I see turquoise blue eyes, dark hair, and a five o'clock shadow I want rubbed over my body. When I pulled up to the bar tonight I didn't see him. But now? Wow! My body sparks again, my breathing increases and not from the running. The song switches to Nickelback's *S.E.X* and I think about climbing that hunk of man like a fucking tree and holding on while I take a ride. Oh shit, I need to get laid soon. A complete stranger has me hot. I run harder, trying to ignore the release my body really wants.

I know I've been running for a while when another set of eyes flashes through my mind. My step falters and I almost eat it right there. I grit my teeth through the pain. The hostage's dark Mediterranean look reminded me of him, but younger. He looked so much like my father, my Abba; I knew he was from the Israeli consulate.

My hands start to tremor just like they did when I held my gun. I can't let this get to me. I jump off the treadmill and walk over to my punching bag. In place of dining room furniture, I've set up a work out room. I pull on my gloves and start beating the bag as the one song I need starts pulsing through the speakers. I hit the bag harder, seeing the bomber I have imagined for years staring back at me right before he takes them from me. I swing my leg in a roundhouse and grab the bag as I throw my knees into the bag. I want to kill him even though I know he is already dead. The song continues and I start yelling to it as I continue to take my pain out on the bag. Marilyn Manson's *Beautiful People has been my trigger for years. It is the* song I let go to. It comes to an end and I drop my gloved hands to my knees, struggling to regain my breath.

My chest heaves and now that I've reached my limit, maybe I can sleep. I head for the shower and let the water sluice off my body onto the floor. I try to think of anything but the man's face. My head drops and again I'm back there. My father was a demanding man. He wanted me to be different. Better. I learned multiple languages before I was in junior high. I studied Krav Maga and Israeli knife fighting. I might look like my mother with my paler complexion, auburn hair, and green eyes, but I was an Israeli killing machine because of him. I was Abba's little Jewish fighter. He wanted a boy, but he got me instead. If they had lived, would he be disappointed that I didn't become a lawyer?

I feel the burning in my throat and nose, and pull my head up and shut off the water. I step out of the shower, quickly dry my body, and head for the nightstand in my bedroom. Jerking the drawer open, I throw things all over the floor, and reach for the bottle of sleeping pills. I hate taking them but there is no way I'm going to sleep tonight. I pop the pills and lie down.

My last thoughts as the numbness fills my body is of dark hair and turquoise eyes. Why do those eyes look so familiar?

# CHAPTER TWO

## MAYA

*Welcome to the Jungle* from Guns and Roses blares from my phone and startles me awake. I don't even say hello as I slide my finger across the screen.

"Get up and meet me downstairs in twenty minutes."

"No!"

"If you are not on the curb in twenty minutes I'll come up there and drag your naked ass out of bed. Dress nice for brunch. I don't feel like arguing, sweetheart, but I will if you insist."

I sigh as he hangs up and I roll from my bed. Greg has been the parent I've lacked for years. I look at my cell phone and don't remember bringing it to bed with me last night. I shake the thought from my head and start to get ready.

Greg helped pick me up when I wanted to give up. He's treated me like a daughter and will even scold me like I'm his child. I smile at some of the memories. He's helped me get into several of my specialized training classes for sharp shooters. He didn't want me to become a police officer, but to work with Secret Service instead.

Twenty minutes later I enter the lobby and glancing at the doorman, I cringe—he isn't my favorite employee here.

"George, send those to the hospital," I grit through my teeth when I see the delivery on the counter. Every year he and I go through this.

"Ma'am, they're so beautiful. Every year you turn them down. I know I'm only supposed to catalog them and send to the hospital, but I thought this year you might want to keep them."

"I tell you every year, get rid of them, now."

"Yes, ma'am. And you have another delivery," he stutters.

I swing around and grab the large manila envelope from his hands and rip it open. It's a stack of photographs. The first picture makes my blood stop. It's of Derek and me outside the bar last night, talking to that man. A bull's-eye is drawn over Derek's face. My hands start to tremor and I turn to the next picture. *Oh God, no!* It's of me in my ERT gear. My breathing increases, and I can feel a panic attack coming. The fear and terror. I can't stop it. The need to run is overwhelming. I'm just about to act on that last thought when the photos are ripped from my hands.

"What the hell, Maya, why are you touching these?" Greg's voice pulls me from my shocked state. He turns and starts railing at the doorman as Derek pulls me into his arms. I melt into him and wish I was strong enough to pull away and leave him. *Can I protect him with my own body? Can I make my fucked-up-ness spare him?*

"You have been told many times that Ms. Aaron isn't to have any direct deliveries. All her items are to be noted and sent to me, unless it's flowers." Greg flips through the pictures, each worse than the previous. Me in uniform, me running on my treadmill, me on my bike, in my truck, talking to the stranger last night, and finally me in my bed sleeping, the sheet barely covering my nakedness.

I cringe into Derek and his arms tighten. Greg is on the phone, calling his contact with the FBI Behavioral Analysis Unit.

Welcome to my life. Every June I get flowers I hate, but this, this is different. This person is angry with me. The last picture, the one of me in bed has a message. *Maybe you will never wake up. Look how easy it is to get to you.* I bury my face into Derek's chest tighter and wait for the panic to start again. It doesn't come this time, instead a slow burn starts in my blood. I pull away and straighten my deep brown, silk tank and dark wine slacks.

I'm done. I put up with this stalker in college and changed my life, not again.

"Come here, darling," Greg says as he pulls me into his arms. "I'll make this right. We will get him. This time Derek will move in."

"No." I pull away and take a big cleansing breath. "No, this time I live my life."

"Now you listen here, darling, I'm not going to jeopardize your safety. I knew exposing you to the ERT could put you back in his sights. It's bad enough that we don't know who has been sending you flowers for years but now to have this one back." He shakes the photos in my face.

"I'm going to brunch," I turn and step outside. I stand on the sidewalk and look for Greg's car but instead see Derek's black Charger.

"Maya, Dad is just worried about you. Let me move in so I can protect you better," Derek says as he opens the back door for me to slip in.

I cringe. I love Derek like a brother. Without him, I wouldn't be here now. But I love my privacy. I like my independence. Plus, if Derek knew how much I struggled with sleeping again he would be calling our friend up north.

I know that my life is crazy. How this happened to me is beyond me. I was a normal seventeen-year-old girl until my parents were killed. Then my life went to hell. I live with the fear that whoever killed them will come after me. That whoever sends me flowers will one day want to meet me. I get the same bouquet every year, every day of June. Thirty days of the same flowers. I had hoped that when yesterday came and went without one I was good, but I guess I was wrong. I was just too busy and distracted to notice.

Now the pictures. This is the work of another. The handwriting, the manner, and the anger are all different.

~

AFTER BRUNCH we head to meet with Greg's friend, SSA Jones, at the Mall. They like to meet out in the open around the National Mall because we are trying to keep this from my superiors at the department. We are down by the Lincoln Memorial. I'm about to ignore the conversation that will interrupt my life when one of the pictures catches my eye. *Wait a minute.* I turn my head and look at the picture from a different angle. *Could it be? Son of a bitch.*

"Greg, hand me those."

I take the photographs from him and set them on the hood of the vehicle. I lay them out in the order I know they go. Me in my truck on the way home from my last class, in my uniform preparing to head to the convention center, me on my bike after the shooting, talking to the stranger before Derek shows up, Derek and the stranger arguing, me running on my treadmill last night, and finally me in my bed passed out.

"Shit!" Derek exclaims as he turns to stomp over to the sidewalk that leads to the Lincoln Memorial. Guess he saw it too.

"All of these were taken yesterday."

"Are you sure?" Jones asks and I nod. "Well that changes everything. Maya, I will have to look at these in comparison to the writing from last time. Any idea how he got into your apartment? What is your schedule like right now?" He fires off his questions in a flurry and I cringe.

"Derek and I are off today and can go back on shift as early as tomorrow if they clear my shot as justified. I forgot to set my alarm last night."

"What?" Greg and Jones yell at me.

"I was distracted." I know it is no excuse.

"She will be staying with me or Derek will be moving in, Tom. Don't worry, she won't be alone any longer."

"I already told you no, Greg. You might think you're my father but you don't control me. I'm going to London in two weeks and I will continue to live my life. My Way!" I yell the last as I storm off after Derek.

"If this gets any worse, I'm moving in. I can't lose you too, Maya." Derek sighs when I walk up.

"I know."

"Why is he back? I thought we convinced him to leave you alone the last time."

"I don't know. I thought I would just have to deal with the flower sender for the rest of my life. Now the angry one is back. Last time he sent me notes, pictures, and threatened me until you moved in. I don't think he is going away as easily this time."

"Maya, who is this man?" Greg asks as he walks up, and I look at the man in the picture.

"Just a guy asking me for a drink."

"He asked her about the shot," Derek clarifies.

"Have you seen him before?"

I look closely and again I'm struck with déjà vu. I know I've seen him somewhere else. "No, other than last night, I've never met him."

# CHAPTER THREE

## MAYA

It's been two weeks of slashed tires, red paint on my door, and more pictures. I've changed my alarm codes and so far have kept Derek from moving in and my work from finding out. Jones has brought in a couple of his team members to help.

I need this break to London so bad. I need to get away from all the craziness. It's been four years since I've been back. I returned every summer after my parents died for a couple of years, then life happened. My hell followed me here and I couldn't do that to the ones I love. I will never put another person in danger if I can prevent it.

Now I'm here for my best friend's wedding. I can't wait to see Ana and her dad, my other father figure. We've been best friends since we were both seventeen, turns out our parents grew up together. Ana and I met in Tel Aviv at a party at the museum. My mom was shocked when she saw who I was talking to. Ana's father, James, and my mom had drifted apart during the years. Ana was with me when my parents died. Lately I've been worried about her. I don't know her fiancé. We barely talk on the phone or Skype anymore.

Clearing international security, I hear someone shout my name.

"Maya!" Ana yells again as she launches herself at me; she seems thinner than I remember.

"I can't believe you're getting married, woman! Ana, I've missed you so much." I hug her and her shoulders shake as she starts to cry. What the hell?

She rarely cries. Out of the two of us, Ana is the emotional one, but still, this is crazy. Must be the stress of the wedding.

I hold her a little tighter and her short, five-foot frame clings to me.

"Calm down, sis," I tell her.

I look over her shoulder and my body tightens. I grab her arm and pull her behind my back fast. The stranger from a couple weeks ago grins at me. What the hell is he doing here?

"Are you following me?" I say as I prepare to hand him his nuts through his throat.

"You two know each other?" Ana claps and starts bouncing on her toes.

I flick my head back to look at her but keep my focus on him. He reaches out and takes my hand. Flipping it, he bends to kiss it, keeping his eyes on me the whole time. I'm in shock and can't hit him. *Ana knows him.* His chuckle pulls me from my thoughts.

"Duncan Preston, and you must be Maya Aaron," he says as his lips skim the back of my hand, sending tingles up my arm.

"You're Duncan?" My jaw drops and I now realize why he looked so familiar. In the years that I visited London we never met, the timing was always off. His father still has never explained why our parents stopped visiting each other.

"When did you meet Duncan? I know you two have never met in all these years, but how?" Ana asks in a piercing girly shriek. Yep, she is a girly girl.

"We actually didn't meet. She was on the team that helped at the convention center a couple weeks ago. I asked her for drinks, but her boyfriend declined," Duncan explains as he drops my hand and goes to grab my messenger bag. I shake my head and turn to Ana.

"You have a boyfriend? Since when? I thought you wouldn't have another after that Carl arsehole?"

"No. I don't have a boyfriend. It was Derek."

She nods in understanding and we begin to walk toward the parking garage. I take the time to really look at him. He has starred in many of my fantasies since I saw him last, all six-foot-eight of him. I forgot how big he was. His large muscles strain against his black jacket and slacks. I turn my head and try to pay attention to Ana going on and on about catering and flowers, but not before he turns and catches me checking out his ass. He just smirks at me. After a few minutes I turn to look at him again. His close-cropped dark hair and five o'clock shadow make him off the charts hot. He has a chiseled jaw and prominent cheekbones. His hands are so large. The old saying about hands makes me smile. *Oh God, did I just think that about my best friend's brother?*

We make our way out to the parking garage and the heat has me pulling off my lightweight leather jacket. I'm still wearing a black blazer beneath with a white t-shirt and jeans. My necklace can be seen and I know that Ana won't say anything about it. I only wear a few bits of jewelry—this locket with my parents' wedding rings, a ring that was my grandmother's on my middle finger, and my father's watch. Today I'm also wearing a necklace that Greg got me for Christmas last year, it's long and hangs to my belly but I know that I look decent enough for Ana. Ana is wearing a pale pink skirt suit with a white blouse. The jacket is long enough to cover her hips. She looks sophisticated and demure.

"I can't believe you couldn't get here sooner. You're supposed to be my maid of honor. You know...relieve my stress? The rehearsal is this evening." Ana is talking away, but I'm not paying attention again.

I shake myself and look at her. Time to pretend her brother doesn't affect me. A slow grin slides across his features. He knows I was checking him out again. Damn!

"I'll make it up to you. Let's go to our pub tonight and get trashed like old times."

"I can't do that. Jonathon won't allow it. Besides we've got the rehearsal and dinner tonight."

"What the hell, who cares! You aren't married to him yet."

This is why I don't care for Jonathon. He treats her like a child and doesn't let her do things. She doesn't call me anymore. We never Skype and worst of all, I know that this is his style she is wearing not hers.

"I agree with Maya. You need to let your hair down and go out," Duncan pipes in.

"No, I can't. Thank you anyway, but no. Besides, Maya, I don't go to that pub anymore."

"What pub?"

"One in Surrey we liked to go to. The bartender knew our favorite drinks and even kept a bottle of mine set aside for me. He was a hoot," I laugh.

"Surrey? My friend Joshua is from there. We can all go together. Come on, Sis. Think of this as your hen party."

"Her what?" I ask confused

"Hen party, I believe you call it a bachelorette party." Duncan smiles at me.

His smile causes me to take a deep breath, and I feel like I'm his complete focus. I shake it off and turn back to Ana.

"No, I'll not say it again. I can't...won't go. Jonathon will be upset if I go." Ana's breaths are coming fast and she starts to hyperventilate.

I know the signs of a panic attack and I'm wondering what else is going on to cause this. Wedding planning is stressful, but not like this. Well at least I don't think it is. Ana starts to shake and I don't know what to do to stop this for her. What the hell is going on with my best friend?

"Okay, Ana, don't worry. We don't have to go."

She calms instantly, her shoulders relaxing. I pat her on the back and try to figure out a way to distract her.

"So tell me about the best man. Am I going to need to use the Jaws of Life to keep him off me?" I smile at her. I know all about panic attacks and how to avoid them or deter them.

"Stephan is okay. I really don't know a whole lot about him. We've only met a few times. He works with Jonathon. The few functions I've seen him at he has been with different girls."

"So you're saying I get to hang out with a player?" I joke.

She grimaces. "No, I'd never say that. I just don't know him well," she defends.

"I was just kidding, Ana girl."

Duncan watches his sister with a critical eye during the whole exchange. His head is cocked to the side and he raises an eyebrow. I can see he's concerned too.

We stop next to a black Range Rover when Ana turns to me. "Duncan borrowed a friend's automobile because his little car wouldn't hold all of us. Hope you don't mind?"

"No, it's okay."

I reach for the back door to open it and Duncan whips his head around to give me a fierce look. I step back and wait for him to open my door as he helps Ana into her seat.

Once I'm settled into the car I lean forward to talk to Ana some more.

"So, Ana, are we heading to the dress shop now?" I had to trust her with picking my dress.

"Yes, you'll love the dress Jonathon picked for you." She turns to me, bouncing in her seat.

She almost seems too happy, I hate that my job makes me second-guess people.

"He picked my dress?" My eyebrows fly up.

"Yes, he's very hands-on in planning this wedding. What're you wearing tonight for the rehearsal?"

I know a topic change when I hear one.

"I have a dress, don't worry." I pat my messenger bag.

"Okay? Is it appropriate? Do we need to have the hotel press it?" Her skeptical look of my bag has me gritting my teeth.

"Ha-ha, you're so hilarious. No, it doesn't need to be pressed. It's appropriate, you'll approve. I rolled it."

When we were teenagers she was appalled that I just stuffed my clothes in my suitcase. She promptly taught me to roll my clothes to save room and less wrinkles.

~

LONDON HASN'T CHANGED at all. It's still bustling with life and one of my favorite cities. I love the mix of cultures that reside here with the historical styles. If things had been different I'd have settled here.

My mind wanders back to the last time I was in London. Even though it's been four years, I remember it like it was yesterday. It was the first time my flower stalker sent me a different bouquet then he normally did. It was also the day I realized it wasn't just flowers, it was a relationship.

I was at James and Ana's home when the delivery came. James never allowed me to stay anywhere but their home. He said his wife and my parents would be rolling in their graves if I stayed somewhere else, I was family. I'd already been getting my June deliveries, but I thought they were innocent. This delivery was the first time I had to explain them, and I was scared. James kept asking me why someone would send me a dozen black roses with a single red rose. This was the first time I'd received black roses, my other deliveries were a different arrangement. I explained that I was arguing with my then boyfriend, Carl. I of course found out later he didn't send them.

However, it was the note that arrived at my apartment after my London trip that made me decide not to come back. It was a plain typewritten note, simply saying if I were smart I wouldn't include James and Ana in our affair. I had no clue who would do that. That's when Greg got involved.

I'd known Derek for a year by then and we had become fast friends. With Greg's job at the Secret Service he knew the right people to call, and he contacted a friend at the FBI. My life has never been the same. My life went to hell when my parents died, but it got fucked up when my stalker decided I was his.

Derek and Greg didn't want me to come on this trip, but I wasn't going to let this asshole interfere with my life...again. I couldn't miss

Ana's day. My phone pinging in my pocket from an incoming message interrupts my thoughts.

I pull it out to see a text message from an unknown number.

*You can never get away from me. I know where you are.*

I forward the text to Greg and Derek.

*Greg: I told you this was a bad idea.*

*Me: I'll be fine, Mom, now stop.*

*Derek: Want me to jump on the next flight?*

*Me: No, I'm fine. We are heading to the dress shop now. Love you.*

"Everything okay?" Duncan asks as he watches me through the rearview mirror.

I smile sweetly, hoping to distract him.

"Just my partner making sure I made it safely."

"How is Derek doing?" Ana asks, oblivious to the tension.

"He's good. By the way we made ERT." Hopefully if I act nonchalant she won't panic.

"What is that?"

"It's similar to a SWAT team. I've already been upgraded to primary."

Her head whips around and her eyes are big.

"You're what? Have you told Daddy?"

"No, but I will later."

Thank goodness Duncan pulling up to the dress shop interrupts our conversation.

"Uhh, Ana, you know I'm not a girly girl. This is not the kind of place I shop," I say as I look at the posh boutique. I only own a few dresses, mostly for work or the infrequent date.

"It's okay, Maya. We will hop in quick, try on your dress, and see if any final alterations need to be made. Then we can head to the hotel. Don't worry you won't catch anything." She chuckles.

"Okay, let's get this over with before I break out in hives."

Duncan laughs from the driver seat. His laugh is full and makes my pulse race.

"Are you coming in?" Ana asks him when he calms.

"Do I look like a lass to you, Sis? Besides I need to call Joshua, he just texted me about an upcoming job."

He gets out and walks around to open both our doors and help us out.

~

As we walk into the boutique I instantly feel under dressed. Guess skinny jeans, no matter how you dress them up, aren't stylish enough for this shop. I hate when people judge without knowing. I know I could buy this shop and close it down without putting a dent in my bank account.

The clerk's eyebrows and lips pucker up. Nope, she isn't blowing kisses, she finds me unacceptable.

"Hello, Ms. Preston, how are you today?" Her sugary sweet tone doesn't hide her disdain of me.

"I'm doing well. This is my maid of honor, she finally made it here. I need to have her try on the dress and see if we need any alterations done before tomorrow."

"Yes, ma'am." The clerk turns back to me and does another head to toe inspection. "We have everything for you, Ms. Aaron, please follow me. Ms. Preston, have a seat. It will only take a moment."

The clerk leads me to the dressing room where she unzips a bag already hanging from the hook. She turns to me and stands there staring at me.

"Excuse me!"

"Take off your jacket so I can help you dress," she replies in a snotty tone.

"Get out, I can do this myself." Yep, I'm pissed off.

"The foundation for your dress is there on the chair, and your shoes are in the box, just stick your head out if you need help."

She walks out and leaves me there.

What the hell is a foundation? I see the bustier sitting on the chair, *oh foundation*. I get dressed but am unable to zip it up so I step out with the back undone. The clerk huffs and slips behind me to zip me in before I step up onto the pedestal. The dress is floor length, straight style with lace and tulle in blush. I hate it and know that Ana didn't pick this out for me.

"Oh the A-line style looks pretty on you, Maya. I was hoping the back was high enough to cover your tattoo because Jonathon didn't want it to show." Ana starts gushing as the clerk comes out of the dressing room with the box of shoes. The shoes are a satin, matching the dress with a bow on the toe. Ugly.

"What is an A-line?"

"It's that style. Don't you love it? Jonathon picked a beauty."

"Sure." I want to gag and claw at all the lace on the bodice and sleeves. "Okay I will go take it off now."

I turn to head back into the dressing room.

"No, ma'am, our seamstress needs to confirm if any alterations are needed. I don't see that we need to hem it with as tall as you are in those shoes."

These heels aren't even as high as the ones I'm wearing tonight.

"I can wear flats if you want, Ana."

"No, Jonathon had a plan, and your shoes are fine. I will look tiny next to you."

"It's your wedding, too. I will wear whatever you want me to."

"Ma'am, I agree with Ms. Preston, you look stunning in the heels."

*Damn clerk, go away.*

As the clerk walks off to get the seamstress I look at the dress and watch my best friend in the mirrors. How did she change so much in a few years? How did her style get so controlled? I miss the mini-skirts and leggings, the slacks with five-inch heels, the baby doll dresses and the boots. Where is my Ana? I miss her.

"Ana, did you really let Jonathon pick out my dress?"

"Of course."

"Why?"

"I want what Jonathon wants." She doesn't raise her head to look at me, instead she is looking at her phone. She huffs and pushes her phone back into her designer handbag.

"What's up, Ana?" I ask as she drops her head again and her shoulders curve in.

"Jonathon's meeting is going to run right up to the rehearsal and we still have so much to do. Now I have to complete the things on his list too."

"What do you need to do? I can do it." I'll do anything to get out of my head and away from all this lace.

"Well, I need to check with the florist, confirm our salon appointments for tomorrow, and double check the banquet room for tonight. He was supposed to confirm with the bar and barmen to make sure that all the alcohol is there, double check the menu for tonight and tomorrow, and verify his seating arrangements for tonight."

"Okay text me the list and let's get started."

Hopefully she will do the florist.

"Really!" Her head pops up and she smiles at me.

"Of course, that's what a maid of honor is supposed to do."

"Thank you."

"Don't thank me...I might make sure the bar is only stocked with JD." I smile at her and her face lights up with mischief. There's a glimpse of my best friend.

The seamstress confirms my dress will do and I change back into my clothes. We head out to the curb where Duncan is pacing as he talks on the phone. His gaze lifts to look at me and I turn to make sure he isn't looking at someone behind me with that much intent.

"Gotta go. Make the arrangements," he gruffly replies as he stalks toward Ana and me.

He helps her into the vehicle and turns to me, then wraps his hand firmly around my forearm.

"There was a delivery to the hotel for you," he growls into my ear.

His tone has me whipping my head to look at him. "I don't know what you mean."

"It will be in your room."

I'm confused but worried I know what it is.

The wedding is being held at the Mandarin Orient Hyde Park, it happens to be one of the nicest hotels in London. I know this isn't

Ana's style again. She'd have picked a castle, a small church, or even a garden. Not a hotel with a view of Buckingham Palace.

We pull up to the front of the hotel and my jaw drops, there's a valet in a uniform similar to the palace guard's. He opens Ana's and my doors as another takes the keys from Duncan. Another guy walks up and tries to take my bag, I shake my head at him. Duncan leads us up the stairs and into the large lobby decorated in maroons and golds. I feel like my jaw just hit the floor. I stop and Duncan's hand lands on my lower back, trying to push me in more. Instantly, tingles radiate from his hand and I jump away.

*What the hell?*

"Uh, is this where the wedding is, and where we are staying?" I stutter.

"Yes, isn't it lovely?" Ana replies breathlessly.

"I guess you can say that. I was thinking more like stuffy and pretentious." Oops! Darn verbal vomit. I watch her smile fall. "Sorry, Ana, I didn't mean it. It's stunning." I feel like a schmuck, I can't believe I said that to her.

"I agree with Maya, this is pretentious. Did Father want you to get married here?"

"No, Jonathon wanted to get married here. He said he has always wanted to come here."

~

WE CHECK in and head up to our rooms. On the ride over, I dreaded seeing what delivery Duncan was talking about, but nothing is in my room. Ana and I are in adjoining rooms, with Duncan staying across the hall. James is in a suite a floor up. And Jonathon and his friend are staying a floor below us.

Duncan offered to help me get the last minute details taken care of for Ana. As I hoped, she's going to see to the florist, leaving Jonathon's list to Duncan and me.

DUNCAN

I can't believe my luck. I've dreamed about this woman for weeks now. I help her verify that all the liquor has been delivered and enough barmen have been hired. We then confirm the menus my sister wants. Neither of us knows anything about the seating so we left that, along with the flowers, to Ana.

I watch her move, her jeans hugging her curves, her t-shirt molding to her knockers. Again I think of them in my palms. I adjust myself behind my zipper, trying to hide my erection. I need to think of something, anything, other than this woman right now.

Work! I'm going to be on a detail in France for an aid to the French Prime Minister. After the fiasco in D.C., I thought I wouldn't be allowed on another foreign diplomat, but we impressed people by getting our high value out before the situation got out of control. I still wonder about that shot she took.

"Maya, can I ask about your job?"

"What about it?" I can see the weariness in her eyes.

"That shot you took, have you ever shot that far before?"

"Only in training. Can you go check with the kitchen to make sure that they have all the napkins pre-folded?" She changes the subject. Why she won't talk about it makes me even more curious.

I walk over to the banquet head and confirm that the bloody napkins are folded just as my sister and her fiancé want.

I've only met Jonathon on a few occasions and have never liked him, but my sister wants him so I guess I'll support her. My phone buzzes in my pocket and I look at the text.

*Joshua: I'll come get my Rover tomorrow afternoon.*

*Duncan: Don't put a scratch on my auto, arsehole.*

*Joshua: Wouldn't dream of it. How does Ian and Raul sound as team?*

*Duncan: Good*

I close the text and look over to see Maya with a curious look on her face. She's looking at the flowers that are being arranged for tonight's banquet with disgust.

"Don't like the arrangement?" I look at the pale pink and cream colored flowers.

"Not really."

"What's the matter with them?"

"I'm just not a flower kind of girl, plus these flowers have a meaning that doesn't fit with a wedding."

I stare at her in shock. The meaning of the flowers? What the hell is she talking about?

"Excuse me?"

"Nothing, I just know a bit about flowers, it was something I studied. I'm going to go get ready."

She awkwardly turns away, practically running from the room. I take a picture of the arrangement and decide I want to research what she meant.

# CHAPTER FOUR

## MAYA

The day flies by until we head up to our rooms to get ready for the rehearsal. I'm exhausted now. After the flight and my nerves over the last few weeks, I need to get some sleep and a good workout in before tomorrow so I'm not a complete bitch. I also need to find the time to talk to James about my new position before Greg spills the beans.

I can't believe I reacted like that to those flowers, but I know what the Rose Carolina means, I've had them delivered to me in the past. I know they mean love is dangerous. I decide not to ask Ana about them thinking she just picked them because she thought they were pretty.

As Duncan stated earlier, I did receive a delivery. It was sent to my room while we were all running around. I don't understand his anger, but I don't care. I need to talk to Ana.

"Knock, knock are you in here?" I walk to the adjoining door we left open while we changed.

"Right here," she says from the bathroom. She steps out in a long coral maxi-dress with elbow length sleeves.

"Hey, did you pick the purple hyacinth flowers for my room?" I'm hoping that the delivery can be explained.

"What are you talking about?" She follows me back to my room.

I point to the nightstand.

"Why did you pick those?"

"I didn't get you flowers for your room. They are beautiful though." She returns to her bathroom, putting on a heavy amount of makeup—another thing my Ana didn't do.

My gut turns as I realize that my flower stalker has followed me again. This is the same arrangement that was on my mom's bedside after her funeral. The same flowers I have sent to the hospital every time they're delivered. The same flowers that mean an apology. I don't know what apology or even who sends them, but I get them and I hate them. Jones thinks it has something to do with my parents' deaths, because there is also a delivery to their gravesite in Tel Aviv every year for the whole month of June of dark crimson roses.

I need to get off this crazy train. I follow her back into her room.

"How do I look? Do you approve?" I turn around in my deep purple printed scarf dress with open toe high heels that buckle at my ankle. I have the dress wrapped so the ties cross around my back and waist and end at the small of my back. My dress is daring because the front is open to almost my navel. I have strategically lifted the back so my tattoo doesn't show but my cleavage does. I've got them, so I'm going to flaunt them. My high heels are almost five inches in height, I'm going to be looking down on a few men. Perfect! Well not Duncan. *Woah, down girl, no thoughts of that.*

"I love it, Maya, it's so you, and those shoes are hot."

"I got this while I was in Tel Aviv last year. I bought a couple other dresses in different Mediterranean styles too. I love them because they pack easily."

"I like it."

"Good because I bought you one too in turquoise, here." I toss her the package I'm carrying.

"Oh I can't accept this, Jonathon won't approve. It's not the style he wants me to wear."

"Excuse me. The hell you say. Pick out your own clothes, woman. This is so you."

I want my best friend back, the one that didn't care what a guy thought, or anyone else for that matter.

"He's my soon to be husband and he wouldn't like that much cleavage showing." She points to my chest.

"Fine, I'll keep it for when you pull your head out of your ass and tell him that you wear anything you want. Besides, I bought you a tube top to match, it hides the cleavage," I grumble at her.

"Please, Maya, don't be angry. He's trying for a big promotion and I have to look my best," she begs.

"Okay, this is your dress and I'll have it."

A knock at her door concludes our conversation.

"Coming," she yells. "Daddy, you look handsome and so do you, Duncan."

I walk into the room and see both men waiting for us.

"Maya, sweetheart, look at you. I can't believe it's been over a year since I saw you last. How is work?" He pulls me into his arms, kissing my cheek. This man has been so special to me since I lost my parents. He filled in when I didn't know I needed them. He used to come visit me monthly and was at both my graduation from college and the police academy. He and Greg are my rocks.

"James, I'm good. You know how work can be." I catch Duncan over his shoulder, looking at me. He is wearing an all-black suit. He still needs to shave, but it turns me on, and I want him to rub that scruff over my body. Oh crap, no more of those thoughts. I smile at him and he smirks at me, it's like he can read my mind.

"Daddy, ask Maya about her new job." Ana interrupts my mini-orgasm.

"What new job?" He pulls back and his eyebrows drop. "Greg hasn't mentioned a new job."

"We need to get downstairs before Jonathon thinks Ana is pulling a runaway bride."

"We will be talking about this, darling." He walks to Ana and offers his arm. Duncan walks to me and offers his.

As soon as my hand touches his arm I feel the tingles from earlier. He covers my hand with his and his fingers tremble slightly. Maybe I'm not the only one affected here. I feel him flex his muscular forearm under my fingers and I tighten my grip. We all head down to the rehearsal and I wonder if the best man is going to annoy me as much as it sounds like Jonathon will.

~

JONATHON IS as stuffy and pretentious as this hotel. I knew the instant he decided he was better than me and didn't like me. What can I say, I don't like him either. He brushed me off and started flaunting Ana in front of his business associates that he invited to what is supposed to be a family night. Duncan left me, and James started mingling too. I hate mingling and feel out of place. This is only the drink service, we haven't even started the actual rehearsal and I already want to leave.

"Did it hurt when you fell from heaven?" A male voice says from behind me.

"Excuse me?" I turn and look at the blond man holding two glasses.

He is about six-one with blue eyes and a trim body. He is probably a runner, as in he runs from a fight. There was a time when this type of man would appeal to me for a one-night stand, but now he just annoys me. I turn to walk away.

"Wait, I'm Stephan Landers, Jonathon's best man. I hear you're the lovely maid of honor. I have a drink for you." He pushes the glass of champagne at me.

I raise my eyebrow at him. "I'm Maya Aaron, nice to meet you." I nod and walk away, looking for something stronger to drink. No way am I taking a drink from a man that uses cheesy lines like that.

I make it across the room to the bar and find it's only serving wine and champagne. Great.

For Ana, I'll put up with anything.

As the drink service ends, the wedding coordinator takes the wedding party aside to go over how tomorrow will play out. Jonathon acts as if he's above all this, his nose in the air and chest puffed out.

Stephan is definitely going to need me to use the Jaws of Life on him. He pulls me to his side and locks his arm around me. I twist away from him. He leans into me again and looks down the front of my dress. I step back again.

I need another drink, or maybe six.

Ana's style isn't anywhere in this wedding, it's all about Jonathon. He tried to make sure this wedding was the event of the year, even attempting to get James to push the royalty card and have one of the princes make an appearance. Thank God they both declined.

We walk into the banquet room where the dinner service will be. Everyone is already seated at the tables, leaving me to sit next to Stephan. I notice that Jonathon has seated me far away from Ana. I hate assigned seating.

As the waiter walks by, I stop him.

"Can I please have two fingers of scotch neat?"

"Ma'am, we are only serving wine during dinner."

"Beer? Ale?" I ask hopefully, crossing my fingers under the table.

"No, ma'am." He walks away and I'm more frustrated than earlier.

You've got to be shitting me. Wine. I'm not a wine drinker. I need something stronger if I'm going to have to deal with Mr. Grabass. And just like that, he slips his hand under the table and slides it across my leg.

I reach down and clasp his fingers in mine, and bend his wrist back. Leaning toward him, I smile sweetly.

"Touch me again and I'll break your fucking hand." I bat my eyelashes at him.

I feel the tingles of awareness, like someone is watching me. I turn to see Duncan with a scowl on his face. I smile and tip my wine glass at him.

After dinner, I rise to make a run for it, walking away as fast as I can. As usual, luck isn't on my side.

"Maya, why don't we let bygones be bygones and you come to my room later?" Stephan reaches out to push his key card into my cleavage.

That is it!

I grab his hand with my right, pull him toward me as I turn, stomping my heel into the top of his foot. He groans and bends forward. I jump out of his reach. This time, I don't play all sweet and nice.

"I said touch me again and I would break your hand. You should be happy I'm nice. I could not only break your hand but drop your ass right in front of everyone." I storm off.

We're now doing an after dinner mingling session, according to the wedding coordinator. I need to get out of here. Ana and Jonathon are walking around, and I can't find anyone else I know to talk to. I'm still not very comfortable in crowds. I can feel the tension building in my shoulders.

I finally find a door leading out to the gardens. I can see the lights of Hyde Park across the hedges and hear the sounds coming from there. I want to escape into the smells of the garden. The cut grass smell tickles my nose. I start to relax as I walk off the balcony into the lower garden. Now this would be a place Ana would actually like. It's beautiful with lights wrapped around the bases of some of the trees, but mostly everything is natural.

All the champagne, wine, lack of food, plus jet lag is catching up to me. I need to relax before tomorrow so I can be on my best behavior for Ana. I really need a heavy bag or a good work out. Although, some sex with Duncan would be good too.

*Damn, bad, Maya,* I have got to stop thinking like that.

I'm in a darker part of the garden. The sounds of the party float down to me as it's still in full swing. I hope that fucktard doesn't find me out here. I'm just about to call Derek about the delivery when I hear something behind me.

# CHAPTER FIVE

## MAYA

"Are you hiding from the bride or the best man?" A voice says from behind me.

I don't even think, I just react. My training kicks in, and I plant my left leg and back kick with my right. Avoiding the kick, he steps to the side and into me, grabbing my hips. He pulls me back toward him. Our bodies are pressed together but I continue to fight. I raise my foot, poised to slam my heel into his shoe, but he avoids it.

"Hold up, honey. It's just me Duncan," he whispers in my ear.

I start to bring my elbow back to connect with his ribs. He pulls me in even tighter to his chest, sending my senses into overdrive. I now don't know if I want to kick his ass or fuck him. I feel his erection against my lower back, his hands rub up my waist to under my heaving breasts, and his fingers gently caress the underside of them. I involuntarily moan.

"God, baby, that was the hottest thing I've ever seen. Tell me where you learned to do that?" His voice is husky in my ear. His lips caress my neck then move up to my earlobe. I want to answer him but my brain has turned to mush. What this man does to me is crazy. I rock my hips back into his erection. He groans and bites down on my neck. "If you don't want to end up bent over that bench over there you'll stop that," he growls against my skin. "You're by far the sexiest woman at this bloody do. All night I've wanted to shag you with those bloody heels pressed into my back."

"What if I told you to bend me over that bench?" I boldly reply. "Wait, what the hell is a do?" I ask confused.

He growls again just before his lips return to my neck, right where my pulse is racing. I can't believe I'm instigating this.

I want him.

He drags his teeth and tongue across my skin, gently pulling as he sucks. I know he is marking me but I can't stop him.

I really want him.

"A do is a party," he replies against my neck, making goose bumps rise on my bare, moist skin.

I moan as I feel myself grow wet.

"God, baby, I want to hear that sexy sound again."

"Duncan, please," I groan. "I want you, but we can't, your sister…"

"Baby, my sister is busy. She'll never notice us missing. I have wanted you since I watched you get off that bloody bike two weeks ago. Do you know what it feels like to wake up hard as a rock and no one to relieve it?" He walks me further into the garden where it's darker. "Answer my question. Where'd you learn those moves?"

It isn't a question, it's a command. My breathing increases, my nipples pucker, and my clit throbs in response. What the hell, I've never responded to a man bossing me around. I actually tend to go for the weaker guys so I can boss them around, but Duncan has me hot and panting with his commands and dominance.

"I've studied...Krav Maga...since I was a kid...along with...other martial arts," I pant.

"God, I'm so hot for you. First, tell me if that guy at the bar is your boyfriend and who sent you flowers today," he demands again.

I'm almost shaken from my sexual lust by his question.

"No, he's my partner, only a friend. A business associate here in

London sent them," I lie. I can't tell him about the flowers and I won't tell him anymore about Derek.

"Ever since I picked you up at the airport, all I've wanted to do is push my cock into your tight little body. This dress, with all your exposed cleavage, is turning me on. I want to taste every inch of you."

I'm going to hyperventilate, I'm panting so hard. His dirty talk and kisses alone have me on the edge of an orgasm.

I see a wall loom up, then I'm spun around in his arms and lifted up. My back hits the wall, and I wrap my legs around him. I groan as I feel his erection right where I want it. His hands divide and leave my waist—one going to my neck to control my head while the other trails down my side again. His hand ends up at my knee, where it starts a slow slide up my leg under my skirt. His lips claim mine in an intense kiss to show me who's in charge here. My body is on fire. His tongue rubs my lips and I open to him, allowing him to plunder my mouth. I swirl and stroke my tongue with his. His hand goes into my hair, positioning my head where he wants it.

I've never been kissed with this much intent. I follow his lead, my hands start roaming his shoulders and go to his hair to pull him in closer.

God, can this man kiss.

His other hand is still slowly moving up my thigh, and encounters my bare backside from my thong. He dips his thumb toward my core. I wiggle, bringing his erection closer to where I want it. His fingers are now at the front of my panties and they slide in the side. He rubs my clit and glides his fingers down to my entrance. I moan into his mouth. I'm going to come if he keeps this up.

"Baby, you're so wet," he says as he pulls away and lays his forehead against mine. "Come to my room. I want you spread out on my bed for me. I'm going to eat this bare pussy for dessert." His words pull me under more. He continues to rub his thumb over my clit while he enters me with his middle finger. I gasp and lean my head against the wall. "I need to taste you, I want you, Maya."

"Maya, are you out here?"

Shit, my luck. My head whips to the side where I hear Ana's voice.

"Just a second," I gasp.

He removes his hand from between my legs and licks his fingers and groans. I'm so turned on. He lowers me down as my legs unwrap from his body. His other hand moves back to my neck, pulling me closer to him.

He leans forward, speaking into my ear, his lips brush the shell, "You know where my room is, and here is my spare key." He slides it into my cleavage and is gone before I can say anything else.

Holy Shit!

"Maya, what're doing out here?" Ana asks as she descends the stairs to where I'm standing. I casually smooth out my dress, making sure nothing is out of place.

"Just getting some fresh air. I think the jet lag is catching up with me," I try to explain. Of course I can't tell her I was making out with her brother.

"Well come on, I want a shot with my best friend." She laughs.

I'm reminded of how Jonathon controls her and how much she has changed.

"Okay, let's go, sister."

I follow behind her, hoping Duncan didn't leave too many marks on my neck. I smooth my skirt again and check the bodice, making sure my full breasts are still contained and his key card is hidden.

"So, what're we drinking to that we haven't already toasted? Also please tell me this will be a drink I like?"

"Well, you're my best friend, my sister, and one of the few people I trust. What else would we do shots with?" Her words give me a slight pause. She sounds melancholy.

"What's the matter? You're less than twenty-four hours away from marrying the man of your dreams."

Ana stops and turns to me, her head slightly tipped to the side and down. Her lips form a small frown and I can see the sorrow on her.

"Maya, if anything ever happens to me, will you take care of Daddy and Duncan? They've nothing in common now except me. They barely talk. Since Duncan joined the army they've only fought, please, I need you."

"What're you talking about?" My brain reels. She's actually starting to scare me with the way she is talking.

"Maybe I'm feeling everything is going too well, that something is going to happen. I want to make sure that I never have unfinished business. I've also had too much to drink." She smiles with the last part, but I still feel like she isn't telling me something.

We both lost family at young ages, and we're both serious about never leaving our future kids like what happened to us. Ana's mom was killed in a car accident that Ana miraculously survived. Ana wasn't even six months old at the time. I'm sure I'll never have children. Besides, I'd have to trust someone with my heart for that to happen, and that isn't going to happen anytime soon.

We make our way to the bar. "Two shots of any American whiskey, preferably Jack Daniels," I tell the bartender. He hands us each a shot glass filled with our drinks.

"Okay, to always being on top and best friends forever, cheers," I say, and laugh as I throw back the shot. The bartender pours me another and sets a single red rose down next to my glass.

"For the lovely lady," he says and I smile at him. He doesn't need to know I hate flowers.

"To friends forever and angels in dark places, cheers," Ana says, and throws back hers. That's been her toast since we were nineteen. She's setting her glass on the bar when a manicured male hand grabs her wrist.

"Darling, I think it's time for Mia to take you to your room. You've imbibed too much." Jonathon mispronounces my name.

"Her name is Maya. And for your information, I'm all right." I watch her back straighten, and her petite frame appears to be taller then she is. She's actually going to stand up to him in front of everyone. It's about time my Ana started thinking for herself. Then I realize how many people are watching us. I know that Ana wouldn't want to make a spectacle. But, I'm proud of her for finally finding her voice.

"It's all good, Ana, we can take the bottle and head to your room." I signal the bartender to give me the bottle. I feel Duncan's key at my breast and know I'll not make it there. But I need to diffuse this before people get a show. I also know that Duncan is a bad idea. I reach for the bottle the bartender left beside the rose.

For a moment, I wonder about the rose, it's the only red rose in the venue.

"Maya, Anabel is done drinking for the night." Jonathon's hand lets go of hers and grabs my wrist, stopping the progress toward the bottle. His touch feels like ice water has been injected into my veins. His grip tightens, each of his fingers dig into my skin.

I'm going to kick this English prick's ass. How dare he touch me?

"Let go of me, now," I whisper, staring him in the eye. He's going to remove his hand or I'm going to make him.

"Let her go. Now," the words are snarled from behind me as I feel Duncan's hand on my shoulder.

Ana slides over to her brother's side. I knew without looking it was him. I felt the electricity between us. Jonathon looks over my head to Duncan, then to Ana.

"Anabel, don't cause a scene. Go to your room like a good girl. I'll see you tomorrow. Remember your promise to me?" His voice is cold, his face pinched and eyes narrowed. He is looking at Ana like he wants to hurt her and is disgusted by her. He is not only treating her like a child, but like a child he hates.

How dare he talk to her like that! I've had enough of this asshole.

I grab his wrist with my other hand, and push down as I push up and twist with my captured hand. I bend his wrist back and look him in the eye as I step into his space.

"I don't need to be a good girl. Don't ever touch me again. And if you ever talk to her like that, I will break your jaw," I whisper so only he can hear. The urge to punch him or break his wrist is overwhelming. I let him go before I do either.

Wrapping my arm around Ana's waist, I feel her deflate, her head bows and she instantly becomes the other woman again. Duncan lowers his hand to my waist and turns both Ana and I toward the doors. His hand slides to my lower back as his head turns back to Jonathon. He seems torn between getting us away and going back to fight him. I want to go back and kick his ass. We've barely cleared the doors when I whip around to Ana.

"What the hell was that?"

"What the bloody hell was that?"

Both Duncan and I say at the same time. I nod my head to him to continue.

"Ana, please tell me that tosser treats you better than that?"

I can see him trying to control his anger, his body vibrates from the tension. He doesn't want to scare her any more than she already is.

"He's just stressed with the wedding tomorrow." Her head stays down. I've seen this behavior before. She'd never allow that to happen to her. Right? I've watched many witnesses to domestic violence act just like this. *Not my Ana,* my mind screams.

"Ana, sweetie, does Jonathon get stressed a lot?" I dread the answer.

"I'm tired, Maya, can you and Duncan help me to my room?"

She avoids my question. Now I know for certain she's hiding something from me. She's acting like a battered woman. Oh God, how could I let this happen? Last time I saw her she was energized for whatever life was going to dish out. She was starting art school. Did my being away so much cause her to turn to a man like that?

I shake off the thoughts and follow my training.

"Ana, how about you and I ditch out on this pomp and circumstance?" I know it's bad to ask but I need to protect her. I need to give her what she gave me years ago, a safe place. "Let's give Jonathon a break and you come home with me this time." I know her answer when her shoulders push back and she stands up to me. What's his hold over her?

"Now, Maya, you know I can't walk away from Jonathon. He loves me. Don't you dare push your paranoid bobby barmy on me or your fears of relationships."

Wow, it feels like she just slapped me in the face. No going back now.

"Ana, how about you tell me what the hell your fiancé was thinking talking to you like that? Explain why you're so different? Tell me why it bothers you so much to upset him?" I fire off each question as I step further into her space. I know my anger might set her off more, but I need to know the answers to my questions. I need to protect her. She's my family and I won't lose her too.

Duncan puts his arm between us, pushing me back, trying to calm us both.

"Hey, Sis, Maya's just concerned. He just treated you like a daft cow. He grabbed ahold of Maya and was trying to hurt her, and he enjoyed it." His voice gets gruffer the more he talks about it.

"Okay, I'm sorry for my fiancé. Maya, he just doesn't want me hungover for tomorrow. Now are you both going to walk me upstairs or am I going by myself?" She lifts her chin, nose going in the air, and all I can think about is *Invasion of the Body Snatchers*.

"Okay," Duncan and I say together.

We walk her back to her room and as she enters, she turns to us. "Go back to the party. Get to know each other. I'm tired."

I want to protest. I want to take her from here. Ana closes the door before I can say anything.

# CHAPTER SIX

## MAYA

Duncan turns toward me, I can see him working something out behind those eyes. He nods his head as he comes to a decision. Grabbing my hand, he leads me to his room.

"Let's have that drink and get to know each other," he says as he opens his door.

I can't believe I'm here after all. I shouldn't be, but damn I want this man as I've never wanted another.

I look around the room trying to distract myself from the smell of his cologne. His room is almost exactly like mine, minus the door to a connecting room. This hotel might seem stuffy but it's actually gorgeous, and the decor is something that Ana couldn't stop talking about.

I turn back to him, time to pull up my big girl panties.

"Duncan, we need to figure out what to do to help Ana. We can't do this." I swing my finger between the two of us.

He ignores me and walks to the bar, where he pours us each a scotch. He hands me one and tips his head to the side, his lips pinch like he's deep in thought. I feel my resolve crumbling under his scrutiny, my metaphorical big girl panties dampen.

"Maya, you and I aren't going to change her mind. She's more stubborn than anyone I know. I've been around Jonathon only a couple times, maybe she's right and all this bridal bull is driving him barking mad." He sips his drink. I watch his lips and then his throat as he swallows. Everything about this man turns me on.

"Seriously. Are you making excuses for that asshole?" I lift my glass to my lips and drain it in one gulp, needing liquid courage. He watches me, probably to see if I'm going to react to the significant amount of scotch I just swallowed.

His focus turns to my lips now, where I've licked the remnants of the alcohol. His stare is like a caress. He shakes his head, tosses back the rest of his drink, and takes both our glasses to set on the bar. I watch as he pulls off his jacket and lays it in the chair, his tie comes off next, followed by the top buttons of his shirt.

The exposed skin at his collar mesmerizes me, and I want to lick the tan skin like he did mine earlier.

"No, I'm not making excuses for that tosser. My father is backing him and he'd not agree if there was something up. I won't go against him again." There's a flash of pain in his eyes before he banks it.

"Duncan, please, we need to put a stop to this joke." I shake off the desire and remember how angry I am at Jonathon. How worried I am for Ana. I start to wave my hands around, trying to block out the sexual tension.

He stalks toward me and I actually step back as he reaches out for my hand and gently turns it to look at my wrist in the light. "Okay, baby, now I'm going to kill him. He marked you. Why didn't you say he grabbed you so hard?"

I look down to what he's looking at and see the angry red marks from Jonathon's fingers on my wrist.

"Oh that? It didn't hurt. I bruise easily." I try to pull my hand from his grip. There goes that zap of awareness again as if my body knows him. I need to get away from him before I do something we both might regret.

"Baby, you're so fair, this is going to show tomorrow. You're already sporting my razor burn and love bites on your neck." He points to my neck and I lift my other hand to gently touch it.

"Duncan. Please. Stop." I pant as he caresses my wrist with his fingers, tingles work their way up my arm. Again, I step back from him and he advances. I feel the wall at my back.

"Maya, I want you. I know that I shouldn't but, baby, you've had my attention since I saw you in D.C., and in that dress you look beautiful." He pulls me to him. His arms wrap around me and skate down my back to the fastening of my dress.

The urge to lick him comes over me again, and this time I can't stop it. I lick his neck at the opening of his collar. He pulls the tie of my dress loose and unwraps the silk ribbon that crosses around my body, and stretches the opening over my head. I'm mesmerized by the look in his eyes as he undresses me. The bodice falls, exposing my bare breasts. His eyes fasten on my erect nipples. He lifts me in his arms and carries me to his bed. As he lays me down, he tugs my dress off the rest of the way. Reaching for the ankle straps of my shoes, he unbuckles and pulls them off, then kisses each ankle. His kisses lead up my leg to my center, where he blows gently on me. My hips lift, wanting him there. I push up on my elbows to watch him.

Duncan steps back from the bed and finishes unbuttoning his shirt. As his chest is exposed, I see the edge of a tattoo that wraps from his back over his shoulders. My eyes skate down his chest to his nearly eight pack abs and I spot another tattoo along his right rib cage. He's so sexy. I feel myself getting wetter and worry he can see the effect he has on me. He finishes pulling off his shirt and drops it to the floor before moving to unbuckle his pants. I can't wait, I want him, now.

"Please, Duncan. I need you."

"Soon, baby," he says huskily. His gravelly voice alone is drawing me closer to the cliff. "I want my dessert. I've waited two weeks to taste you."

"No, now! Please, Duncan, I can't wait." The urge to flip him to his back so I can be in control overwhelms me.

"Keep thinking that thought, baby, and I will restrain you to the headboard with my belt." My pussy convulses at the thought.

He pulls his wallet out of his slacks and pulls out a condom before dropping his pants and boxer briefs to the floor. I'm entranced by the large size of his cock, and my mouth waters at the sight of a drop of pre-cum. I lick my lips and he growls.

"Next time, baby."

I get wetter just looking at him. He places the condom next to me on the bed before grabbing my thong in his large hands, pulling the sides and ripping it off my body. He lowers his head and sucks my labia lips into his mouth, then parts them and zeros in on my clit. My back bows off the bed as he coaxes it out by licking and sucking it. I feel the orgasm just on the verge but I can't let go enough to come.

"I've dreamed of this pussy. I've come like a randy teenager from those dreams."

"Oh. Duncan. Don't stop, I'm about to come," I beg.

He growls against my clit and pushes two fingers inside me, curling them to hit my G-spot. I scream his name as I come. He pulls away from my clit and licks up my juices, and fucks me with his tongue. I feel like my body is a live wire, the sensation is too much. I try to pull away but his hands press into my thighs, holding me down. His tongue rims the edge of my entrance, my pubic bone, and my stomach as he licks his way up my body. He sucks on the underside of one of my breasts and I know he left a hickey. He rises above me, then sucks one of my nipples deeply into his mouth, releasing a groan. He pulls away and kneels back on his haunches, pushing me up the bed.

"Baby, you felt tight around my fingers. I'm going to go slow, but this is going to be so fucking good."

I watch as he pumps his hand over his engorged cock once, twice, then rolls the condom on. I'm ready to go again and entranced. Duncan lays over me but not on me. He rubs his cock against my folds, getting it wet from my release.

"Please. Duncan." I squirm, wanting his cock inside me.

"Baby, your bare pussy is the best I've ever tasted, like honey or nectar. I could live off of eating you out all the time. And your breasts are so fucking hot, next time I'll pay them more attention." His words are driving me crazy. Wait...did he say next time, that's the second time he's indicated there would be more than once. Oh hell no! This is just tonight for me.

My thoughts are cut off as he starts slowly pushing into me. I can't think of anything else now. The head of his cock is so broad I feel it stretching me, almost painfully.

"Oh God...Baby, you're so tight. This is going to go faster than I want." He groans, and pushes fully into me with a thrust.

"Mmm, Duncan."

"Maya, baby, I gotta move, but are you okay?" I nod. "No, say the words, Maya."

"Yes, Duncan. God, yes. Move."

That's all he needs. He pulls out almost all the way and slams home again. We both groan.

"Here goes, baby. Wrap your legs around me." I do as he says. He starts moving faster, pistoning into me. I push up into him, too. My orgasm is cresting upon me.

He groans over me. "Now, baby, come now," he practically roars. I come so hard I might pass out. My vaginal muscles squeeze him tight, setting him off. He growls my name into my neck and goes rigid everywhere. His strong arms lock around me, holding me tightly to him, and I return the hold. I don't want to leave him and I get the sense he doesn't want me to leave.

I'm undone. How do I go on from here? This was by far the best sex I've ever had, and I can never do it again. Pain stabs my heart as I hear his voice in the distance.

"Maya." Did I pass out?

Duncan moves off me. My arms fall to my sides, empty. I feel the loss instantly. The warmth and connection are gone. He pads to the bathroom and returns with a wet washcloth.

"Open, baby. I'm going to clean you up."

No man has ever done this. I open my legs for him. The cool wash-cloth rubs my vagina and it feels comforting. No one has taken care of me like this. My past lovers were only concerned about themselves.

He throws the washcloth toward the bathroom, lies on the bed, and pulls me into his side.

"We'll relax for a bit, then round two."

I snuggle into him; I've never been a cuddler, but he's just so comfortable and I feel content. I close my eyes, the jet lag and alcohol catching up. I fall asleep in his arms with one of my hands resting over his heart. The steady beat pulling me deeper into sleep.

# CHAPTER SEVEN

## DUNCAN

"Bugger, what in the bloody hell 'ave I done." I groan. She stirs and cuddles into me more. I knew I had to have this woman but should I is the problem.

All day I've watched her. When we worked together earlier she had me spellbound. She's my siren. Her body is more like a runner's, except for the full breasts. Even her damn cowboy boots were hot. I wanted her legs wrapped around my hips while I drove her into multiple orgasms. I couldn't believe my luck. I've been trying to figure out a way to find out more about her. Now here she is. I'm glad that man is only her partner, because she is mine now.

The fact that she's Ana's best friend is a mark in the wrong. That and the fact she lives in another country, but I will overcome both, I've had worse odds.

My life is starting to work out, finally. I work private security. My boss was my old captain, and today he asked me to be his second in command, just like when we served together. I have a flat in a new building and I'm no longer in the military. Now to work things out with my father.

I need to figure out what to do about Jonathon too. Maya is right, there's something off with Ana's and his relationship. I've never seen my sister so emotional. I've known for a while there was something up with him, but Ana won't listen to me. Maybe Maya can talk her out of this farce tomorrow. Father seems okay with him. However, I haven't spoken to the old codger in over nine years. Today was the first time I've seen him since I got home. He acted as if we weren't in the same room earlier and then ignored me the rest of the night. I want to tell him about my job. I want to fix what I broke. And mostly, I want to have him back in my life.

My mind drifts back to Maya. My body and mind know she is the one, but I'm fairly certain she isn't going to agree. When she walked into Ana's room earlier in that dress that was no more than a scrap of material, I wanted to drag her from there. No one should see her looking that good. Watching her at dinner with that fucktard of a best man was making me angry. I've never been a jealous man until now. The thought of anyone touching her makes me want to break something. That's what sent me into the garden earlier.

I was trying to avoid starting a fight with Stephan. I watched her defend herself when he did something under the table. My hands clinched into fists then and now. When she pulled those moves on me in the garden it got me so hard, I thought I was going to bust my zipper. When my sister interrupted our little tryst, I knew I had to have her. Part of me hoped she'd decline my offer. I knew if I had her like this it would never be enough. My cock begins to harden. I want her again. I've never been ready this quickly before. This girl has me gutted.

I close my eyes and I'm taken back to the day my military career changed. The day I lost my best friend. As Christopher laid dying in my arms, I didn't care about the bullets hitting my body. My armor took so many hits that day that I'm still surprised I lived. I smell his blood and the gunpowder in the air. I can still see Timothy trying to save his life. His words are what I remember the most: *It was worth it.* He left his baby and wife alone. How was it worth it? How was all that worth the sacrifice he made for me? He took the bullet meant for me.

I found the letters in his pockets. It was as if he knew. One for his wife, one for his daughter, and one for me. I delivered them and read mine.

I'm shaken from my thoughts when Maya whimpers in her sleep, draping her leg over mine. Her hand brushes my semi-aroused cock and I want to roll us over to start round two. She needs more sleep. I notice the dark circles under her eyes. She must work too many hours at her job. I lean my face into her hair and smell the vanilla and jasmine scent that's teased me all day. Her hair is soft and spread across her back and over my arm. I run my fingers through the thick mass of hair. She settles back in and my thoughts wander again.

Over the years, I've heard Ana talk about Maya, but she's not what I expected. I feel myself drifting off. Guess I could use some sleep too. I'll wake in a few and take her again, because this is so not done. I remember the look of panic in her eyes when I said next time. I just hope I can keep my nightmares at bay for just one night.

MAYA

I come awake with a start, practically jumping from the bed. I hear a grunt next to me and an arm tightens around my middle. Oh great, what have I done? I move slightly, trying to gain some space. He pulls me back in, even tighter. I shift again, acting as if I'm rolling to my other side; he shifts to spooning my rear. Carefully grabbing a pillow next to me, I hug it to my body for few minutes then roll again to put the pillow between us. Success! His arm wraps around it. I wait for a beat and then slide off the side of the bed. I can't believe he fell for it.

Duncan is sleeping so peacefully and I find myself torn between wanting to run and climbing back in bed with him. Although, sleep is the last thing on my mind. I want to wake him up with my mouth on him, but I can't do that. I have plans for my life and things to take care of. I can't put anyone else in danger from my stalker. Plus, he's Ana's brother.

I search out my clothes and dress, finding my key in the pocket. On the floor by my dress is the key Duncan gave me earlier. I leave it and my torn thong. Grabbing my heels, I back to the door, waiting for him to jump up and stop me. I open the door as quietly as I can, and cross the hall. Walk of shame, yep that's me.

Looking down the hall in both directions, I don't see any witnesses and enter my room to the darkness of my life. I can't be with anyone, but I want to be with him. All day, whenever he touched me, my body would react to him. I've never had that feeling with anyone before.

After a shower, I tie my hair up on top of my head and walk to the adjoining door. Ana left it open a crack, and I slip into her room and crawl into her bed, just like when we were younger. God, I miss her. She shifts to face me.

"I was wondering if you were going to come in here. Still sleep restlessly I see."

"Yeah." What can I say, since my parents died I wait for the other shoe to drop? I'm so afraid of being alone, I don't let people close, except her and Derek. I also very rarely sleep without nightmares.

"Was the bar still open?"

"No, I was walking in the garden again." My lie is to save her as much as me. How could I explain to her about Duncan?

"Maya, I love you. You will never be alone." She squeezes my hand.

"Thanks, Ana. You know I won't judge if you want to talk."

"Oh yes, I know. There is nothing to say. Jonathon just likes everything perfect, even to a fault. Nevertheless, he is my choice and he will take care of me. Please forget what you think you saw."

I smile into the dark and hug her. "Okay, just this once. But if he hurts you again he will die." She doesn't reply back to that and I wonder if I hurt her or if she is just ignoring me.

As I drift off, I realize she didn't say she loved him, just that he was her choice.

# CHAPTER EIGHT

## MAYA

We wake up early and head to the salon where we spend the day being beautified. My hair is piled up on my head with loose curls falling around my face and neck. They did my makeup darker than I usually wear it. Ana is a vision, her blond hair is pulled into a tight chignon at the back of her neck and her make up is subtle, yet also harsher than what she usually wears. I help her dress in a very-unlike-her wedding dress. The ball gown style with lots of beading, appliqués and lace sleeves is nothing like the dress she would talk about when we were younger. I want to ask if *he* picked it out too, but I won't upset her today. James steps into the room and practically starts crying.

"My girls, you both look so beautiful. If your mums could see you now. Anabel, your mum would be so proud of the woman you have become. Maya, darling, you look so much like your mother. In fact, I remember she had a dress just like that, same color and everything, for her sorority formal in college. It's funny that Ana would pick an almost replica of that dress."

Jonathon picked my dress, not Ana. Before I can process his words further, the wedding planner steps in.

"Showtime, ladies and gentleman."

We step into the hall and await our cue. At the start of the song, I walk through the doors and down the aisle, keeping my focus on the minister at the front of the hall. My attention slips to the garden behind him, the doors and windows open. I will never think of that garden the same way. I will never think of Hyde Park the same way either. Part of me wants to look for Duncan but I know that would be bad, he isn't for me and I don't want to hurt what little family I have left. I join Jonathon and his best man waiting at the altar. For the life of me I can't remember the guy's name. He leers at me and I want to vomit in my mouth. I turn to watch Ana and James make their way down the aisle. She looks pretty, but she isn't smiling like I would expect her to. She has a smile on her face but it doesn't reach her eyes. She is looking at Jonathon but it isn't the look of a woman completely in love with the man she is marrying. It's a look of resignation.

As they reach us, James waits for his line, and with a loud voice says, "Her family and I give her away." Tears spring to my eyes as he looks at me when he says family.

The rest of the ceremony is a blur, and when we walk back down the aisle, following Jonathon and Ana, the best man squeezes my hand, making me feel like I need to bathe in a peroxide bath to get the germs off me.

We make our way to the ballroom and watch as Ana and Jonathon start the receiving line. People are walking up, hugging and congratulating them. I see Duncan walk into the ballroom and about swallow my tongue. He looks so good in his traditional tuxedo. I can see his arm muscles flex under the jacket, his legs strain the pant legs, the understated pin striping of the dark charcoal suit adds to the depth of the color. He and James are in matching tuxes with silver vests and ascots. My mind flashes to what Duncan looks like out of it, but he looks so yummy in it too. He catches me looking at him and stalks toward me. I see the intent in his eyes and know I don't want to have this conversation in front of everyone. Needing a quick escape, I head for the wedding coordinator and check on the arrangements for the dances and coordination of speeches. I need to avoid him or I'll be finding the nearest closet to fuck him in.

~

I'VE MANAGED to evade Duncan most of the night. It was easier during dinner, as I had to sit at the head table with Ana and Jonathon. Throughout the night, I've felt his eyes on me, like now. When I look in his direction, he seems upset. The best man is spinning me on the dance floor; he's been trying to get me alone, attempting to pull me toward the balcony and garden several times. I'm about to break his wandering fingers when Duncan's deep voice rumbles behind me.

"May I cut in?"

"Of course, don't keep her too long though, she has maid of honor duties."

Really, this guy is a jerk.

Duncan chuckles and I bristle. He pulls me into his arms and the feelings of want and security wash over me. Why him?

"Finally...are you avoiding me? Or do I need to kick that fucktard's arse to prove he is not for you?"

The growl in his voice immediately makes me wet for him.

"Duncan...please—"

"Now we're talking, meet me upstairs," he interrupts me.

Ah, did I miss something? Where the hell did he get the impression I wanted to go upstairs?

"What?" I ask as he leans down to whisper in my ear.

"Baby, when I hear you say, 'Duncan, please,' I want to bury my cock so deep inside you."

I pull back, putting distance between us. Holy hell, now I'm really turned on.

"No. Stop. What happened between us can't happen again. I'm leaving tomorrow and for that matter, this was only an itch that needed scratching. Plus, I don't do relationships. I don't need or want them."

"Really, Maya, I'm not asking for forever, just tonight. This time you won't escape me. Where did you stay after you left me? I went to your room and knocked. And by the way, I threw away the best man's rose to you."

"I stayed with Ana. Wait...what rose?" I'm not about to explain my sleeping problems to him.

"The red rose that was on the floor by your door. Right now you are mine, I don't share, so I threw it away."

My sense of flight is starting to fire as I realize what this means. My stalker isn't just sending me flowers, he is here. Someone followed me. I've put my family in danger again. The best man would have bragged if he left me a rose. Then I remember the single red rose from the bar last night. I step out of Duncan's arms as the song comes to an end, and fight the urge to step back into them.

"Please, Maya, I don't beg. I need you now, and watching that arse rub all over you has me short circuiting and wanting to kill him."

I'm about to answer when a commotion at the door draws my attention. Ana has a look of panic in her eyes. What the hell? Jonathon is standing with his arm around her, talking to her.

"Duncan, something is up with Ana, I gotta go." I turn to walk away.

"What?" He swings to the door and sees Ana too. Jonathon now has a smug look on his face and Ana is crying.

"What up, girl?"

"Jonathon says we are leaving now for the honeymoon, not tomorrow like what was planned." Her smile drops and the tears continue to fall. I know why she is upset, we were going to have breakfast in the morning before I left. Jonathon's eyes fasten on me then lower to my wrist with the bruises from where he grabbed me. I feel Duncan move behind me. He puts his hand on my lower back. Jonathon's eyes flair wide and his mouth drops open. I can see the wheels turning but can't figure out what he is thinking. He looks at Duncan then over my shoulder. I turn to see what or who he is looking at. Stephan is standing there, glaring at Duncan. What the hell is going on?

"Mia, I'm trying to surprise my bride with an early honeymoon getaway, but of course all she is worried about is *you*," he sneers.

"Okay, this is the last time wanker, her name is Maya. Does she need to wear a bloody name tag for you?" Duncan growls.

Ana is trying not to smile. I'm just trying not to yell at him for being so obvious.

"Thank you, Duncan, but I can handle this." I step to Jonathon's other side and whisper so only he can hear. "I can find my way around London so don't worry. Like Duncan so eloquently said, my name is Maya, you might want to get used to it because I will be keeping an eye on you." I step back and look at them both.

"Jonathon, I understand what you're trying to do. It's okay. Ana, we can get together for Christmas like you want. I'll come back. When I get home, I'll put in for leave. I'm flying out tomorrow and I know how to get to the airport myself. I'll also make sure the wedding coordinator gets all your gifts delivered to your place."

I smile at her so she will calm down.

"Maya, this is the first time we've been in the same city in years. I was hoping to spend time with you tomorrow."

"You go. I promise I will be back. Let me go find your father while you say goodbye to Duncan." I watch Duncan take his sister into his arms as I walk away.

"James, Ana and Jonathon are ready to leave."

"Maya, darling, oh yes, let's go say our goodbyes. When do you fly home?" he asks.

"Tomorrow evening." I smile at him. I wish I could stay longer but feel the need to get my life in control and protect those I'm close too.

"I'll be in D.C. next week, we must have dinner. How about Georgia Brown's. I know how much you love that restaurant."

"I'm off on Tuesdays and Wednesdays. And I think it's you that loves that restaurant. But yes, we could do that." We stop our conversation as we come up to the group.

"Ana, I am so proud of you. I know your mum is too. She's here, darling, looking down on all of us."

"Awe, Daddy, thank you."

"Of course, give me a hug and we'll see you in two weeks."

"Daddy, can you and Duncan take care of Maya? You should have Maya tell you about her job." She smiles slyly at me. She reminded me when we were getting our hair done that I still hadn't told James about my new position. I know he will worry more than before. I planned on telling him via text or right before I boarded the plane tomorrow.

"Of course, darling, I'll make sure she gets to the airport. Duncan, would you like to join us for a drink?" Ana and I both look at James and Duncan.

"Yes, sir, I'd like to join you." Duncan looks a little shocked.

"Okay, off with you two lovebirds. Take care of my girl, Jonathon." James pats Jonathon on the shoulder.

"Yes, sir," he smiles. His smile gives me chills.

"Love you, Maya. I'll call when we get home, text me when you land." Ana hugs us each.

"Yes, Ana, I'll text when I land. We'll discuss Christmas when you get home. Love you!" I don't want to let her go. I feel like something isn't right and I want to just hold onto her. We smile at each other and she turns with Jonathon to leave.

# CHAPTER NINE

## MAYA

James and Duncan lead me to a table in the bar area where it's quieter. James watches as Duncan pulls out my chair.

"So, Maya, what's going on with your job?" James starts as soon as we're seated. No hello how are you, just right into it. He knows I'm a police officer and he knows about my special training, but this man is a very protective father figure. How will he react to my latest job choice?

"Um, okay, James, please don't freak out." I start.

"Why would I freak out, darling?"

"Because ever since my parents died you've tried to fill in for them. I know you want me here instead of the States. I know both you and Ana hate me being a police officer. But—"

"Can I get you all a beverage from the bar?" A server walks up and interrupts our conversation.

Thank goodness. I need this distraction.

The server is trying to get Duncan's eye and I want to claw out her eyes. Where did that come from? I don't do jealous, and I really don't care who he sleeps with next. Well, maybe I do.

"He and I will have a scotch. What about you, darling?" James asks, looking at me.

"I'd like a bourbon, if not, Jameson is fine." She leaves to get our drinks, adding a swing to her hips.

"Stop stalling, Maya," Duncan says, of course he'd notice that.

"So...I've been with Metropolitan Police for almost two years now. Because of my background, the extra training sessions I've taken, and my additional knowledge and skills, the captain of the Emergency Response Team approached me back in February. While in the interview, they also asked me to double over in the Special Services Units. They want me to do both with my skills. That's how Duncan and I met actually. I was on a call that he was at." I turn and smile sweetly at Duncan. I know I'm bad.

"WHAT!" James blurts out, so much for English manners. "Greg promised me he would keep you from danger. He said he would make sure."

"Excuse me?" The hairs stand on end on my neck. How could they do this to me?

"Don't get in a fit. I asked Greg not to interfere with your job, just to make sure you were always protected."

"Dammit, James..." The server returning interrupts me.

I take a hefty swallow of my drink as I watch both men stare at me. Avoiding their gaze, I look down to see a message on my napkin.

*You left my rose at the bar last night. I took it to your room. What did you think?*

What the hell? I look around the bar as I pull the napkin into my lap so the men don't see it.

"Darling, please, I can get you a job at Scotland Yard or the consulate. With your linguistics skills and education they'd both want you," James states, interrupting my panic. I love this man so much, but I'm going to disappoint him. I look at Duncan, he appears to process this a little more. I bite my lip and hope he didn't see the note and they both don't push me about my jobs.

"Maya, what linguistic skills and training is my father talking about?" Okay, here goes. Most men run for the hills when they find out about me. This is how I'll make sure he doesn't want another night with me.

"Wait, before I answer that, James, explain about Greg."

"He didn't mean to hurt you, he was doing what I asked. I will try to understand why you want to do this, but it is my job to make sure you survive all this."

"Derek is with me, I'm fine."

"Okay."

"Now, Duncan, other than the Krav Maga, I went to the FBI training classes for side arms and sniper training. I've been a competition sharpshooter since my teens when I was in the biathlon. My father wanted me to go to the Olympics. I speak fluent Yiddish, Hebrew, Arabic, French, Gaelic, Spanish, and Italian. I'm currently learning Pashto, Dari, Mandarin, and Farsi. Plus, I have a bachelor's degree in Criminal Justice." I feel like I'm reciting my resume. James looks so proud. On the other hand, Duncan appears to want to either rip my clothes off right here and have his way with me, or lock me in a cage to protect me. Okay, only part of what I expected.

"Maya, I just got out of the British Army. I'm working for a friend who runs a security company. He'd love for you to work for him. Ana and Father would love you to come to London." By the look in his eyes, he'd like me here too. I swallow more of my bourbon.

"No, no both of you. James, you know better. Duncan, I'll give you the benefit of the doubt. I need to finish what I've started. I like my condo. I love my life in D.C." Even if it's a bit lonely. "I can't drop everything. Besides Uncle Marcus would be lost without my visits up to Boston. I don't want to buy a house or make any decisions until after Savta's solicitor gets everything figured out." I can't tell James I haven't been to see Marcus in months. I've been too busy and something has changed between him and me. The last time I was in Boston he tried forcing his nephew on me. Even after I said no.

"I'm so sorry, Maya, I forgot. She was an amazing woman. What she lived through and accomplished is astounding." James says with a sympathetic pat on my shoulder.

"May I ask what's Savta?"

"Savta is Hebrew for grandmother. She liked me to call her that, as a nickname. James, it's okay, she needed peace. She'd buried most of her family and some extended family. I'm the only grandchild and family she had left." My heart does a slight drop when I think about losing her last winter. She was so ready to leave this world.

"Did you go back to Tel Aviv for the funeral?"

"Yes, I stopped by and blew a kiss toward Momma and Abba too."

"Oh, child, loss of a loved one is very hard. You didn't go alone did you?

"No, Greg and Derek went with me."

"Your mother and my Isabella were such good friends, for that I loved your mother like family. As for Marcus, he can skip the pond once in a while too."

"Wait, Uncle Marcus in Boston," Duncan chimes in startled.

"Ya," I say and smile. "He and your mother were neighbors with my mom growing up."

"So that's how this all fits. Father would go see his cousin...what's his name again?" Duncan pauses and looks at his father.

"Oh, you mean Shawn." I see the wistful look in James's eyes when he thinks of Shawn.

"Yes, that one, he lived near Mum and Uncle Marcus," Duncan states.

"That's right. Marcus isn't my uncle, but he won't let me call him anything else," I laugh.

"Duncan, Maya, come to the house for brunch tomorrow, before you need to leave, Maya." I want to decline, I can't be around Duncan. All I want to do is climb into his lap and make out with him. Then Ana's words begging me to help her father and Duncan come to mind.

"Okay, James, but only if Duncan doesn't mind giving me a ride there. I can get a taxi to the airport from there. I also have a message from Greg, he said to tell you hello. Something about getting together with you next week." I look to Duncan and back to James.

"Of course, what time?" Duncan is almost stuttering as he looks to his father. Is he nervous? What's this?

"How about eleven? Gives you time to get checked out. Yes, I'll see Greg next week. Anything you want to confess before he spills the beans?" James smiles at me.

"He was in the interview insisting I double over into Special Services," I confess.

"Alright, children, I'm going to head home. One night in a strange bed is enough for me. Too many years of traveling, now I like my own bed. Have a good rest of your evening. Maya, I'm proud of you like you were my own daughter. I worry about you, but I know this is what you want. I also know Greg will keep an eye on you." He bends over to kiss my forehead. I know where Duncan gets his height. He shakes Duncan's hand and walks out, looking tired.

"Between my sister getting married today and you basically telling him you want people to shoot at you, he just aged ten years. He thinks of you as one of his children. Since your parents passed, he has told my sister and me how important you are and how much he regrets their deaths. I don't know why but I think he blames himself." Duncan states as he looks at his scotch.

"Do you know how my parents died?"

"Only that all of you were in Tel Aviv, I can imagine though."

"My parents were having dinner at a restaurant, just minding their own business, when a suicide bomber walked into the bus station across the street. Collateral damage is what they were called. If I can prevent just one suicide bomber or an idiot from taking a parent from a child, I will. I'm excellent at what I do. I shoot better than most of the men in the current ERT unit. You know about that shot I took. It was the furthest any sniper on the D.C. ERT has ever shot. I don't like to brag, but if I'm that good, it should be used for good." I rise to leave, feeling emotional all of the sudden. I won't cry and I won't let him see me break down. I crumple the napkin and drop it into my glass so the words will smear.

I love James and the fact that I hurt him hurts me, but I'll not lose him and Ana too. I hurry out of the ballroom and reach the elevator. I'm pushing the button repeatedly when I feel Duncan stand directly behind me. The door opens and I try to rush in to close it on him. Of course, that doesn't work. He pushes in as the doors close. Duncan presses the button for our floor and crowds me against the back of the elevator. I turn my back on him, hoping he'll get the clue. He pushes into me, putting his hands on the railing in front of me. I'm pressed into his chest, trapped between his body and the wall. I normally only do one-night stands, if that at all, but he's all I want. Why is he still in my system?

"Maya, I know loss. Loss of a parent, loss of a lifelong mate, and loss of men I led. I get it. However, I don't like the thought of you in danger, no matter how hot it is. How did you get into my blood so deeply?"

"Please, Duncan, I told you no."

"Maya, I'll see you again. We'll figure this out. I want you and I know you want me. Your pulse is racing right now because I'm so close." He points at my neck.

"No! I can't do this!" The elevator dings at our floor. I push past him and run to my room. I'm pretty fast, but I don't have his legs and I'm wearing heels

"Maya, wait," he grabs me and pulls me back into his chest. I want to go on the defense and attack him, but my mind short circuits. His big body surrounds me, his masculine scent engulfs me, and those damn tingles when he touches me sends my heart racing, blood heating and my body readying for him.

"Please, Duncan, no." I feel him resign himself. I want him so bad but right now, I'm too raw. Seeing Ana leave and James hurting is messing with me

"Okay, I'll see you in the morning." Groaning, he lets me go and I walk to my door.

I enter my room, take off my heels, and remember I forgot to talk to the wedding coordinator. I slip my heels back on and peek out the door to see the hall is clear. Deciding to take the stairs just in case, the burn of energy will help my senses. As I'm almost to the bottom, the door opens and a couple falls into the stairwell. They're heavily kissing and groping each other. I ignore them until I notice the best man...Fucktard.

"Hey, Mia, see what you're missing. Why don't you come join us? I like threesomes, bet you will too," he slurs.

I walk right up to them. His companion is the server that was checking out Duncan. I get right in his face and bring my knee up.

"My name is Maya, you fucktard." I push past them and into the hall, leaving him groaning and crying like a girl.

Yep, a fucktard.

After arranging everything, I decide to go back to my room and relax for the night. Maybe a bath in the huge tub and some whiskey will calm my nerves. As I enter my room, I look to the nightstand and see another arrangement of flowers. This time, they're gardenias. Taking out my cell phone, I snap a picture and send it with a message to Derek and Greg.

***Me: Got these, my annual flowers, and a single red rose delivered to me in the last two days. What do they mean other than I've a stalker?***

***Derek: I'm moving in again. No ifs, ands, or buts about it, sexy. I'll make sure Dad keeps it on the DL. I'll research the meanings and let you know. Having fun? Tell James I said hi!***

***Me: Not really. Miss you.***

***Derek: Me too. I'll pick you up at the airport. Be careful.***

***Me: Love you.***

***Derek: Me too.***

***Greg: I see the messages. I will forward it on to Jones.***

I end the chat, walk over to the flowers, and drop them into the trash. I then notice the note left behind.

***My Darling,***

***I'll not allow you to get away from me like she did. You looked so lovely in that dress tonight. I was sure you would. You're more beautiful than she ever was.***

***Oh, the memories. Oh, what I'll do to you when we finally meet.***

***Love Always.***

My skin crawls and I immediately get out of the dress and stash the note in my backpack to research later.

~

*I'M WALKING DOWNSTAIRS. I recognize the hallway. This is Savta's home in Tel Aviv. I step into a room of strangers and they all stare at me, making me feel like I'm on display. Maybe they're staring at me because I've not been able to look in a mirror in days to do my hair. I slide my hand through my hair, feeling the tangles. I don't want to be here. They will turn on me any moment when they realize I murdered them.*

*It's Shiva, and no one talks about her, only him. I walk through another room to see Savta. She looks so lost, her head bowed and the wig she wears a little askew because of all the hugs and crying.*

*"Savta, can I talk to you?" I say in Hebrew*

*"Motek, come, my dear." She leads me from the room. My grandmother only speaks Hebrew and Yiddish anymore; she knows English but refuses to speak it. Motek means sweetheart in Hebrew—she's called me that since I was little. Pain blossoms in my chest and I feel a pain in my arm. I look down to see a bloody, boney hand gripping me. I look up and Savta is scowling at me. I'm lying in my bed.*

*"Maya, wake up." Her voice is frantic and sounds breathless.*

*"What, Savta? It's not morning yet," I say in Hebrew back to her.*

*"Maya, there has been an accident."*

*"Accident? What?" I revert to English in my terror.*

*"You killed them. You spoiled child. My son would still be alive if you hadn't pushed them to go out."*

*"Savta! I didn't know."*

*I'm yelling it wasn't my fault when I look around and find I'm standing in a market. People are pushing past me. I'm dressed in my gear, my balaclava pulled under my chin. I hear a voice and swing around to see no one.*

*"Maya, darling, you look so beautiful. What I'd do for you...I'd kill for you. You're my one and only." I look down at my feet to see Ana and James dead.*

*"Maya, wake up! There's been another accident," Savta says. Duncan is dead. His beautiful black hair is covered in blood.*

*"Maya, no, Maya, why, why did you do this?" I'm bleeding in the tub.*

I come awake as the voices yell in my dreams. Crap this is twice in two nights the nightmares are back in full force. My stalker has brought them out. No going back to sleep now. I get up and change into shorts and a workout top and head to the gym. I need a good run.

# CHAPTER TEN

## DUNCAN

Well, that went well. She shot me down. I need another drink. As I'm sitting at the bar, I hear a commotion from the hall. Maya has just walked out of the stairwell, and I hear someone crying and carrying on. I'm about to go check on her when I notice how calm and regal she looks. She's fucking beautiful. And as I confessed earlier, she's in my blood. My blood runs hot and my cock throbs. I want her again. I then see the best man being helped by one of the wait staff out of the stairwell. It's the girl that Maya got jealous over earlier. Oh yes, I noticed that. I was so turned on by her jealousy. The best man is groaning and tears are streaming down his face.

"I'll make that bitch pay. When Jonathon finds out what she did, he'll make sure she's taken care of," he yells. What a fucktard. Maya completely ignores him. I want to go silence him but know that will only make the situation worse.

Part of me wants to chase her, but she already turned me down once. I ignore the server as she eyes me again. Only one woman is going to be in my bed if I can help it. I'm done for the night and head to my room to try to get some sleep.

I come awake with a start, my heart beating so fast I think I'm going to have a heart attack. My stomach starts to roll and I jump up from the bed, barely making it to the loo. I retch until I'm dry heaving. I can smell the coppery blood and remnants from the gun battle in the air, along with the smell of burned flesh from the bomb going off near us. I rub my hand across my sternum where I can still imagine some of the bruises from all the bullets hitting my vest. Every time one would strike me, I'd fall back until Ian pulled me back. I can still feel Christopher's limp body in my arms as I dragged him along with me.

I stand on shaky legs, gripping the tile of the counter until I feel my legs working again. I brush my teeth and splash water over my face. I want these dreams to end. I want my life back, but how can I go on when he died?

As usual, it isn't even five. I decide to use the hotel's gym—I've heard its state of the art. Before my normal nightmares started, I dreamed of Maya in my arms again. Taking from her body, her hot pussy rippling around my cock. Just thinking of the dream has me hard again. Maybe I can run off this damn erection and blimey sexual frustration. All I want to do is bury myself in her again.

I enter the facility to hear classic rock playing as a woman runs on a treadmill at a fast pace. Her hair is pony-tailed up high, but the length still has it landing about mid-back. I know her without her turning around. *Maya.* Her tiny, black shorts are tight and show off incredible muscular legs and thighs, not to mention a firm arse. She's wearing a close-fitting, yellow runner's bra. There's a large Star of David tattoo on her lower back with writing around it. How did I miss that the other night? Bloody hell, my erection is in the danger zone. I could nail boards, I'm so hard watching her muscles flex as she runs. This woman is so gorgeous. Her back and arms pump with her legs. Her muscles flex and I want to watch myself pump into that tight, little body.

"Bugger me!" I groan.

Maya all the sudden jumps onto the sides of the treadmill and turns. Woops! Guess I said that out loud. She slows her treadmill and jumps back on and starts to jog. She reaches for the phone playing the music and turns it down.

"How long have you been here?" From the sweat sheen, I'd assume a while.

"A bit," she states.

"Don't you sleep?"

"I work nights, so I can't sleep right now."

"Baby, it's almost midnight in D.C. You're all turned around."

"Ya well, it's how I'm wired." She looks a little guilty, and I wonder what that's about.

"Mind if I run next to you?" Not sure I'll be able to run with this hard-on.

"No, I don't mind. I won't be much longer, I need to head up for a shower anyway." I groan at the thought of her all soapy and wet. "Did you say something?" Maya turns her head to me.

"No." I start running full out, hurting my already hard cock more. I need to distract myself from all her skin and sweatiness.

Bugger off, I want to work out another way right now. She slows her treadmill even more, steps off and stops it. She grabs her phone and shuts it off before putting it into a pocket at the waist of her shorts.

I watch her in the mirrors surrounding the gym as she turns and stretches. Maya bends and rests her hands on the floor, her arse in the air. Fuck this, I jam the emergency stop, jump off the treadmill, and am on her in a second. She gasps as my erection hits her pussy in this position, and rises up and leans back into me.

"Duncan, I'm sweaty. I've been running for hours."

"I don't care! Come on, baby, we can take care of both of us." I rub my cock against her arse again. She groans and turns to me. That's it. My mouth is on her, claiming her. I wrap her ponytail around my wrist and march her back to the exit, my tongue in her mouth the whole way. I drop the ponytail and my hands roam over her body to her arse. Her skin is smooth and slick from sweat. I can't take it anymore and pick her up, feeling her right where I want her as she wraps her legs around me. Bugger me!

I don't know how we make it into the elevator or back to her room. All I know is I can't stop kissing her and I want to imprint myself on her. I'm sure anyone that saw us got a good show. I stop kissing her as we reach her door. She pulls her key out of her bra and my eyes fall on her breasts.

"Open the door now, baby, I need those in my mouth." My voice is husky with the need for her.

She opens it and I carry her in, kicking the door closed behind us. I enter the bathroom and kick this door closed too as I kiss her lips again. Sitting her on the counter, she pulls back, unzips, and unlatches her double-layered bra, letting it fall from her shoulders. My mouth closes on her breast and her head falls back. I suck her nipple into my mouth and press the distended little bud against the roof of my mouth as I caress and play with the other one.

"Mmm, Duncan, please. I need you."

I continue to suck on her nipple, pulling it hard into my mouth. Her breasts are perfect and the sweat on her is turning me on even more. I pull away with a pop and turn on the light. I turn to the shower and turn it on to warm.

"Stay there. Don't you dare move, baby." My voice sounds harsh, I want her so much. "Why two bras?"

"Because one isn't enough with these girls," she says as she lifts a full breast in her hand. I laugh and grab her again, loving on her breasts as she writhes around on the counter. I pull her legs apart and step in between, pulling her to me. She starts grinding against my erection. I'm about to embarrass myself by coming in my shorts.

"Baby, if you keep that up we're not going to make it into the shower."

"Duncan, honey, I need you now. I wanted you last night. I should've never told you no." *Honey.* Maya called me honey. I want to hear her say that to me again. My chest swells with the endearment.

"You'll get me soon enough. Let's get in the shower." I step away to pull my shirt over my head and drop my shorts. She starts to stand to pull off her shorts, but I grab her and lift her up. Holding her with one arm around her waist, I pull her shorts and thong off with my free hand. Her phone hits the floor, unfazed, Maya wraps herself around me again. I latch onto a nipple, pulling it into my mouth and sucking hard. As I pull off, I gently bite the tender bud.

"Oh God, Duncan, please." I switch to her other breast and treat it the same. I'm standing in the middle of the bathroom with her wrapped around me and my mouth on her. What a better morning is there?

Then it hits me, I don't have a condom. "Bugger me!" I set her down.

"What? Please don't stop. I want you so bad." She starts trying to climb up me again.

"My condoms are across the hall in my room. Sorry, baby. Unless you've some?"

"Duncan, I haven't been with anyone for a while and I'm clean," she begs.

"Baby, it's been awhile for me too, and I just had a bunch of tests, including those, for my job. I'm clean too."

"Then fuck it, take me now!"

"Maya, are you sure?" The thought of her tight sheath without any barrier wrapped around my cock has me struggling to breathe.

"I'm on the pill."

"Oh Bugger, I can't wait to feel you bare." I lift her up where she again wraps around me. She's like a spider monkey crawling higher up me. I plant her back against the shower wall and push up against her.

"Baby, I need to make sure you're ready for me, you're so small and tight." Reaching between us, I finger her clit until she moans loudly.

"Please, Duncan, I need you now."

I insert a finger into her. She's so tight, I feel my balls start to pull up. She can make me come without even being inside her. I pull my finger out and suck off her juices and groan.

"Sweetest damn pussy." I lift her higher, anchoring her against the wall, and slowly enter her. Her head rolls back and her eyes close.

"Maya, open your eyes. Look at me. I want you to see who owns you right now."

"Oh God, Duncan." Her eyes snap open. The green of her irises is so bright. I reach up and gently pull her hair out of the band as she slides further onto my cock.

I feel the burning in the base of my spine. I need to make her come before I do.

"Baby, I love your hair." I can't take any more of this torture and fully pull her down onto me. We both groan in pleasure. "Hold on. I need you to come, I need to feel you squeezing my cock."

She wraps her arms around me as I start to lift her off me and plant myself back in her deep. I begin to pump her up and down on me. Her thighs hold on tight, but I feel her lifting her hips as I pull out each time. She leans back into the wall, hitting it a bit as we go. Her vaginal walls start to tighten around my cock. God, she feels so silky smooth and smashing wrapped around me. Her bare pussy lips rub against my groin when I push her down on me. I'm about to blow my spunk into her and she still hasn't come yet. I lean forward and take a nipple into my mouth and she instantly tightens around me. She throws her head back, keeping her eyes on me as she starts coming.

"Duncan, Duncan. OH God, yes!" she cries out and digs her nails into my shoulders. I pump into her harder and her head hits the wall.

"Ahhh, Maya!" I come on a loud growl. My arms lock around her. I've never gone bareback before and I've never come so hard before. I'll never use a condom with her again. We both hold onto each other tightly. Our breathing begins to normalize. I feel our combined juices leaking from her and it starts to turn me on again.

"Baby, we need to wash up."

"Okay." She sounds sleepy. I release her legs from my hips and turn her into the spray. Her hair is almost all wet when she looks up at me, all shy and sweet.

"Will you stay with me as I sleep?" she asks quietly.

"Of course, baby." Okay, what's that all about? I want to know this girl. I want to protect her and keep her with me. I know she'll not allow that, but I can't help how I feel.

She looks so vulnerable right now. If being in that blimey war taught me anything, it was to grab onto what feels right. To not think twice when you're given a chance like this. I shake off the thoughts as I remember something.

"By the way, what happened to the best man in the stairwell?" I ask.

Her back straightens and she looks me in the eye. She smiles, and sweetly says, "That fucktard called me Mia and tried to proposition me into a threesome while making out with someone else. So I kneed him in the balls."

I can't help but laugh so hard and loud. The funniest part is she called him what I call him. "You should do that more often," she murmurs.

"What?" I look at her questionably.

"Laugh. You look so handsome and young when you do it." Her words stop me. It's true I don't laugh very much anymore.

"For you, I'll try. By the way, do I need to worry about this Greg chap?" She bristles slightly at my statement. I know she doesn't do relationships but I'll be heading to D.C. every chance available.

"No, he's a friend of your father's." She doesn't say any more.

We finish washing each other and get out. She dries off and puts her hair in a bun on the top of her head. I see her tattoo again and want to ask, but I don't want her to close up on me. I know enough to figure out there are names and part of the writing is Gaelic. Interesting. We climb into bed and I pull her to my side, where she cuddles up. It's going on six in the morning now and we don't need to be to Father's house until eleven.

"Sleep, baby. I'll wake you up in a couple hours."

"Thank you, Duncan. I just can't sleep by myself unless I take sleeping pills or am exhausted."

What the fuck! She'll be explaining that statement later.

"Baby, just don't run off again."

"I won't."

I settle in and close my eyes, enjoying the feel of her in my arms. This is the best feeling in the world. I don't want to ever stop holding her.

# CHAPTER ELEVEN

## MAYA

I'm sitting in the first class lounge at London Heathrow thinking back over the day. The nap with Duncan was wonderful. I usually can't sleep like that, and it was nice to wake up feeling rested. Not panicked. He made love to me slowly when he woke me up. I wanted a hard and fast fuck, but he controlled the whole experience and now I feel all confused.

He lives here, I live in D.C. We both have jobs we love. With my stalker coming back in my life, changing this can't happen. I can't let another person die because of me.

We looked into each other's eyes the whole time and I could feel him banging into the walls around my heart. The loss is unavoidable, but I'm not ready to experience it again. I killed them. I'll not hurt someone else.

Derek texted me the meaning of the flowers. Gardenias represent a secret love and the single red rose means life-long devotion. Great, I've got an admirer who wants me for life. This has to be the same person. I can't have two stalkers with two different agendas. I shake off the negative thoughts and remember my day with Duncan.

On the way to James's home, I rode in Duncan's classic Aston Martin. His car mesmerized me. It was the hottest car I've ever seen—black with sleek lines and leather interior. His big body fit behind the wheel like a glove and the car purred. Shit, I felt like purring.

*"Duncan, this car is so fucking hot, I want to drive it. What year is it?"*

*"Baby, that won't happen today, because when I see you behind the wheel of this car, I'll want to fuck you so hard the neighbors will ring the ole bills"*

*"I was thinking about fucking too, watching you drive. I want to climb on your lap and take a real ride." He groans.*

*"Baby, I can't believe I want you again, but I won't risk you getting hurt. So unless this car is parked, you aren't climbing into my lap." I laugh at him.*

Shit, I laugh again, thinking back over that. He's serious about keeping me safe. Crazy man.

Brunch with James was fantastic. I forgot how much I missed being around him. I might have gone up to Boston regularly to see Uncle Marcus, but I'm closer to James. He was with me at the hospital, and I know my mother talked to him right before she died. Maybe someday he'll tell me about that conversation. I miss her so much, and Abba too, but she was always there even when I didn't do as perfect as he wanted. Plus, James is one of the few that were with me when the pain almost won.

James tried to talk me out of staying with the ERT, even Duncan attempted to get me to talk to his friend, Joshua. I told them both that my mind was made up and if they didn't want me to walk out, they'd stop right then.

The best part was James and Duncan talked and seemed to get along really well. Ana will be excited when she comes home, they'll have a good foundation for a relationship started. I just hope they keep it up. I know when James comes to D.C. next week I'll talk to him more about working the situation out with Duncan for Ana's sake.

Duncan and I were unable to spend any more time alone. James kept us at his home until I needed to check in for my flight. It was good. I didn't want to feel any more emotions than I already was. That's what I kept telling myself. James even wanted me to use his service to get to the airport. I almost took him up on the offer, but Duncan insisted he'd take me.

I could see him trying to work up to something on the way to the airport. Duncan kept squeezing the steering wheel and fidgeting. As we got closer to the airport, he got quieter and his mood seemed to darken. I needed to end it, but I couldn't say the words. He walked me right up to the security checkpoint. I was looking around, trying to avoid the feelings I was having. My chest was so tight I thought I'd have a heart attack.

*"Maya." It takes me a second to realize he's stopped a couple steps behind me and is pulling my arm back.*

*"No, Duncan, I can't stay. Don't ask me to," I say, trying to break his hold. He just tightens his grip more. I turn around to look at him.*

*"Maya, stop," he interrupts me. "I know you've got to go back. I know you have plans. I don't want to stop them. I know what it's like to have people you care about try to force you to make decisions you don't wish to. Can we do a long distance relationship? Just talk and get to know each other? I can't imagine being with anyone but you right now. I know this is fast, but being in the military and seeing what I have, I know you can't take life for granted. Please, baby?"*

*I walk the two steps back to him and right into his arms. I can't help myself, he's right, life is short, and I know this. I want him too and only him. I've never felt like this. I'll just have to take care of this stalker on my own.*

*"Okay, Duncan, we will try," I say into his chest.*

*"Give me your phone," he says as he pulls back.*

*"What? Why?"*

*"I want to be able to reach you. I'm going to be heading to France tomorrow, but I'll be in touch."*

*"Okay." I hand him my phone and realize I've dropped down to a single syllable language. This man muddles my mind. He dials from my phone and hands it back after a moment.*

*"Now I've got your number too."*

*"Duncan, we shouldn't tell the family yet."*

*"Why not?" His eyebrows drop and his face pinches suspiciously.*

*"What if this doesn't work out?"*

*"Oh, baby, I'm going to make it work."*

*I laugh. "Okay, Big Guy, whatever you say." I smile at him.*

*We kiss each other goodbye, no promises of when we will see each other again, but at least we're trying.*

"British Airways flight 184 with service to Washington D.C. Dulles Airport will begin boarding shortly." I'm jolted from my thoughts by the overhead announcement.

As I take my seat in the first class area my phone pings with a text message.

***Duncan: Are you on the plane?***

***Me: Yes, just got to my seat***

***Duncan: I just got to my flat. Going to have Ana do some decorating when she gets home.***

***Me: What're you doing?***

***Duncan: Walking around and finding every surface I want to fuck you on.***

***Me: Okay***

My panties are instantly wet. Man, can he sext.

***Me: I'm going to have to do that when I get home too.***

***Duncan: Baby, I hope this isn't a long wait because I'm hard as a rock just thinking about you.***

***Me: I know what you mean. I'm so wet for you.***

***Duncan: Ah, baby, I think I'll be coming to D.C. soon. I need you. Urgh.***

I smile and switch my phone to airplane mode. I lay my head back against the headrest and think about what I'm doing. I hope he's not in danger from me. This feeling of finally being alive is new and I like it. I know that I'll need to figure out my life.

Greg has been helping me for years and here's another favor I'll need to ask from him. I'll need to make sure Derek doesn't try to force the issue about moving in again. When he moved in the last time, he scared all guys away. I won't have him scaring Duncan away, although, Duncan might have a problem with him staying with me. I'll need to explain soon.

Duncan told me how he'd be heading to France to work for a

diplomat there. We didn't discuss very personal facts, but I'm sure we will soon enough.

I can't and won't tell him about my stalker. I need to determine if there really are two or just one playing a sick game with me. I need to take care of this situation before it hurts people I care about. Care? Do I care for Duncan already? If I did, wouldn't I open myself completely to him? I keep so many details about my life to myself, very few people know me completely. Greg and Derek do. Ana knows a lot but not all of it. James knows more than Ana but...wow! I think about it carefully, not even Greg and Derek know me completely. Not even the one man I tell a lot to knows everything. Can I let Duncan be that person?

I rub my wrist and think about my nightmares. I need to get those under control again. When I woke in Duncan's room the other night it was from a nightmare, and this morning was too. I'm going to have to keep an eye on them. If they get too bad, I'll have to call *him* again.

I need to change my thoughts before it's too late. I can't go down that rabbit hole. I grab my phone, pull up the music app, and plug in my headphones. The rock music is like a balm to my soul. I close my eyes and rest until we land.

# CHAPTER TWELVE

## MAYA

I came home to a new flower delivery, adder's tongue, which Derek says means jealousy. Since then, every day, I get a dozen crimson roses along with my usual arrival of hyacinths. They're forwarded to the hospital every time. I don't want them here. I'm being followed most days, but as soon as someone tries to intercept whoever it is, they take off. Derek wants to move in and I keep telling him no.

It's been over a week since I left London. Duncan and I talk and text when we can. I've been trying to figure a way to head to London for a quick weekend or even Paris where he is. Duncan is guarding a diplomat's daughter; he complains that she's a handful.

Tonight I'm getting ready for dinner with James when my phone beeps with an incoming message.

***Duncan: Baby, I miss you so much. Sorry, I couldn't text sooner, had to work. Just got to my room. Can you call?***

***Me: Can't. Your father is waiting for me at Georgia Brown's for dinner.***

***Duncan: Lucky man.***

***Me: I miss you too.***

***Duncan: Have you been made primary permanently yet?***

***Me: Yep. My partner and I are going to celebrate after dinner tonight.***

***Duncan: Why him? Why not some girlfriends?***

***Me: Jealous?***

***Duncan: Fuck ya! I feel like you just gutted me. That man gets to spend time with my girl.***

***Me: Stop. I sleep with you and work with him, besides he isn't into relationships.***

***Duncan: All guys are into you.***

***Me: Well just for that, I won't try to fly to Paris next week when I'm off.***

***Duncan: Wish you could, baby, but we're heading to Nice, France. Sorry.***

***Me: Okay, well I gotta run. Text me tomorrow.***

***Duncan: Okay, baby. Good night.***

~

I RUN into the Southern cuisine restaurant to see James taking a seat in a booth across the way. I point to him and bypass the hostess. He stands and hugs and kisses my cheek.

"Have you heard from Ana at all?" I ask right away. She never texted me back after I got home. I know she's on her honeymoon, but this is so not like her. Duncan and I have discussed this and he's worried too.

"No, but they're probably having a good time. Barcelona is beautiful in the summer."

"I guess. It's just not like her."

"Her life has changed. Jonathon is her priority now. Someday they'll have a child. Just like someday you'll be married too."

"Not likely."

"Okay, I'll change the subject. Have you been up to Boston lately?"

"No, I've been so busy with work."

"I've been so busy too. I was thinking of heading that way after my meetings tomorrow to see him."

"How are your meetings so far?"

"Good. I'm working with the Israeli delegation to have a delegation set up next month along with a ball. I'm hoping this will ease tensions after what happened a couple weeks ago. I heard you were the sniper on that call."

"Yeah. I was just doing my job."

"I heard they're talking about bringing in David Harel to lead their security."

"I'll have to make the time to see him while he's here if he does."

"How's Derek?"

"He's good, I can still kick his butt. He's thinking of moving in with me again."

"Why is he moving in?" I see the questions in his eyes he's not asking.

"He doesn't like the place he's staying at now, my place is quiet. He doesn't want to move back in with his dad. I'm fine, stop worrying." I smile at him.

"Uncle Marcus is going to possibly be coming to London for the holiday too."

"When was the last time Uncle Marcus crossed the pond?"

"Been years. I think he's hoping to see you, he seems lonely. Actually, I believe the last time he crossed the pond was when Isabella died."

"I'll call him soon." I can't react to his comment about Isabella. I know how much James misses her.

I can't tell James that Derek wants to move in because he's worried about my stalker. The rest of the meal goes by without any more talk of my job or Derek.

As we walk out to the curb, he hugs me and kisses my cheek again.

"Maya, it was rather enjoyable to see you. You appear happy, are you seeing someone?"

"Uhh, what?" I almost fall over.

"You've a special smile I've seen off and on tonight. I thought you might be thinking of someone."

"Oh no, I'm just super excited about my new position on the ERT." How can he tell? I was thinking of Duncan and missing him.

"Okay. Will I see you at Christmas for sure?"

"Yes, I'll call when I've made my reservations," I promise.

"Take care, darling, please be careful, and remember I love you."

"Thank you, James. I love you too." I hug him again. I'm happy about the job, but the relationship that's starting with Duncan is making me feel more human than a robot. Having James notice makes me aware I need to be more careful, but I also feel guilty for lying to him.

# CHAPTER THIRTEEN

## MAYA

"Use the momentum of your opponent to send them past you. Deflect the punch and give them a little push. They'll end up on their ass and wonder what they did."

I demonstrate the move for the class, sending a student gently to the ground. I smile and help the student up as a shadow falls across the doorframe. I turn to see who it is and my smile widens. It's been a long time since I've seen my father's old friend.

"Hello, child, can you talk for a moment?" he says in Hebrew.

"Give me a minute," I reply back. My Hebrew flows off my tongue as though I've spoken it every day when I haven't in months.

I set up another student who knows the moves I want to teach next, and walk out into the hall with my towel and water bottle.

"Hey, stranger. What are you doing here?" I greet him in English.

"I am good. I need a favor," he continues in Hebrew and I begin to worry.

I look around us and not seeing anyone, I raise an eyebrow at him in question.

"I'm teaching this class until four, then we can practice." Again I reply in English. I want to see if he will cave and tell me what's going on.

I've known David Harel most of my life. He served in the Israeli Army with my father, before David went on to be Mossad and my father to become a lawyer. David helped teach me my knife fighting skills, as well as fine-tune my Krav Maga training. After my parents' deaths I very rarely saw him, although he was always like an uncle to me. Him showing up here doesn't surprise me because of what James said over a month ago, but him only speaking in Hebrew tells me that he is hiding something.

"Why practice? I'll win every time. I might have taught you a lot but not everything I know," he says in Arabic and I become more confused.

"Keep it up, old man. I've learned some new skills," I respond back in Arabic.

"I need your help tonight, 2000 hours. You will wear this and pose as my date. No one here knows about our relationship. You will be checked, so no knives. If something happens you will have to use your hands," he says in Yiddish. Yiddish is a language not many people know and that's when I figure I need more of an explanation.

"Why?" I say in German. I've been studying German lately so I'm testing him now.

It's not that I don't trust David, it's that I don't understand why he is being so evasive.

"We are going to the ball the Israeli consulate is hosting before they sit down to talk about the Egyptian border attack. There will be ambassadors from several consulates, along with other political faces. I need to attend as a retired operative with my much younger date to distract from the fact that I'm looking at their current security," he continues in Yiddish.

"I don't dance," I say in French.

"You will. I don't ask you for much but I need you for this. I will have a limo pick you up at nineteen thirty." He turns and walks away. The box he handed me hangs limply in my hand and I wonder what the hell he is getting me into.

At exactly nineteen thirty I'm waiting in my living room for the call saying the limo is here. David picked a very sexy black dress with thick straps over my shoulders that also hang down onto my arms. There is a peekaboo panel between my breasts showing my cleavage, and the waist is cinched in, accentuating how small I am. The most daring part of the dress is the split up my thigh. He also threw in a pair of black pumps with a strap over the top of my foot. They're over four inches and will bring me up to his six foot height. I pulled my hair up into braids and a bun, showing how thick my hair is.

I can't get over the fact that I know David is up to something, but what? I won't know until we can talk privately.

The front desk rings, informing me my ride is here.

I grab my thin shawl and handbag, and check myself in a mirror one more time before I walk out.

I haven't heard from Duncan at all today, and with David's visit, I'm on edge. I know Duncan would call me if he could, but I'm at a loss as to why he hasn't when we've spoken every day. Yesterday he mentioned there might be a chance that he would be in New York next month, and I'm planning to take the time to go see him.

"Ahh, my darling, you look amazing. I knew that dress would flatter you," David says in English as I step up to him. He kisses me on both cheeks as he takes my hand and leads me out to the stretch limo waiting at the curb.

As he holds the door for me, I feel a tingle of awareness, like I'm being watched. I scan the area, trying not to alert David.

"Get in the car. We need to talk."

I slide in and wait for him.

"We do need to talk. Tell me what's going on. Why all the cloak and dagger, David?"

"About three weeks ago someone started searching your family's background. He was American and he knew enough about you that it didn't trip anyone up until he questioned your father's background."

"What about Abba's background alerted someone?"

What secrets did my father keep that someone from Mossad wouldn't want known?

"Don't fret, darling. Your Abba was a good man. He was a friend of Mossad, and mine most especially."

"Then what?"

"How about you tell me why a BAU team has a file on you?"

"Dammit, David, you can't just go searching my background. That is none of your business."

"Anything that does with you is my business. Your Abba, Yoseph, would never forgive me if I let something happen to you. Now spill."

"I guess I have two stalkers. One that has been sending me flowers and a couple notes, nothing serious. The second is a little more serious."

"I would say. The BAU has him listed as the potential to become violent. I knew about the first, I've been keeping an eye on that one for years. As for cloak and dagger, like I said earlier, I need to watch the operatives without them realizing I'm evaluating them. What a better way to distract them then with a beautiful woman?"

"Thanks, Uncle David." I sneer, using the nickname I've called him since I was a kid.

"No Uncle David tonight. Act like you like me."

"Fine. By the way, I love the shoes. I'm keeping them."

I hold up a foot, displaying the high heels. He smiles.

"That's fine, kiddo. Here we go."

The limo comes to a stop outside the hotel where the event is being held. David's door opens and he gets out, then holds out his hand for me. I take his hand and put myself into the role of being his date. His large six foot frame is still muscular at sixty, and I could see young women being attracted to him. He's completely bald with no facial hair and a few wrinkles that make him look like he's fifty. His dark brown eyes are always looking for danger. He puts his arm out and I take it, thinking of Duncan. At the coat check, I give them my shawl but keep my little black handbag as we walk into the ballroom.

There are more than just a couple consulates here, it looks like every political figure in D.C. and other major countries is here. I scope the area, looking for Greg, but don't see him. He or some of his team should be here with the number of big wigs in attendance. We make our way to where the Israeli ambassador is standing.

"Sir, the lovely Maya Aaron," David says in Hebrew.

"Sir, it's nice to meet you," I say in Hebrew, shocking him. He proceeds to ask me where I learned Hebrew and about myself.

"I live here in D.C. My father was from Tel Aviv."

The music starts up with a waltz.

"Come, Maya, let's take a turn."

David leads me to the dance floor and holds me close so we can talk.

"Okay, what do you think?" he asks on our first turn.

I'm looking around the room; the only person that keeps pulling my eye is a tall Hispanic man that appears to be part of the French dignitaries guard. Something about him is familiar.

"Why was it so easy for you to get close to the ambassador after what happened in June? If you're not working for them yet, you shouldn't be able to get close."

"Good eye. I trained you well. Looks like you are attracting attention like I hoped."

I smile at him and continue to scan the room.

# CHAPTER FOURTEEN

## DUNCAN

I can't wait until I can take a break and text Maya to tell her I'm in town. My current job is to protect the undersecretary to the Prime Minister of France's daughter. Because this trip includes the prime minister and the undersecretary, we were radio silent, so I couldn't warn Maya I was coming to town. Then we had to attend this gala. I walk in from taking a call from Joshua to check on my team before I call Maya.

"Raul, where is Ian?"

He nods across the room to where the Israeli contingency stands. "He's going to see if he can lure a woman away from an old codger." He smiles and shakes his head.

I turn to see where Ian is heading. A tall bald headed man is standing beside a beautiful woman whose very presence calls to me. "What the bloody hell?"

"What, Big Guy?" Raul looks at me, his eyebrows dropping and his face tightening; he knows my tone.

"I'll be back." I stomp off, stalking the woman that keeps me up at night. She turns to look at the man and smiles. That's a smile meant for me, not some old codger.

I barrel down on Ian. "Go back to Raul now!" I bark at him as I pass him.

She has her back to me and I realize I need to be careful how I do this. I focus on something other than her lithe body in that dress. As she turns to accept a glass of champagne, I notice the slit going up her leg. Son of a bloody hell, what is she wearing? I pause and try to focus again.

"Excuse me, may I have this dance?" My voice comes across ruff, more demanding then questioning.

She turns and the shock on her face is evident. The man standing next to her goes to pull her behind him. Oh hell, he didn't. "Maya, please!" I demand, bowing my head slightly.

"Uhh...just a moment, David. I'll be right back," she says, smiling at the bloke who is going to die if he doesn't release her.

"Sweetheart, are you going to be okay?" he asks while looking at me. That's when I realize he's more than some old man. I can see the training pouring off him with the way he stands.

"I'll be fine. Duncan's a friend, he's James's son."

He still looks at me warily and I grit my teeth at him, trying not to growl my hatred to his touching her.

She puts her hand out to me and I haul her into me, pulling her behind me. My body is humming with energy. Instead of turning around, I push her as I back us up onto the dance floor, spinning her around until she faces me.

"Did I miss something or did we break up?" I growl.

"I'm helping a friend, that's all. What are you doing here?"

"I was going to call and tell you I'm here for the night. But instead I see you fawning all over that old man." I swing my arm in the direction of her date.

"Don't let David hear you say that, he's still just as dangerous as he was when he was a Mossad agent."

"Baby, did things change?"

"No, I said I'm helping David, but you're going to blow our cover if you don't give me some space. What hotel are you at? I'll meet you there after the gala."

"At the Crowne Plaza, room 1121. I want to kiss you right now."

"You can't. I missed you too. Goodbye."

She pulls away from me and turns to walk back to her date. Just before she gets to him, her head turns to look at me and I see the desire in her eyes. I fight the urge to go grab her and run.

"Bugger me, Big Guy, who was that lovely lass?" Ian interrupts my thoughts.

"That is my sister's best friend, Maya."

"Looks like you know her more than just 'she's my sister's best friend.'"

"That is none of your business. Come on, we have work to do."

I turn to look over my shoulder once more and find she is looking at me again.

"My father does not pay you to dance with hookers. I want to leave," Alisa, our protectee, yells. Her voice grates on my nerves.

"She isn't a hooker, she's my sister's best friend, and I thought I could say hello as Raul and Ian were here."

"You're not paid to think. I want to leave, now."

I nod to the guys and we head out, before I reach the door, I look back once more. Maya is watching me again. Her head nods slightly and I can't wait until later.

MAYA

My nerves are still raw from seeing Duncan. I can't believe how turned on I was by his show of jealousy. When he walked out and I nodded at him, I saw the woman he was guarding giving me a look that I can only describe as evil. I push that thought back as I think about him in that black suit with the guns he was carrying. Most people might not have known he was carrying, but I could tell he had a single gun in a shoulder holster and another at his back. I'm fairly certain he has an ankle piece too. But the thing that turned me on the most was the number of knives I could see on him. I want to lick his body as I pull each out and test it.

"Earth to Maya. Want to tell me about the man?" David's voice interrupts my fantasy.

"He's Ana's brother. We met at her wedding in June."

"Is that all? You know I could have his whole dossier before morning."

"He's a friend. Don't worry about it."

"He could have been the one searching your background."

"No, it wasn't him. He just..." I feel the sudden urge to flee. "David..." I hear the panic in my voice.

My tone must put David on edge, he turns and then his body is falling into me. I pull him with me as I grab my cell phone from my purse and pull us behind a bench. We decided to walk through the park near my condo so we could talk. Two more bullets hit the pavement near where we are hiding. I feel the bite of rock hitting my skin, more importantly I feel the stickiness of David's blood as it runs from his body.

"9-1-1, what's your emergency?"

"This is Officer Aaron of the ERT. Shots fired, one person hit. We are at the park near Massachusetts Avenue and 3rd Street in the Triangle. Request ambulance and ERT for a possible sniper."

"Maya..." David groans. I look down to see the shot entered his back on the right side and exited through his chest.

"How bad?" I'm worried about him.

"Not too bad. I won't be able to show you up in the gym tomorrow."

I hear the sirens and realize no more shots have been fired.

An hour later I'm still standing in the park answering questions. I'm tired. I have plans. And I want out of these heels. I texted Duncan to tell him I was running late. I didn't tell him what was happening.

"Maya!" I turn as Derek and Greg stalk toward me. Derek is yelling my name as he moves faster. I know this is one of his greatest fears.

"What the hell happened?" Greg demands.

"David and I were taking a walk when he was hit. I think someone at the gala figured out what he was up to."

"And what was that?"

"We were just checking the ambassador's current security."

"Are you hit?" Derek pulls me into him and I shiver with the fear coming off him.

"Here take this." Greg hands me his tuxedo jacket. I look up at him and realize he saw me tonight.

"He asked me to help him. He also wanted to talk about someone researching my parents."

"I saw what you were up to. We'll talk about that later. Someone just searched your address here."

"What?"

"Yep, come on, you're going home with me for the night."

"I can't and I won't."

"What do you mean you can't? I'm not going to argue. You're not safe."

"I'll stay in a hotel for the night."

"Did the EMT check you out?" Derek asks.

"Yes, just scrapes and scratches, I'm good. I will be at the Crowne Plaza, see you tomorrow at brunch."

I turn and walk away, heading toward my condo. I pull out my cell phone and am glad I had it in a protective cover. When I threw my clutch earlier, I thought it was broke.

***Me: I will be there in 20 minutes. Need to change.***

***Duncan: I've been waiting. Is everything okay?***

***Me: I'll explain when I get there.***

# CHAPTER FIFTEEN

## DUNCAN

It's been a half hour since the gala ended and over two hours since I saw her. My skin crawls thinking of her in another man's arms. I need her. My phone dings from the wardrobe and I open the text window.

***Maya: Going to be late. Something has come up.***

***Me: Where are you? I'm on my way.***

***Maya: No. I'll be there as soon as I can.***

***Me: Is everything okay?***

She doesn't respond again and I'm left wondering what is going on. An hour later I've had enough and open another text screen.

***Me: Need a D.C. address for Maya Aaron.***

***Timothy: Just a second***

Five minutes later my phone is ringing.

"Timothy, you could've texted it to me."

"Big Guy, I don't know what you're up to, but you just had me pinged by the FBI. Who the bloody hell is this lass?"

"What do you mean?"

"I searched her address as you requested and the next thing I know the FBI is trying to hack into my system. I led them on a hunt but they will still know that someone in London searched her information. Is she an operative or under FBI protection?"

"No. Thanks, man."

"I've got to report this to the Boss Man."

"Bloody hell, okay, I'll explain tomorrow. I gotta go."

I pace the room for a few minutes and decide to walk down to the bar. I'm just ordering my drink when my phone goes off again with multiple texts.

***Joshua: You will be explaining to me later why Timothy hacked information I could've given you.***

I ignore him; I can deal with him tomorrow. The next text is more important to me.

***Maya: I will be there in 20 minutes. Need to change.***

***Me: I've been waiting. Is everything okay?***

***Maya: I'll explain when I get there.***

Oh hell yeah she will be explaining. I drink the scotch and decide to wait for her out front. Standing out in the humid air makes me glad I changed into cargo shorts and a t-shirt. I'm enjoying watching the activity of the valets and how busy the hotel is at midnight when I hear a V8 engine pulling up. I look up to see a black four-door truck with tinted windows. The driver's door opens and I hear the rock music as I watch my girl step out. The valets watch her as she rounds the hood in short cutoff jeans and a V-neck t-shirt. She is carrying an overnight bag. I don't step out of the shadows, I just watch her and feel myself calm.

"Scratch it, dent it, or all around damage it and I will break every bone in your body. Put it somewhere where another car's doors won't hit it. Got it." She tells the valet as she hands him the keys.

"I've died and gone to heaven, baby," I growl as she turns to see me.

"Hey, honey. Don't die. I like you just the way you are." Her smile lights up her face and I stalk to her.

My lips hit hers before I remember we are standing outside.

"Come on, I need to be inside you, now."

Lacing my fingers with hers, I lead her into the hotel and straight for the elevator. The doors close and I pull her back into my front, running my hands over her body. I hear her breath catch and thinking she is turned on, I rub her arms again. This time she pulls away.

"What's the matter, baby?" That's when I see the bandages on her arms and nicks on her face. "What the bloody hell happened to you?"

"David was shot and I was hit with cement from the ricochet. I'm okay and David will be too."

"What do you mean David was shot?"

"He thinks someone figured out what we were up to tonight at the gala."

"Explain."

The elevator doors open and I pull her behind me to my room. As the door closes I turn on her, my arms cross, my back straight and my legs are spread. This works on my team, I even lift the brow.

"Okay, stop being so bossy," she grumbles as she drops her bag onto the chair. "David owns a security company in Tel Aviv, he was hired by the Israeli government to keep the ambassador safe after what happened in June. They're not taking any more chances. He thinks someone on the current team is leaking information. I was supposed to pose as his date as we checked the current security. We left the gala early and were walking through the park near my condo when we were shot at. He took a bullet in the back of his shoulder, the next two hit the pavement as I pulled him to safety."

"God, baby! Why do you have to do this?"

"Why do you do what you do?"

"Okay. Come here." She tips her chin at me in defiance but I see her breathing increase. Finally she steps to me. I spin her around so her back is to my chest and slide my hands from her collarbone, over her breasts, down her flat stomach and stop at the button of her shorts. "You made me worry tonight. Made me jealous again. And made me get in trouble with my boss. I want you naked and on that bed, now."

Maya's head falls back against my chest. I tip her chin up, leaving my other hand holding her body to mine. She turns her head and I claim her lips again. She opens and our tongues dual. I nip her bottom lip and pull back. "Now, Maya."

She pulls away and pulls her shirt over her head as she slips her sandals off her feet. She reaches behind herself and unhooks her bra. Her back is still to me and I see the muscles play across her shoulders. She unbuttons her shorts and they fall, leaving her standing in front of me in a black thong. The muscled globes of her arse tighten as she steps to the bed. She stops and looks over her shoulder at me with a smile on her face.

"Are you going to stand there or fuck me like you want to?"

I strip out of my clothes so fast the button for my cargo shorts flies across the room and hits the dresser.

"Kneel on the bed and show me that arse."

She removes the thong and positions herself on the bed, using her elbows to hold her up. My eyes zero in on her weeping pussy and my mouth waters. I drop to my knees behind her and bury my face in her heaven. I lick her clit and waste no time fucking her with my tongue.

"Duncan, please. I want your cock."

"Baby. I love when you say that."

Standing, I push on her shoulder blades, getting her into position as I slowly thrust into her. Heaven. I missed this. Her pussy contracts around my cock and I pull out slowly, and push back into her with force, pushing her forward on the bed. My hands wrap around her hips tightly, holding her where I want her. I continue to glide out slowly and slam back into her. I look down at where we're joined and almost lose my spunk from the sight of her body opened to my tunneling cock.

"Baby, are you close?"

"Umhm."

I smack her arse and her head comes up off the bed, and she screams as she comes around my cock. The contractions of her pussy pulling me in deeper has me losing it. I pull out and slam into her again and again, faster as I come deep inside her. I growl her name as she comes again.

I hold my body from falling on her and wait until she comes to herself. I slide out slowly, our combined juices leaking from her body. I get a washcloth and clean her up. Lifting her up, I crawl up the bed with her in my arms. She is mine and I'm not letting her go, ever if I can help it.

"Duncan, what did you mean by you got in trouble with your boss?" Her voice is a whisper. I thought she was asleep.

"When you didn't answer me I had our tech guy search for your address."

"Wait, that was you?"

"What?"

"You searched me?"

"Yeah, why does the FBI have a tracer on you?"

"Because of my job." She mumbles and I know she is lying to me.

"Really?"

"Yeah. Why else?"

"You tell me."

"There is nothing to tell, because of my job all agencies keep an eye on us."

I'll take it for now, but I know there is more to this.

# CHAPTER SIXTEEN

## MAYA

I wake up feeling warm and rested. The smell of leather and something spicy tickles my nose, and I open my eyes to see Duncan's chest. I kiss the pec my cheek is resting on. His body stirs and I feel his erection against my knee.

I gently slide my leg across his body as I rise above him, straddling his hips. He smiles up at me and I give him a devilish grin as I lean forward and kiss his collar bone, my lips tracing down his pec until I'm over his nipple. I lick it and gently bite it. His hands land on my hips and press me down onto his erection. I feel myself getting wet from our erotic play, my fluids leaking onto his cock.

"Baby, stop playing or you're going to end up on your back."

"Mmm...you taste so good." I slip down his body and lick every plain and linear line of his perfect abs. I pull further from his hands and hover over his erection, gently blowing on the crown weeping with pre-cum. Groaning at the site, my mouth waters more as I look at his beautiful cock. The head is broad and reddening with need, the shaft thick and long. Wrapping a hand around the base, I lean forward and lick off the evidence of his desire.

"Baby...take me...in that beautiful mouth." He groans.

I lick him from base to tip along the thick veins. When I reach the top, I treat it like my favorite ice cream cone and lick it over and over. His hands clench the sheets and I give in and take him in my mouth as far as I can. I suck in my cheeks as I pull up off him and his moans have me doing it again. With my other hand, I fondle his balls, rolling them around in my hand as I bob up and down on his cock. I'm so lost in my task of making him come I don't hear his words, but the next thing I know I'm yanked from my new favorite toy and he is impaling himself into my weeping core. I feel the contractions and a bite of pain with the intrusion.

"I said enough, woman. I come inside your hot pussy, you hear me." He growls as he lifts me up and slams back home.

"Please, Duncan, fuck me harder."

He rolls us without leaving my body and pulls my legs up to his shoulders. His strong arms hold him up as he pushes into me harder. Our bodies slapping together, the evidence of my pleasure heard in the room with the wet sounds, his balls hitting my ass in this position. He doesn't relent. He thrusts faster and harder. My world focuses on the orgasm hovering on the edges. He leans into me further, bending me, and hits a spot inside me that has me screaming his name. My orgasm blows through my body like an internal explosion centered at my core. He continues to thrust through my pleasure, prolonging it, until I feel his muscles lock and he grits out my name as I feel his come hitting my insides. He releases my legs and falls onto my body, his elbows keeping his full weight from landing on me. I'm trying to catch my breath when I hear my phone going off in the distance. I know the ringtone and let it go to voice mail. I don't want to talk to Marcus right now.

"Guess I better let you up so you can see who called."

"No, stay right where you are." I sigh. I want to keep this feeling. I want to relish this time with him.

"Come on, let's go shower. I need to get ready for a meeting."

"Must we? Can't we stay in bed all day?"

"I wish, baby, but the brat wants to go to Milan today. Are you still going to try to come up to New York next month?"

"If you want me to?" I smile shyly at him.

"If I want? Woman, I want you!"

He pulls me up off the bed with him and carries me to the bathroom.

The rest of the morning we spend making love in the shower. I watch him dress in another black suit with a thin black tie and white shirt. I watch him arm himself and squirm through the whole process.

"Baby, keep doing that and we won't be leaving this room."

"I can't help it. Watching you put guns and knives on turns me on."

"Please stop, woman." He groans as he turns to look at me. "You dressed in leather turns me on."

I smile as I look down at my brunch outfit. Brown tweed, wide leg slacks; a camisole top in plum paisley with a black leather, slim fit jacket; and plum strappy high heels.

"So you like?" I twirl for him and he grabs me.

"I like you best naked and under me, but yes, I like you in this."

He leans forward and nips my bottom lip. I open and we kiss like we won't see each other for a while, which is true. My tongue slides into his mouth, memorizing every inch of it. My hands slide into his hair, pulling it slightly as his tongue takes over my mouth. He pulls back with a groan.

"I need to meet the guys down in the restaurant, and you want to keep us secret, so guess we part here."

My gut clenches. I want to be on his arm. I want people to know about him and me, but I know that it would hurt the ones I love.

With a deep sigh, I pull away. "Okay, I'll head out first. I'll see you next month. Goodbye." I grab my bags and head for the door, feeling like the world is caving in around me.

Duncan grabs me from behind and swings me around. "It's never goodbye," he declares as he kisses me again. I pull away, averting my eyes and turn to open the door.

I'm going to have to put a stop to these feelings soon. I can't kill him too.

As I wait for the valet to bring my truck, I turn to see Duncan enter the lobby with the Hispanic man from last night.

"Hello, lassie, didn't I see you at the gala last night?" I turn to see a blond man standing behind me. I step away and recognize him as one of Duncan's teammates. The man is as muscular as Duncan but not as tall.

"I believe you have me mistaken for someone else. Later."

I walk up to the valet and tip him as I turn to see Duncan standing in the entrance, watching me. I want to nod my head at him. I want to blow him a kiss, but I was the one that put these restrictions on our relationship.

"I never forget a beautiful lass." The blond says, trying to follow me.

"Ian, leave the woman alone," Duncan practically growls.

I swing up into my truck, turn on the music loud, and open my window and sunroof. Nickelback's *S.E.X* blares through the speakers. I turn to see Duncan smiling at me as I pull into traffic.

"WHERE HAVE YOU BEEN?" Greg demands as I sit down at the table.

"I was at the hotel." I'm still smiling, thinking about the message I left for Duncan as I pulled away.

"I called, they didn't have you registered."

"I used a false name."

I can't believe I'm lying to two of the most important people in my life. Like I said before, I was the one to put this restriction on us. I can't even let Derek know.

"I tried your alias."

"Well, I wanted some time by myself."

My phone pings in my pocket and I look to see a text from Marcus. I ignored his call, didn't return it, and now he's texting me.

***Marcus: When will you be coming up next?***

"Just a moment, Greg, let me respond to this text." I excuse myself as I pull the phone out completely and respond.

***Me: Busy for a while, don't see myself making it up there any time soon.***

***Marcus: I want to see you.***

***Me: I'm busy with work. Need to go, having brunch with friends.***

***Marcus: You have time for them but not me?***

***Me: It's Greg and Derek.***

***Marcus: They take up too much of your time, they aren't even family. Come home. I want to see you.***

***Me: I told you, I'm busy. Bye.***

Therein lies the problem, Boston isn't my home, Marcus isn't my family, and lately I've felt uncomfortable around him.

"Everything okay, sweetheart?"

"Yeah just Marcus pushing for me to go to Boston. I'm too busy right now."

"I have you both set up to take the Air Marshal training in October."

"Okay," both Derek and I answer.

I love when Greg sets me up with additional training.

"I'm heading to the hospital later to check on David."

"He's been moved to the consulate with a private physician."

"Well, guess I won't see him before he leaves. I can't show up there or it will really blow our cover."

"I can't believe you agreed to that."

"He needed help, I couldn't tell him no."

"Do they have any more information on the shooting?" Derek asks.

"Not as far as I've heard. All the security guards that were under investigation have been cleared."

The rest of the meal progresses without any more heavy discussions. I get a quick text from Duncan letting me know they are taking off. I send him a kissing face emoji and return to spending time with my friends.

# CHAPTER SEVENTEEN

## MAYA

I'm packed and ready to go tomorrow evening. Duncan and I talk every day, and even though it's only been a month, I'm excited to see him. He will continue to work, so I've done some research on different places I want to go explore. This isn't my first trip to New York, but I'll get to go where I want.

"Officer Aaron, can you come with me please?"

I'm in the ERT gym working out. I turn to see a man in a suit watching me. Just then the captain and sergeant walk up.

"We told you to let us talk to her first." My captain says to the new guy.

"Officer Aaron, my name is Olsen with Internal Affairs. I need to ask you about your whereabouts last night."

I step away from the rope I was in the process of getting ready to climb again. Pulling off my gloves, I look at Olsen with wariness. Why is IAD asking me questions?

"Do I need a union rep?"

"Do you think you need a rep?"

"What is this about?"

"Tell me where you were last night."

"I was teaching a self-defense class from 1900 hours to 2100 hours. After that I was at home until this morning, when I showed up for training."

"Can anyone corroborate that?"

"There were twenty students in the class. As for being home, you can check my security system and the building's cameras."

"You were at the class for the full two hours?"

"What time do you need to specifically know where I was?"

I hear the anger in my voice and know I'm about to lose my temper. I also know that he is doing this on purpose, trying to trip me up.

"Twenty thirty hours."

"My partner, Derek Williams, was also an instructor. One of the helpers has been training with me for almost a year. What is this about?"

"Do you know Justin Yancy?"

"Yeah. Officer Yancy was Echo One before my partner and I took over the positions. He's currently Victor Two."

"He was murdered last night outside his apartment."

"What does this have to do with me?"

"He was killed with a knife. I understand you studied Israeli Knife fighting."

"Yes."

"Witnesses say someone in all black was seen leaving the area. A tactical knife was found with your initials engraved in the hilt and an ERT patch was in the victim's hand. As if he ripped it off in a struggle."

"Was he stabbed or sliced?"

"What does that matter?" he asks angrily.

"Well, I was taught to slice not stab in a fight. I only stab as a jab or if I'm surprising them. If there was a struggle, I would've been slicing. As for the knife, I have several, and my locker was broken into two weeks ago. Two of my tactical knives are missing. As for the patch, all mine are accounted for."

"She's correct about her locker being broken into," my captain supplies.

"I understand you're leaving town tomorrow. I would like you to voluntarily hand-over your passport. I know you travel internationally quite often."

"I won't relinquish my passport. I have an alibi, and what motive would I have?"

"I understand you and your partner took over Yancy and Nelson's positions in the team."

"That wasn't my fault. I'm happy with my new position, but I never meant for them to lose theirs. Nelson is the one that chose to disobey orders, he was suspended indefinitely. Yancy still had his position and he and I were okay. I've practiced with him. I wouldn't ever hurt him."

"May I ask about your travel plans?"

"I'm going to New York for the weekend."

"Why?"

"Why not."

"Olsen, she has answered all your questions. Williams is right there, and he can corroborate her alibi. Next time notify us and meet her with a union rep," my captain says as he steps in closer to Olsen.

"She was with me. When she got to her condo she called me. Check her phone records," Derek interjects.

"Fine. I will be talking to you again, Aaron."

"I look forward to it."

He walks away and I'm left to wonder who would try to frame me for this. My stalkers have both been quiet, but I don't understand what they would gain from framing me for murder. The rest of the day goes by without incident.

I spend the evening running on my treadmill as I watch the Food Network. Duncan texts me before I go to bed. I can't wait to see him. I forget about Yancy's death for a little while.

THE NEXT DAY I'm boarding my flight to New York when I'm

reminded of Yancy and the fact that IAD wanted me to forfeit my passport. This needs to get figured out before I leave for London in December. With it only being three months away, they should have it cleared up by then.

My plane lands and I grab a taxi to the hotel where Duncan is staying. We decide that I will get my own room to keep our cover, he wanted to pay for it but I don't let him. Some day he will find out about my money, but for now I keep those cards close to my vest.

***Duncan: How much longer until you get here?***

***Me: In the taxi now. When I check in I will give you my room number.***

***Duncan: We're at dinner now.***

***Me: I'll get room service. Text me when you are done.***

***Duncan: Can't wait to see you, baby.***

The taxi pulls up to the hotel and I get out after paying him. As I walk into the lobby, I think about the fact that Duncan and I have never been to each other's places. We are each other's dirty little secrets, using hotels only. I booked a suite, so I'm not surprised when I enter the room to see the large bathroom, fireplace, private balcony and king-size bed.

I decide to take a quick shower before room service arrives. After my shower, I'm walking around in the robe when I notice my cell blinking. I smile when I see Duncan's text.

***Duncan: What's your room number, baby? I'm back.***

***Me: 1407***

***Duncan: That's a suite.***

***Me: Just get your ass up here.***

I'm waiting for my food and my man. Wait...*my man*. No, he can't be my man. A knock interrupts my thoughts and I go to the door. I pull my robe tightly around my body and allow room service to enter the room as Duncan knocks and enters behind him. He grumbles at the waiter for looking at me and I smile. I tip him and he leaves. Duncan wastes no time and is on me in a second.

"Why did you answer the door in this?"

"I thought it was you."

"Do you want to eat first?"

"No, I want you."

He reaches down and unties the robe, revealing my naked body. He makes love to me twice before I get a chance to eat. Duncan helps me finish my cheeseburger and cold fries, then we fall asleep wrapped in each other's arms.

~

"WHAT ARE YOUR PLANS TODAY?" Duncan asks me the next morning as he is getting ready to head out. I enjoy watching him dress and arm himself again.

"I'm going to the Guggenheim today, then maybe to the 9/11 Memorial. What time are you going to be done?"

"I asked the team to take over dinner duties, I'm taking you out tonight. You're not my dirty little secret and I want to go see some of New York with you. I'll be done at three. Can I move most of my things up here?"

"Oh dirty little secret. I like that. I'm a bad girl." I smile seductively as I crawl to the end of the bed, naked, to him.

"You're definitely a bad girl. I'll spank you later. Now answer my question."

"Of course. Where are we going for dinner? I didn't pack anything really nice."

"Nothing too fancy. I made plans, so wear something warm."

"Ooh, I can't wait."

"Now get up here and kiss me, I need to get to work."

I rise from the bed, making sure I swing my hips seductively, and stand directly in front of him, my breasts brushing his suit jacket. I look up into his lust filled eyes as his mouth slams down onto mine. He groans as I tangle my fingers into his hair. His hands on my hips lift me and I wrap my legs around him. He turns and pushes my back into the wall behind him. I pull back.

"You need to get to work."

"Fuck work. I need to fuck my woman."

"Go to work, we have tonight, honey."

He groans again as I slide down his body and he backs away. He leaves and I slip on my robe to go lock the dead bolt behind him.

After a shower, I have a bagel and coffee from a shop close-by and decide to walk to the Guggenheim. It should be opening by the time I get there. My walk is crowded with tourists and locals, and I enjoy the warm weather of September.

My day goes by in a blur of artwork and sadness. I make it back to the hotel at two thirty and realize my mistake when I see Duncan's team in the lobby. I lower my head and rush to the elevators, hoping they don't recognize me. Luck is with me and I make it back to our suite where he is waiting for me in a pair of jeans and a t-shirt with a jacket over the top.

"Hey, baby. How was your day?"

"Good. I almost ran into your team, you should've warned me."

"Sorry. They should be gone. Ready to go?"

"Yep."

We spend the afternoon on a cruise to the Statue of Liberty and dinner at the Empire State Building, along with listening to the local music and enjoying the sights. By the time we get back to the hotel, we are both ready to rip each other's clothes off. He caressed my body every chance he got and I was just as ruthless, brushing against him whenever I could.

Sunday morning I wake in his arms again and we shower together, enjoying the last moments with each other. Between now and Christmas, I don't know when I will see him again. I want to see him but his schedule is changing all the time because of his high value.

"I want to see you again before Christmas." His gruff voice sounds from behind me as I load up my bag. He's in another suit because of the fashion show going on today.

"I want that, too." I turn in his arms.

"I'm glad you took a chance on us."

"So am I."

He kisses me gently and pulls away before taking my hand and walking me out. His team is at breakfast somewhere in Times Square, so we have a few more minutes together as I check out and grab a taxi back to the airport. I had to book an early flight because I'm on shift this evening.

I turn in his arms and kiss his chin.

"I miss you already," I tell him honestly.

"Me too, baby." He bends down and kisses me. Our kiss is interrupted when his name is yelled.

"Shit." I climb into the taxi. "Airport now." I slam the door in Duncan's face and see the hurt, but I can't have James or Ana find out about us.

## DUNCAN

My gut clenches when I hear Ian yell my name, but that's nothing compared to the pain in my chest when she dives into the taxi and leaves me standing there.

She turns to look at me and I see the shock on her face, guess I couldn't hide the hurt. I need to convince her that we're no longer going to keep us a secret. I'll tell my father and Ana myself. I want this woman always. This weekend was one of the best of my life.

"Hey, who was the lass? She looked familiar."

"No one," I say as I turn away, my phone pinging with a text.

***Maya: I'm sorry. I'm not ready for anyone to know yet.***

I don't respond right away because it still hurts. I've never felt this way before, but I know that what I feel isn't going away. When I finally decide to text her, I know she's at work and won't respond back.

***Duncan: I don't want to hide us anymore.***

# CHAPTER EIGHTEEN

## MAYA

The ringing of the phone brings me out of my restless sleep. I reach for it, feeling the lack of sleep catching up with me. I'm off tonight, so I'll take a pill and get some rest.

"Hello." In my heart I'm hoping it's Duncan, but that was not the ringtone I set for him, maybe he's using another phone. Things have been strained the last month since I left him on a sidewalk in New York looking like a fool. He wants to tell everyone but I'm not ready. I don't want to lose him.

"Maya, sweetheart, I haven't heard from you since August. What've you been up to? Are you seeing someone? Answer me, child." The frantic voice comes across the line. No hello, nothing.

"Uncle Marcus, slow down and I'll answer you. I've been working. Lots of extra training with the ERT."

"Are you seeing someone?" he asks angrily.

"Why?"

"That's not a no, sweetheart. No man is good enough for you."

"Uncle Marcus, what do ya want?" I don't want to lie to him, but I'm the one that made Duncan keep our relationship quiet.

"I want you to go on a date with my nephew, Lawrence."

"I thought you said no man was good enough for me. Besides, I can't." I roll onto my back and stare at the ceiling, smiling at my phone. This is new for him, usually he doesn't want me to date anyone. He doesn't like the time I spend with Derek.

"Lawrence is an exceptional young man. He'll treat you right."

"Uncle Marcus, I'm not interested." I roll to look at the clock. "I've got to get going, I have training I need to attend. Take care. I'll call you soon." I hang up before he can say more, and rush to get ready.

I need to be at Quantico in just over two hours for another training session Greg has lined up for me. Greg has been helping me fine-tune my skills in several areas. Derek will meet me at Quantico so we can go through this training together.

I love going to Quantico and seeing all the training and soldiers in the area. I've trained with several of the Marines during marksmanship school. I talked to many of them during and after their deployments. I've learned a lot from them. Some of them have become good friends. I have contacts in so many fields of D.C. politics. It's never a bad thing in this city.

DUNCAN

I dial the number and hear it ringing. "Hello," the sleepy voice says from the other end.

"Oi, Bossman."

"Why are you calling me at 0300, Duncan?"

"Thought I'd let you know that I'm sick of this job and if I don't kill this little brat, it'll be a miracle."

"Thank you, Duncan, for your patience. Her father is paying us a lot and you're the best." I hear the sarcasm in his voice.

"She's a conniving little snot. She's trying to make her boyfriend jealous by using me. I'm seeing someone and she will not understand."

"Wait, what do you mean you're seeing someone? You never told me. Which French model is it now? Or is this the woman you searched in D.C.?"

"I told you that is a friend of my sister's and since I was in town I thought I would say hello. I can't tell you my girl's name. We're keeping our relationship quiet for a bit longer. She's not a model. I need the Christmas holiday off so I can spend some time with her."

"Fine, but finish this job. Be careful, brother."

"I'll try."

I hang up and open a text screen. I need to hear her voice but know she's probably sleeping, it's her night off.

***Me: Hello, baby.***

***Maya: Hi, handsome. I have this weekend off of work. How about I fly to Milan to see you?***

***Me: Wish you could, baby, we're flying to Athens in the morning.***

***Maya: I could fly to Athens. You name it and I'm there. It's been too long. Plus, I should apologize in person after New York.***

***Me: Baby, I want to see you too, but that won't work.***

***Maya: Okay. I've got to go, we're heading into a meeting.***

I know she's lying to me. I'm hurting her but my assignment is being difficult and I don't want to bring Maya into that. Moreover, the threats against my assignment have escalated and I don't fancy Maya near any danger if I can prevent it. Her job is dangerous enough, but this I can control. I go to sleep worrying I'm screwing up the best relationship I've ever been in. I forgave her for what happened in New York right away. I know I'm wearing her down about telling my family about us.

# CHAPTER NINETEEN

## MAYA

I look up from my phone to see two sets of twin eyes watching me carefully. Oh shit, the gig might be up. Lying to either of these two is hard, and I've already been doing it for months.

"What?" I ask sweetly.

"Want to tell me who you're texting? And, who upset you?" Derek asks.

"No." I turn to Greg waiting.

"Who is it, Maya? With everything going on you can understand why we're worried? Has the stalker resorted to calls and texts?"

"No. For your information it's a friend. I'm upset because our schedules never work out so we can see each other." I can't give them too much information.

"Who? You aren't seeing anyone. You've not even picked up any of the guys from the gym since you came back from London months ago." Leave it to Derek to point that out.

"Picking up random guys at the gym, young lady?" Greg asks.

"Now you two listen...first, I'm not going to explain my nonromantic relations with either of you. Second, look who's talking, Mister Slut." I glare at Derek.

"Okay, children. Let's get back to point. Maya, we won't be able to keep this stalker quiet much longer. If something big happens the department needs to know." As usual, Greg jumps in and scolds us. I glare at Derek. He'll get his ass kicked at the gym next time.

"I know, Greg, but I can't let James or anyone else find out."

I head back to my condo after our late dinner and run on the treadmill, wondering if Duncan is cheating on me. I need to take a pill and get some sleep, but I need to get this excessive energy out of my system. I couldn't even spend his birthday with him—work came first for both of us. I still see the hurt in his eyes when I left him in New York.

EVERY TIME I've tried to head to see Duncan, he ends up having a change of plans and heads to another location. I was just thinking it was bad timing, until this morning when I woke up to see his face plastered all over the news with the French diplomat's daughter in his arms. She's no young girl. She's a grown woman. And I want to rip her arms off. This is why I don't do long distance relationships, one of us can't take the temptation.

Who am I kidding? I don't do any relationships. Oh well, guess I was right, this wasn't going to work out. I can't believe he couldn't tell me he wanted to be with her. She's gorgeous with her blond hair, curves, and softness. I bet she listens to him and doesn't argue at every chance. It's obvious she doesn't care who knows about them.

He and I have talked or texted almost every day, maybe we're just friends. That's it. We're better friends who have had a couple fantastic weekends. I know so much about him, how he feels about the losses of his mother and fellow soldiers. How he and Joshua met. How he and James talk weekly. What I mostly know is he's honest, so it really hurts that he couldn't tell me about whatever her name is. I'm bustling around my condominium when Derek walks out of the guest room.

"Why the hell are you slamming cupboards, sexy? And jeez, the music is loud enough to wake the dead."

"Nothing, I'm heading to the gym for a workout. Want to come?"

"Naw. The last time we went to the gym when you were in a mood you handed me my ass. Thanks for letting me stay here last night, my roommates like to party a lot, and you know I don't."

"No problem, that's what friends are for." My phone rings, *S.E.X.* from Nickelback blares out of the speaker. I look at the caller ID and hit ignore. I can't talk to him right now. It immediately starts ringing again, and I reject his call…again.

"Someone you don't want to talk to? Want to discuss it with me?" Ever since our dinner last month, Derek's been trying to find out whom I talk to all the time.

"I don't think it'd be a good idea. But thanks."

"Hey, I'm not trying to pry, just know you can't hold it in. You've listened to me. Let me return the favor. Like Dad said, it better not be your stalker. He hasn't resorted to calling you yet has he?"

"No. Got another bouquet of roses I sent to the hospital last night. Maybe later we can talk." My phone continues to ring off the hook. I silence it and send him a quick text.

***Me: Get the hint I don't want to talk right now.***

***Duncan: I swear it was nothing. I need to explain, please.***

Before I can send a reply, both Derek's and my cell phones go off with the paging tone. Crap, time to work. He returns the call as I grab both our go bags and start to head for the door.

"We're on our way, about ten out. Meet you at the location. Text it to my phone. Yes, sir." He hangs up.

"What's up?" I ask as I set the alarm and lock the door behind us.

"Hostage situation. They want us to meet them on location. Is all your gear here?"

"Yep. Good idea I had yesterday in bringing it home."

We load into the SUV and head to the location the precinct texted him. As we pull up, I look around the neighborhood. It looks like an average blue-collar neighborhood, but I can see that a perimeter has been set up around a house at the end of the block. I can't see where they're going to want me to set up but figure they'll let me know.

"Captain," we both say as we walk up to him.

"Sierra and Echo, we want you to set up on the roof of that home over there." He points to a house about three down from the target. I notice other ERT members getting ready around us.

"What's the situation?" I ask.

"Father has already killed his wife and is holding his two year old son hostage. I'll signal if I feel that we need you to take the shot. First, I want you to get some infrared on that home and tell me what you see with both of your scopes. Officers last saw him in the living room in the front Eastern quadrant. Got it? We've got Team Two set up on the south side of the house."

"Yes, sir." I walk back to my SUV and pull open the back. I get out my bag and start pulling on my gear. I didn't have time to change out of my workout clothes, so I put the cargo pants over my shorts and the black shirt on over my t-shirt and button it up. My phone vibrates across the cargo area and I leave it. I need to focus on this situation, not Duncan. I put my tactical vest on and pull my hair into a bun at the back of my neck. I then strap on my belt and holster, snap my sidearm into its thigh holster, and hook my comm piece into my ear and around my neck. I open my gun case and look at my most trusted piece of equipment. She's like a friend. When I hold her, I know what my purpose in life is. I shoulder my rifle and put on my glasses and black ball cap. Because we are away from all the activity, I don't need to wear the helmet. Derek is geared out about the same as me, except he doesn't carry a rifle. He has a spotting scope and a machine gun strapped to his back. I watch as the entry teams get into position.

A new Team Two has started with us. It just so happened that two other guys on the unit could meet the marksman skills and they got moved up into the open positions. Yancy's murder is still unsolved, but I'm no longer a suspect. I know that there is still another knife of mine out there and someone was trying to set me up.

We head to the home the captain directed us to. When I get to it, I see some more team members waiting. They help boost me up to a low roof so I can climb up higher. I make sure to keep my riflescope protected from bumps and the sunlight doesn't reflect off it. I get into position with Derek next to me. The roof isn't very sloped and I'm able to lie on my belly.

The homes are older construction with shingled roofs. The day is cold with a little bit of a breeze; and I hope it doesn't start to rain. I slip a mag into my gun and chamber a round as Derek pulls out his data book and starts writing down all the distances and ratios I give him. I twist my ball cap backward so it's not in my way. I line up with the house and start checking each room before finally stopping on what appears to be a family room. Sure enough, he's there and holding the boy to his chest with a gun in his hand. I press the button to open the comm.

"I see him in the living room. He's holding the boy and has a nine millimeter loosely gripped, hanging down next to his leg. Do you still want me to check the house with infrared?"

"Yes, Sierra, I want to make sure the little boy is the only hostage. Also, what's your shot like?"

"I've got a clean head shot, but he'll drop the boy to the floor, so not a good idea. I could aim for the gun hand, although the little boy's leg is right there, and if he moves it could be worse. I've no chest shot."

"Copy that," he says as I click off my comm.

"Okay, Echo, infrared." I flip some switches on my scope and make the necessary adjustments to be able to see heat signatures within the structure. The secondary part of the scope slips into place. Again, I scope the whole house and finally the living room. I'm still telling Derek different measures and distances as I search. He's looking through his scope too and doing the same, confirming the measurements as he writes them into our data book.

I can make out the last vestiges of heat from the mother's body on the floor of the room across from the father, but the small heat signature in the corner stops me. I focus more and curse softly before flipping on the comm again. Derek looks where I am and curses too.

"Captain, we've got a situation. There's a second hostage in what appears to be a crib in the corner of the room."

"Son of a bitch. We were hoping the neighbors were wrong when they said the family just had a baby. The father hasn't even mentioned it once. Is it alive?" I can hear the anger in his voice, and like me, I feel the tension ratchet up more with this discovery.

"Captain, this is Bravo Team Two, we don't have any confirmation from our side as we have the brick wall back here." My teammate says into the comm.

"Appears to be sleeping. Active heat signature, so not dead and not currently making itself known," I say with as much hope as I can muster.

"Okay, Sierra, we're going to have to figure out a way to get him to put the boy down so we can get in there before we have a serious tragedy."

"Yes, sir." I click off my comm.

"Damn, sexy, glad I'm not you. You know I can't handle kids and guns in the same area." Derek sounds stressed and I want to turn and look at him, but I keep the father in my scope and my eye on him. I switch my scope back to regular and look for any way to end this.

Wait, did I just see that? I watch him a bit longer and realize what's happening. I click my comm back on.

"Captain, I think he's up to something. He's talking to the boy."

"Keep an eye if you need to end it. You know what I mean. That's an order. Everyone clear."

"Yes, sir," I say as I hear each of the team members respond with an affirmative. I watch carefully as the father lowers his head to kiss the little boy. I see his eyes look at me and know he's found me. Shit, this isn't good. He puts the little boy down, steps back, and looks directly at me. How did he see me? I know we didn't give away our position.

"Shit! Sorry, sir. We got suicide by cop about to happen," I relay into my comm.

The father says something to his son again, looks at me and points his gun at the little boy. Well shit, just another thing to fuck up my day. I take the shot. Good for him I'm the best. My bullet hits him in the upper right of his chest. It makes him drop the gun and fall down, but hopefully he doesn't die. The rest of the team rushes in the minute the shot left my barrel as Derek informed the team. I keep my team and the perp in my sights.

When the coast is clear, I start to relax. I couldn't take the kill shot. Deadly force was necessary but not needed. I knew my bullet was going to be close, but I couldn't, no matter what, take the kill shot. I wasn't going to leave those children without another parent.

Oh yeah, sure he'll go to jail and the kids will go somewhere else, but he'll live with what he did and his kids will, at least, have a parent alive. I wish we'd been called earlier to prevent the mother's death, but that could have been what started this whole situation.

I lie my head down on my gun and feel my heart harden a little to this newest pain. It's always like this; I get bitterer with each shot. Am I actually making a difference? Is being alone so worth it? Oh yeah, my pseudo boyfriend just cheated on me. Maybe alone is better. I feel Derek's hand on my shoulder.

"Come on, sexy, let's blow this Popsicle stand." He laughs. I know he's pretty messed up about what just happened, but this is the way he deals with the pain. I twist my ball cap around to cover my face and start packing up my gear.

We climb down and head back to the SUV. Other officers are patting me on the back and congratulating me on an excellent shot. I just feel empty and lost. I look out to see the news crews zeroed in on me. I don't want to be featured in a news story and pull my cap lower on my face.

"Sierra, right call. He had more bullets in that gun but is screaming that you should've killed him."

"Sir, I didn't see a reason to kill him."

"Sierra, you did fine. See you at the station for debriefing."

# CHAPTER TWENTY

## MAYA

After what seems like forever, I'm released from debriefing and head to the SUV. I remember I left my phone in the cargo area on silent. I open up the hatch and grab it. It's dead now, so I plug it in. As the screen lights up, I see there are literally over one hundred text messages and multiple voicemails. Wow, he doesn't give up easily. I guess I gotta face him now. I'll just make a clean break. Okay yeah, I'm a chickenshit, I text him instead.

***Me: Duncan let's just be friends. You and I as a couple weren't going to work anyway.***

I wait for the response, but nothing comes, so I head home. Derek went out with some friends. I park the SUV in the garage and head up to my condo, sitting by my door is a bouquet of flowers. I pull my sidearm and check my surroundings. This shit's getting serious. Someone was on my floor again. I have a penthouse apartment. No one should be up here unless I let them.

I reach into the pocket of my cargo pants and pull out a black latex-free glove. This bouquet has a ribbon, maybe we'll get lucky and find prints on it. I carefully lift the bouquet and walk into my condo and straight to the kitchen, where I pull out a bag and drop the flowers into it. I dial the number I've had memorized for years and know that I'm not going to get away from him moving in now.

"What up, sexy? We just got to the bar, want to come?"

"No, I just had a delivery waiting for me outside my door."

"That's it, Maya, no more! I'll be there in a couple hours. I'm moving in. Set the alarms. Did you keep them?" I can tell he's agitated and upset with my defiance to letting him stay, but he's right, this is getting out of hand.

"Derek, I checked everything, I'm good. But, okay, you can move in."

"See you later, sexy. Be careful. Call Dad and let him know." I hang up and know that my life is changing, and not for the better. My stalker has finally gone to the next level.

I dial Greg's number and hope he can keep this secret too.

"Hello, I saw you on the news. Excellent shot. What's up, sweetheart?" he says, and I know that he is going to go all protective on me now.

"I had a delivery waiting at my door. There's a ribbon tied around them this time."

"Did you bag them without touching them?"

"Yes."

"Okay. Is Derek heading that way?"

"He'll be here shortly. Can we keep this quiet?"

"Not for much longer, sweetheart. I'll be over in the morning. Get some rest. Love you, kiddo."

"Thank you." I hang up and head for the fridge.

I pull out the stuff to make a sandwich when my cell phone starts ringing. I see the caller ID, hear the ring tone, and cringe.

"Hello." Indifferent is how I'll pull this off.

"What the fuck do you mean friends? Are you cracking up, Maya? Have you lost your bloody mind? Because I'm not giving up on us. That girl was trying to make her boyfriend jealous and paid the paparazzi to take a picture. I swear on everything holy if you were here I'd spank your arse for even thinking those words."

"Girl? That was no girl. That was a full-fledged wet dream. The picture clearly shows you with your arms around her. She's looking at you like you hung the fucking moon! I've had a horrible day and I just want to eat a sandwich, run on the treadmill, and try to go to bed." I yell back at him.

"No, you're not getting out of this. I've been trying to call you all day, I'm not going to let you run. I was shot at and took one in the vest. I also saw my girlfriend on CNN in a hostage situation."

"WHAT?" I scream into the phone, my legs give out as I fall to the floor and start breathing slowly. He can't die; he can't leave me too. One minute I want him out of my life and the next I can't live without him.

"Maya! Baby, calm down! I'm okay. The vest took it. The boyfriend thought he was going to get rid of his competition. What happened to you today? The news only said a female sniper stopped the situation." He sounds calmer than I feel. I feel like the bottom fell out of my world.

"I had to shoot the perp today in front of his kids," I murmur. I don't want to tell him about my stalker. "Duncan, are you really okay?" My voice sounds shaky and whiney to my ears.

"Baby, I swear I'm okay. Tell me more about what happened to you today, and then I'll explain what happened to me." His voice sounds so calm and soothing. This is what I needed, to tell someone about my day. To talk through how I feel.

"I shot a father in front of his toddler after he pointed the gun at the little guy. This is after the father killed the mother. I almost left both of those children without parents, hair to the right or lower and he'd be dead. I'm becoming the monster I fight." I sigh loudly.

"Maya, baby, you're not a monster. It sounds like a justified shot. Explain to me why you think you're a monster."

"I was called to the scene after the mother was murdered and he barricaded himself in the home. Little did we know he wanted to die too. The perp had his toddler boy in his arms and a baby girl sleeping in a crib. At first, I didn't understand how he saw me, but later we found out he had a radio tuned to our frequency, so he knew when I got on scene. Of course, he wasn't waiting personally for me, he just wanted to die. Suicide by cop. He wanted me to kill him. He put the little boy down, stepped back, took aim, and waited for me to shoot him. I ended up shooting him just to the left, between his second and third ribs, and fracturing his shoulder blade. The bullet did ricochet and puncture his lung, but he'll live. He dropped the gun. During the post-briefing, he called from the hospital demanding to talk to me. He refused surgery until I'd speak to him. He was going to die, so I spoke to him."

"What did he want?" Duncan asks quietly.

"He wanted to know why I didn't kill him. He said he deserved to die and I was supposed to be his executioner. He said if I'd been a man he'd be dead." I feel raw telling him this, but at least I don't feel like I can't breathe anymore.

"Baby, you made the right call. What did you tell him?"

"I told him that it wasn't my job to be judge and jury. Even though he's probably going to spend the rest of his life in prison, his children would have at least one parent alive. I said as a person who lost her parents to violence, he's lucky it was me looking through that scope at him and not a man. His children would be able to ask him why the hell he did it and they could maybe learn about their mother from someone who at some point must have loved her. I told him I wasn't going to leave his children orphaned, that's his choice. Then I told him to grow the fuck up, put on his big girl panties, have surgery, and rehabilitate himself."

"Maya, it was a justified and clean shot. By leaving him alive, he'll face what he did."

"Duncan, what happened with that model? I don't share and I don't want to be in a relationship based on lies."

"I swear nothing happened. I go to bed at night thinking of only one woman...you. I think of you all the time. I can't wait until I see you. I'm gutted that this spoiled girl has hurt you. She threw herself into my arms. When I looked down and saw the look in her eyes, I stepped back and told her I have a girlfriend. She laughed and said probably not after this, then pointed to the photographer. I got so angry I had Ian take over the close protection while I took the background. I wanted to call you before the pictures came out, but she demanded we fly to Milan. While we were there, we took her shopping, and ran into her boyfriend. He pulled a gun and shot me in the vest. I broke his hand. The whole time she's telling him how proud she is of him for sticking up and fighting for her. I hate games."

"I'm sorry. I just saw those pictures and freaked. Wait, did you call me your girlfriend?"

"Bugger off! Yes, Maya, you are my girlfriend, at least, I hope you are. I miss you and want to be with you. Joshua pulled us from the detail and told her father we weren't in the business of paparazzi shots. The father is mad at her."

"Duncan, I'm not sure about this. We've not seen each other since September. I can't do relationships. I've been told I'm bad at them."

"Baby, we will make this work. I promise. Just, next time, let me explain before you try to break it off. Why'd you not let me earlier?"

"All I saw was that model looking at you like I wanted to, she's where I wanted to be. I got so jealous, I actually thought of killing her. I thought you got tired of waiting for me. Plus every time I've tried to come see you, you make an excuse or change your mind."

"Baby, I didn't change my mind. I want to see you so bad. The client kept having us travel around. Believe me, I want to see you. I'm tired of using my hand to get off because I keep remembering our last weekend together. I want to actually take you to dinner again and walk hand in hand with you in public."

I want all those things too. Maybe more, but I can't tell him. He'll run for the hills and I can't jeopardize his life by being with me. Plus, I can't share my darkness yet.

"Baby, are you there?" he interrupts my thoughts.

"Oh sorry, I was thinking how nice a date sounds."

"Do you know how close I was to getting on a plane and coming to you today? Joshua made me stop because he has me moving to another detail in Paris so that I can have the whole Christmas break off with you. When I saw you on the news and saw your partner, I was so upset and then your text. Baby, don't do that to me again."

"You know Derek is only my partner and friend."

"I know. Have you bought your ticket yet?"

"Got it on hold, I'm trying to figure this all out."

"Figure out what? Just bloody buy it."

"Well, I'm going to have to do the night flights again so I'll be in early in the morning. I want to spend time with you as we planned without the family knowing, but Ana knows the schedules better than I do. Would you like to spend the whole day with me at my hotel before we make an appearance at your father's on Saturday for brunch? That's the day that Ana wants me to fly in."

"Of course I want to spend the day with you. Tell me when and I'll be there to pick you up."

"Well, I work week on week off, and I get off at 1700 on Thursday, December twentieth. I'll land the twenty-first at zero seven thirty in the morning. Okay?"

"Buy it, baby, I can't wait to see you. How long will you be able to stay?"

"If you can stand it, I fly home on January fifth."

"Can you afford to take that much time off?"

"Of course, I have plenty of time banked." I cringe and hope he isn't asking about my money situation, he and I have never discussed money. I don't tell many people I don't hurt for money.

"I can't wait to see you."

"Okay, I'll get everything booked if you're sure about this?"

"Baby, I've never been more sure of anything."

"Okay, I gotta go. I need to eat and work out. Hopefully, I'll be able to sleep."

"You do sound tired. I'll see you soon. I'll text you tomorrow. Take care, baby." He pauses before the last part.

"Take care, Big Guy." I'm still sitting on the floor and not sure if I want to get up. I'm actually not hungry anymore. I stand up, put the food away, and head to bed.

*"Maya, darling, wake up, there's been an accident."*

*"Accident?" I ask.*

*"Yes, they're all dead, and you could have stopped it if you hadn't been a spoiled child."*

*"You killed my daddy!"*

*"You let my mommy die!"*

*"You're mine, forever. I'll kill all that stand in my way."*

I COME AWAKE WITH A START. Shit, more nightmares. It's been months since I had these nightmares. Why? I roll over, my room is dark, and I look at the clock. 3:00 a.m. Well crap, no sleep for me now. I'm getting ready to have my off week, one more day then I'll take a sleeping pill to sleep tomorrow.

I get up, head for the living room where my treadmill is, and run like the devil is chasing me. I have my headphones in with Skillet's *Monster* playing loudly. I know Derek is in the spare room sleeping.

I've tried therapy and everything else. Until I learn to relax at night without the dread or nightmares, this is my life. I was able to fall asleep with Duncan every time we've been together, before that, only his sister could get me to relax enough to sleep. When Carl and I dated in college, I couldn't sleep with him either. He thought I was crazy.

# CHAPTER TWENTY-ONE

## MAYA

I'm showered, caffeinated, and ready for my shift today. As I head across the parking garage to the SUV, I hear my name yelled. This is a secure garage and after the flower delivery, I'm on edge.

"Can I help you?" I turn to see a man about six one with shaggy brown hair standing by my truck. Okay, jackass, get away from my baby.

"Maya, you don't recognize me?" That voice sounds familiar and he looks familiar, but I feel like I need to be careful. Something about this man makes me feel uneasy. He walks out of the shadows to me and in the months since he lost his job, I see he's let himself go. His hair is longer and he is sporting a shaggy beard. He's thinner and his clothes hang on him.

"Carl. What are you doing here?" I step back from him in unease. Great, I thought of him earlier and now he's here. He walks closer and acts like he's going to kiss me. I step back and put out my hand to shake. I don't want to touch him, but know he will push the issue if I don't.

Something feels really off right now.

"Maya, it's been months. Now that we don't work together, want to have dinner sometime?" He tries to pull me in but I yank my hand from his. Since he quit after the suspension, he has told anyone that will listen that I stole his job. I don't trust him.

"Sorry, Carl, I have a boyfriend. How did you get in here?" I decide Duncan is right, he's my boyfriend and that should get rid of Carl.

"Oh your doorman let me in. I told him we were old friends. You've got a boyfriend? The doorman said that was your partner, Derek."

"Excuse me. Are you checking up on me?"

"Well, I was checking to see if there was any competition. Can't blame a guy. Girl, you look smoking hot. Come to dinner with me."

"No, I'm seeing someone. I need to go, bye." I turn to leave, but he grabs my arm. "Carl, you're going to want to let me go, remember I can hurt you," I say as I prepare myself to attack him.

"I seem to remember it was my hands on your throat, girly. However, you'll come around. I'll see you soon." He lets go as he turns to leave.

"What happened to you telling everyone I stole your job?" I demand.

"I forgive you, it wasn't your fault." He continues to walk away.

I feel like taking another shower. The garage that I've always felt secure in now feels like a black hole. I'm going to have to talk to the doorman.

## DUNCAN

"Duncan, tell me why someone is searching your whereabouts?" Joshua's voice comes across my cell and I can tell he's upset.

"I don't know what you mean."

"Is your girlfriend checking up on you after yesterday?"

"No. What did they search?"

"Someone tried to find your London address and then did a search to see if you were still on the other job."

"I don't know why. My girl is fine."

"Are you sure? I've been doing some searching myself. IAD has questioned her, plus she has a BAU team on a case involving her."

"I'll talk to her when she gets here in a couple weeks. For now don't worry."

I hang up and go to sleep wondering what could be going on with Maya.

~

*"Hey, bro, watch your back."* Christopher's voice jolts me from my sleep. The last image I saw before I opened my eyes was Maya's body lying just like Christopher's across my body. Her chest heaving for air as her blood leaks from the gapping wounds.

I sit up and feel the pain again. I run to the bathroom and fall to my knees. I dry heave, smelling her blood and seeing her beautiful hair matted from the blood. My hands press on her wound and the blood seeps through my fingers.

"No! God no!" I mumble through my raw throat.

I feel someone in my space and look up to see Raul standing in the doorway. He soaks a washcloth and hands it to me, along with a cup of cool water. I rinse my mouth and wait for the judgment.

"How often does this happen?"

"Not as often as it used to."

Right after Christopher was killed, Raul helped me hide the PTSD from our C.O. He and the other guys in our unit all have our issues with that mission. That was a shit-storm of epic proportions.

"What set you off tonight?"

"Don't ask."

"I did." He bends over and helps me rise up on shaking legs. I brush my teeth and walk out to slip on a pair of sweatpants over my boxer briefs. Raul is sitting in the chair waiting to talk. I see the two tumblers of scotch. I know my stomach is going to protest it but my nerves need it.

"Joshua called and said that my girl might be in danger. I saw her in Christopher's place and he told me to watch my back."

"What kind of danger?"

"I don't know. She hasn't told me. For some reason there is a FBI Behavioral Analysis Unit with a file on a case she is involved in. She has some kind of security on her that if you search her name they back trace you. I accidentally tripped it by having Timothy do a search on her. Then to top it off, Joshua says the Internal Affairs Division interviewed her a few months ago. These are things I think she should talk to me about. Right?"

"She's a cop?"

"Yeah."

"Was she the girl from the gala and hotel the next day?"

"Yeah, that's her. She doesn't want anyone to know about us."

"Why? She embarrassed to be seen with you?"

"No. Our families know each other. She's worried that if we don't work out she'll hurt them."

"That was her in New York too?"

"She came up for the weekend. I want to be with her, but she won't give up her job and I can't give up mine."

"Lasses always make it trouble. That's why I'm going to stay single."

"Man, when you fall it's going to be epic."

"Doubt it, haven't found a lass that was worth more than a quick shag."

"Like I said, it will be epic. Maya makes me feel like a better man. When I sleep with her I don't have nightmares. She heals the open wounds I carry. But I know she is hiding a lot about herself."

"Maya? That's a nice name. Wait, why was she with the codger at the gala?"

"They were checking the ambassador's security detail. He's an old friend of her father's."

"She skilled?"

"Double black belt Krav Maga, sharp-shooter, and knife fighting."

"Double black belt. I'm impressed. She could teach me some

things." He nods his head as he finishes the last of his scotch. I look at my empty glass and don't remember drinking it.

"Thanks, mate."

"That's what I'm here for. I'll see you in the morning. By the way, we all still struggle with it, you're not the only one."

He leaves the room with that parting shot and I realize how much I've shut the guys out lately. Well no more, we are a team.

# CHAPTER TWENTY-TWO

## MAYA

I'm so excited and turned on to see Duncan. I was practically walking on clouds through my shift; the captain asked me if I was high. I laughed at him and said I had big plans for the holiday. I actually packed a real suitcase and some dresses.

I have several surprises for Duncan. Checking in at the airport was fun; I got to use my new certifications to carry a sidearm on the plane. Of course, that meant I was acting as a second to the air marshal in the first class cabin.

As I walk out of the secure area of the airport into the crowded arrivals area, I see Duncan towering over everyone. He looks better than I remember. He's wearing dark jeans with a maroon, pullover sweater. His hair has grown out and hangs around his ears. His eyes are boring into me. That spark is still there. I want to do the movie running leap into his arms but control myself.

"Maya, baby. God, I missed you." His arms come around me and hold me to him. He bends down to sniff my hair and then pulls me up to press our bodies together, my feet dangling. Our mouths slam together, kissing like there's no tomorrow. His tongue is marking every part of my mouth. I feel his erection against me. I want to wrap my legs around him here in front of everyone. One of his hands is on my ass, the other is gripping my ponytail. He pulls back and looks into my eyes. I smile shyly at him. I've missed him so much.

"Baby, we aren't waiting another three months to see each other. I feel like I'm going to have marks from my zipper on my cock. No more Skype or sexting, just you and me together for the next two weeks."

"Yes, Duncan. I've missed you so much. Please, get me out of here. I need you," I say breathlessly.

"You don't have to ask twice." He puts me down and grabs my suitcase in one hand and my hand in his other. His long legs start eating up the distance to the parking garage.

"Honey, slow down, my legs aren't as long as yours, plus I have heels on."

He looks at me from toe to top of my head. Under my father's soft leather bomber jacket, I'm wearing a black wrap dress with a pair of sky-high fuck me calf boots. He groans and growls at me when he looks me from head to toe again.

"No slowing down, you either keep up or I'm throwing you over my shoulder. I need to be buried inside you in the very near future or I'll be permanently unmanned."

"Okay, honey." I giggle and speed up, my steps trying to keep pace.

We make it to the garage where no one is around. He stops, grabs me by the waist, and hoists me over his shoulder. I'm being carried like a sack of potatoes while he runs with my rolling luggage to a Rover. My pony-tailed hair is hanging down almost to the ground.

"Hey, where's the DBS? I was hoping to get lucky in that car."

"Baby, I knew you'd have luggage, plus this way, if I don't make it home, I can pull over and pull you into the back."

I laugh again, the happiness to finally being here with him is almost overwhelming. I was anxious we might get bored with each other and we'd just become good friends. He puts me down by the passenger door, pushes me up against the vehicle, and starts kissing me again.

"I need to get you out of this damn airport." He opens the door and lifts me in, then loads my luggage in the back.

We head out into the London traffic and I think we're heading for the hotel when I realize we're driving in the opposite direction.

"Where are we going?" I ask confused.

"My place."

"Duncan, I can't stay with you."

I know Greg will be flying in to attend meetings in a couple days. We're staying at the same hotel. How will I explain Duncan to him and Derek?

"Yes, you can, and you will. Remember surfaces."

"What about your father and Ana?" What about my friends I want to say.

"Who cares, I'm going to tell them tomorrow, fuck this. I'm bloody tired of hiding."

"Duncan, please."

"Baby, when you say, 'Duncan, please,' all I want to do is ram my cock into you." I groan.

"Honey, I know I tell you that when I want your cock in me. But right now, I don't want to hurt you or our family. Your family is like my family. James and Ana are some of the only family members I have left." I also want to prevent him from knowing about my stalker. The last time I was in London I got deliveries, I'll probably get them again. I'm still getting them back home. I don't like the thought of him getting hurt because of me.

"I know, baby, but think how hurt Ana will be when she does finally find out. I don't plan to end this anytime soon. Do you?" He turns to look at me.

"I want to be with you. I wish it were easier and we could see each other more, but for now, this is the way it has to be. We both love our jobs and our cities."

We pull into a garage and I see his DBS parked in a spot. I love that car. I don't have one but maybe someday. I drive my badass truck right now because it's practical. He jumps out. Before I can get my door open, he's yanked it open, reached into unbuckle me, and has me in his arms.

"I can walk, Duncan." He's practically running for the elevator. "Hey, my luggage."

"I walk faster than you can, no time to go slow. Your luggage is fine, I'll get it later. I need to be inside you, I can't even see straight. It's a wonder I didn't wreck the car on the way here."

I laugh. "Okay, honey."

"I'm sorry, baby, this is going to go fast this first time."

"It's okay, you aren't hearing me complain. Besides, we have two weeks."

We come to the elevator and as soon as we're inside, he turns me to straddle his hips and pushes me into the corner. His hands rub into my leather bomber jacket, right to my gun.

"Honey, how'd you get on a plane with this?"

"I can conceal and carry on a plane now." I kiss his neck and slide my tongue up the column to his chin, and take a bite before leaning in for a kiss.

"You'll be explaining that later, but first...wearing a dress was a splendid idea. Bloody hell, Maya, you're going to make me come in my jeans if you don't stop." I giggle, waiting for him to find the first part of his surprise. His hand glides up my left thigh when it encounters my completely naked pussy. He groans.

"Baby, please tell me you didn't fly on a plane like this."

"No, I stopped into a restroom to freshen up and change."

"I'm definitely going to have zipper marks from that image. No wonder it took you so long to come out of security."

"Better hurry then." I laugh and wiggle against him.

"Stop, Maya, I'm about to hit the emergency stop in this elevator."

"Honey, there's a camera." I nod to the opposite corner.

"Yes, there is, but I know the security company and the owner of the building. I almost forgot we're having dinner with my boss, Joshua, tomorrow night."

"Uh, okay. I have a job and we discussed this before. I have a friend flying over in a couple days who wants to have dinner with me, would you like to come?" This is a huge step for me.

"My boss wants to meet you. Joshua is very interested in the woman that's had me celibate for the last three months. Of course, I wish to meet your friend, is she a cop too?" He continues to rub my folds and I'm moaning as we talk. His fingers don't enter me or play with my clit, they torture me by just rubbing my labia lips.

"No, he works for the Secret Service and is a friend of your father's, remember us talking about Greg? As for dinner with Joshua, all right, honey. By the way...the elevator stopped." He has been so focused on my lack of panties he didn't notice we stopped. He whirls around with me in his arms and runs down the hall.

"Grab my keys from my front pocket." I unlock the door. "Push 457392 into the keypad," he says as the alarm beeps. He kicks the door closed and I find my ass on a table right in the hall by the closet.

"Surface number one, baby," he says as I giggle again. We've sexted several times about the surfaces he wants to take me on. I slide my jacket off and then my holster. I hand him the gun. "Damn, baby, that's so hot."

"If you think that's hot, wait until you see what else I'm packing," I say.

I reach toward the waist of my dress and untie it. As my dress falls open, his eyes focus on my breasts. They're barely contained in the low-cut demi bra, and then his eyes fall on my garter belt holding my stockings up. When his eyes narrow on the knife in my right nylon, he groans, pulls it out and puts both the knife and gun into the coat closet. I pull my boot knife from my boot and hand him it.

"Bugger me! What the hell are you trying to do, kill me?"

"I went shopping at Victoria's Secret and was thinking of you the whole time." He groans and undoes his belt, followed by his jeans. I reach for him and pull the sweater over his head, then his t-shirt. He tugs me to the edge of the table, his pants have dropped around his ankles.

"Lie back, baby." He lies over me and sucks a nipple through the very sheer lace of my bra. He then notices the small knife clipped to my bra. "Baby, you like knives?" he asks, then sucks my nipple harder.

"Ahhh, yes." He pulls back with a pop, yanks me off the table, and pulls my dress off my arms to fall to the floor. He flips me over and grabs my ponytail, pulling my head back. Duncan kisses me as he enters me from behind. We both groan.

"Oh, baby, you're so tight. I've waited months to be inside you."

"Oh. Duncan. Please," I pant.

"That's it, baby, told you what that does to me." He pushes all the way in. At this angle, it feels like he's touching my soul.

"Now, Duncan. Fuck me now," I beg. He stops and lies on my back, my hair still wrapped around one of his wrists.

"No, baby, I'm making love to you now. Rough but still making love, no more fucking."

"Argh, PLEASE, DUNCAN, MOVE NOW!" I yell, my voice cracking with need.

He pulls out and rams into me again, we both groan. He repeats it several times. The torture of the long thrusts has me on edge. The table begins to move slightly. I feel the orgasm building. My hands go behind me to grab him. I need just a little more.

"Please, Duncan, I'm so close. I need something more," I beg.

He pulls back slightly and with his other hand smacks my ass and then rubs the spot.

"That's for trying to break up with me," he growls.

"OH GOD, YES, DUNCAN!" I scream as I come so hard I see stars. My vaginal muscles spasm around his cock. He starts groaning and growling.

"MAYA, BABY, YES!" he yells as he comes. I feel him pulsing inside me and his movements have become erratic and uneven, as if he can't stop himself from still pumping into me.

We lie there for a while catching our breath. He pulls out of me and steps out of his shoes and pants. He turns me over and unhooks the bra with the knife still attached, and my stockings. He reaches down, unzips my boots and slides them and my stockings off. I unhook the garter belt.

"Come on, baby, you want to sleep? We can take a nap then we can play some more. We have many more surfaces to christen. We also need to talk about you walking around London loaded for war, plus a few other things." I giggle and go to stand. He picks me up, grabs my purse, and carries me into his room.

I ignore his last statement because I don't feel like explaining now. I just want to be in his arms to sleep and be with him.

# CHAPTER TWENTY-THREE

## MAYA

Duncan places me on the massive bed in the middle of his room. I'm glad I'm not too short or I'd need a ladder to get into this bed. His room is all gray and silver tones. I like it, it's him. He pushes me up more on the bed and crawls up with me. He lies on his back and pulls me to his chest. I really do want to sleep but I'm worried about the possible nightmares. I've had them every night since the shooting.

"Where'd you put my gun?"

"Hall closet, we'll put it in the safe later."

We're just about to drift off when my cell phone rings. I roll to the nightstand where he placed my purse and reach for my phone. It's an unknown number. I worry that my stalker is calling me, but without Duncan finding out, I need to answer it.

"Hello?" I answer tentatively. I also remember I need to text Greg and Derek.

"Maya, its Ana, are you ready to get on the plane tonight? By the way, Duncan volunteered to pick you up." Ana mutters into the phone.

"Ana, where are you calling from? This isn't your cell number."

"This is Jonathon's cell, my cell phone broke."

"Okay. Ya, I'm getting ready to go into a briefing right now. See you tomorrow morning."

"I love you, Maya. We need to talk, oh I got to go." She hangs up. I thought I heard Jonathon saying something angry to her in the background. I need to talk to her, too.

"Ana checking up on you?"

"Yes. Duncan, is she okay?" I bite my lip.

"I don't know, but I worry. We need to talk to her."

"I worry too, and yes we need to speak with her. She doesn't call me like she used to. When she does, it's cryptic comments."

"What do you mean cryptic?" He rises up on his side to look down at me.

"She keeps telling me that if anything happens to her, she'll make sure I know what to do. She asks me to take care of you and James. She even talks like she's dying or going to die."

"Really?"

"Yes. I'm terrified. Something is wrong. Duncan, if something happens to her what will I do?"

"Baby, you've got me too. Don't worry. We'll talk to her tomorrow after we tell her about us. Why don't you invite her to go shopping with us the day after that?"

"Okay."

"Get some rest, baby." He leans down and kisses me, and I melt into him more. He breaks the kiss, kisses my nose and pulls me tight against him. He's looking at me carefully.

"When was the last time you slept more than napping?"

"It's been awhile," I confess.

"Why?"

"Why can't I sleep? Or why haven't I slept?"

"Okay, both."

"I can't sleep because of the nightmares. The night my parents died, I was asleep. I woke up an orphan. I don't want to fall asleep and wake up to more people I care about dead. Lately, I've been having nightmares about those two children yelling at me that I killed their parents." I can't tell him about my stalkers and the dreams of him dying too.

"Baby, that was a justified shooting and you were right in not killing him. As for your parents, I used to have nightmares about my mum. Now, I have nightmares about a friend dying in Afghanistan. I know how hard it is. Do you talk to someone?"

"When I need to. It only seems to work with you and your sister."

"What works?" He looks at me, his eyebrow raising.

"Me being able to sleep. When your sister brought me here after they died, I woke up screaming. Ana crawled into bed with me and held my hand. I slept for the first time in weeks. Now, I need to drink till I pass out, take sleeping pills, or just doze. Except for with you, I haven't been able to sleep on my own."

He puffs up his chest. "Oh yeah, baby, it's all me." I giggle. I know he's trying to lighten the mood.

"I'm serious. In college I attempted to sleep with Carl and I ended up slugging him when he held me down."

"Who's Carl? And why would he hold you down?"

"Well...he was my boyfriend in college. We were in biathlon together and dated for a couple years. One night I decided to see if I could sleep all night with him in my apartment. He tried to hold me down when I started thrashing around. He ended up with his hands around my throat because of the way I was moving around in my nightmare. I slugged him, breaking his nose. He broke up with me right then, telling me I was no good at relationships and he was seeing someone else. He only stayed with me that night to get lucky he said. My roommate threatened to kill him if he ever touched me again."

"What a wanker, serves him right for holding you down. Now relax and try to sleep, baby." I lay my head on his chest, he pulls my hand to his heart, and I actually fall asleep.

## DUNCAN

I have to keep this woman with me. I didn't realize how much I really missed her until I saw her walking out of that terminal. She had my complete attention, both my heart and my cock when I saw her. I'm hoping that Joshua can convince her to take a job with Securities International. It turned me on to see her packing, but I was also scared for her. The thought of her in danger makes my insides twist. My gut clenches with memories of the nightmare I had in Paris. I can't lose her. I won't lose her.

I was curious about her sleeping issues, and the fact that she's having nightmares after that shooting only makes her other issues worse. I really can't believe I went all this time without her. The Skyping, texting, and phone calls weren't enough. I'm going to take her out on dates and show her how perfect these two weeks can be. Just like that one day in New York. No fear of being caught. Just her and me. Maybe she'll decide to stay and will move here permanently.

Her comments about my sister have me concerned. Ana was always so headstrong and independent but in the last six months, I've seen her pulling back and into herself. I'll kill that bloody arse if he has hurt her.

A couple times while we're resting, her phone goes off and I ignore it, letting her sleep.

I spend the rest of the day making love to Maya. We shower and dine in. After dinner I catch her standing in the winter garden area of my flat, staring out at the Thames.

"Baby?" I approach quietly and know she doesn't realize I'm behind her when she startles.

"I'm just enjoying the view."

I can tell she is hiding something from me and I want to push but I know she will close up on me.

"Want to talk about it?"

"About what?"

"Whatever you're not saying."

"I'm peaceful and I don't normally get to be. Even in my own condo I feel like I'm under stress."

"From what?"

"My life, the expectations of doing my job. Many other things."

"Baby, I only want you." I wrap my arms around her and pull her back into me. "Want me to help you relax?"

"Please."

I hear the tremor in her voice. I know what she needs but will she let me do it?

"Lean forward and place your palms against the glass."

The winter garden part of my flat is an area that has a bench and indoor fireplace. I can close a double thick glass wall to shut it off but I usually keep it open. It's cooler in here and with her in just my t-shirt, I see her nipples poking through the shirt.

She listens and presses her hands against the glass. I lift her up and press my sweatpants covered cock into her arse. She moans and her head falls back. I spread her legs and notice she still doesn't have any panties on. I release my cock and slide into her slick heat. Pressing her harder into the glass wall, overlooking the gardens below, I make love to her slowly. My thrusts are unhurried and deliberate. The last couple times I've gone slow with her she has begged me to hurry, but this time I see her biting her tongue not to beg. I want to take her slowly so she can see how good it is. I want to breach her walls. I want her forever. She is my worth it. Her moans increase and as my pace continues, she finally starts clenching around my cock and I lose my spunk in her. I pull out of her and turn her and sit on the lounge.

"Baby, you can tell me anything."

She doesn't respond. Just nods and buries her head into my neck.

Tomorrow is going to come too soon. I'll have to share her with my family, and I know she's going to fight me on telling them, but I'll win this. She ends up sending a few texts and I wonder what my girl is hiding.

# CHAPTER TWENTY-FOUR

## MAYA

I wake up to the morning light shining through the blinds. I can't believe I slept all night. Duncan isn't next to me. At first, I start to panic and roll to look for my gun, then I hear the shower from the adjoining room. I pad quietly into the bathroom. Through the glass doors, I see his back. He turns and sees me and pushes the door open. I climb in and drop to my knees. I've been waiting months to get his cock in my mouth again.

"Oh, baby," he growls. I gently take his cock in my hands and rub it. I lick the small drop of pre-cum off the head. I'm always amazed he fits in me, he's so large.

"Umm." I moan as I slide my tongue from base to tip. I grab his balls with one hand and hold his wet cock with my other as I slide him into my mouth. He's too large for me to take him completely in my mouth, but I swallow as much of him as I can. As my throat contracts around his broad head, I hear him groan. I hollow my cheeks as I pull off and then suck him back in while my other hand massages his balls. I concentrate on breathing through my nose so I can take him deeper.

"Baby, I don't want to come in your mouth, slow down." Like that's going to happen. I let go of his balls, wrap my arm around him, and start moving faster. I swallow him down into my throat as far as I can. He groans again, grabs my hair and starts guiding me. He pushes back in, going further back into my throat. I swallow his head and my throat contracts around the head of his cock again. Tears pop in my eyes as I fight my gag reflex. I look up and see his head has dropped back. He's close. I quicken my pace.

"Baby, stop." I ignore his plea, pull back and do it again, sucking him further into my throat this time. "Enough!" he practically yells. He grabs me under my arms and lifts me. My mouth pops as I'm pulled off him. He plants me on the bench and kneels down in front of me. He spreads my labia and immediately sucks my swollen clit into his mouth. I start to grind myself against his face.

"Oh, Duncan, please," I scream as I orgasm. He lifts me up and pushes me against the wall as he enters me. God, I love it when he loses control. He's pistoning himself into me, his hips are moving so fast.

He growls. "Baby, God what you do to me. I want to be so deep in you all the time." He starts to slow his pace and I feel another orgasm coming. He leans down and sucks my nipple into his mouth, hard, and I'm gone. I feel like I'm flying. I scream his name over and over.

"Maya, yes," he groans and comes with me. My pussy is convulsing around his cock and I feel him shooting jets of semen into me.

He holds me against the wall for a moment. I feel his cock still in me. He pulls out, lowers my legs, and starts to wash me off. This man insists on taking care of me. Can I let him do it? I want him to, but can I? It has been just me for so long. Yeah, I have Greg and Derek, but I even keep them at arm's length. I look at him and he's looking at me with a small smile and a thoughtful look.

"What're you thinking, Duncan?" I ask worriedly.

"Don't freak out, baby, okay?"

"Okay." I hope I can keep that promise.

"I was thinking how nice it would be to have morning showers like this all the time."

I pause. He's thinking along the same lines I sort of was. I smile at him. How do I say this?

"I wish that were possible." Immediately his face falls.

"We need to get ready," he says gruffly. I see the disappointment in his face and grab his arm.

"I didn't say I don't want it, Duncan. I just don't know how to make it happen yet. I'm not ready to give up my job and I couldn't stand the thought of you giving up yours."

"I know, Maya, but, baby, I can't go another six months like these last. I want to be with you all the time, not just on random weekends. I'll also not be able to handle seeing you with someone else."

"I only want you, Duncan. That's a certainty. I'm not seeing anyone else and I don't want to."

"Who were you texting yesterday?" I have to tell him. I have to give him a little of me.

"I was texting Derek and Greg to let them know I landed safely."

"Why?"

"They're like my family there. Derek is my friend and Greg is his father." Honestly that should work.

"What? I knew about Greg, but his son is your partner?" He looks confused.

"Yes, someday I'll explain more, but please believe me. They're my closest friends there. Okay?"

"Okay."

We finish washing and get ready to head to James's place. I decide to wear a white sweater dress with a shawl jacket in tan and my knee-high boots. I feel a little overdressed for brunch, but I know this is perfect. He's watching me dress and smiles when he sees the complete look. I start to put my knife in my boot and he laughs, shakes his head, and turns around. I put on only a minimal amount of makeup and braid my hair into a long plait down my back.

"You've panties on right, baby?"

"Yes, honey, I couldn't torture you like that at your father's. Besides, I wouldn't be able to sit still with you in the room and me with no panties. I'd also be afraid to bend over in this outfit." He laughs again and hugs me to him, kissing me.

"You're so beautiful. This is an old style jacket. I haven't seen one like it in a while."

"Thank you, you aren't so bad yourself. It was my father's jacket. I always loved it and it keeps him close to me." He's wearing a similar outfit to the first time I met him. He's in black slacks, a gray Henley, and a black jacket. His dark hair is pushed back from his face and he's unshaven again. I like the complete look, it appears like I just had my hands in his hair and I want the burn on my thighs from his scruff. I'm pretty sure he knows what I'm thinking because he groans as he grabs my hand and pulls me out of the flat.

We're at James's for an early brunch. He thinks I just got off a plane. I know I don't look like I did and he looks thoughtfully at Duncan. I guess Duncan is right, we can't lie to them anymore.

"Darling, is my son treating you okay," I choke on my tea. "Maya, are you alright?" He reaches across to hand me a napkin as I set my teacup down.

"Yes, sorry, James, went down the wrong pipe." Duncan is smirking next to me.

Treating me right, well I could say after multiple orgasms, of course, he's treating me okay. However, I just smile at James and ignore the question.

"Did I hear my Maya girl," I turn to see Uncle Marcus walking down the stairs.

I've only talked to him one other time since his call in October. I'm not sure, but something has changed between us. I'm more uncomfortable around him than I've ever been. He also keeps pressing me with questions.

"Uncle Marcus, you made it here. When did you get in?" I walk over and give him a kiss on the cheek. He holds me tightly to him and I feel uncomfortable. His hands stroke my back. He finally pulls away but still holds my hand.

"Yesterday morning. How was your flight this morning?"

"It was good." I hope he wasn't on a flight near my time, if so the secret would be out. Uncle Marcus is worse than an old lady about gossip. We walk back to Duncan and James; I pull my hand from his. I sit next to Duncan again with Marcus sitting in a chair next to me. He's looking at Duncan and me.

"So, how did your date with Lawrence go?"

"Date?" Duncan growls. James looks at us with a twinkle in his eye.

"Uncle Marcus, I just had dinner with him once, while he was in D.C. It wasn't a date. For one, I'm not interested and for two, I can't." I look at Duncan, trying to calm him down. I know he has a bit of a jealous streak, that's why I didn't tell him about dinner. Plus it was just dinner, there's no way Lawrence is my type. After Duncan, no man but him is for me. Wait? Did I just think that? Yes, only Duncan. The comfort of that thought soothes me.

"Why? I want you officially a part of this family. I invited Lawrence to the New Year's Eve party." I groan and hear Duncan growl again. He's going to give us away.

"Who's Lawrence?" he asks angrily.

Again, I look at James and he's smirking and winks at me, he knows. The jig is up.

"He's my nephew. Why do you ask?" Marcus answers rather snootily. His fingers laced in front of his face like he is contemplating something huge.

"Well for your information, Uncle Marcus, Maya is my date for the New Year's Eve party," he states.

I'm dumbstruck. How could he say it just like that?

"Really?" Ana says from the entry.

James has a very pleased look on his face while Marcus looks like he swallowed nails. I don't know what to say.

"Ana, I've missed you so much." I walk over to her and give her a big hug. She's lost weight and her eyes appear sunk in. She's not her vibrant self and as I pull away and see Jonathon over her shoulder, I know why. I want to hurt him. I want to cut off his balls. How dare he hurt her? I actually want to kill him. He's doing something to my Ana. Duncan walks up behind me and puts his arm around my waist.

"Yes, Sis, she took pity on this English wanker and is going to the

New Year's Eve party as my date. Plus we're having dinner together tonight."

"Really, I'm so happy for you both." Her smile is so bright and all I want to do is keep that smile on her face. Jonathon walks up behind her and puts his hand on her shoulder. She flinches at the contact, and the light in her eyes disappears. That's it.

"Ana, darling, come with me." I lead her out of the library, up the stairs, and toward her old bedroom.

"Maya, don't run off with my wife. I've heard you can attack people with little provocation." The whole room gasps. I stop on the stairs and turn.

"If you're referring to your asshole best man, whatever his name is, he deserved what he got. He's lucky I was unarmed."

"Oh yes, there's that. I've also heard you and Duncan have issues with public displays of affection."

"That's enough! What Maya and I do is our business and not yours or your fucktard friends!" Duncan yells. Someone saw us together. When?

"Language son, please there are ladies present. Jonathon, you need to watch what you're saying. Maya is a part of this family. If she and Duncan are in a relationship, I'm pleased for them. They're both grown adults and have shared interests." Ana looks at me.

"Maya, what's he talking about?" She looks lost.

"Ana, please come on, I'll explain." I direct her to continue upstairs.

"All right." Her voice is quiet and sounds so childlike. What's this man done to my vibrant friend?

When we get to her room, I explain that Duncan and I have been talking for months. How we met at her wedding and there was a spark. I explain how we've met up twice since then. I apologize and explain how I flew in yesterday. I also tell her if she wants, if it makes her uncomfortable, I'll end my relationship with Duncan. But I tell her that I do care for him.

"Oh no, Maya, no, I'm so happy for you both. Please don't end it. I think he can help you as much as you can help him."

"Thank you, Ana. Tomorrow Duncan is taking me Christmas

shopping and to see my solicitor about some property Savta had here in London. Please come with us. We can shop and hang out. Please?"

"Oh I don't know, Jonathon likes his dinner right at five and I have chores I need to do."

"Please, Ana. I was hoping you'd manage this property for me until I figure out what to do with it. Plus I need your help finding dresses for the parties coming up."

"Okay, but let me ask Jonathon."

"No, I'll ask him," Duncan says from the doorway.

"What, no privacy?" I ask with a smirk.

"I missed you and I haven't got to hug my sister yet." He walks over and wraps her in his arms. He looks over her head at me, he feels and sees the signs I did too. I nod and sigh.

"Maya, would you have ended us if my sister had a problem?"

"I would. I wouldn't like it, but I'd do it if she wanted." I smile at him. "But she's happy for us and now we don't have to sneak around anymore."

He smiles and walks over to me, where he takes me in his arms. "I wouldn't like it and I'd have to change both of your minds. You're my girl now, Maya." I lean up and kiss his cheek. "Father wanted me to come and get you girls. Someone is here to see you, Maya." I feel the tension in his body and worry.

Before we head downstairs where brunch is being served, I explain about the best man. Ana laughs and agrees he deserved what he got.

We head downstairs and I stop in my tracks as I see who's in the sitting room. I want to drop Duncan's hand but know that would hurt him again. I walk into the room with him beside me and see Greg stand. He looks at me and then to Duncan. His smile dies. Oh crap, here it comes.

"I decided to fly in today and James invited me to brunch. How are you, sweetheart?" he says as I dislodge my hand from Duncan's and walk into Greg's arms. I felt Duncan stiffen when Greg called me sweetheart.

"Did Derek come with you?" I know the answer to the question.

"No. Will you introduce us?" His smile has still not returned and

Duncan is still standing there like a statue. Okay, I can do this. James accepts us, maybe Greg will too.

"Duncan Preston, my boyfriend, this is Greg Williams, a man who's as close to a father as yours is to me." Duncan steps up and wraps me tight in his left arm, shaking Greg's hand with his right.

"Sir, nice to meet you. Maya has told me very little about you." The dig hurts.

"That's my girl. She keeps her cards close to the vest. Don't worry, she never told me she's seeing someone. I guessed like your father, but I wasn't sure. It's nice to finally meet you. I saw you at the Israeli Gala in August. Your father has told me a lot about you, as has Joshua Donovan." At the drop of Joshua's name, I gasp and Duncan looks at him warily.

"How do you know Joshua?"

"He and I have known each other for a while. I believe you helped on a job I sent his way with the diplomat's daughter from France. Sorry to hear things didn't end so well." Oh shit, oh shit, oh shit. What does Greg know? Does he know about New York? Does he know about D.C.? When he is quiet like this I worry.

I watch him warily as he sizes up Duncan, what is he thinking?

"Brunch is being served," James says, releasing us from the tension.

We're all sitting at the table eating our brunch. Duncan is sitting next to me with his hand brushing my thigh under the table. I look across the table at my family, well almost. Uncle Marcus still seems like he's upset about something. I hope I can talk to him but I'm not too concerned. I feel the rift between us getting bigger. Greg is sitting on my other side and is watching me carefully. I know he's interested in my relationship with Duncan.

"So I guess Lawrence has competition," Jonathon states while we're eating.

"Excuse me," I say. "We never dated. It was dinner amongst friends. How'd you know we even had dinner?"

"That's not how he talks about it." He ignores my question. I see him look at Uncle Marcus. What's that all about? I thought these two just met.

"I'll let him know she's off the market," Duncan states.

"How'd you know about Lawrence anyhow?" I ask again. This is getting to be annoying.

"Lawrence is a part of our U.S. division. Plus I heard Marcus talking about it," he quickly adds. When did he and Marcus talk? I'm beginning to feel like there's something more going on here.

"Again, Duncan and I have been seeing each other for six months. As far as my dinner with Lawrence, I met him at his hotel's restaurant and we had a quick dinner before I went on shift. Nothing more. If he said there was more, he's wrong. My partner, Derek, even showed up." Jonathon looks at me thoughtfully. I look to Greg for confirmation.

"It's true, Derek was talking to me on the phone when he showed up to pick up Maya from the dinner. She only had dinner and left for a call with Derek. I believe that was one of the nights you made the news after the November shooting. Right, sweetheart?"

"Yes, a suicidal on the roof of the Watergate. I was called in just in case. We got him off without getting hurt." I say with little emotion. Greg reaches over and takes my hand, Duncan squeezes my thigh tightly.

"Maya, don't you practice Judaism? Isn't it against your religion to celebrate Christmas?" The whole table gasps and everyone turns to Jonathon as if his head is on fire. Maybe my look is causing his head to burst into flames. Duncan and Greg both stand up immediately.

"Well, Jonathon, what I do or don't practice is my business." Ever since Duncan told him we were picking up Ana tomorrow he has decided to make me public enemy number one. I have strong shoulders, let's go, asshole.

"Oi, Father, I think Maya and I are done eating. Ana, we will see you in the morning at eight to pick you up. Marcus, it was a pleasure seeing you again. Greg, pleased to meet you. Jonathon, do not ever try to insult Maya again." He reaches for my hand to help me up. I apologize as we walk to the door. I turn to see James and Greg following us.

"Kids, I'm very sorry. Please, come over for dinner tomorrow or call me and I'll meet you somewhere. As for your relationship, I couldn't be happier." James says as he kisses my cheek and hugs Duncan.

"I agree. Duncan, thank you for giving her a smile I've never seen. As for the bastard in there, I'll take care of him. How about lunch tomorrow? Do you still want me to come to the solicitor's office with you, sweetheart?" Greg adds as he shakes Duncan's hand and pulls me close.

"I should be okay. I'll text. Please let me tell Derek. Love you, Greg." He kisses me on the cheek and nods.

"Thank you, Dad, we'll be in touch." He leads me to his car where we leave and head to Duncan's place in Southbank.

# CHAPTER TWENTY-FIVE

## MAYA

"I'm sorry you felt we needed to leave, Duncan. I regret that I never told you about Greg or about my dinner with Lawrence." I'm worried he's upset with me.

"Baby, don't apologize. Jonathon was being a royal wanker. Besides, I want to head to the flat for a nice shag before dinner. As for Greg, you made up for it when you introduced me as your boyfriend. Are you sure he or his son isn't in love with you?" I smile at him and lean over in my seat.

"I'm sure. They love me but not like that. Honey, we can still have a nice shag in this gorgeous car of yours." I stroke the leather seat and reach across the console to his leg.

"Baby, don't tempt me." His voice lowers with his arousal.

"Well, let me see what I can do to tempt you." I reach up under my short dress and start to pull my panties off. Even with the slack in the seatbelt, this is hard, but I get them off and toss them at him. He groans as he sniffs them.

"Baby, you're going to cause us to be in an accident if you don't put these back on."

I push up my dress, almost exposing my pussy, and start rubbing my thighs and moaning.

"Honey, please I need you so bad. I want your cock so far up inside me, please." I continue to rub up my thighs and seek out my labia, rubbing it before moving on to my clit. "Ahhh, Duncan, I'm so hot for you." He growls in reply and the engine accelerates.

"Baby, I'm going to spank you for this. Slip those fingers in yourself, then give them to me." I do as he says, pushing my fingers into myself. I drop my head back against the headrest, my eyes fall close as I bring myself to the brink.

"Now, Maya! Give me those fingers, now," he demands.

"I'm so close, babe. Let me come first," I beg.

He growls again and takes his hand off the gear shift to grab my arm.

"No, you will come on my lips or cock only."

"Oh," I groan as I feel myself starting to tighten. I let him pull my hand away and he pulls it to his lips. He sucks my fingers into his mouth and starts sucking off my juices.

"Ah God, baby, I've got to be inside you, now." He pulls into his parking garage, slams the car into park, and tilts his seat back. Then he unbuckles me, picks me up, and lifts me onto his lap.

"Honey, I need your cock." I pull up his shirt to get to his buckle. I undo his buckle, button, and then the zipper. He springs free, he went commando today. The whole time I'm messing with his pants, he's pushing back my jacket and lifting my dress higher to get to my breasts.

"God, I love these tits. Get ready, you did this to me." He pushes me down onto his erection, both of us groaning as we feel the connection. I'm so drawn to this man, I'd give up so much for him, and that's what scares me the most. My knees are bent on each side of his hips and I start to ride him, this sexy car has been turning me on to do this. He's meeting each of my thrusts; when my orgasm hits, my thrusts slow down. He doesn't like that, so he uses his hold on my waist to lift me up and down harder on him. This prolongs my orgasm more and I arch my back into the steering wheel. He groans as he comes on the next thrust. I fall back and set the horn off. We both laugh as I jump.

"Oh, baby, I'm never going to be able to drive this car again without thinking of this right here."

"Good, just as long as it's me you're thinking about, I'll take it."

He laughs. "Baby, you're the only woman in my mind like that." I lift off him to get back into my seat so we can get out and head to the apartment. He groans. I look at him and see his eyes are trained on my pussy and thighs. "Baby, seeing my spunk all over you turns me on so much. We need to get inside the flat so we can try out another surface." Crazy man is horny all the time.

"Oh, honey, I don't know if I'll make it out of the elevator without dropping to my knees for you."

He groans and pushes himself back into his pants before turning and getting out. He reaches in and grabs me, throwing me over his shoulder.

"Come on, baby, we're making it to the flat. Someone needs some spankings for starting that little stunt in the car." I try to grab my purse and panties. He sees my intent and grabs them for me.

His long legs are eating up space to the elevator when we hear a throat clearing from behind us. I look up from my upside down position to see Lawrence.

Duncan swings around, asking, "Can I help you, sir? This is private property?" Duncan's arm is resting against my ass so I'm not giving anyone a show.

"Well I was looking for my girlfriend, but I seem to have found her."

His what? Oh no, he didn't.

"I'm your what?" I ask and wiggle so Duncan will put me down. I stand and stare at Lawrence as if he's talking in tongues. He looks at my disheveled appearance, Duncan carrying my panties and purse, and his dark eyes darken further, making him look almost evil. I step closer to Duncan.

"I thought we had an understanding, Maya." He sneers at me.

He doesn't even compare to Duncan, at his only six foot height and slim build. He's a boy while Duncan is a man.

"No, we didn't. We had dinner…as friends…for Uncle Marcus. It was nothing more." I'm practically yelling.

How did he find out where I was? Was he following me? He can't be my stalker, I just met him.

"You must be Lawrence. I'm Duncan, her *boyfriend*, although there are much better ways to put that. Her man, her sweetie, honey, her lover, and whatever else she wants to call me. Do not look at her and don't even think of trying to get in touch with her again. I'll not only break your legs, but I'll also break you." Jealousy and anger pours off Duncan in waves. I put my hand in his and squeeze so he feels me with him. He looks down and I see the fury in his eyes. I want to step back, but I know it isn't about me.

"I'm Lawrence Baker. Maybe you should clarify with her how she feels. She asked me to come to London to be with her for the holiday. We had a very intimate dinner." He doesn't extend his hand to Duncan for a handshake. Maybe he thinks Duncan will break it. I want to punch his face. Intimate dinner, what the fuck?

"No, I didn't. You asked what I was doing for the holiday and I told you I was going to London. As for intimate dinner, we sat in your hotel's main restaurant. My partner showed up to eat my leftovers and give me a ride to a call."

"That's not how I remember it. Why don't you tell him the truth? You told your partner you were going to be late and walked me to my room. We had a very intimate and private goodbye. But I see you've found yourself a Neanderthal to control, I won't be here when you want me back, darling."

"You can wait until the world ends. She's mine, you bloody piss ant. Now get out of here before I have security escort you out. I'd do it myself, but I don't want to accidentally kill you when I put my hands on you." Duncan growls at Lawrence, just then a guy in a suit walks up and takes him from the garage.

"Duncan, I swear I've been only faithful to you. I ran into Carl once after he was fired, he asked me out and I told him I was in a relationship. I didn't tell Lawrence I was in a relationship because I didn't want it to get back to your father. I didn't lead him on though. I didn't go to his room. I didn't ask him to come to London. I told him I wasn't interested in him. I swear, please don't be mad at me. We can call Derek and he'll confirm what I said. You heard Greg, I was on a call that night." I'm practically begging. How do I get that angry look out of his eyes? I put it there. This is my fault for hiding our relationship.

"Maya, baby, I'm not mad at you. I'm mad at the situation, and I'm angry that that bloody wanker decided to come here. By the way, how did he know you were here?" We both stop and then it comes to me.

"Jonathon." We both say at the same time. That motherfucker is going to be a problem. We both shake our heads and make our way to the elevator to head upstairs.

We've barely cleared the door when he's on me again. He lifts my dress over my head, unhooks my bra, and then drops to his knees where he unzips my boots, removing the knife I slipped in there and pulling them off. His tongue snakes out to the apex of my thighs, licking our combined fluids from my thighs. He stands, lifts me up, and carries me to the dining room.

"It's time for a snack." My ass hits the table with my legs still wrapped around him. He releases my legs and sits them on the table, opening me up to him.

He sits in the head chair and pulls me to the edge of the table, and proceeds to lick down my thighs. He stops every so often and bites or sucks on them. I'm moaning and writhing on the table and he pulls the chair up closer to lick and suck my pussy lips into his mouth. He spreads my labia lips and latches onto my clit. I come up from the table and scream. He pushes me back down without losing his suction on my clit, and gently bites my clit, making me come so hard. He starts licking up my juices as they flow from my body.

"This is my pussy, baby. No one else's, just mine."

"Yes, Duncan, only yours." I'll tell him anything he wants as long as he gives me that wonderful cock.

"Please, Duncan, I need you," I beg.

"Not yet, baby, one more time."

"I can't!"

"Yes, you can. God, I love this pussy, so pink and succulent. It's like a beautiful flower opening to me." His words and his tongue are working me as no one ever has.

He moves back up to my clit and swirls his tongue around it, but doesn't touch it. I feel like I'm having an out of body experience. He growls against me and I grab his head to pull him to my clit. When he latches on, he sucks on it so hard I think I see stars. I start screaming his name repeatedly, and I hear myself change languages. The next sound that reaches my ears is the chair scraping against the floor and falling as he stands. He enters me in one long thrust. I cry out again and he groans.

"Look at us, baby. See that cock so far in you and you opening for it. That cock owns you. That cock owns this pussy. You hear me." He leans down to lick and suck on my breasts. I know he's marking me, I feel his teeth against my skin. There will never be another for me after this.

I can't believe how easy it was for him to breach my walls. He rises up and starts thrusting into me harder. The table scrapes along the wood flooring. I look down at where he's in me and come again from the erotic sight. I'm still screaming his name at the top of my lungs when he comes with a roar. He actually roared. Holy hell, I'm so turned on. He falls onto my chest, his breathing is labored.

"Baby, did I hurt you?" His gentle but breathy words have me looking into his eyes and smiling.

"No, not at all. We do need to talk about this possessive streak of yours though." I laugh at him.

"Baby, don't make fun of me when my cock's in you." For emphasis, he flexes his hips, making me groan.

"Okay, you win. This time." He pulls out and both of us whimper at the loss.

We spend the rest of the afternoon making love on many more surfaces. I don't know if I can stop my heart from falling now. His bout of jealousy has him marking me everywhere. He leaves love bites and hickeys on my breasts and thighs. As we get ready for dinner, I'm laughing at him and his caveman ways.

"Honey, its good you only marked me where people can't see."

"Sorry, baby, just the thought of those two wankers has me all wonky."

"I told you, don't worry. It's just you." I lean up to kiss him. He bends down and claims my lips. My cell phone buzzes from the other room. I walk over to grab it and gasp at the picture.

I then notice the unknown number.

"What's up, baby?" he asks from behind me. "Holy shit! Is that your flat?"

"Yes. Just a moment, I need to call Derek." I dial the number.

"Hey, sexy girl, how is London? I didn't expect to hear from you already. Did Dad meet up with you yet? I told him you wouldn't like the surprise—"

"Where are you?" I don't have time to play, someone has been in my space.

"At work. Why?"

"Get a team and head to my condo. Someone broke in and left me a present. I'm calling your dad now."

"Son of a bitch! I'll take care of it and change all the codes. I'll also file the reports. You know this will come out now."

"I know, but I can't have my space invaded like this again. Thank you, Derek." I hang up and drop my head. I need to get this asshole. I dial Greg's number next.

"It just escalated. Someone broke into my condo again and left me a butt load of roses. Derek is on his way with a team. It's going to come out. I'm sorry."

"Are you okay, sweetheart," he asks.

"No, Duncan's here. He saw the picture. I'll call you back later." I hang up.

"Want to tell me what's going on? And what this is?" Duncan asks. I know he heard most of the conversation.

"I'd like to say no, but I need to go to a hotel now. I won't put you in danger. I've had a stalker for a while now."

"A what? How long?"

"About six months, but honestly I've had one since my parents were killed."

"Bloody hell, Maya, why didn't you tell me?"

"Because of this. I didn't want you to worry. It's only been flowers and a few notes. The other one started just after we met the first time. He broke into my condo and took pictures of me while I was sleeping."

"What? Two?"

"Yeah, two."

"Is this why you have a BAU case? And an FBI alert?"

"You know about those?"

"Bloody hell, woman. Yes, I know."

"Greg has had a friend with the BAU keeping a watch at everything for years. Nothing was serious until June when they determined it was two of them. The newest one is more serious, that's why I need to leave."

"What notes? And you are not leaving here. This building is more secure than any hotel."

"Don't worry. Greg, Derek, and I have it under control."

"I'll bloody worry. Now bloody hell, tell me what's going on. This is far from under control, based on that picture."

"We have a dinner to go to. We can talk about it later. Derek is having a team go to my condo now."

"I'm telling Joshua tonight. Timothy can look at some security feeds and find something your team can't."

"Duncan, I can take care of myself," I snarl. I won't let him run my life.

"You're my woman, I'll not allow anyone to hurt or scare you."

"Duncan, stop now." I'm huffing.

He stalks toward me and pushes me into the glass wall of windows behind me that overlook London. I'm instantly turned on by his aggressiveness but also angry because he's pushing me around.

"Baby, I can't control your job, but I can control this. I'll prevent you from getting hurt. I'll be talking with my team. And you will be staying here. Got it?"

"Yes, Duncan." He's right, another set of eyes can't hurt. Greg has had a team on it for years and nothing has ever been found.

# CHAPTER TWENTY-SIX

## DUNCAN

As we head down to the Rover her cell rings with the popular American song, *Bad Boys,* and I smile as I help her in. I watch her answer and she bristles. I nod and she nods back, so I set the phone up to connect to the Rover's Bluetooth.

"Derek, do you want to repeat what you just said?" She looks nervously at me. I wonder what she's thinking.

"Am I on speaker phone now?" A male voice answers back.

"Yes." Again, she looks at me nervously.

"There was a note with all the roses. It said ninety-nine roses because I'll love you for the rest of my life. You will never be rid of me. I've watched men come in and out of your life for years. He is just another that I will control or get rid of too. You're mine. I'll possess you like I wanted to possess her." He pauses so we can absorb it. "No prints, no images from the cameras, and nothing from cameras in the neighborhood. I'm having the security system set to do a rolling pass-code. I called Dad and told him. He's pissed. He's having SSA Jones called in with his team. He's even threatening to have you moved into protective custody. Maya, this is out of control now. Keep my sister safe, Duncan. I'll kill anyone that hurts her." He'll kill? Sister?

"I'll keep her safe. Who the bloody hell is this?" I growl back at him.

"I'm her partner, Derek. She and I have been close for many years. My father and I would go to the ends of the world to save her. Maya, sexy, please be safe. I'll continue to run searches. I need to go. I'll call in a couple days."

"Bye, Derek. I'm sorry." She murmurs. She turns to look at me with a look of guilt. "He's staying at my condo. I've known him for years and like he said, we're like brother and sister, nothing more. He and his father are like my family. Okay?"

"Okay for now," I growl at her.

This jealousy I feel when another man says he cares for her bothers me. I've never been like this with any woman. I'm protective of my sister, but the thought of this man calling Maya *sexy* makes me want to rip his tongue out of his mouth.

I feel sorry for marking her as I did, but bloody hell, what was I supposed to do? That wanker called her his girlfriend. I wanted to kill him on the spot. She's mine and I'll make sure the world knows that. My eyes burn as I remember seeing that image on her phone of her condo covered in roses. Heart shaped with candles and rose petals in front of her windows. Her bed covered in them too. My stomach rolls from the anger. I'll kill whoever this is if they touch her.

I pull up to the restaurant and worry I'm going to lose my shit. My chest hurts just thinking about how much she's kept from me. First Greg and Derek, and now two stalkers are after her. I look over at her as she looks at me nervously. She knows how angry I am right now.

She resembles a schoolgirl in her short mini skirt with black tights, dark sweater, and leather jacket with those damn boots. I want her again, right here. I want to show her what she does to me.

We walk into the restaurant where we're meeting Joshua. I should have told Maya he intends to talk to her about a job with the company, but I didn't wish to wreck the afternoon any more than it already was. You'd think I'd want a break, but I want to clear off the nearest table and take her again. I never did spank her for her stunt in the car. I know it turns her on when I do, so I'm waiting her out.

We approach Joshua's table and I see he's on the phone.

"What do you mean you don't have eyes on him?" Blimey, this isn't going to be good. I hear his southern accent peeking through and know he's close to losing it. "Find him! I'll be there later to take over. If anything happens to her, Ian, your head will roll. Not only will I be after ya but so will Michael when he gets done with his errands." He growls and hangs up.

"Ian lose eyes on Nathan? Where's Michael?" I ask, trying to diffuse the situation.

"Yes! Michael is Christmas shopping for Mum. I hate to do it, but I might have to add a second guy. Michael won't like that. He's been her only guard for years now, she'll not like it either. So sorry, my mum raised me with better manners, I'm Joshua Donovan." He stands and extends a hand to Maya. When she puts her hand in his to shake it, he turns it and kisses her knuckles. I can't help it, I actually growl at him. This is my best friend, but damn this is my woman.

"Maya Aaron. Don't mind him. He's in a full-on jealousy mood today." My woman is actually making fun of me.

I lean toward her ear and whisper, "Want to see what mood I'm in right now? I still owe you a spanking from earlier." She actually squirms, possibly to relieve the pressure of the erotic image I left. "That's right, baby, mine," I say the last a little louder so Joshua can hear me. The bloody bastard actually laughs.

"Come sit you two before I have to pay the maître d' to clear the room." He laughs again.

"I'd not be jealous like this if she had just let me tell everyone she's mine back in June. As for you, baby, you know why I'm like this right now." I growl at both of them. Now they both laugh.

"Jealous much, Duncan." He laughs at me harder.

"Oi', what're you laughing at, ya bloody bastard? You've been a barmy wanker for one girl since I met you?" That shuts him up. He doesn't like references to his "Angel", at all. None of us has ever met her or knows her name. I only know about her because he got drunk one night and spilled the beans. I watch him rub his side.

"So can I ask who Michael is?" Maya asks. Oh great, here it comes.

"Michael works for me just like Duncan, but he's on a special assignment, protecting my mum," he states.

"Can I get you something to drink? And would you like another Jack Daniel's, Mr. Donovan?" The server interrupts.

"Yes, another for me, Maya, Duncan?"

"I'll have the same as him," Maya answers with a smile.

"Scotch," I say.

"An Englishman that drinks good Tennessee whiskey, I like you already." Maya is smiling at him.

"Yes, but to make it perfectly clear, I'm only half English. I was born in Georgia and lived in North Carolina for a while until my grandfather brought us here when I was twelve." He says no more, but I know he drinks Jack for a reason, something to do with his "Angel" again.

"Well, you won't hear any complaints from me. I either drink JD or Jameson."

"An Irish girl to boot, Duncan you're in trouble. Reddish hair, green eyes and Irish, mate, you do have your hands full." He laughs.

"I'll take it, she's worth it." I smile at her and wink.

She is worth it. I'll prove I'm not leaving her to this maniac. Even if Greg and Derek think they've got it handled, I'll help or take over.

"So, Maya, tell me a little about yourself. The way Duncan talks I was expecting a very different woman to walk in here. You're too small and beautiful to be the spitfire that he speaks about."

"He talks about me? Awe...how sweet. What do you want to know? Not my resume I assume."

"Actually, I'd like to know about your background. I'm interested in seeing if you'd be a fit with Securities International." I cringe, knowing what's coming next.

She swings her head to me, and I smile.

"Excuse me...I'm not looking for a new job. I've got two good jobs already. And you, Big Guy, just because of what happened today, make no mistake I'll go back to D.C. in a heartbeat."

"Two?" Did she just say two? What's she talking about?

"Well, Duncan, we haven't had a chance to talk yet, but just before I boarded the plane, I interviewed for a second more permanent position with Secret Service. Greg finally got his wish. I won't be on his team, but I'll be working with the service. It's a new idea and it helps with relations between both services. It will mean I could move permanently to Secret Service if I wanted to eventually."

"What? Baby, you're already ERT and Special Service, why now Secret Service?" I watch Joshua out of the corner of my eye, and he looks thoughtful.

"Yes, but I'll only be called on a Secret Service call if they need a sniper. I already double over with them when they need close protection for Special Services. That's how I was able to come across the pond with a sidearm and am able to carry in London. Greg set Derek and me up to be air marshal qualified too. I had to call ahead and let the locals know I was heading over. I took the Quantico course to be able to double with the air marshals if I fly with a gun. I was able to partake in the most advanced training with the Secret Service sniper school. I'll carry two badges and it'll be such a plus for me. With my language skills, they'll utilize me more often now. Plus, I think its Greg's way of keeping an eye on me." She smiles at me. She thinks this is funny. Bloody hell.

"Let me get this straight. You're an ERT sniper with Metro and now a sniper with Secret Service? Also, are you talking about Division Chief of Investigations Gregory Williams?" Joshua asks her.

"Yes, I've known Greg for several years, his son is my partner. I've not gotten the job yet, there was some extra paperwork and special considerations to make for both Derek and myself to double over. Nevertheless, yes I'm a sniper. I also help with Special Services as a close protection operative. I have extensive training in most handguns, hand-to-hand combat, and I'm a second-degree black belt in Krav Maga. I've also trained since I was a teenager in Israeli tactical knife with David Harel. I speak many languages. What more do I need to say? I'd say whip it out and let's compare, but you know I don't have one and that would be too much for my man."

The way she says my man makes my chest swell. I want this restaurant cleared so I can show her how her man feels about all that. Joshua starts laughing.

"Okay, Maya, you made your point. I'm sorry to infer that you're less than you are. What languages do you know?"

"Well, I'm fluent in Yiddish, Hebrew, Arabic, French, German, Gaelic, and Italian. I know Pashto, Dari, Farsi, Spanish, Mandarin, and I'm currently learning Indonesian and Japanese."

"Bloody hell, woman, are you a linguist?" Joshua exclaims, making me smile with pride at my girl.

She's added a couple more languages to her knowledge base in the last six months.

"Well, yes, I have a photographic memory and was raised speaking many languages. My mother taught me Irish Gaelic. My father spoke Yiddish, Hebrew, and Arabic. We spoke them regularly in our home. He also expected me to learn more." I see the bitterness and hurt in her eyes. I know from our phone conversations she feels her father took much of her youth from her. It was his attempt to make her as perfect as he wanted. I reach under the table to hold her hand. She turns and smiles at me.

"You know David Harel?"

"He was an old military friend of my father's."

"He runs a security company too."

"I know. He's asked me on occasion to help him."

"I'll admit, I've done some checking on you."

"You have?"

"Well after Duncan accidentally hit the FBI security net on you, yes."

"I explained to him about that."

"What about that IA investigation?"

"How do you know about that?" I watch her spine straighten. She's wary about something.

"I have my ways. Care to explain?"

"It was a misunderstanding. My locker at ERT headquarters was broken into. Two of my tactical knives were stolen. One was used to murder another ERT officer. I was cleared."

She says everything with little emotion but I can feel the energy radiating off her body.

"How did they know it was your knife?"

"I had my initials etched into the base of the blade."

"Did they find the suspect?"

"No." I can tell she isn't going to say more but my hand tightens on her thigh. She turns to look at me but her eyes and feelings are blanked. She is hiding something. Joshua interrupts my thoughts.

"Well, Maya, I'd love for you to come work at Securities International. I'd make it worth your while and I'd pay for all your belongings to be shipped here. I know Gregory will have a fit, but I'd personally love to see him pissed off. He beat me at poker badly a couple months back."

"Thank you, but I'm not interested. Oh, you're the Englishman he beat. He loved that."

I stiffen next to her. I want her here with me. I can't go without her. The thought of her returning to D.C., where this arsehole is, makes my skin crawl.

"Well, the offer stands. Let's have dinner and get to know each other. I can't believe you have my mate here tied up as he is. If it's not too personal, what happened today that has you both skittish?" She actually looks at me and I nod before she begins.

"My condo in D.C. was broken into and ninety-nine red roses were left for me with a note, candles, and rose petals. I've had an admirer for years, but they've never done this."

"You have an admirer and you aren't concerned?" Joshua looks at her shocked.

"I'll take care of them or they'll go away on their own. They were harmless until recently. They're getting closer and more daring."

"Tell him about the other one," I grit out.

On a huge sigh, she says, "In June, the morning after Duncan and I met for the first time, I was left a package of pictures. This is another person who is angry with me. Greg walked in and saw them or I would have handled them on my own. It was pictures of my whole day, including meeting Duncan outside the bar and one of me sleeping in my condo."

"Someone got into your condo?"

"I was extra tired and forgot to set my alarm. Since then, he has slashed the tires on my bike, painted my door red, and sent me pictures of my day. I believe that the IA investigation is a result of him, but I can't believe he would kill another ERT officer. Officer Yancy was on the call that night in June, he was suspended shortly after, but he and I were friends. He called shortly before he died, asking to talk to me."

"What did he want?"

"He never met with me."

"How did they clear you?"

"I was teaching a class during the murder. Plus, I gave them reasons why it wouldn't be me."

"Such as?"

"Look, do you fight with knives?"

"Yes, as a matter of fact I do."

"Then you know that most knife fights result in a slashing cut, very rarely are they stabbed unless you sneak up on the person and take them by surprise. I'm trained enough that I would have slashed him from his navel to his neck or across his abdomen. I wouldn't have stabbed him in the chest due to the ribs, unless I throw a knife. Also, the perp was close enough that Yancy pulled a patch off them."

"You never told me this." I pull away slightly.

"It was right before I met you in New York," she says by way of explanation and I realize that explained some of her mood then.

"Joshua, can you have Timothy run a soft check on her flat and a few names if I give them to you?" I ask quietly.

"Of course. Are you sure you're okay? Most women would be freaking out."

"My partner is condo sitting for me and I don't go anywhere

without protection." He looks at her carefully, seeing if she'll give up anything else.

This is why Joshua is in charge, he can wait out anyone and can read people so well.

"Look, I'm not worried. I think the flowers are from someone that knew my mother or father because every year, for the whole month of June, flowers are delivered to their graves in Tel Aviv and to me in D.C." I knew there was more. She keeps hiding herself from me.

"Is that all, Maya?" he asks her, his eyebrow arches. He knows there's more.

"What else? I think they might be working together. One of them has followed me to London several times or knows where I'm at here. Also, they can get onto police property."

"What?" I huff out. The more she says, the more I worry.

"Okay, after the shooting in November, there were flowers left at my condo door. I was also sent pictures of myself from the news reports. The photographs were left on my SUV and truck while they were parked in the police department parking lot. That's why Derek and Greg have been so protective. I think that's why Greg came over for the holiday. He's worried. He knows that I've received flowers when I was visiting here before."

"Of course. Not because he thinks you should be with his son." I can't help myself, I'm so jealous right now.

"Duncan, enough, Derek isn't like that to me. I told you Greg is like a father. Stop now."

"Why not let this rest and we will have an excellent dinner." Joshua cuts into our argument.

The rest of the evening goes by without a hitch. I finally begin to relax and feel comfortable. I see out of the corner of my eye how many men check her out, but I know that I have to control my jealousy or I'll push her away.

"It was wonderful to finally meet you, Maya. I hope you know the offer will stand as long as I'm in business. I'd be daft not to hire someone with your talents. I'll also be in touch after Timothy runs his checks," Joshua says when we're leaving.

"Thank you, Joshua, but for now, I'm happy where I'm at." I'm not happy, but I can't push her.

"Lunch tomorrow, mate?" I ask him.

"Sure why not. I'll see you both then."

"Duncan, we will have Ana with us and possibly Greg," Maya states. I see Joshua pause and turn to look at me with a strange look on his face.

"Your sister will be with you tomorrow?" Joshua asks.

"We're picking up Ana in the morning to go with us to Maya's solicitor's office. Maya has some paperwork to go over. The ladies wanted to go shopping after that, and I want to get my sister away from that smarmy arsehole for a little while. I swear something is going on with him." I didn't mean to say so much, but I know Joshua would understand.

"What do you mean something is going on?" he asks.

"She's lost weight, her eyes look sunk in, she flinches when he touches her, and worst he controls her," Maya provides.

"Has she talked to you, Maya? Do you suspect what I think you're saying?" Joshua asks.

I know he has experience with situations like this.

"Yes, Joshua, I think he's abusing her, but I don't ever see any signs. Although, she wears different clothes than she used to."

"Duncan, why didn't you tell me?" Joshua swings around to me, his body is vibrating with tension.

"Well, let me see. I don't always tell you what's going on with my family. Plus, she doesn't talk to me."

"I'll try to speak to her tomorrow. Okay, guys, just relax, both of you. When she figures out what an asshole he is, it will be as plain as Rudolf's nose. All right?" Maya tries to snuff out the rapidly growing fire between Joshua and me.

I don't know what his problem is except his personal background with abusive people. Maybe that's it, although, he seems more agitated about my sister.

"I'll see you tomorrow, Duncan and Maya, goodnight."

I hope I don't get a phone call later from him at the pub trashed. I decide to call Ian and put him on notice. I pull out my cell and dial Ian's number as I walk Maya to the Rover.

"Hella," Ian's thick Scottish accent comes over the phone.

"Mate, tell me you're not already mullered? Did you not just get off guarding Ms. Patrice?"

"Na, Mate, just thinking about where to head. Yes, I was just with her. You with Bossman or something?"

"Will you call Bossman and go with him. Something is up and he's not going to call me to come get him."

"What, don't want to leave those lass' legs tonight? Got some shagging to do?"

"Something like that, mate. Now take care of it, he's there for you."

"Don't go there, mate," he angrily replies.

"Okay go!" I hang up on him and swing my girl around to me and kiss her thoroughly. I want to infuse myself all over her skin. I want every man around to know she's mine. Mostly I want my ring on her finger and her carrying my name. I can't believe I feel this way, but after today with those wankers, I know she'll be mine.

"Sorry, I wasn't ignoring you, baby."

"What's that all about with Joshua?"

"I've no blimey idea. I've never seen him like that. He has situations in his past that he might share with you someday."

We head back to my flat and I make sweet love to her all night. I'll worry about my sister and Maya's stalker tomorrow.

# CHAPTER TWENTY-SEVEN

## MAYA

I feel like I was blindsided at dinner last night, but guess I can't blame Duncan for trying. If there were a chance I could get him to D.C., I'd do it. I want to be angry. Why do I have to give up my life? Why can't he move? I know I'm starting to care for him, but how much? I can't put him in jeopardy by being with me. My stalkers are stepping up their game, and I won't allow anyone else to get hurt. I'm cursed and broken. I don't even know if I can love or care for someone other than Ana and Derek.

I haven't even told him the important things about me. I want to, but I'm afraid. I rub my wrist and look out over London from his beautiful enclosed deck. The cooler air makes me shiver but I love the view. I have on a lightweight, gray wrap sweater; a black, long-sleeve shirt; and jeans and my boots again.

I've had my coffee, ran on the treadmill, and even called the solicitor to set up a few pieces of paperwork. I texted Greg this morning about meeting us for lunch. Duncan woke up early and is in his office doing some work from home before we need to leave.

As I sit out here and take in the view, I braid my hair over my shoulder in a fishtail. I like being able to wear my hair down and in elegant styles versus my tight buns and ponytails for work.

We made love off and on most of the night. I know I'm falling harder for him each day. He got a text from whoever he called last night that Joshua went to a pub and got trashed. I wonder if he'll back out of our lunch today.

~

WE'RE on our way to pick up Ana. I have a plan and I won't take no for an answer. I need to protect her and take care of her. She is my family. The thought that Jonathon is hurting her makes me want to kill him.

We pull up to Ana and Jonathon's building and head in to get her but instead find her waiting in the lobby. She walks out wearing gray slacks, a printed blouse, a mid-length trench coat, and black high heels. She looks so prim and proper again. I want my friend, the fashionista, back.

"I'm ready." She looks frantic and her movements are stiff.

I wrap my arms around her and she flinches slightly. I lean in to whisper in her ear, "Do I need to take you home with me?"

"No, why would you ask that?" She looks scared as she pulls away.

"Never mind, let's go. I was hoping to see your flat though."

"Oh, sorry, Jonathon doesn't like me to have visitors without him here."

Really? Okay, now I know he's a controlling motherfucker. We get in the Rover and head to the solicitor's office. I had asked Greg to let me do this by myself, I didn't want him to know my plans.

"Ms. Aaron, your grandmother has properties all over the world. It will be years before I find them all and get her estate settled. The property here in London is only one I've found so far. I've written the address down, I suggest you go look at it and decide what you plan to do with it." It's only Ana and me in the office.

I asked Duncan to wait outside, I wasn't sure how I was going to react and haven't told him about my money. He's not happy about being left out.

"Thank you, Mr. Flemish, I'll go look and let you know. Do you have the other paperwork drawn up?"

"Yes, ma'am." He pulls out a stack of papers and looks at Ana and me. She has no clue I did this and Jonathon will never know either. He then pulls out the cell phone I called him about this morning and several boxes.

"What's all that, Maya?" she asks.

"Those are your Christmas gifts. Ana, I just made you and any of your children my beneficiary, but Jonathon can't touch any of it. I also bought you a special purse that has a hidden compartment. You're going to hide a burner cell phone, enough cash to help you get to me or away, and anything else you don't want him to know about in there."

"I don't understand what you're saying, Maya."

"Please, Mr. Flemish, will you give us a moment?"

"Yes, ma'am." He walks into the lobby where Duncan is.

"Look, Ana, don't lie and don't try to deny it. I know he's hurting you and until you're ready to leave, you will carry this bag. I'm here to help you. I'd take you back with me now if I knew that would help, but I think you'd go back to him. If he's threatening any of us, you know we'd want you safe. I've also included a second passport and ID for you. I had my solicitor get you second copies of each in case Jonathon has yours. I love you and I will protect you. As for the money, you know as well as I do that there's more than enough in there for all of us. Also, at the very bottom is another special compartment with a gun, it's a small Sig with laser sights so you won't miss. If you fly, get rid of it. It's safe. Just remember what I taught you before about guns. If you point it, be prepared to use it."

"Maya, why would you do this? A gun? Why?" She doesn't deny what I hinted at, so I know it's true.

"Because you're my family. Why can't you leave him now?"

"I can't leave," she says as she drops her eyes. She won't look at me and I know she'll have to come to me.

"Okay, when you're ready, you have the means to." I don't push her any further. I grab the paperwork and show her the evidence. I then grab the paper with Savta's London address on it. I lead her out to the lobby where Duncan and the solicitor wait. Ana and I made sure to put the purse together so no one knows what it is and Jonathon won't get suspicious.

"Ready, beautiful ladies," he says to us, his eyes searching mine. I smile at him and take his hand. I know he'll be asking me later about what was discussed in there. And I know I'll lie to him. I can't tell him yet.

"Here is the address we need to check out. I'm ready. How about you, Ana?" She still looks dumbstruck. I made her promise not to tell Duncan about any of it. She agreed.

We decide to head to Harrods to do some shopping before we go to the property. I ask Duncan to leave us alone for a bit so I can look for his Christmas gift. I'd already decided to get him a leather bomber jacket. I think he'll look so hot in it. Ana helps me pick out two dresses, one of which is for the formal Christmas Eve party at the consulate that James goes to regularly. He invited Duncan and me to go with him when we called him this morning.

I also settled on a sexy dress for the New Year's Eve party. Of course I bought formal eveningwear, so I needed shoes and accessories to go with them. I talk Ana into a beautiful, red dress for the party. I told her it was another gift from me. She's starting to get some color in her cheeks and is actually smiling more. I miss her so much. She brings out the girl in me. Harrods will deliver my purchases to Duncan's flat.

"So, why are you not going to the consulate Christmas Gala?" I ask her as I try on shoes.

"Jonathon didn't get invited and I'm tired of him using Daddy's influence," she says bitterly.

"Does he use James's influence a lot?"

"Yes to a point. He had Daddy introduce him to some dignitaries from Tel Aviv and the Philippines." I notice she's not trying on any shoes.

"Don't you want some sexy, red high heels to go with that new dress?" I ask her.

"I already have some perfect silver ones I'll wear. I'm good." She smiles shyly and drops her eyes.

We're walking through a gift section, where I'm looking for some cigars for Greg, when Duncan walks up.

"All right, ladies, I'm done making myself scarce. What did you buy? I don't see any bags."

"They're delivering them." I smile at him as he pulls me close for a kiss. He kisses me until my toes curl, laying his claim on me publicly.

We head to the area of London where the home is that Savta owned. I'm floored. It's not a flat, it's a huge Victorian house with five bedrooms. There's a terrace and sunroom with a small garden out the back. The property has been empty for a couple years. Mr. Flemish said there were renters in it for a while. He thinks I should sell the property, but it will need a thorough cleaning and some minor maintenance before it can go up for sale. I could stay here instead of a hotel when I come to London. The area is a Jewish community, so I'd be able to feel close to Savta and Abba here.

"Your grandmother left you a house?" Duncan asks.

"Among other valuables. She was always worried the Nazi's would come to power again so she had properties all over. Mr. Flemish said it's going to take some time to find all the resources. He believes there are at least two more properties here in London. Please don't freak, Duncan, but I inherited it all."

"Why would I freak, baby?" He looks at me perplexed.

"I'll explain soon but for now, just trust me. Please?"

"Baby, for you, anything." He leans over the console of the Rover to kiss me, and brushes his hands down my braid and pulls it slightly. I instantly feel the need for him.

We get out and walk around the property. I know I'm going to have to tell him the truth soon, but right now I like not having to worry he's with me for the money. In the past, other's only dated me because of the money.

"Ana, if you could work with Mr. Flemish to hire someone to fix this place up so I can sell it, I'd like that. Also, if you want to practice your interior design, go right ahead. Before I leave, I'll give you Power of Attorney. That way you can access my accounts here to pay any bills."

"Maya, you don't need to do that." She tries to fight me.

"Yes, I do. I want you to be able to fix anything without me around. Okay?"

"Fine." She huffs. But I can see her excitement in transforming the property.

"Although, please don't do any major construction. That way I'll have a place to stay when I come for visits, at least until it sells. Okay?"

"I can do that."

We load back up into the Rover and head to lunch. Joshua is going to meet us after all. I text Greg to let him know where we're going, but he declines as his meetings are running late. We pull up to the restaurant and I see Joshua pacing outside, he looks nervous. I hear a gasp from the back seat and turn to Ana.

"What's the matter, Ana?" Duncan asks.

"Nothing. I thought it was just going to be us for lunch."

"No, I invited my boss, Joshua. Remember me talking about him? He was my lieutenant then captain in the Army."

"Yes, I just...maybe I should get a taxi home?"

"No, come have lunch with us. Then we can go back to Duncan's and try on our new dresses. You can help me figure out my make-up and hair for tomorrow night." She's not running back to him if I can help it.

Duncan jumps out and opens our doors for us. As he opens Ana's door, I see Joshua stiffen. Okay, now I'm curious as to what's going on. Ana is dragging her feet as she walks behind us.

"Come on, slow poke," I tease her. She smiles at me and then I notice her make an internal decision. She has something weighing heavily on her, more than the situation with Jonathon. She straightens her shoulders, brushes her hands down the front of her outfit, and walks with her head high.

"Okay." She smiles at Duncan, and then looks at Joshua again.

"Hello, ma'am, I'm Joshua Donovan." He takes her hand and kisses her knuckles. I see her smile shyly at him.

"Joshua, my sister, Ana Davidson."

Joshua puts her hand on his arm to lead her into the restaurant.

We slide into a booth with Ana and me in the center and the guys on the ends. I've always wanted to come to this restaurant.

"I'm excited to be here. I have to admit *Hell's Kitchen* is one of my few guilty pleasures, I watch while I run."

"*Hell's Kitchen*?" Duncan asks me curiously.

"Yes, a Gordon Ramsay show where he yells at cooks. I love it. I've wanted to come to one of his restaurants for a while now."

"We can go to his other restaurant for dinner tomorrow before the gala." He smiles as he takes my hand.

I feel like a fangirl, but I love cooking shows. I don't cook like Ana does, but I can and I'm learning more from the cooking shows.

Lunch goes on without any hitches until the very end when Lawrence makes an appearance. Ana bristles and Duncan looks ready to kill.

"Well hello to you all again." He acts like the cat that swallowed the canary. What's going on?

"Hello, Lawrence, are you following me?" I ask because I'm beginning to worry he is. I also wonder if he knows what happened at my apartment in D.C.

"Well, darling, no, but if you want me to, I'll comply." He smiles smugly at me.

"Do I need to tell you again that she's mine and you're not to be around her?" Duncan growls at him as he stands to look down at Lawrence. Lawrence cringes and steps back. Go, Big Guy.

"Listen, caveman, this is a public restaurant. I just stopped by to say hello to Mrs. Davidson." I see Ana struggle next to me. This guy knows Jonathon and he could cause problems for Ana the way she's acting.

"I was just getting ready to head home to Jonathon. Would you like me to pass him a message?" She pushes me out to rise. Joshua stands too and looks like he's going to stop her. She just looks at him and then to Lawrence and back to us.

"I'll give you a lift, I was heading there for a meeting with him." She winces and looks panicked at me.

"Ana, would you prefer Duncan and I give you a ride home?"

"Um, no, I'll ride with Lawrence. Thank you for the enjoyable day and the early Christmas gifts, Maya," she says as she lifts her purse.

"No problem, sweetie." I lean over and kiss her. Duncan kisses her cheek and Joshua kisses her knuckles and smiles at her.

Shortly after Ana leaves, Joshua runs off, leaving Duncan and I alone.

"Okay, baby, ready to go mark off more surfaces from my list," he says as I laugh at him.

We head back to the flat and are greeted by the concierge with my purchases. There are several garment bags and smaller bags with the gifts in them. I bought James's Christmas gifts and something each for Derek and Greg.

"Baby, did you leave anything at the store?" He laughs.

"Yes! Can I borrow the spare bedroom to hang these? You can't go in there, though." I want to surprise him.

I don't generally dress formally unless it's for work. I'm very nervous. Ana set me up to have my hair and makeup done.

"Of course, use the room across from ours." My insides tighten at him calling his place ours.

This is a life I want but know I can never have. I need to change the subject and focus on him.

"Honey, I bought you a pocket kerchief that matches my dress. Is that okay?" He walks over to me with the long garment bags in one hand and several other bags in the other.

"Baby, I like you picking out stuff for me." He leans down to kiss me. "Now go change into some jeans and something warm, I'm taking you out."

"I thought we had surfaces to try out?" I quip back.

"Baby, I'm going to have you on some more surfaces later. First, I want to take you out to do something fun, just you and me. I'll hang these in the room if you want to head in there after you change to open the bags. I'll stay out." His smile is devious as he looks me up and down. I know he's thinking of the surfaces yet to try.

# CHAPTER TWENTY-EIGHT

## DUNCAN

My plan was to come back to the flat and bury my cock in her sweet heaven, but when I peeked into one of the bags and saw a wrapped gift, I stopped. I had bought some gifts for her too, but I realized we didn't have a tree to put them under.

I walk into the spare room and hang the bags up high. I hope she's okay with money because I know these weren't cheap. I can't wait to have her on my arm tomorrow and show the world she's mine. Some of my Christmas gifts for her will be delivered to Joshua today instead of coming here.

Joshua will be at the party tomorrow with us, he'll be doing some work. His odd behavior today is concerning me. The infatuation he has with his "Angel" has gotten worse. Ian called me earlier to say he's putting Raul on standby for tonight. This is the most he has gone on a binge in a while. I walk back out to the sitting room and look out the windows, thinking about how lucky I am to have Maya.

I'll do anything to keep her here with me. I worry about her stalker and wonder about her relationship with Derek. I don't want to even think about her leaving me in a couple weeks, she'll be closer to that danger. I'm hoping Joshua will talk to her more about working with us.

She walks out of my bedroom in a pair of low-rise jeans with the legs shredded up, a green sweater that's off her shoulders showing a skimpy tank top, and those bloody cowboy boots. I know she's got a knife in her boot again. I've talked her into not carrying her sidearm for the last couple of days.

She looks so good, the green of the sweater makes her eyes look brighter. I'm about to change my mind, but then I remember I need to show her she's more than just a shag. My chest pulls and my heart thumps harder. What the bloody hell is going on with me?

"Baby, you look good." I hear the growl in my voice.

"Thank you, handsome." She smiles and walks toward the spare room. I really want to see what she's wearing tomorrow.

### MAYA

We actually went Christmas tree shopping and ice skating in Hyde Park, then had dinner at a little bistro near the park. I hadn't done anything like that since before my parents died. One holiday season my mom talked my father into letting us have a tree. It was so much fun. My heart aches a little as I think of them. I'm fingering their rings when Duncan looks over at me in the Rover.

"Are you okay with a tree, Maya?"

"Yes."

"What's the matter?" He sounds concerned.

"I don't want to bring down the remarkable evening we've had. Thank you for the skating, dinner, and tree shopping, it was fun. I've never been on a date like that." I know I don't sound as happy as I felt earlier.

"Maya, baby, please talk to me." He pulls into the parking garage of his condo and turns to me.

"I just remembered the Christmas season when my mom talked Abba into letting us have a tree, I was fifteen. She told me stories of her growing up and her family's Christmas celebrations. She even made homemade eggnog and cookies. Abba had fun once he realized she wasn't trying to replace Hanukkah but give me a little of her. I miss her so much. Don't get me wrong, I miss him too, but she was everything. She believed in me all the time. I kept all those ornaments. They're at my condo. I bring them out and look at them occasionally. She got me an angel ornament that year, and every year after until she died."

"I wish I could have known them. Dad talks about her and Mum a lot now. For a while there, it was like talking about her brought around memories of Mum, and he'd not do that. Now though, he speaks about them all. He liked your father."

"I'm happy you and your dad have worked out your problems." I don't acknowledge his comment about my own dad. I loved him very much but am still not sure why he pushed me as hard as he did.

"I think he suspected us back at the wedding or he hoped, because he was all about me asking you out. He's also realized that I joined the military for my country, not to spite him. I'm not a diplomat, I'm not an executive, but I am a soldier. He worried I'd not come home, so he felt better to push me away he said. After losing Mum, he doesn't handle loss very well. You know all about that." He smiles at me.

"Yes, I know about pushing people away. I'm glad you're who you are. I wouldn't be with you if you were a businessman." I laugh at him.

"Come on, baby, let's head up."

We unload our purchases from the Rover. Duncan even bought decorations for the tree. He's carrying the tree, a small but full one. I'm carrying the other bags. We're heading toward the elevator when my cell starts ringing. I look at the caller ID, knowing who it is from the ringtone.

"Hey, Derek," I say as Duncan makes a face. I whisper for him to be nice and he nods.

"There's been another delivery. This one better be a joke. You promised me the last time you wouldn't go back to him." I can almost feel his anger through the phone.

"What're you talking about, Derek?" I'm actually nervous; Derek and I have been through so much and for him to be this angry with me isn't common.

"Well, your ex-boyfriend Carl sent you a dozen roses. You promised me I could kick his ass if he came sniffing around again. With everything going on, and you having Duncan, why would you go back to him? Wasn't his behavior on the unit toward you enough?"

"I ran into him once after he left the unit. I told him I had a boyfriend. I'm not interested in Carl and I want you to get rid of those flowers. Was there a card?"

"Yes, it said he'd always love you. Jeez, girl, you went from no men but me and Dad in your life to two stalkers, one hang on, and a boyfriend. What the hell?"

"Derek, I'm only with Duncan. I'm not with anyone else or trying to see anyone else."

"Damn it, Maya, we need to get control of this. Have you noticed anything there? Has your stalker started sending you stuff there yet? I'll get rid of Carl and his flowers."

"No. I haven't gotten anything like the last time I was here."

"Seriously?" Duncan hisses, he's looking at me carefully and watching the emotions cross my face. Why would Carl do this? I didn't tell him I wasn't going to be home.

"By the way, the doorman told him you were out of town, too. You need to talk to that dumbass." Derek says, distracting me from my thoughts.

"Motherfucker, I'll call the condo association as soon as I can. Take the flowers to the hospital and donate them. How are you doing?"

"I'm good. Hate the holidays. Thanks for all the distractions, but enough is enough."

"No problem, that's what partners are for. Call me if you need to talk." I hang up the phone and step into the elevator with Duncan. He looks pissed.

"Maya, who's sending you flowers now? And, why would your partner need to talk to you? Is that not what his father is for?"

"First, don't get jealous, I told you I ran into Carl and told him I was seeing someone. He still sent me a dozen roses to my condo.

Second, my partner doesn't do this holiday very well. It brings him bad memories. He and his father don't discuss this time of year. He's also condo sitting for me to keep away from the celebrating."

"Bugger me, why does every man feel he needs to take what's mine?"

"Excuse me? Yours?" I ask as I raise an eyebrow at him.

"Maya, you're mine. Like you, I don't share. I'm getting tired of these blokes coming out of the woodwork. Come on." He still looks upset.

Well, I'm going to show him he doesn't have to worry about any other guy.

# CHAPTER TWENTY-NINE

## MAYA

We walk into the flat and Duncan goes to set up the tree in front of the windows. I put the bags down and help him. When he acts as if I'm not there and seems angry, I decide to take matters into my own hands.

"Duncan, I'll be right back."

"Okay." He doesn't even turn around to look at me.

His jealousy is in full force. I know he wants to mark me up like he did yesterday, but is mad at himself for taking me that way. He's also upset about me hiding us for so long.

I walk into the bedroom and over to the dresser he had me load my clothes into, and put on another gift for him. I tiptoe back out to the living room.

He's staring out the windows.

I lean against the wall and take in my surroundings. I love his flat, it's all windows except for the exterior walls with views of London. It's a very modern style with clean lines, blues and grays throughout. He has a gourmet kitchen and a formal dining room. It's four bedrooms, three and a quarter baths. His bathroom *en suite* has a soaking tub big enough for the both of us. The winter garden has a fireplace in it. I could really get used to being here.

"Hey, handsome, want to show me that view?" I hope my voice comes across as sexy, but it sounds rather rough to me.

He turns to look at me and I watch his eyes widen. He's struggling to stay there and wait to see what I'm up to.

I'm wearing a sheer black negligee that barely covers my ass. His eyes scan over my lace covered breasts, following the ribbon that hangs down to my belly and stops on the matching sheer panties.

I bite my lip as I slowly walk to him, swinging my hips seductively. I left my hair down and flowing around me. My heels make a soft clicking sound and his eyes drop to see the feather tufted bedroom heels. I walk right up to him.

"Baby, what's that you're wearing?" I hear the growl in his voice.

"Don't you like it? It's called a babydoll nightie." I smile coyly at him.

"Baby, I love that nightie, but you're not going to be wearing it much longer."

"That's okay, it did its job."

"What?"

"Well, you were so distracted and upset, I thought I'd show you something. I bought this just for you, no one else. I thought of you ripping it from my body as you pushed your beautiful cock into me. I have a few others too. You see, you don't have to worry about me leaving you for any of these jerks. You're in my head. Now I want you in my body." With that, I reach down to the ribbon between my breasts and raise it to him. "Unwrap your early Christmas Eve gift." My voice sounds sultry to me. I hope I'm telling him what he needs to hear. I don't care about anyone but him.

"Baby, you're the best gift I've ever gotten, but you need to understand something."

"I already know, Duncan. Go ahead, mark me, claim me, and make me yours." I say breathlessly, I love when he loses control. I know he needs this. He reaches out and grabs me around my waist in a swift motion, and turns us to plant me against the glass wall.

"I'm going to take you right here, baby. Don't move while I undress us both."

"Oh...okay" I pant.

He rips his clothes from his body, but gently pulls off my little nightie, sliding his hands down my arms as he slides it off. When it falls to the ground, he kneels down and glides my sheer panties down my body. He doesn't touch me except for the rub of his thumbs down my legs. I squirm and know I'm already wet for him.

He pushes me up against the cold glass and I gasp as the heat from my body and the coolness connect. He leaves the heels on and lifts one of my legs over his shoulder, opening me up to him. He slides a hand to my center and gently rubs me.

He leans forward and kisses my belly, and then lightly nips me. I moan and wiggle against him for more. He looks up at me. His eyes have darkened with desire and I know my face is flushed.

"Baby, you're mine. I want you so bad right now, but I'm going to take you as you deserve."

"Please, Duncan, just take me," I say breathlessly.

DUNCAN

Bugger me, she's going to kill me. When I turned I thought my heart was going to explode in my chest. This woman is so mine. I love how fucking hot she is. I kiss down her flat stomach and lift her up until her other leg wraps over my other shoulder. I press my face into her core, and push her open and against the glass. I then find her clit and suck it into my mouth. She moans and I growl.

"This is mine, baby. No man gets you like this." I then lose it and start finger fucking her while I suck on her clit.

She squirms and pulls my hair. I feel her start to squeeze around my finger and I know she's close. I pull back and she groans. I stand with her still wrapped around me. I pull her legs off my shoulders and wrap them around my waist. I lower her to my cock and slam into her as I push her into the glass. She's crying out my name and screaming as I feel her come on my cock. I start rocking into her like a man possessed. I'll not lose this woman to any bloody wankers. She's mine.

"You're mine, you hear me, Maya. You. Are. Mine! No man but me." I growl at her.

"Oh God, yes, Duncan. I'm yours and only yours," she screams as she comes again. I can't hold it this time, I come, shooting so much of my spunk into her, marking her from the inside. I press my forehead to hers and we both sigh.

"Do you feel better now, Big Guy?" She smiles at me.

"Hardly." I turn us around, still planted deep in her and sit on the sofa with her straddling me. I'm getting ready to work on round two when my cell phone starts ringing.

"Bloody hell!" I pull her off my lap and walk to my pants to fish out my cell. "This had better be important, mate. I'm a little busy." I bark, knowing he'll explain quickly.

"Duncan, we've got a problem. You need to meet me at the pub in Surrey right now. Joshua is trying to kill the barman."

"Bloody hell, I'll be there in forty-five." I turn to Maya as I hang up.

"Let me shower quickly and I'll go with you."

"No time, baby, just get dressed."

"Honey, I smell like sex and you."

"Damn straight. Get dressed, Maya."

She doesn't argue with me, she just goes into the room to dress, then meets me at the front door. She's dressed in her jeans, tennis shoes, and my maroon sweater. I grab her hand and we head out.

Joshua must be plastered to cause a row with the barman. He's known that guy for years. It ends up taking us over forty minutes to get to the pub. When we pull up, Maya has a strange look on her face.

"Why are we here?" she asks.

"This is where Joshua comes when he wants to get plastered and reminisce about the past."

"Really? Weird. This is the pub that Ana and I used to come to. It's the one we were talking about before the wedding."

"Small world, I guess." I grab her hand and we walk into the pub. Raul is holding Joshua back. Joshua is yelling at the barman.

"You bloody bastard, do you know what you've done? He'll kill her." Joshua sounds like he has definitely partaken in too much.

"Maya, is that you." The barman rushes to my girl, pulling her from my grasp and into his arms.

"Listen here, you blimey bastard, let my girl go or I'll break your arms," I growl, and Maya just hugs the smarmy bastard back.

"Patrick, it's been so long. Duncan, honey, this is Patrick." She acts like there isn't anything wrong with the fact that now both Joshua and I want to kill this wanker.

"Baby, please step back." I try to control my anger.

"Duncan, stop, he's an old friend. Your sister knows him."

"Ana was here today. My lucky day, both my beauties coming to see me." Patrick pipes in.

"What?" Both Maya and I say to him.

"Yes, she stopped by for a visit."

"He bloody called her husband," Joshua slurs. "That bastard is probably hurting her right now. Duncan, please let me kill him." Joshua reaches down to his boot and I know what's coming next.

"Not happening, Bossman, come on, let's leave before they call the coppers." I reach down and bat Joshua's hand away from his boot knife. I grab him away from Raul and throw him over my shoulder, wrapping an arm around his legs so he can't move around.

"You hurl down my back and I'll drop your arse," I tell him. "Come on, Maya, baby." I reach for her hand with my other hand, glare at the bastard, and pull her out the door. Raul is pulling up the rear.

"My car is around the corner, you got him?" Raul asks.

"Not a problem. I'll take my turn. What set him off?"

"I pulled his GPS earlier when Ian called and found him in the neighborhood. He was following some skirt and when she got in a taxi, he went into the pub and proceeded to get shit-faced. I stayed in the background until the bastard told him something and he went after him. I called you as soon as I could. Sorry to ruin your night."

"Not a problem. By the way, this is my girl, Maya Aaron." I introduce them and she shakes his hand. He helps me load Joshua into the back of the Rover. I open Maya's door and she gets in and turns around to look at Joshua, who's now passed out. He's mumbling in his sleep about Angel.

"Oh my God," Maya says from the passenger seat.

"Baby, please don't judge him. He lost someone and has never gotten over it." I try to explain. When I turn to look at her she has a look of shock on her face and is still looking at Joshua. "Baby, are you okay?"

"Uh yeah, I'm fine. Who did he lose?"

"Some girl he thinks he loved. Something about one day and he knew. He calls her Angel. I don't know anything else." She still looks like she's in shock. "He doesn't do this very often. He's just having a rough time lately. In the last six months something has set him off." She nods and looks out the window to the pub as I pull away and head back to my flat.

# CHAPTER THIRTY

## MAYA

I'm sitting at the bar in Duncan's kitchen nursing my coffee. I woke up early after another nightmare—this one was different from usual, Ana was screaming for me to help her.

I left Duncan sleeping and ran on the treadmill in the study. I tried to sort out why my nightmare changed, something set me off last night. I've been spoiled. Although I do feel safe in his arms and want to stay with him, I can't. I can't expose him to my problems.

I need to figure out what I'm going to do about the Joshua revelation. If Duncan knew, he'd kill him. I also know that Joshua had his chance and ruined it. That explains Ana's behavior at lunch yesterday.

I decide to text Greg and check in with him.

***Me: Lawrence is following me.***

***Greg: Okay. What do you want to do?***

***Me: I have an idea. I'll be in touch.***

***Greg: I'm in meetings all day and have an event tonight.***

***Me: What event?***

***Greg: Can't tell you. Love you, sweetheart.***

I hate it when he gets all secretive with me. I continue to sit here at the bar, waiting until a decent hour in the States to call the condo association about the doorman problem. This latest fuck up with him is probably going to cost him his job, but I don't like just anybody having access to my home. I need to be on guard because of my job and now this second stalker. I also have been a bit paranoid through the years.

I sense movement and look to my left where the bedrooms are located near the front door hallway. I expect Duncan to be looking for me. Instead, Joshua walks out of the guest room. He's in a pair of low-slung shorts and nothing else. His chest is chiseled and full of muscles. He might be the boss, but he's in as good of shape as Duncan. I cough so I don't startle him.

"Oh hey! Umm, I guess I ruined your night, sorry." He coughs out.

"You stay here often?" I want to say more. I want to question him.

"Yes, even though my condo is a couple floors up, sometimes I sleep it off here."

"You go on benders a lot?"

"Not really!" He sounds defensive.

"Really, that's all you're going to say, *Lieutenant*?" I sneer, I know I'm a bitch but damn him.

He fucked it all up and now, he must feel guilty or something to go on this many benders. He stops at my statement and looks at me carefully. He then looks back toward the master bedroom.

"Don't worry, Duncan doesn't know. I didn't tell him, but if you get her hurt, I'll end you."

"Got it." He walks into the kitchen and reaches for a coffee mug, exposing his left side, and I gasp. He turns to look at me.

"What are you fucking looking at?" he growls. Guess I deserved that.

"Hey wanker, don't talk to my girl like that," Duncan growls from the hallway. He's in a pair of shorts and bare-chested too. Joshua and I turn to stare at him and then each other.

"Sorry, Maya," Joshua grumbles.

"Sorry, Joshua," I say back.

"Baby, you don't need to apologize to him." Duncan walks up

behind me to wrap his arms around me. I lean back into his body. Wait, I can't become comfortable in his arms. I pull back and try to pull out of his arms, but he pulls me in tighter.

"Yes, I do need to apologize. I made a bitch comment before you came in. Joshua beautiful tattoo." I say to let Joshua know I saw it.

Maybe he still cares.

"Thanks. Good coffee, who made this?" Joshua is looking around like there's someone else here.

"I did. Just cause I'm a tomboy doesn't mean I can't cook. I just choose not to cook. But coffee, that's a science I know very well." Both of them laugh at me.

"So what are you two's plans for the day?" Joshua asks us as he tips his cup up for a sip.

"I need to go to my depository so I can get into my safety deposit box. I also need to call the damn condominium association and I have a hair appointment. Then, for your information, I'm going to seduce my boyfriend, seeing as how we were interrupted last night. We also need to decorate our Christmas tree. Is that okay with you?"

"Jesus, Maya, TMI." Joshua laughs as he sputters his coffee.

"Safety deposit box?" Duncan asks as he steps around the counter to pour himself a cup.

"Yes, most of my mother's jewelry is in it. I want to wear some of it tonight. Plus, I need to exchange some paperwork from the attorney yesterday."

"Care to share?" Duncan is looking at me hopefully. Share? Me? Can I do this without raising red flags? I'm aware I hurt him the other day at the solicitor's office, but I didn't want him to know yet. Plus, I wasn't sure how he'd react to how I'm helping Ana; I need her to be safe. Just as I'm about to answer, my phone starts in on the song *Welcome to the Jungle. I know* who's texting me. I look at the message and cringe with worry.

***Greg: Lawrence isn't either of your stalkers. We got nothing back from the search of your condo. I also got a delivery of dead roses here at the hotel.***

***Me: I'm sorry to pull you into this. Leave London now. I'll see you soon.***

***Greg: No! I'll not leave you to this lunatic. Be careful, please.***

***Me: I will.***

I look up to see both Duncan and Joshua watching me. How do I explain this? I don't share well.

"Well, first, before I share, Joshua I want to hire Securities International."

"Why?" They both say at the same time.

"You two are funny talking together like that, do that much?" I laugh. "Don't worry, I can pay. I'm going to need several complex background checks done. I'm considering surveillance too. How much?"

"Maya, what else is going on? Who's texting you? I know it isn't Derek, unless you changed his ringtone." Duncan is getting angry.

I didn't talk to him about this, but I know now that Ana is in danger and I need to protect her. I also know that my stalker is escalating if he's sending stuff to Greg.

Joshua ignores Duncan. "I can do it for free if you were my employee." His reply is so matter of fact.

"I have a job. I don't want to be asked again. If I wanted a job, I'd come to you. For that fucking matter, I can go to your competition. I'm not playing around here. Don't push me again!" I'm angry now, I'm sick of this shit. Why do I have to give up my life? Why do I have to end my dreams?

"Bloody hell, Maya, I was just making the offer, but if you want to do this, meet me at the office in an hour, or for that matter take me, I don't have my vehicle."

"Maya, explain this to me now." Duncan is outraged.

Well too fucking bad.

"Fine, go shower. See you shortly. As for you, *honey*, I'll discuss this with you at the office too. For your information that was Greg, nothing turned up in the search of my condo. Also, if you pressure someone else to offer me a job or push me again, I'll leave. Got it? No, ifs, ands, or buts about it, I'll be gone." I don't tell him about Greg's delivery.

"Bloody hell!" He storms from the room. Joshua walks into the spare room and then leaves with his clothes in his arms. I can't believe I lost my shit that way.

I wanted to yell and rail at Duncan. He wants me to sacrifice my life in D.C. for him. I stop and pause as a troubling thought comes to mind, is he trying to ask for something longer than boyfriend-girlfriend. My chest constricts and I feel like I can't breathe. I can't and won't hurt him that way. Damn it! I call Derek.

"Hey, sexy, how's it hanging?" He always makes me smile.

"I think I'm fucking it up already. He wants me to get a job here and I got mad at him. I don't want to leave my job yet. I have more to do. I can't leave you or Greg. I can't put him in danger if my stalker does follow me."

"Listen, Maya, you need to make that decision. Dad and I will be okay without you. You and I both know our job is making us both unhappy. We thought we were making a difference, instead we're helping those we fight. As for your stalker, I hope we can finally get that under control soon. Love doesn't happen all the time, is that what this is?"

"I don't know, maybe. My chest hurts because he's in the shower and mad at me right now. I feel like I'm going to pass out."

"Ya, that sounds close. Take it from someone who lost it all, don't let it slip through your fingers."

"Derek, I can't trust myself or someone else again. You know where I'll go if I lose him. I couldn't handle his death, too." I rub my watch against my wrist and worry about killing someone else.

"Maya, let go and fall. I need to go, take care, sexy."

"What're you up to?" I ask, sure I know the answer.

"Today is the twenty-fourth, I have my yearly date. Maybe someday I'll not feel the need to go through this." He sounds so lost.

"Be careful. I'm here if you need me. Call our friend if it gets bad. Bye." I hang up and think of all he has lost and all I've lost. Can I really take that chance with Duncan?

I'm standing by the windows looking out at nothing. My head drops and I feel the pain as if it was yesterday. I killed them.

"Derek on the phone again?" Duncan asks from behind me. I raise my head and turn.

"Yep. It's the anniversary today and he's hurting, plus I needed to talk to him."

"So you can speak to him but not me?" He sounds jealous and angry.

"Sometimes. He's my sounding board, and my best friend. He's hurting bad today; I'm usually there for him."

"You keep telling me not to worry. But then you say things like that. In a relationship, the other person is your sounding board. What am I?"

"I've known him since I was nineteen. Please, don't be jealous of him, I don't think of him that way. I've explained to you that he and Greg have been a part of my life for a long time. Your father introduced us all."

"But he thinks of you that way."

"No, he doesn't. He sees me as an annoying little sister."

"All men look at you and think that, baby. You aren't only gorgeous, but you're very special. Trust me, I'm male and I watch how other men look at you."

"Well thank you, but no, he doesn't look at any woman that way. Not anymore. Maybe someday he'll see someone, but not today."

"He into guys?"

"No. He lost everything, and I mean everything, on Christmas Eve many years ago. He doesn't see any woman but her."

"Oh bloody hell, that's got to hurt. I can't imagine his pain."

"Yep, please don't ever tell him I said anything. It's why he became a cop. Like myself, he wants to keep others from feeling what we do." Duncan walks to me and pulls me in his arms.

"Okay, baby. I just want you to talk to me. You keep yourself so closed off. I want to be your sounding board too." He leans down and kisses the top of my head. Joshua walks back into the flat.

"All ready to go?"

"Yes," Duncan says, taking my hand. I grab my purse as we walk out.

~

WE HIT the depository first in Knightsbridge. I got Mother's ring and earrings, put in the new Power of Attorney and Will, and pulled out some of the stashed cash. I want this off the books. I look into the bottom of the box and see my father's Commando Bowie knife. I pull it out and look at it carefully. I test the weight, it's heavier than my other knife, but I feel close to him holding it.

Maybe it'll remind me why I can't let Duncan get close. I worry about the danger Greg is in now because of me. I don't want Duncan or Greg's families to go through what I'm going through now. I can't let that happen. I put the knife into my right cowboy boot, as my personal knife is in my left. It is bulkier, but I don't have any other place to carry it.

Duncan has asked me not to walk around armed and I'm trying, so I only carry knives instead of my gun. Until this stalker is taken care of, I'll be armed at all times. He'll have to understand this part of me if he wants to be with me.

# CHAPTER THIRTY-ONE

## MAYA

As we pull up to Securities International, I'm quite impressed with the building. The location is a newer, secure building near city hall in the London Bridge area. We head up to their office and I like the decor, Ana could decorate it better though. There's a receptionist at the desk, both Duncan and Joshua nod at her. Her very red hair and striking green eyes are the first I see, but then she stands and towers over me, and smiles.

"Hello, Rebekah, tell Meghan, Merry Christmas. Did my gifts get delivered?" Duncan says to her.

"Yes, Duncan, we got them. You didn't have to do that." She smiles at him and my gut clenches. This is the woman he could have if not for me.

"Take care, give Meghan hugs from me," Duncan says as we round the corner into Joshua's office.

"You make your staff work on Christmas Eve?" I say snarkily. I know it was not nice, but I'm jealous now.

"Rebekah is only here for a couple hours today. She needed the hours and I needed her to answer the phones for a little bit." Joshua heads to his large desk to take a seat and indicates for me to take a seat across from him. "Okay, Maya, what can I do for you?"

I calm my nerves by taking a quick look over his shoulder at the view of London. I can see the river, the bridge, and many other sights from here. It's breathtaking.

Straightening my shoulders, I turn to Joshua and look him square in the eye. "As I was working out this morning, I came up with some ideas. I want you to do a background check on Jonathon Davidson and all his friends. I want you to fine-tooth comb his life. He's into something and I know my gut is right, he's abusing Ana. I also know that Lawrence is following Duncan and me. I saw him again last night when we were leaving the flat to come get you. I'm not sure yet if I want a tail on any of them. As I said earlier, my stalker left no prints, so I'd like to know what your man was able to find. Also, if you tail Ana, they've got to be real good because if Jonathon finds out, it could be bad. I also find it interesting that right after Jonathon and Lawrence found out about Duncan, my condo was broken into. Somehow my stalkers and these idiots are connected." Both men look at me carefully.

"You think that bloody git is beating my sister and this is your solution? You also noticed a tail and didn't tell me." This is why I waited to tell Duncan my plans.

"I don't think, I know. However, she needs to want out, we can't pull her out yet. If we pull her out now, she'll run right back to him. I think he threatened us to keep her with him. She won't confirm it, but I can tell she doesn't love him as she should. I've made sure he can't do permanent damage. As for the tail, I was watching him and you'd have noticed if not for me distracting you."

"Bloody hell, Maya." Duncan is angry, but Joshua is silent. He looks like I do when I'm waiting for a mark in my scope. He's the reaper and death is waiting for someone. Yet I also see a flash of something else in his eyes. He knows something. Joshua pulls a key from the center drawer, opens another drawer, and opens a box with the key.

"Here. I already ran him. I'll put a detail on him and Stephan. As for Lawrence, I'll have him run now. Anyone else?"

"You ran Jonathon already?" I look at Joshua with a mix of surprise and concern.

"I ran all of your backgrounds."

"What?!" Now I'm angry. He ran my background?

Oh crap! He could have found out what I've been hiding from Duncan. The past I wasn't planning on telling him. I start to rise and feel the panic prickling my skin. I need to get out of here. Running has always been my way of escaping.

"Yes, Maya, I know." He looks at me carefully.

Oh God, he knows. My breath comes out in a gasp and my chest constricts in pain. Greg helped me bury that so deep the MPD couldn't find it, how did he? The only knowledge my job has is that I have a counselor on retainer in Boston. I continue to rise out of my seat.

"Know what?" Duncan asks, looking between the two of us angrily. He pushes me back down into my seat. I push back against him, trying to pull away. I don't want to go through this here. I can't. I rub my watch against my wrist, trying to center myself.

"This is for Maya to tell you, Big Guy. It's not bad." He tips his head to the side and raises an eyebrow.

Is he telling me he understands? He's also challenging me to tell Duncan. Okay, fine, I can share a little. I don't have to reveal everything. Duncan would run for the hills if he knew.

"I have an inheritance, Duncan, that's what he's talking about." Joshua raises his eyebrow again.

He wants me to confess the other parts but I can't. Only four people know about that, well now five, damn him. Not even Ana knows all of it. She knows most, but not all.

"So, why hide that? I know about your grandmother's inheritance." Duncan is starting to really get upset, he steps back closer to Joshua and away from me.

I can see the veins beginning to pop on his neck, his breathing has increased, and he's standing taller. He thinks I'm hiding more stuff. Okay, I am, but really now, I can't do this here. I look at Joshua in panic. Why did he do this?

"Damn you, Joshua, seriously? How dare you invade my privacy this way? Only a few people know about that. I was able to keep it off my police application."

I hate being put on the spot. I feel cut open and exposed, fitting for this situation. The hot seat isn't where I was planning on ending up.

Joshua leans back, waiting for me to explain. Duncan looks like he's going to kill someone. I look over Joshua's shoulder again and see the view. London was always my calming place, until my stalker started threatening my family here. I pull my phone from my pocket and look at it, wanting to call Derek or Greg to help me. I'm such a coward.

"Honesty is the best policy in a relationship, Maya." Joshua taunts me. My eyes snap up to him.

"Really, Joshua, maybe you should take your own advice." He bristles and looks at Duncan, who's watching us like a tennis match. Head bob one, head bob two.

"Fine." I make my mind up to tell him what I can. This will get him to run and protect him from me. I pause. Am I protecting him or myself? "Duncan, come sit down. Joshua, you're a royal pain in the ass."

"I'd rather stand." He growls.

"Duncan, remember how I didn't listen to you about that French model? Calm down and think before you judge. You asked me that, now I'm asking for the same consideration, please."

I wait. I'll walk out if he doesn't give me this chance. I can't handle the pain again. We've not even made it a week together and we're crumbling. Maybe this is a bad idea. I stand and walk to the door. I don't need this shit. Running is so much better, why face what I did and who I became before. I've tried to bury that girl. I've done everything I could to be better than her.

"Maya. Stop. Now!" His words hold an edge. I turn to look back at him.

"No, Duncan, I don't need this. I don't think this can work if we can't trust each other enough to let the other explain. I was wrong. I can't tell you more. I don't WANT to tell you more. It hurts too much."

I hear the catch in my voice and don't believe the words coming from my mouth.

"Always with the running, Maya, stop. I was just taking a moment so I didn't say something bloody wrong. My pause was bloody wrong, though." He walks to me, lowers his shoulder to my stomach, and lifts me over his shoulder.

He carries me out of the office and into another. He turns to face the door and locks it before putting me down. My hair is loose and falls around my face. I'm trying to push it from my face when he backs me against the door, caging me in with his body.

"Maya, now you'll explain and you won't run from me again." His hands rest against the door by my shoulders, pinning me in.

"Fine!" I know I sound like a child, but I don't need to justify myself to anyone anymore.

I take a deep breath and worry he's going to run. I'll have to tell him most of it or Joshua will rat me out.

"Duncan, I haven't had to explain myself to anyone in years. I do have a pretty good size inheritance, from my parents and now Savta. Your sister is my sole beneficiary as of now. I had an ex-boyfriend date me in hopes of getting my money. I didn't want that between us, but I guess I put it there by not telling you. I'm sorry." Okay, part of it out, only two more facts Joshua could have found.

"Why hide it, Maya, I'm not like that wanker, Carl. What else is there? I can see you preparing. Let me in, baby," He begs.

"Duncan, please, the rest doesn't matter. It doesn't change us."

"Yes, it does, Maya. You keep yourself from me by not letting me in. I want to know all of you—physically and emotionally."

"I'm not sure what Joshua has found. I can guess some because, no matter what you do or how much money you throw out, your past will never go away."

"Just let me in. Tell me something. Anything."

"Derek isn't just housesitting for me, he's my roommate."

"He's your what? I told you...YOU. ARE. MINE. I don't share very well when it comes to you."

"I'm very much yours. Derek couldn't keep staying where he was, so I offered him a room. Plus after my stalker showed up at the wedding, he bugged me until I let him move in again. He swore he'd not lose me too. I told you, he and Greg are like family. We used to live together, only as roommates while I was in college. I care about him, but not like I do you."

He pulls back slightly. I can't believe I just admitted I have feelings for him.

"When I met Derek, he had just lost everything he held dear. I was struggling with my loss too." I look down as my voice lowers.

"Okay, but what are you not telling me? I can read you, Maya, I know your tells."

"I tried to commit suicide." I choke out.

Duncan pulls back a little, looking confused. Now he'll run. The panic is starting again but this time, I'll allow it. I need him to flee. I need him to not want me.

"What, when?" He shakes his head.

"After I went back to the States I was so lonely. I missed Ana, James, and my parents so much. I struggled in school and I just wanted the pain to stop. I was angry, hurt, lost, and unwilling to talk to people. I couldn't sleep and that was playing a bigger role than I knew at the time. I was talking to your sister the night before what would have been my mom's birthday, I told her I was tired of all of it. She must have heard it in my voice. The next morning I skipped my classes and cut my wrist. Just as I was getting ready to cut the other, your father busted in the door and busted my ass. If he hadn't stopped me..."

I pull my watch away from my left wrist. It's large and utilitarian—ugly—but it covers the scars of my pain, how low I'd sunk into my grief. I never take it off. Now, I use that injury to ground myself and remember how low I can sink. I show him the scar. "I was screaming for help instead of trying to actually kill myself they say." He pulls my wrist up to his lips and kisses the mutilated tissue.

"Oh God, baby, I'd have lost you without knowing you. I'm so glad Ana and Dad were there for you. This doesn't change how I feel about you. I can't imagine your pain."

"This is why I have to help Ana. Your dad took me to the hospital. He called Greg, an old friend he knew through work. Greg told him about a grief counseling group his son was in. Your father got me into counseling and that group, that's how I met Derek. Your dad started making monthly visits to check on me, and didn't stop until after I got on the force. He's become my dad too. He still calls me regularly. I was so weak and he didn't judge, he just hugged me and told me it would get better. He won't let me go back there and I've done a lot to make sure I never will either. He, Ana, Derek, and Greg are all I have in this world."

"Wrong. You have me too." Duncan reaches down and lifts me into his arms. I wrap my legs around his hips. I don't ever want to leave here. This man is starting to mean so much to me. He kisses me so gently. I feel his emotions in that kiss.

"Duncan, I want you."

"Soon, baby, we need to finish with Joshua." He puts me down and I turn to notice this is his office. It's decorated in his gray tones and there are pictures of Ana and James around.

"Duncan, before I head back to the States, I want you to take me on that desk so you'll have a good memory until I come back." I point toward the large masculine desk. He growls and grabs my hand.

"I can arrange that." We head back to Joshua's office, time to get this finished.

"EVERYTHING GOOD?" Joshua asks as we walk back up to his desk.

"Yes," we say together. I look up at Duncan and smile. He didn't run for the hills.

"Joshua, we need to run background on a Carl Nelson too. He's also been following Maya around. He was a former member of her ERT unit. All these bloody wankers coming out of the woodwork makes me think they're connected or something," Duncan states. I'd thought that earlier too.

"Before we talk any more, Joshua, you need to understand something, what's in that report happened a long time ago. I've grown and am much stronger now. I know what my limits are and I'm not mental or depressed. If I need to, I have someone I can talk to. I'm surprised you found it though because Greg helped bury it good." There, I defended myself.

"I never would have thought anything else. You didn't have to explain, we all have hit rock bottom at least once."

"Thank you. As for Derek, he isn't what you think, he's my friend."

"I know that too. You only have eyes for the big guy there." He smiles. "We all have pasts and we all need to learn from them. Hiding isn't the way around it." I see knowledge and understanding in his eyes.

"Joshua, Duncan, I need to explain to you what I've already done. Ana has a burner phone, cash to get her anywhere, a spare passport and ID, and an unregistered handgun. She's promised to use them if necessary. She also, as Duncan partially knows, is my sole beneficiary and has Power of Attorney on all my London holdings. The paperwork is in a pseudo name so Jonathon can't find it."

"A pseudo name?" Joshua asks.

"Yes, a name only her and I know. For now, I'll keep it to myself. Sorry, Duncan, but it's safer this way for her."

"Maya, I think we can do this without any upfront costs. If I need anything, I'll let you know. I had Timothy hack into your security feeds to see what he could see. He found some inconsistencies that need to be covered. Can you call Derek so we can talk to him too?"

"Now wouldn't be a good time. Can we do this without him?" I pause and decide to share the rest. "Also, Greg told me today that he was sent dead roses. They mean 'it's over'. I'm not sure what's over with him, but I'm worried. I tried to talk him into going back to D.C., but he won't." I look at my watch, noticing it's about eight in the morning in D.C. I know today Derek will be at the cemetery and around the park, reliving his hell. I didn't tell him about his father. Am I hurting them all?

"I'd like to say we could, but I'm afraid that someone on the inside is helping your stalker. I need to talk to Derek, but if today isn't convenient, we can do it after the holiday. Okay?"

"Thank you, Joshua. I can pay too."

"No, I'll do this because it's right," he says.

I look at him and want to know why he walked away from her in the first place.

"Who do you think is on the inside?" I need to know.

"Well for one, the head doorman appears to be on the inside. I also think there's someone on the force. I know you don't want to hear that, but as of an hour ago, all the evidence from the break-in at your condo has disappeared."

"What?! Not possible. Derek didn't say anything when I talked to him earlier. He's not on duty right now but still, he'd be checking in if there were a problem. Even Greg didn't say anything."

"I got the text from Timothy when you were at your depository."

"Shit. Okay, after Christmas we'll call Derek. I can text Greg shortly, he's in meetings right now."

"Baby, are you sure you should be going back there?" I wondered if he was going to push it.

"Yes, I have a job and I'll fix this." He nods, grabs my hand, and leads me from Joshua's office back to his.

Duncan closes the door and strides toward his desk. He pulls the chair out and looks at me thoughtfully. I stand there, in the middle of the room, looking at him over the desk, thinking how hot he looks. He's wearing black jeans with a black t-shirt and black cable knit cardigan. He pulls off the sweater and drops it to the floor.

"Strip, baby." Without pause, I drop my jacket, pull off my shirt, and slide off my boots. Pulling both knives out, I place them on the desk in front of me. Duncan smiles at my knives. I unsnap my jeans and drop them. I start to walk to him in my bra and thong. He pushes a button on his desk and stands, pulling his t-shirt off and dropping his jeans. He's again commando.

"I said strip, that means everything." I smile, unhook my bra and slide off my thong. I walk to him. He's now seated with his legs spread. I step between them. His thick erection is pointed at me and I see the pre-cum. I drop to my knees and lick it off, then I suck him into my mouth as he groans. "Enough, baby, hop up on the desk." I deep throat him one more time, pulling off with a pop, and stand. I sit on the edge of his desk.

He stands between my spread thighs and pulls me to the side of the desk, and enters me in a long thrust. I'm breathing rapidly and trying to control my moans so as not to give us away as he pumps into me, driving me closer to my orgasm. He leans over me, sucks a nipple into his mouth, and then gently bites the turgid bud.

"The office is soundproof and the door is locked. Tell me who owns you," he says in my ear.

"OH GOD, DUNCAN, YOU OWN ME," I scream.

"YES, I DO, BABY!" He continues to pump into me, each thrust harder. He suddenly pulls out and flips me over. He enters me again, pulling my hair and lifting me up with my back to his chest. My legs are trapped on each side of his.

He pumps harder and I explode, as I'm coming, I hear and feel his release. This man really does own me—body and now soul. He wormed his way into an area that no one has ever touched. How could I let this happen?

# CHAPTER THIRTY-TWO

## MAYA

The rest of the day goes by without incident. Duncan and I head back to the flat to make love before I get my hair done, and have lunch. We finished decorating the Christmas tree. I call the Condo Association to complain about the doorman.

I'm now standing in the spare room pacing nervously. I have my mother's Sapphire Claddagh ring and earrings. I'm also wearing her Rolex that my father got her for her birthday before she died instead of my other watch. I'm in a blue, silk chiffon dress with a halter neckline and silver choker collar with a keyhole opening between my breasts. My hair is up in an elaborately braided updo at the back of my head. I'm wearing silver, open toe, sparkly stiletto shoes.

My makeup is very dramatic but not too much. I'm worried about what Duncan's going to say. I grab my new fox fur wrap cape, sparkly handbag, one of Duncan's Christmas gifts and walk into the living room where all three men are waiting for me.

They all turn and each of them takes a breath. James is in a traditional black and white tux, looking so regal and handsome. Joshua is in a white tux with black accents and black pants. Oh my God,

Duncan is in an all-black tux with black shirt and shoes. He's scorching and I just want to peel that tux off him.

"Maya, darling, as usual, you're beautiful." James walks over and kisses my cheek. "Duncan told me you told him. I'm proud of you, Daughter. You and Ana are the lights and loves of my life," he whispers in my ear while hugging me. Tears come to my eyes and I blink rapidly to make them stop. He always knows what to say.

"I love you too, so much, James. Thank you!" He steps back and looks at his son. Duncan hasn't moved. He seems like he hasn't even breathed.

"Duncan, honey, are you okay? Do I look that bad?" He groans and walks to me with a wrapped box in his hand.

"Oh, baby, you don't look bad. You, by far, are the most beautiful woman I've ever seen. I'm going to be beating the men off. I was utterly speechless when you walked out of that hall." He pauses, takes a breath and tries again. "I have a gift for you." I smile as he hands me the box.

"I have one for you too. First, let me put your pocket kerchief in so all the women know you're with me." I gently put the folded scrap of material in his pocket and reach up to touch his cheek. "Here you go." I hand him my gift and put my cape on the chair so I can open the one from him.

I open the wrapping to a velvet jewelry box. My hands shake as I open it. Nestled in it is a beautiful silver and diamond bracelet with matching earrings. I'm speechless. I pull out the silver loops bracelet and admire it. It looks delicate, but after a closer inspection, I see that it's actually quite heavy duty. I'm instantly in love with it. He takes it from my hands and puts it on my wrist. I remove my mother's earrings and put on the matching diamond loop ones.

"Thank you, honey, they're so beautiful." I lean up to kiss him. He pulls me close and kisses me hard. "Open yours."

"Okay." He opens his to a velvet jewelry box and laughs. "If this is a bracelet and earrings we can match, baby." I smile at his joke. He opens it to the silver *P* cufflinks and button slips. "I love them, baby, I'll wear them."

"Okay, enough of the mushy stuff, I'm hungry," Joshua says from by the entry. I smile at him and he nods back to me.

We take the elevator to the lobby and out to the limo to head to dinner. We eat at another Gordon Ramsay restaurant, as Duncan promised. I'm excited and thrilled with our dinner, and the start of what feels like an enjoyable evening. All three gentlemen keep me included in their conversations. Joshua asks me if I can translate for him at the consulate gala, as there will be dignitaries from all over the world. I offer my services and smile at Duncan.

We arrive at the gala and immediately I feel Duncan tense. Other men are checking me out and he's making sure not to leave my side, even to get me a drink. Finally, Joshua takes my arm and leads me away to help him network. We've only talked to a few people when I feel an arm wrap around my waist. I turn smiling, thinking it's Duncan, but see Greg.

"Hello, my darling. You look exquisite," he says with a smile, knowing he startled me. "Come, let's dance." He takes my arm and leads me away from Joshua. We've circled the floor a couple of times when I see Duncan over Greg's shoulder.

"Excuse me, sir, but you're dancing with my girlfriend," Duncan snarls. I can't help myself, I start laughing at the situation.

"Duncan, look who found me." I say through giggles as Greg turns around and Duncan realizes who he's jealous over.

"Duncan, how is your evening? I hope you don't mind I saw my daughter and thought I'd dance with her. Generally, whenever she's dressed up we're working, so I don't get to dance with her."

"Excuse me. May I cut in?" Duncan tries to say without sounding too gruff.

"Actually, I do mind. Give me a few more minutes and I'll bring her right back to you. No one else will dance with this beauty." Greg pulls me close and I watch the indecision on Duncan's face as he turns to head for the group.

"Okay, Greg, what's going on?" I ask, feeling a little put-off. Why would he push Duncan like that?

"Sweetheart, we have a problem. All the evidence in your break-in has disappeared from the D.C. Metro evidence locker."

"I know, Joshua told me today."

"There's more...your security company was hacked."

"Damn it. What can I do?"

"I'll start looking at getting you another. I wish you'd come to the hotel where I can keep an eye on you."

"I can take care of myself."

"I know." Greg turns his head and looks at Duncan. "How much have you told him? James said you told him about your attempt. How are you doing?"

"I'm good. I've told him a lot." The song ends and he leads me to Duncan.

"Duncan, thank you for letting me dance with her longer. Joshua, I'll be in touch, we need to talk. Darling, I love you. Can we have dinner tomorrow?" He looks at Duncan as he says the last part.

"Come to my house and we'll have a ham dinner tomorrow evening with all the kids," James says to cover the awkward silence.

"See you tomorrow," Greg says as he leans down to kiss my cheek.

Duncan immediately pulls me to his side and continues to growl at any man that comes near me. Joshua brings people to me to talk to him.

I forgot how much fun it was to speak all these languages. Duncan has only let me go dancing with Joshua or James since Greg has been busy talking with the American dignitaries that are present. He didn't ask what Greg and I spoke about, but I know he wonders.

We're standing by the patio door when an older man walks up to us. He's talking in rapid-fire French to Joshua, who's struggling to understand him, something about him needing to come back to work for him. I translate for Joshua to calm the man down. I explain to Joshua this man wants Securities International to return to protect his daughter. I then see her—she's in a slinky, skintight slip dress. She walks right up to Duncan and plasters herself to him. She's blonde, curvy, tall, and so beautiful.

"Bonsoir, ma chéri," she says in an overly sweet voice. Duncan gently pushes her back.

"Alisa, I'm not any chéri to you." He's severe and looks ready to eat nails.

"Is this your new protection detail?" She sneers at me. His arm is behind my back, resting low. If this is how close he gets to his details, I'm going to have to have a talk with him.

"No, this is my girlfriend, Maya."

"Oh, darling, did you tell her about us," she says with feigned innocence.

Duncan looks around and then down to me.

"Baby, come dance with me." We walk away from her. I hear her gasp and notice the photographer in the corner.

"She isn't going to stop, Duncan." I can't believe I didn't claw her eyes out.

"This will stop her." He bends down and kisses me in front of everyone. When he pulls back, he pulls my hand up and flips it over and kisses the inside of my wrist. My blood is rushing through my veins and I'm practically panting. As we start to dance, I see Greg watching us with a smile on his face.

"Duncan, if you don't stop we're going to make a scene when I jump you here." He throws back his head and laughs so hard.

Crisis averted, this man is mine. We finish the dance and he stays by my side with his hands on me the rest of the evening. I see her looking over at us a few times, but I know she's never had him as I do. I can feel his dedication and faithfulness to me.

I walk to the restroom a little while later. I'm just about to walk out when she walks in. She steps up to the mirror where she preens for a moment.

"You know you won't be able to keep him satisfied. You're the girl from New York. You're not in my league, petite." She sneers at me.

"I already know I can satisfy him, you, on the other hand, are the one out of your league. Au revoir!" I respond back in fluent French. She must have saw us. I smile as I walk out of the restroom and go find Duncan. He's waiting beside the coat check with my wrap.

"What took you so long?"

"I had to take care of some French trash." I smile sweetly as Alisa walks by us. She brushes by Joshua and gives him a look. I watch as he doesn't even give her a second glance.

"I think we lost her father's business, Joshua."

"Don't worry about it, Duncan. We've plenty of companies, we don't need to be hired by petty people. Plus, Maya helped us get many more jobs tonight."

I smile at both of them as we head out.

When the limo pulls up to Duncan and Joshua's building, after dropping James at home, I'm so tired but I feel a prickle down my spine. The guys step out and Duncan reaches in to help me out. The spark of unease hits even harder. I've learned to listen to this agitation throughout the years.

"Duncan, where's Joshua?"

"He just stepped into the entry, he's waiting for us. Why, baby?"

"Something doesn't feel right, lean down here." Just as Duncan leans down, a bullet whistles through the air past him, I hear the glass shatter behind him into the lobby.

Duncan drops back into the limo on top of me. My breath rushes from my lungs from his fall onto me. He's covering me with his body. Oh shit, he's hit. Was I too late? My heart accelerates and my mind starts to race. I can't lose him.

"Duncan, are you hit? Duncan, please talk to me!" I'm practically screaming. He pulls his head up and looks down at me.

"I'm okay, how about you?" He looks at me worriedly.

"Good, where's Joshua?" We both turn to see him lying on the floor of the lobby.

I reach down Duncan's leg and pull his backup from his ankle holster. This gun is almost a miniature to my usual sidearm. I check it and cock it as we prepare to move.

We scramble to get to Joshua, using the limo as cover. Another bullet wings past Duncan and me as we prepare to run the last bit. I make it to Joshua's body and grab him and drag him behind the counter. Duncan is on his phone with someone, he has his 9mm in his hand. He's trying to get between the shooter and me. Several more bullets rain down on us. Glass shatters around us.

I'm checking Joshua for bullet holes, pushing my skirt into a position where I can work on him. I finally find where the blood is coming from, he's shot in his upper arm, just below the shoulder, a through and through.

"I'm fucking okay, let me go and take cover." He comes to, he must have hit his head when he fell. "Damn I hate getting shot, and this is my favorite tux." Yep, he's okay. Just then, the elevator door opens and I swing my gun that way. "They're mine, Maya."

I lower my weapon and notice the same dark haired man from the pub—Raul—holding a compact machine gun and a tall guy with longish brown hair carrying an assault rifle. They take defensive positions aimed at the door. Duncan is trying to get in front of me again, this time so they can't see my exposed legs. I'm going to kick his ass if he doesn't stop this bullshit.

"Bossman, I ran security checks and called the coppers. It appears that the shooter has run, do I need to ring an ambulance?" The tall guy says.

"No, Timothy, you can patch it up. It's just a scratch. I hit my head when I fell forward, though. Maya and Duncan, are you both okay?"

"We're good. Maya, asked me a question that had me lower into the limo and saved the bullet from hitting me." All eyes turn to me.

"I just had a feeling I was being watched. I can't figure it out, but something told me to ask you to bend down." I know it would sound crazy to most people, but to trained soldiers who rely on that sixth sense, it was okay to say.

"Timothy, Duncan, get me off this floor and upstairs. Maya, you go to Duncan's flat and we will head off the police. Maya, hand that gun back to Duncan before we have more problems. Where's Ian?"

"He's on a bender. I was getting ready to go get him," Raul says.

"Okay, Raul, go get him, meet us in my flat. We need to discuss this. Maya, I'll have Duncan text you when it's safe for you to come to my flat."

I hate being told what to do. I know he's doing it to avoid the police bringing me into the situation, but I fight for myself. I start to fight him when I see Duncan. I hand Duncan his gun, pull up my dress on one leg, and pull out a Bowie throwing knife. All the guys are watching me.

"Bossman, I'm going to take Maya to my flat, I'll meet you at yours in a few." His eyes are smoldering, he wants to make sure I'm okay and plant himself inside me to prove we're both alive. I've seen this look before, but never had it directed at me. I feel the same way. I want to strip him naked and make sure that none of the bullets touched him. Joshua looks between the both of us.

"You have thirty minutes," he growls. "Timothy, pull up all the surrounding cameras and see if you can find our shooter."

Duncan helps Timothy pull Joshua to his feet and we all pile into the elevator. Raul takes off for Ian.

Duncan and I get off on his floor and walk toward his flat. We're barely in the door and Duncan is leaning over me.

"I've wanted you since you walked out of that room earlier, but now, I need to make sure you're okay. Strip and show me." His commands have me wet and breathing heavily.

I want him so bad. I put my knife on the hall table as I walk through to the living room. I reach behind me, pull the zipper down from my lower back to my butt, unhook the halter collar with the heavy jewelry, and drop my dress. I'm standing in front of him in my matching deep plunge strapless bra, panties, garter belt, stockings, and heels. I turn so he can see my back.

"All off, baby. If I knew you were wearing that under your dress, we'd have never made it out of the flat this evening," he growls as he strips his tux.

I pull my leg up on the coffee table, unhook my garter and slide my stocking to my shoe. As I unhook my shoe, I pull it and my stocking off. I do the same on the other side and unhook my garter belt and bra. I finally grab my panties with my thumbs and slide them down my body. I can hear his breathing increase as each garment is dropped.

He steps closer to me, picks me up, and I wrap my legs around his naked hips. He pushes into me as he lays me on the coffee table. It's a large piece of wood with marble accents and holds both of our weights as he buries himself deep inside me. He's pulling out and pushing in before I even have caught my breath from the first entry. The energy is charged with both our adrenaline rush and passion.

"Oh God, baby, when I heard that bullet whistle by me, all I thought was I was losing you." I hear his words as my body starts to tighten around him with my first orgasm.

"I know what you mean. When you fell on me I thought I lost you. Duncan, please don't leave me." This is the most I've confessed to him, but I can't keep the feelings to myself anymore. I couldn't stand to lose him. "I'm worried that shot was meant for you because of me. Duncan, send me away! I don't want to leave you, but I don't want to lose you either."

"Baby, it's going to take more than a wanker with a bad aim to take me from you," he growls as he continues his assault on my body.

He's pushing into me so fast and hard now, I'm starting on my second orgasm when he reaches down and pulls my legs up to his shoulders, causing a deeper penetration. He thrusts into me a couple more times and I scream his name as he yells mine. He lets my legs drop and rests his knees on the floor, lying on my body. He broke our connection right after he came. I feel the loss. This man does something to me. I can't be without him and I forget my wishes to stay away. I need to protect him. Am I willing to leave him to save him? His arms tighten around me as if he knows what I'm thinking.

# CHAPTER THIRTY-THREE

## DUNCAN

I leave Maya to take a shower and head up to Joshua's penthouse flat. I didn't want to leave her. I knew those bullets were meant for me, but they were close to her too. This person wants to hurt her in any way possible.

I can't believe she said for me to send her away. The thought of her not being a part of my life makes me crazy. When I enter the flat, it's a flurry of activity. Ian is getting sobered up, Joshua is pacing, and Timothy is tapping into his computers.

"Are you okay, Bossman?"

"Yes, how is Maya? Did she say anything?"

"She wants me to break it off with her, she's sure that the initial bullet was meant for me and it was because of her. Please tell me she's wrong."

"Well, it wasn't that bloke Lawrence you spoke about, but it could have been this Carl wanker. She's right though, if you didn't bend back into the limo, you'd have had a head full of bullet. It was not a really good sniper, though. He'd have anticipated you bending down.

Call Maya and have her come up here, I need to ask her questions. The bobbies are gone. Are you done proving you're both alive?"

"Never. I thought she was gone and she was sure I was hit. Joshua, I can't breathe thinking about her being that close to a bullet. None of the other bullets hit her. Thank bloody hell!"

"Hey, Big Guy, she's constantly around bullets. You're going to have to get over that to be with her." He looks over his shoulder. "Raul, just put Ian in the spare room and tuck him in. He's not going to sober up anytime soon. Damn him and his fucking anniversary."

"Boss, his anniversary was months ago. I don't know what set him off tonight," Raul says.

"Okay. Duncan, ring Maya now, I need to hear what she thinks."

"What's this girl going to tell us, Bossman? Besides, why she's pulling guns and knives? If she has a stalker, the shooter was after Duncan because of her." Timothy interjects.

"Just you wait and see, Timmy Boy, she'll impress even you. Don't tell her I said that," I say.

I'm so proud of my girl, even though I want her as far from danger as I can get her. I call her and she's up within minutes. She's in yoga pants, one of my t-shirts, and barefooted. Thank God she put a bra on. I'd have to kill these wankers if they saw that. She walks right to me and steps up on her tiptoes to kiss me. I know I'm in love with her, I'd give her anything. She's my everything.

Tonight when Alisa pulled that crap, I wanted to drop to my knees and beg Maya to take my name so no one else could claim either of us. I want her and I'm sure she wants me. Why else would she want to leave me?

Maya leans back down and laces her fingers with mine, and turns to the others. I immediately notice the slight bulge at her back. She's packing her gun.

"Timothy is at the computers, Raul over there is surveillance, and Ian is ballistics, but he's sleeping off a bender. Guys this is my girl, Maya Aaron, an all-around bad arse." I smile at Joshua and then to her. She smiles back at me.

"Thank you, honey, but I don't want to prove myself to them right now. What do you need, Joshua?"

"What's your thought on the shooting?" He doesn't pull any punches, he straight up asks her the central question he wants answered.

"Okay...non-pro, probably using a single shot, sounded like a 770 30-06 instead of a professional rig. They're easy to get and cheap. If I were taking the shot, I'd use a jacketed bullet with my SR-25, position myself on the roof of the building across the street, and I'd have made sure to anticipate Duncan leaning down. It would have been a chest shot, none of this head shot shit if I wanted to kill him. Like my Marine buddies say, go for center mass—more ground and less chance of missing. Although maybe he wanted to scare me by just injuring him, this shooter also didn't consider any external factors. He shot through glass and didn't take the wind or snow into account, correct? I heard the glass blow, so he didn't use a cutter. He also made sure his remaining shots were more a cover than to kill. It reminds me of another shooting I was recently involved in. I would say he doesn't have a collapsible gun, so you should be able to pick him up carrying a big case. Regular scope, no modifications. I didn't see any lasers or red dots, so not a modern gun guy. Returning to the comfortable, cheap aspect, he'd use a cheap scope."

"Bloody hell," both Timothy and Raul say. I'm so proud of my girl.

"That was so hot. When she was talking guns and ammo, I forgot to think," Timothy says, smiling at her.

"Timmy Boy, she's mine," I growl at him. Damn this is the only woman I've ever gotten jealous over like this.

"Timothy, show her the surveillance footage," Joshua says.

As Timothy pulls it up, Maya points out a few more thoughts. The guy was definitely not a professional, he shot from a room across the street, and she's right about the gun. I watch her as she tries to get a clearer picture of the shooter.

"I think I know this shooter. Timothy, can you find out if someone has entered the country?"

"Don't insult me, gorgeous, of course I can. Who am I looking for?"

"Carl Nelson. He was just in D.C., though that doesn't mean anything. He was on the ERT unit with me and does own many guns."

"I'm looking now."

"Okay, Maya, thank you. Duncan, you can take your girl and head back to your place. I'll call if anything comes up. Also, Maya, does the police know you're carrying either the guns or knives?" Joshua sits on his large sofa watching us. I can tell he's processing something in his mind.

"Joshua, I have clearance to be armed in London. I've already declared myself and some of my weapons."

"Really? Can you use those knives with accuracy?" Maya reaches into the band of her yoga pants, pulls out a thin throwing knife, and throws it at Joshua. It plants into the pillow to his right.

"If I wanted to hurt you, it would be impaled in your arm. If I wanted to kill you, it would be in your throat. Again, I'm not whipping it out." She sounds angry.

"I'm sorry again for doubting you. I'm not used to anyone but myself being good with knives. How many do you carry?"

"Right now I only have two and my gun. Normally I can have five or more, depends on the situation. I have a spot in my vest and my boot so I can hide them at work."

"Bossman, what's the plan?" I try to change the subject. I don't want to know how much danger she's normally in.

"Duncan, take your girl, we can handle the rest, and just keep playing like nothing has changed. Maya, why don't you call your roommate and confirm with him that this Carl guy hasn't been by your condo today. Also, the day after tomorrow, we will call him about that inside person."

Just then, Maya's cell phone rings with the ringtone I've associated with Derek.

"Hello D, what's up? I didn't expect to hear from you today." She pauses and I see the look of fear cross her face. "What? Oh my God! Derek, I'm so sorry." I signal for her to hold on. "Just a second, Derek, Duncan wants to say something."

"Baby, put it on speaker phone." She pushes the speakerphone button and my stomach clenches as I know this can't be good.

"Derek, do you want to repeat what you just said? If you can't, I understand. I'm in a room with the Securities International team. There was an incident here tonight too."

"Son of a bitch! This. Is. Done. I'm done standing in the back waiting for the next message to be your dead body. I won't survive that, Maya. You know I won't. But damn, my family is off limits. I'm calling Dad and having him come get you."

I need to lock down this anger I feel for this man. He practically just professed his love for her in front of my boys.

"Derek, stop! Duncan didn't hear the first part, tell him what you found." I hear the sigh come across the line.

"Duncan, what she isn't telling you is this has been going on for years. In the past, she got letters, flowers, and small gifts. When I moved in with her in Boston, she was being followed. It stopped and they went away, except for every June. You know what June is. But this latest shit is out of control. Tonight I went to a place I go to every year at exactly eight at night. This time, I found a single black rose lying on the ground where I usually stand. I ran back to the cemetery and, in the short time I was gone, a dozen dead roses were left there. Those are both apparent threats to me. I can handle that shit, but when I got back to the condo, there were another dozen dead roses outside Maya's door. I entered the condo to find another bouquet of daffodils and yellow hyacinth with a note. I've called the team here, but this ends now. After the delivery to my father earlier today and now this, she's being targeted and so are those close to her." He concludes with another long sigh.

"Derek, you need to go to a hotel. Get away from the condo. I already told your dad I was safe with Duncan for now. He needs to get away from me, too. Maybe I need to get away from all of you."

"No, Maya, I'm not leaving you, and you know how Dad feels about that," Derek snaps.

"Derek, what did the note say?" Joshua asks.

I can't speak, these two have a bond that I had no clue about. But the fact that this day of pain for him was turned into a horror is something I couldn't understand.

"Who's this?" Derek asks angrily.

"I'm Joshua Donovan, owner of Securities International."

"Well, your team had better be good because Metro has a snitch. The note said, 'I love you and I'll kill anyone that comes between us. You're mine, Maya, no one else's.'"

"Derek, go to a hotel, now." Maya pleads.

"No, sexy, I'm not leaving you alone with all this. You know me better than that."

"Look, Derek, I'll only say this once, Maya is mine now," I say into her phone, then look into her eyes. "You're not leaving me, Maya." I can't help myself, I need it out there.

"Hey, Big Guy, she can be all yours, but she's my family. I'll kill you if I must. I'm almost as good as your girl there. You won't know I'm there when you die," Derek says calmly.

"Is that a threat, you bloody American arsehole?" I yell angrily into her phone. Maya pulls the phone away from me.

"Duncan, enough, please stop." She's angry with me. What the bloody hell is going on with them?

"Come get me, Duncan. It was a promise. I don't threaten. Joshua, are you going to help her or do we need to do this ourselves?"

"Derek, I give you credit for attempting to stand toe-to-toe with Duncan, but I'll not go against him. He's my teammate. Do I need to warn you what I can do to you? Are you and Maya more than what you say?" Joshua asks.

Maya has a look of complete shock on her face. The phone is silent for a moment and I dread the reply that I worry is coming.

"Do I love her? Yes. Does she love me? Yes. Are we a romantic couple? No!" There's a pause as he sighs. "Have I been between her legs?" Another pause and my blood runs cold. "Hell yes. She rides my motorcycle with me, we also practice jujitsu. She's my sister; we've battled our demons together and fought through fire for each other. I'll not ever let any harm come to her. As for sexual...yuck. That's so wrong. She's *MY* sister, you dumbasses. My father and I adopted her into our family a long time ago." I let out a sigh and pull her to me. I know he isn't lying.

"Okay, Timothy will pull all the security footage and feeds in the neighborhood. I'll be sending a friend over in the morning with a new security system, it will link to our offices there and here. Maybe we can get some eyes on this wanker. As for the bobbies, go along with them, but send us copies of the evidence too." Joshua replies.

"Okay, tell me what happened there tonight."

"Derek, there was a shooting, it looks like it was Carl. Joshua got hit but is okay. I'm okay. Don't worry," Maya supplies.

"Fucking asshole, I wish you'd let me take care of that bastard the last time he hurt you. I'll kill him this time, Maya. Did you know he's a suspect in Yancy's murder?"

"I'm on this one too, Derek. You and me, we can break a few of his bones." I vow.

"Did you call Dad yet, Maya? He'll worry," he asks her.

"No, I will soon."

"Okay, Big Guy, keep her safe, the team just got here. I'll forward pictures shortly. Call Dad now, Maya, before he finds out and gets upset." He hangs up and her shoulders drop. I look at Joshua and nod, he nods back, and I lead her from the room.

We've barely cleared Joshua's door when I pick her up into my arms, cradling her to my heart, and carry her all the way to my flat. When we enter my hall, I turn her to straddle my hips. I pull her gun from the holster at her back. She reaches between us and releases the Velcro holding the band the holster is tucked into. Interesting. I then pull my shirt, that hangs like a dress on her small body, over her head, and pull the knife from between her breasts. I suck a nipple through her bra and hear her gasp.

I carry her into the bedroom and lay her out on the bed. Grabbing her yoga pants and thong in my hands, I pull them both down, baring her to me. I pull her hips to the edge of the bed and kneel down, licking her sex in a long sweep. I zero in on her clit and circle it with my tongue as I push a finger into her. She moans and writhes on the bed, begging me to take her. I need to show her how much I cherish her. How much she means to me. My finger curls to hit her G-spot while I suck her clit hard into my mouth. She comes on a cry of pleasure, yelling my name. I lap at her until she calms, and then kiss her thighs. Standing and lifting her hips off the bed, I pull her to me, and impale her in one long thrust. Her inner muscles clench around my thick cock.

"Maya, baby, you're mine and I'll never have enough of you."

"Oh God, yes, Duncan."

I continue to hold her up as I thrust into her. She comes again and my balls pull up, wanting to release. I need to draw this out. I pull out of her, lift her off the bed, and lie down with her above me. She sinks onto my cock and I watch as she slowly fucks me. I reach up to unhook her bra and throw it across the room.

She leans back, placing her hands on my legs behind her. The new angle has me hitting her in a new spot and I watch as she starts to lose herself in another orgasm. I grab her waist and roll us over so she's under me now. Pulling one of her legs up and resting the ankle on my shoulder, I push into her harder, and lose myself in the ecstasy of her body.

This time when my balls tighten, I drive even harder into her. She screams my name and I come with a loud roar. I will not lose her.

I want to tell her how I feel, but know she'll push me away. I also won't let her think this was her fault.

We fall asleep in each other's arms, tangled together, forgetting to call Greg.

# CHAPTER THIRTY-FOUR

## DUNCAN

The next day we exchange our gifts. I hand her a small package, and explain as she opens it. "When you told me the story about your mum getting you the angels, I couldn't help myself, is it okay?"

"I love it. Thank you, Duncan."

I got her a delicate blown glass angel ornament when she was getting her hair done yesterday. I also got her a heavy-duty body armor vest to protect her. She got me a leather bomber jacket and 25-year-old Scotch.

The telephone rings as I'm just about to lean forward to kiss her and find the next surface to take her on. I jump up and answer it as I smile at her.

"Hello."

"Mr. Preston, there was a gentleman here, who bypassed me. I tried to detain him, but he hit me. He should be coming to your door now." The guard from the security desk huffs out.

Just then, there's a banging on my door. I walk to the door, grabbing my gun from the hiding spot under the entry table. I turn to see

Maya has her gun and is right behind me. I try to push her back as a voice comes through the door.

"You'd better let me the fuck in there. Maya, I'll shoot the locks and come in for you." I turn to see she has a look of complete shock on her face.

"Who's that, Maya?" I ask her.

"It's Greg. We forgot to call him last night," she says sheepishly. I turn to look into the display and see he's getting his gun out to do as he said. I push the intercom button.

"Just a moment, Greg, I'll let you in." I walk back to the entry table and hide my gun again, then unlock the door and let him in. He barely crosses the threshold when he takes a swing at me. I step back, raise my hands up to block, but he drops, and sweeps my legs from under me, sending me to the floor. I hear the elevator doors open and Joshua busts through the door.

"What the bloody hell is going on in here?" Joshua asks as Greg goes to kick at me. Maya throws herself between us and deflects it with her shin.

She steps into Greg and wraps her arms around him.

"I'm okay. I'm fine. Calm down," She begs him. I jump up to grab her away from him, but Joshua pulls me back. I watch as Greg instantly calms and wraps her close.

"Sweetheart, I thought I lost you too. I heard about the shooting and all I could see was you dead just like her." Tears run down his face. I'm torn to the core watching this man come undone.

"I'm okay, I swear. I'm so sorry I forgot to call you. I'm okay." She soothes again.

I watch his hands slide up into her hair and tip her head back to look into her eyes. My instant moment of jealousy is followed by complete awe as I watch him look her in the eyes and see his love for her. She's not as alone as she thinks.

"Maya, sweetheart, I can't lose you too. I love you as if you were my own flesh and blood. Please don't scare me like that again." he begs her.

"Okay, I'm sorry." They both turn to look at Joshua, who's still holding me back.

"Joshua, sorry for the guard downstairs. Duncan, part of me wants to take her from here right now to protect her, but I know you'll protect her," Greg says as he still holds her tightly to his side.

"I'll make coffee," Maya says as she steps from his arms and walks the short distance to me. She kisses my cheek and walks away before I can hold her close.

"Greg, come in and sit, we can talk about what happened," Joshua says, snapping me from my stupor.

"Yes, please, Greg, come sit down." We all walk into the living room.

After explaining the incident last night and confirming with him his thoughts, we enjoy an excellent breakfast and decide to keep everything status quo to see what happens. Greg leaves without explaining his behavior and I wonder more at their bond. I know that she's not sleeping with either of them, but what's going on?

We head to my dad's home for Christmas dinner. Jonathon calls to say that Ana is sick and sends her love. I can see Maya isn't happy with this any more than I am. We don't tell Father about the shooting or the break-in of her condo.

I watch Greg as he keeps a close eye on Maya, and walk over to him and pull him to the library.

"Greg, is there more you're not telling me?" I ask casually.

"Duncan, she's going to push you away. She thinks the only way to protect those she cares for is to keep them at arm's length. The way she looks at you tells me she's trying to work it through. You'll want to keep an eye on her closely and know that she cares. I actually think she loves you."

"I care about her too. I'll not allow her to push me away," I say confidently.

"You really need to understand her better. You'll have no chance to stop her." He laughs at me.

"What's that supposed to mean?" I ask angrily. How dare he tell me I don't know my girl.

"Okay, you try. She'll run. I know her better than most. She tried it with Derek and me; she won for a short time and got away from us. I fly out tomorrow to head back to D.C. Take care of her and be careful." He shakes my hand and walks back to the parlor where Maya and my father are talking about the upcoming New Year's ball. He still didn't explain to me what was going on. Instead, I now worry about her pushing me away.

MAYA

The next week Ana doesn't come around at all. Finally, it's New Year's Eve and I call her to confirm she's coming here to get ready. She shows up at about three and looks so pale. Maybe she is sick. I show her the bracelet and heavy-duty tactical vest Duncan got me for Christmas. She says Jonathon got her earrings and some other presents but doesn't elaborate, and I don't push.

We're dressed and getting ready to step out into the living room where the men are waiting. Well, except for Jonathon, he'll meet us there. I can see that Ana is nervous. She insisted on dressing in the bathroom, which makes me worry that she's visibly bruised and hiding it from me. The lace back and cap sleeves of her red, slender, straight dress is breathtaking.

If she had any wounds, would I notice them? Damn, I hope I would. She's so very shy and distant now. I want her to come away with me so I can bring my friend back.

I've left my hair down and flowing down my back in loose curls. Ana did my makeup. She gave me what she calls a smoky eye. If I wear makeup, it's usually a powder, mascara, bronzer, and a little lipstick. Ana has done a complete makeup job on me and I feel beautiful and sexy, not overdone. As we walk out, the raised voices of James and Duncan stop. Duncan starts shaking his head as he looks at me.

"Baby, you look gorgeous, but there's no way you're leaving my flat in that dress. I'd kill any man that looked at you." I smile and twirl for him.

"Honey, I thought you'd like it." My dress is white with a bright blue and green baroque pattern, a deep plunging neckline, open back, and a slit up the front he hasn't noticed yet. I'm wearing the silver stiletto heels and stop and push out one of my legs through the slit so he can see the whole effect.

"Bugger me, Maya, are you trying to get me arrested? I'll kill any man that looks at your legs like I am right now."

Ana and I both giggle and James just rolls his eyes.

James is wearing another traditional black tux and, this time, Duncan is in a gray one.

"Son, I'm glad to see I'm not the only Preston man to have a jealous streak, but you're not going to get her to change. I've known her many years and it's nice to see another man try to control her." He turns to look at me. "By the way, Maya, I love the dress. Ana, you look exquisite too, I like the red." James smiles at both of us, and walks to Ana so she can take his arm. She smiles sweetly at her father, then looks at her brother.

"Duncan, be nice. Maya is wearing a dress. I picked it out."

"Thank you, dear sister, because I swear this night isn't going to be easy. That dress from Christmas Eve was bad enough, but this one is over the top sexy. For all your information I'm not jealous, I'm territorial. I'm protecting what's *MINE,*" he growls at me and walks over to put my cape on, then bends down and kisses me.

"I swear, Maya, they'll die, so warn anyone that looks at you."

"Yes, darling." I giggle back.

When we arrive, Jonathon takes one look at me and rolls his eyes, he then looks at Ana, and I can see the anger in his eyes. He grabs her arm and drags her off. I can't hear what he's saying but she's nodding and it looks like apologizing. For the rest of the evening he keeps her in the back, except for the one time I see James dance with her. Duncan couldn't get her to dance and he has barely left my side. Both Lawrence and Stephan have tried to cut in or ask for a dance, but Duncan sent them packing. Uncle Marcus asks me to dance and as we're gliding across the floor, he pushes me away and into Lawrence's arms. I immediately step back from them both.

"Marcus, what're you doing? I will not dance with Lawrence," I say and stand in place. I look around for Duncan. Marcus is becoming a problem for me. Lawrence is just a pain.

"Yes, you will. He wants to apologize and try to win you back." Marcus then proceeds to walk off.

"I'm not dancing with you, Lawrence."

"Yes, you will, Maya. You don't want to cause a scene." He sneers at me. People already have to dance around us and are giving us a wide berth.

"Want to make a bet. I don't care, and I'll make a scene. Step away from me now." He reaches for me and I grab his hand and twist it behind his back. "I told you to step away. Don't touch me or I'll break this arm." I push him away as I feel Duncan come up behind me.

"Oi, you little wanker, you better get the bloody hell away from my girl. Don't make me say it again." Lawrence walks off and Duncan pulls me into his arms as we finish the dance.

I feel like I'm being watched. The prickles of unease have been happening all night but are more so now. As Duncan and I glide around the dance floor, I look out on everyone to see if anyone stands out. I don't recognize anyone until a lone person at the back of the ballroom, hidden in the shadows, catches my eye. I turn my head to look at him as we glide away to the other side of the dance floor, and he's gone. My unease continues.

At midnight, I kiss Duncan and pray he's in my life next year too. He smiles after our kiss and looks me in the eye. Maybe he's thinking the same. I know I need to protect him though.

"Baby, I want to take you home and show you what this dress has done to me all night," he whispers in my ear.

"Okay, let me say goodbye to James and Ana."

"Jonathon dragged Ana out of here while you and Lawrence were arguing. That was what took me so long to get to you. Father is over there."

"He took her out before midnight?"

"He said she wasn't feeling well. She looked pale, but she always does when she's around him." We walk over to James and I kiss him good night.

Marcus is sitting with him and I just nod to him. I don't trust him anymore. Something has changed between us and he isn't the same man I thought he was. Maybe he's never been the man I thought. I want to think that over more but I also only want to think of the man who's holding me to him.

# CHAPTER THIRTY-FIVE

## MAYA

New Year's Day we had dinner with Joshua and spent the rest of the day making love. I think we've christened all of the surfaces of his flat now. We don't talk about the attacks or my stalkers. We don't even discuss Derek and Greg, who've only texted me off and on. We're supposed to have dinner with James on Thursday.

Duncan had to go into the office today to talk to Joshua about his next assignment, so I'm at the flat by myself getting my stuff organized and dreading the next couple of days. I decide to show Duncan I can cook and am making a Bolognese sauce with angel-hair pasta. I have garlic bread in the oven and my sauce is just about ready.

The doorbell rings and I look into the camera as I palm my gun, checking the security feed. There's a deliveryman on the other side.

"Can I help you?" I use the intercom.

"I've a delivery for Ms. Maya Aaron."

"How did you get up here?"

"I was told to come through. Do you want the delivery or not? I need a signature."

"Just a moment." Something doesn't feel right. The doorman would have stopped him, and something in the deliveryman's voice sounds off and bothers me. I debate what to do and know what I must do.

"I will not sign. Put them down or leave."

"It says they're from a D. Preston." I know that Duncan wouldn't have let this man past the doorman and he knows how I feel about flowers right now.

"Let me call him and see what he says."

"Okay, never mind. I'll leave them here." He gives in too quickly.

I watch him put them down and continue to watch as he leaves the view of the camera. I see a man enter the elevator and wait a minute more. I unbolt and open the door after I check my gun and holster it at my back. I step out and am immediately hit as I bend down to pick up the box. My gun is pulled and thrown into the apartment. I roll, knowing they have the upper hand now that I'm on the floor.

"I knew you wouldn't open the door. I knew that you'd wait until that damn delivery guy got into the elevator. I didn't expect it to be so easy to get you, though." That voice, I've heard that voice before. He kicks at me, but I roll away from him.

I pop up onto my feet and get into my stance. I notice he's wearing a mask, but his eyes look familiar. As I'm sizing him up, I see he's preparing to punch. He steps into a straight punch aimed for my face. I slide to the side, dodging his hit and use both my forearms to deflect his punch. Using his forward momentum, I throw him into the wall across the hall and dive back into the flat, slamming the door closed with my feet. I rise up to my knees and engage the locks. Turning to the panel, I hit the panic alarm and notice the delivery is lying on the wood flooring next to me. I open the box to the familiar delivery of a dozen black roses and a single red rose. The note catches my eye.

*Maya darling,*

*You'll always be mine. I'll kill Duncan if you don't leave him now. I've had a sniper, a good one, on him for days now. You have twenty-four hours. No more warnings, Maya. Leave him now.*

*Love always,*

*Sir*

My insides clench. I will not lose him too. I put the note in my pocket as I hear pounding on the door.

"Open up, Maya. It's Timothy." I check the camera and let him in. He looks at me as the fire alarm starts blaring through the apartment. I turn and run for the kitchen. My Bolognese is ruined. I dump it into the sink and turn off the burner as Duncan comes storming into the condo.

"What the bloody hell is going on? Why are the panic and fire alarms going off?" He looks at me and instantly stops, seeing the flowers on the floor. "Bugger me. Baby, are you okay?" He rushes to my side and pulls me in. I feel all the bumps and bruises, but I feel the terror for him more.

"A delivery man came to the door. I refused to open the door and he left the flowers outside. I opened the door and a second man attacked me. I knew the voice, but I couldn't place it. He was wearing a ski mask. He had to have passed Timothy."

"No, baby, the corridor is empty." He looks at the flowers. "What do they mean? Was there a note?" He looks at me carefully. I need to lie. I will not be responsible for his death too.

"No note. The black means ending, death, a new beginning. The single red rose means life-long devotion. I think he's telling me he'll try harder. The attack was new, though."

"I can't let you go back to the States with this stalker after you. Timothy check the feeds, find out how he got in here and how he escaped."

"I tried to cook you dinner, sorry, in the attack it burned." I attempt to change the subject so he won't see the actual terror in my eyes. I scan the windows and wonder where a sniper could get to us here.

"It's okay, baby. Come on, let's get you cleaned up." He pulls me back into the hall toward his room.

It takes over an hour to get everyone out of the condo and us to get some food. Duncan and I are now in the tub soaking and relaxing. I know he's upset about the attack.

"Baby, what does your tattoo mean?" I wondered when he'd ask.

"Well, of course, the Star of David is for my heritage. My parents' names are in Yiddish at the side points. My father's name is also in Hebrew below the Yiddish, my mother's in Gaelic, to represent their cultures. The top is Savta's name, Uriella, in Yiddish as the head of the family. The bottom is French and says, 'Until everyone accepts all God's personas, there will be fighting.' It was something I did while in college and I've added on to it. Now tell me about yours." Distraction is the best key. I don't want to end this, but my clock will run out fast.

"Baby, I love it. The one on my back is of course for my mum, she's the angel protecting Ana from that car accident. No one knows how Ana survived when Mum was killed. Plus I feel she's always watching my back. The one on my ribs is the SAS emblem with a mate's name below it."

"Whose?"

"Christopher. He and I had been friends since grammar school. He died in my arms while I was serving under Joshua." He takes a big breath behind me as I rest between his legs. I know he's dreading me flying home. Every time we make love, he acts like he's imprinting himself on me. He doesn't know, but my soul is his. I just can't let my heart go there.

"Tell me about Christopher."

"Our team was pinned down after we were ambushed. All the guys were there around us. Joshua and Raul were both shot—just minor hits. Timothy was working on Christopher. Ian was providing our cover fire. Christopher had an eight-month old baby and a young wife. He looked me in the eye and asked me to watch over his family and told me it was worth it. He then died."

"I'm so sorry. Is he the one you have nightmares over?"

"Sometimes. I served three more years trying to put that day behind me. I can still smell the guns, blood, dirt, and death. I pray I never have to go through that again, but he taught me to live by dying." Duncan inhales and exhales slowly. I don't know if he's struggling with the memory or something else.

"I'm so sorry," I rub his thighs as my heart hurts for him.

"Maya, have you thought of Joshua's job offer?" he whispers.

Well, now I know what he's struggling with.

I bristle. This was not supposed to be brought up, I thought I made myself clear the last time. I rise up out of the water. Can I use this to pull away and save my heart? Can I push him away to protect him? Damn straight, I'll use this. I need to get away before this sniper comes after him.

"Duncan, we discussed this, I already have a job, possibly two."

"Baby, I want you here."

I stiffen. He does want me to give up my life.

"Why can't you move to D.C.?" I quip back.

"Do you want me to?" he says without hesitation.

Wait, what? He'll move for me? I didn't see that coming. He can't follow me, they'll still kill him.

"No, but it's a good question. Why must I give up my life?"

"Why, Maya? Why can't I move to D.C. with you? Why can't you move here?" He stands too.

I step out and start to dry off. I turn my back so he doesn't see the desolation in my eyes. I'll do whatever it takes to protect him.

Wait, oh God, no...I love him. I'll do this for my love.

As if reading my mind, his next words throw me off guard.

"Maya, I love you! I want to protect you from these stalkers. I want to have you in my life and my bed every day." I swing around to look at him, this really can't be happening.

Did he just say that? Oh God, no! I need to get out of here. I can't lose him too. I walk from the bathroom to the bedroom and start dressing. I will not jeopardize his life. He can't love me, that's how they died, and now with the threat of losing him, I've got to do this.

"Maya, where are you going?"

"I'm packing so I don't have to tomorrow."

"STOP!" He yells at me.

"NO, Duncan, you can't love me. It hasn't been enough time. You live here, I live there. We have demanding jobs. One of us could die." There's the crux of my phobia.

Someone else dying and leaving me all alone again.

I struggled with this during therapy and even more so since the shooting after the consulate gala. I've woken every night from nightmares of losing him. Now after today and the threat, I will not lose him too.

"Oh, baby, stop. I'm not going to die. If that war couldn't kill me, only you leaving me will." He walks to me but I back up.

"No, Duncan, we said we'd keep it simple. This isn't simple, this is all FUCKED up. I have a job."

"Baby, I have a job too. One that I love as much as you love yours, but I'll quit and sell everything to become a bloody American if it means I can keep you."

"Stop, Duncan, I need to process all this." I throw on some yoga pants and a bra and t-shirt. I grab my now packed clothes and run for the door, grabbing my purse and leather jacket.

"MAYA, STOP! If you walk out now, you better be real sure before you come back." He's standing there naked, in all his glory, watching me. I grab my gun from the coat closet and place it in my purse.

"What the fucking hell does that mean?"

"You can only run once."

"Damn it, Duncan, I need some fucking time." I run out the door, leaving my heart right there. I left him. My last image of him is watching him fall to his knees as I walk out.

Oh God, what have I done?

I make it to the lobby and hail a cab to the airport. I break down in the cab and cry for what I give up.

I'll only ever love that man. I'll only ever want him, and I can't have him.

## DUNCAN

How the bloody hell did this happen? I'm sitting in a pub and going over it in my head. One minute I had her heavenly body pressed up against mine, the next I was watching her walk out the door with my heart. I feel like my heart is dying. I signal the barman for another shot of JD. How the hell does she drink this bloody crap? I turn to the door when I hear it open, hoping she found me. I have no idea where she went, the doorman said she jumped into a taxi and was gone. Of course, it's not her, but Joshua.

"Timothy just called. She jumped on a flight to D.C. right after leaving your flat. She sent a text to Derek to pick her up at the airport." Joshua looks like he doesn't want to be relaying this message to me. Why is Derek always there to pick her up? As if he can read my mind, his next words stop me cold.

"Derek called me right after that and said there's something more going on. He thinks that the attacker today gave Maya a message. He says that you need to stay away until he can figure this all out." She never said anything about a threat. I throw back the shot and wonder if there's evidence I missed. He continues, "Look, Duncan, from what Timothy found out, there really isn't anything going on between them. She's faithful to you. This Derek guy is just her partner. It appears what he said last week is true, they're like siblings. He and his father are the only people she interacts with socially in D.C. We need to search your flat again and have Timothy pull the footage and take a closer look."

"I know she's known him since college. They lived together for years while she was in school. She told me, but like I bloody care. I told her I love her and she ran."

"You told her you loved her right after your life might have been threatened? You and I both know she struggles with the death of her parents."

"What's the difference? I love her. I'll protect her. Greg told me she'd push me away. I told him I wouldn't let her. He laughed at me, guess he was right."

"This might be how she's protecting you."

"Don't make excuses for her! I know that. I thought she was going to give us a real try when she told me all that stuff on Christmas Eve." I signal for another shot. I know the alcohol is hazing my thoughts and not letting me see the full picture, but I've lost the one woman I never knew I needed.

~

A COUPLE HOURS later Joshua and Ian are trying to help me to my flat. He called in Ian when I guess I got a little out of hand. I want my woman back home. As soon as the door to my flat opens, I smell her and I'm instantly angry again.

"Bloody hell, I can't stay here. It smells like her, I need to go get her back. Pour me on a plane, mates, I'm going to get my woman and drag her home, kicking and screaming."

"Can't do that bloke. Those bloody Americans won't let ye on a flight in this condition." Ian points out the obvious.

"Why the bloody hell not? They'll not keep me away from her," I slur.

"Well, mate, you're drunk."

"Hey, I helped you once, now you help me. And as for you, Boss-man, I quit. I'm going to be a bloody American for my girl." They both look at me as if I'm crazy.

I've watched both of these men pour their hearts out to me and now they're not going to help me. Well bloody hell, I'll leave on my own. I start to step around them and see Timothy walk into my flat.

"Okay, Timothy, take him down." I don't see the punch coming, but I know it's going to happen. We've had to do this to each other before. This is the first time I was knocked out by one of them though.

When I come to the next morning, I'm in my bed and the pillows smell like her. I groan and roll out of bed. It had to have been a night-mare; she's in the bathroom or dining room. My cell phone is blinking and I look at the message.

***Maya: Please don't come after me. Give me time and space.***

Bloody hell, yesterday wasn't a nightmare. She left me. My girl is gone and doesn't want me to come for her. I walk out to the kitchen, pick up the coffee pot, and throw it at the wall. I then walk back into my bedroom and trash the room.

When Ian and Joshua find me later, I'm sitting in my spare room staring at her dresses she left behind. She also left her throwing knives and all her jewelry. I'm holding the angel I gave her in one hand and the note that must have come yesterday. She ran out so fast she left everything. My God, she's the most beautiful part of my life. I can't live without her.

"How did you two bloody gits make it through this hell?" They both just shake their heads and call a cleaning service.

"I'd say time heals the pain, but I'd be lying," Ian says.

"Here, I found this in here. She left because I was threatened. What did the footage show?" I hand the note to Joshua.

"She fought off the intruder and he followed her to the airport. He didn't get on her flight, but a private jet. No name. My money is on Carl. You can't go to her yet, we need to figure this out first."

## CHAPTER THIRTY-SIX

### MAYA

I sent him the text as soon as I landed at my connection in Copenhagen. Because I jumped on the first available flight, I got flown into Copenhagen and had to overnight there. I need space and time to process this. I need to find out who this is and take care of them. I look out the front of the airport and see Derek in his car. I've always liked his Charger.

I smile weakly at him. I have another couple of days off before I have to be back at the station. I hand him my gun and both of my big knives. I left my throwing knives in London.

"Take me to the closest bar and don't leave me, no matter what I say."

"You got it, sexy. Do you want to talk about it?"

"Do I look like I want to talk about it?" I turn to him and let him see the devastation in my gaze. I feel like I'm torn apart from the inside.

"Well, no. But as someone who's lost as much as I have, don't let it go if it's real."

"I had no choice."

"What?" His head swings my way.

"Don't worry about it. Take me to the bar." He's watching me carefully. I can't tell him about the note. I can't believe I left it at Duncan's. Hopefully, he won't find it.

I spend the next two days in a drunken haze, finally passing out before I have to check into the station. I can't believe I left him. What an idiot, I had it all and I let it go because I'm afraid. My father would kick my ass. Derek only listens and shakes his head, he's lost more than me, and he thinks I'm stupid for giving up as he calls it. Greg calls me, trying to get me to talk too. No one will ever know why I truly gave it up.

I feel like Duncan is all over my skin and all over my soul. I go about my life and working out at the gym and studio as much as I can. Sleep, as usual, evades me, except now it's worse. I wake up with nightmares of Duncan yelling for me and me running from him. I feel like I'm living a half-life. I ended up getting the job with Secret Service and so did Derek. I spend money on my truck and avoid anything personal.

Carl calls me a couple times, but I avoid him and end up blocking his number. Lawrence also makes an appearance. Why won't they leave me alone? I block him too. Marcus calls to ask me if I'm going to come up to Boston, I decline. The one man I want to bug me won't. I don't even see him on the covers of the gossip rags; he must be working somewhere else.

James calls me a couple times and I assure him I'm okay, just needed some time to think. Two weeks after I left him, James calls to tell me he put my stuff in my safety deposit box again. James asks if I need to call our friend, it's his way of asking if I need to see my counselor again.

"Maya, darling, my son is stubborn like me, whatever he did, please forgive him. He loves you."

"That's the problem, James, he loves me. I kill everyone that loves me. I can't take him away from you."

"Maya, no. You didn't kill them. Do I need to call Derek or Greg and have them take you back?"

"No, James, I don't feel like hurting myself like that. The pain I'm in right now feels like death."

"That's love, darling." He hangs up and leaves me to think about what he said.

## DUNCAN

I stay at my flat for a week, drinking and lying on my sheets, smelling her on my pillows. The scent is fading. It's leaving me like she did. I love this woman and she walked away from me. I want to be with her. I contemplate leaving and going to D.C. to track her down, but Joshua says to give her space.

On the second week, my father comes to get her jewelry and knives to take to her safety deposit box. I put her dresses in my closet where they belong. I keep the angel on my nightstand. She belongs to me.

I ask Timothy to come to my flat and wire up my laptop to the cameras in her neighborhood so I can watch her. The only man coming and going is Derek. She goes to work and works out. I watch her running on her treadmill all hours of the night. Her nightmares have returned.

I'm watching her empty flat one evening when a sleek motorcycle pulls up to the garage entrance of the building. I see the passenger get off the bike, I know it's my woman. She has on a white helmet with some design on it and the guy is in all black. They both pull off their helmets and my blood stops. She's so sexy in all that leather. She hands him the helmet as she pulls off her pack and pulls out a set of keys. She puts the pack back on and grabs her helmet. I watch as she walks into the garage and he puts his helmet back on.

In moments, she's pulling out of the garage on her Harley and they both take off fast down the street. I watch for a little while longer and decide to take a shower. When I get out of my shower, I rewind the feeds and see nothing new. I click to current and watch as they pull up on their motorcycles. I switch to the garage feed and watch them park the bikes, get off, and head in. She looks relaxed and smiles at him, but the smile doesn't light up her eyes, it's fake.

Father and Joshua come to take me out the third week for dinner. Ana calls to check on me, but she won't tell me if she talks to her or not. I finally go to the office the next day and immediately walk out the door, and go straight to Joshua's office.

"I'll work in the conference room or tech room; I can't function at my desk."

"This is why office sex is wrong."

"Shut up, you git." I walk out and instantly decide to head to the gym. I'm beating the heavy bag as if I'm a madman when Ian walks in.

"Want to spar?" he asks.

"I could kill you."

"I'm game. You let me wail on you once. Time to return the favor, this is what being a mate means."

We gear up then step into the ring and I proceed to hand him his arse. Timothy walks in, geared up, and steps in the ring next, I take him out. When Raul walks in, I know I'm going to hurt.

"Okay, mate, let's do this." He knows Krav Maga too.

"She knows Krav Maga, I can't fight you." The memories rush back of watching her defend herself at my flat.

"Yes, you can, pansy wanker. Nut up and try to beat me." He's pushing my buttons.

"I'm going to kick your Spanish ass, wanker."

"Name calling is beneath you, wanker."

I lunge for him but after Timothy and Ian, I'm worn out. He deflects and takes me down with multiple double-fisted punches to my diaphragm. I'm lying on the mat, wishing for death. "Do you cede?"

"Never." I huff through the pain.

"Then get up and fight me." He taunts me again.

"I cede to you, but I'll never give up when it comes to her." They all sigh heavily.

"That's what we thought, now give her space and let her come back to you," Joshua says from the door. He watched the whole time.

"Okay, what now?" I roll and look at him.

"Let her figure it out. When she realizes that the threats will continue even with you out of the picture, she'll come back."

"I actually think she will. She's lost weight already, and no one will spar with her anymore," Timothy says.

"She's lost weight? I need to go to her."

"No, Duncan, she needs to figure it out. Give her time. We need to figure out who's threatening her."

"I don't know if I can wait much longer."

"I sent the cleaning service back to your flat, they're cleaning everything. The dresses are being moved to your father's house. We're removing her from your life for a while. It needs to look like you gave up on her."

"I need her. If you touch that angel, I'll beat you, Bossman."

"She doesn't want you right now and it needs to look like you're over her. I have it in my office, you can have it back later."

"All she needs to do is say it and I'll go to her. I'll give it all up."

"Yes, but until she figures it out, you can't force it. Ask Ian."

We head to the pub after we all shower. I'm ready to do what it takes to get my girl back. If it means I give her space, I will, but only for a little while. I wish she'd text me or call.

IT'S BEEN over a month since she left me. Joshua has put me on Maya'a and Ana's details. I mostly spend my time in the tech room listening to phone taps we've set up on both of them. I'm listening in on conversations when her cell phone rings. It's a standard ringtone, so I know it isn't a friend or her work. Who's calling my woman? She answers, her voice is soft and sounds tired.

"Hello."

"Maya, darling, can I take you out tonight?" Lawrence's voice comes across the line.

"I already told you, Lawrence, I'm not interested. How did you call me, I blocked your number? Don't call me again." I hear the fire in her voice.

"I know you broke it off with the Neanderthal. I'll forgive you for slumming it. Come back to me."

"Never, Lawrence, he's the only man I want. There was never a you and me. Go to hell." She hangs up on him.

Wait, she wants me? Why won't she call me? Why are we suffering through this if she wants me? I start to plan, I'll be going to her soon enough. She's too stubborn to come to me. Moreover, I need to protect her.

She starts dialing another number, but the sequence puts a jam on my signal. Interesting. My girl knows how to block out wires and traces. I turn on the feeds to her flat and watch her pace. Because of the block, I can't hear what she's saying, but I can tell she's relaxing as her pacing becomes less and less. She finally sits down and continues to talk to this person. I wonder if it's Greg. He wouldn't want us to know, but he was just as confused by her as we were until we found the note. I asked Joshua not to tell Derek or Greg about the threat. If they confront her, she'll pull away from them too. She needs someone. In my mind, I flash back to that night she and Derek went for their ride, she relaxed and looked less stressed. I can't take them from her life. She might be mine, but they are her life.

# CHAPTER THIRTY-SEVEN

## MAYA

I can't believe he actually called and asked me out. I want Duncan to call, but his last words ring through my head again.

*"If you walk out now, you better be real sure before you come back."* I don't know if I'm confident in our future. I then hear James's voice. *"That's love, darling."* I've run on the treadmill so much lately I'm afraid I'm going to break it. I look at my phone and know I need to make the call. I dial the number, being sure to add the codes to prevent a trace or someone to listen in. I wait for him to pick up, and start to pace my condo.

"Maya, it's been a long time. How are you doing? James, Greg, and Derek are worried about you. They told me about your man."

"I knew they'd call you, Dr. Mason. He isn't my man anymore. I know you told me over and over it wasn't my fault, but how can I believe that? What if he dies? I could kill him too. Now with this stalker threatening him, I have to protect him."

"Maya, your parents' deaths were a tragic accident. Death is inevitable, it happens to us all. You can't outrun it or outfight it if it's your time. Yes, he could die, but is loneliness worth that? What's not to stop your stalker from killing him even now with you away from him?"

"No. I can't let that happen. He can't die. I need him. I hurt so much."

"Pick yourself up and do what you're good at, fight for what you want. Do you want him?"

"Yes." I feel calm and sit on my sofa, looking out into the D.C. skyline.

"Then you know what you need to do. As for right now, go to the gym and work off that tension I hear in your voice. Use your release. I'm always here for you. As for your stalkers, find them and put a bullet between their eyes. Come on, Maya, fight. You know how to do that."

"Thank you, Dr. Mason." I hang up and grab my gym bag, then head down to the garage and jump into my truck.

It takes about twenty minutes to get to the gym. I walk in and say hi to the guys as I walk to the locker room to change. I know that no classes are going on right now, but people were practicing. It's Friday night, so there will be fights starting soon and I'm hoping to get involved. I stretch out, bouncing on my toes and warming up, when the owner walks up.

"Want to fight tonight, Maya?" Vic asks me.

"Yes."

"I have a new guy that asked specifically to fight you." He points to a corner where a man is standing in the shadows watching us.

"Who's he? What level?"

"He says he knows Krav Maga and is an MMA fighter. He came in the other day and asked if you do the Friday night fights. I told him you do them every other week. I warned him that none of our guys would fight you anymore. Guess word is getting around to the other gyms that we have a master with a lot of talent."

"Okay, I'll fight him." I smile at Vic. I'm not a master, but I'm good.

"Maya, are you sure? He looks like he wants to actually fight you, no holds barred."

"I got this, Vic. Put on the song." I continue to stretch and warm up my muscles.

Vic comes back to start helping me put on my safety gear. I enter the matted area where we grapple and fight. I don't know my competitor. He's about six feet with short blond hair and brown eyes. He smiles at me as I put my mouth guard in and my helmet on. He puts on regular open-faced headgear, my helmet has face protection. Vic steps to the center of the mats.

"Okay, let's keep this clean and show the newbies how this works. Maya, please be gentle." He looks at me. I smile through my gear and mouth guard.

My opponent doesn't shake my hand or introduce himself. He steps into the center, holds out his gloves, and I bump them with mine. The music I like to release to starts and I barely hear what my opponent says.

"Let's go, girly." He slips in his mouth guard. Why would he say that to me?

He immediately kicks out without warning. Thank God for all my training, I barely avoid the kick as I drop down and come up with a punch to his low stomach. He drops his elbows onto the back of my neck and I feel the pain ricochet through my head and body. I fall back and see his leg come at me again. I turn to take the brunt of the hit on my right shoulder. I twist back, step in, and nail him in the solar plexus with my left and then bring my right into the side of his headgear. He staggers back for a second. This is just a show of training, so I don't advance on him. I start to tell him how to avoid that hit when he rushes me. He grabs me around the middle and lifts me up. My body flies through the air, and when I hit the mats, I immediately roll to avoid the knee coming down for my face. This guy is dangerous. I pop up to my feet and look at him. I turn to see Vic rushing in to stop the match. The man swings and hits Vic in the face. Vic goes down, and others rush to his aid. I see a doctor I know kneeling by Vic to help him. I turn back to my fight.

My opponent comes at me again. This time, I'm ready. He kicks out, and I spin and miss the kick but am ready with my own. He obviously isn't aware I also study other forms of self-defense. The karate roundhouse hits the guy on the side of his headgear. He shakes it off and rushes at me again. I'm able to keep him from picking me up with a shin kick and punch I angle up into his diaphragm. I grab his head and bring his headgear and face to my knee. He swings and hits me on my side, and my breath rushes from my body. I fall on my hands and knees. He leans down, bent over my back, trying to trap me to the mat.

"Girly, I have a message for you. Stop your investigation or Anabel will be hurt. Also, don't go back to Duncan unless you want him to die too." I see red.

I spin explosively to my right, throwing my elbow back as I spin, hitting him in the stomach. I then proceed to land several punches on his back and kidneys. He falls face forward to the mat. I drop onto his back, but he rolls, throwing me off him. I also roll to my back and grab his arm as I pull my feet over his body. I use the leverage that Derek and Greg taught me. I feel him start to fight me as I pull the arm-bar tighter. I keep pulling until I hear him yelling he gives. I let go of him and roll to the side. He rises up above me and I see his intent. I roll away from him and push up. He comes at me again, his arm dangling uselessly. I kick out, knocking his legs from under him, and wrap my forearm around his neck, using my other arm for leverage. I hold him in the chokehold for the required time until he loses consciousness. I spit my mouth guard to the side of my mask. I'm yelling at him the whole time. I know he can't answer me, but I'm so angry. They threatened Ana and Duncan.

"Who the hell are you, asshole? How do you know Ana and Duncan?"

I dive for my bag, where I have a pair of cuffs for training. I cuff him and rip off my headgear.

"Are you okay?" I say to Vic after I spit out my mouth guard completely.

"Good. You?"

"Who the fuck is this asshole?"

"I don't know. Police are on the way."

"Hey, doc, want to check him before the ambulance arrives? Make sure I didn't kill him." I turn to the doctor. She bends down and checks his pulse.

"He'll live. Have a headache and he needs his shoulder relocated." She smiles at me.

The police arrive and take the guy away. I answer their questions as best as I can. My body hurts everywhere from the few hits I took. The doc checks me and says I am just bruised up.

I head home with new thoughts in my head. Something is up with Ana. Why did he threaten Duncan? I left Duncan and he's still in danger. I send a quick text to Joshua and let him know about the threats. He doesn't respond back, which I expect.

I'm walking up to my door when I notice it.

Stabbed into the door with my other missing tactical knife is a note.

*Maya,*

*He thought he would warn you. I've killed for you once, injured another, you will be mine soon. How'd you like my friend? Hope you're not too bruised. I'm coming for you.*

*Your true lover*

I step back from the door, knowing that my world is about to blow up in my face. I dial Greg.

"Hello, darling. I didn't expect to hear from you tonight."

"I've had a visitor at my apartment."

"I'll call SSA Jones. I'm on my way."

"Call IAD Officer Olsen for me too please."

"Why?"

"My stalker killed Yancy."

"Shit. On my way."

I'm waiting outside my condo for backup to arrive when my cell phone starts ringing. I don't recognize the number but answer it any way.

"Sweetheart, we need to talk."

"Uncle David?"

"I wasn't shot because of what I was doing. I was shot because of something you're involved in. Want to tell me?"

"I'm dealing with it. Stay away. Gotta go, Greg is here."

"Take care."

I hang up and realize what the note means more so now.

Oh my God. Who else did he hurt?

Derek runs past the others and right to me, taking me into his arms. I pull away as all the bumps and bruises make themselves known.

"David just called. He said that his shooting was about me not him. That's what the note means."

"What do they mean about friend and not too bruised?" Greg demands.

"I was attacked tonight at the gym."

"Officer Aaron, this is getting to be a little unsettling. I just got off the phone regarding the situation at your gym tonight. I'm talking to your captain now about relieving you from duty for a little while," IAD Officer Olsen says as he walks up.

"I don't want to be relieved. Find this asshole so I can get on with my life."

It takes hours for everyone to leave. Finally it's just Derek and me. I go take a shower, hoping that it will release some of the muscle pain.

After my shower, I'm icing my body while I watch the Food Network when Derek walks in.

"Did you call him?"

"Yes." I groan.

"Well at least the fight got you some release of all your energy." He laughs at me.

"Sure it did."

"So now you think you really are a danger to them?"

"Actually, I don't know how I feel other than sore. It feels like I'm missing something. By the way, Lawrence called again today. I blocked him again so keep an eye out. I have to tell you something but don't be angry."

"What's up, sexy?"

"I left Duncan because the attack at his condo was a message, I had twenty-four hours to leave or a sniper was going to kill him."

"Son of a bitch! I knew it. Did you let Joshua know?"

"Yeah, I texted him just a bit ago."

"As for Lawrence, there were already a dozen red roses in the lobby. I sent them to the hospital."

"Damn it."

"Did you let Joshua know about the threat from before too?"

"Yes. I have a meeting with the chief tomorrow about the attack. They want to make sure it's not someone I put away."

"Do you want a beer? By the way, Dad is on his way back up."

"Yes. Why?"

"He wants to talk to you? He didn't say anything other than he needed to speak to you."

"Guess I'm going to have to make a decision. Even when I'm not with Duncan, he gets threatened."

"I know, sexy."

Greg shows up and questions me more about both attacks. I know he wants to ask me about calling Dr. Mason but he respects my privacy too much. We relax for the rest of the night, but my thoughts are filled with questions. Who was that man and why did he attack me? Who left the note on the door? It has to be another cop, and that pisses me off. Guess I'll find out tomorrow. As Greg is leaving, he hugs me close.

"Heard you used an arm-bar and almost dislocated the guy's arm," he says proudly.

"Thank you for teaching me that move. According to Dr. Nic, I did dislocate it. I should've just put him into the sleeper hold first, though."

"How bad are you hurt?"

"Just sore. Good-night."

"Night, sweetheart. Love you."

I go to my room until I hear Derek head to bed. I then walk back into the living room and run on my treadmill until I feel like I'm going to drop.

# CHAPTER THIRTY-EIGHT

## MAYA

Another month passes. That's three months, three fucking months, and nothing. I miss him so bad. I think I'm losing my mind. All I do is work and workout. Unfortunately, no one will spar with me anymore. After the fight, everyone became scared of me.

The investigation has come to a standstill and I know it's because of the fact that it's a cop. How can I keep my job? I wasn't relieved of duty but every day they think about it as more photos turn up of me. My knife had no prints on it. The man who attacked me was found dead in his cell the next morning. They say it was an unrelated jail attack. I never got my questions answered.

After the attack, Lawrence kept coming to the condo. I filed a restraining order against him. I go to the range and practice shooting all my firearms. I've gone to Quantico a couple times to work with some of the instructors and push my skills.

My life becomes a series of days blending into work one week and working on forgetting the next week. I finally can't take it anymore; today I'm making a change. I brace myself as I dial the number I've memorized after staring at it for weeks.

"Securities International Incorporated, this is Rebekah. How may I direct your call?"

"Joshua Donovan, please."

"May I tell him who's calling?"

"Can I just surprise him?"

"Sorry, ma'am, I'm going to need your name." I don't want to give my name in case it's too late and he's in a meeting with him.

"Okay, tell him...it's another angel in a dark place."

"Excuse me, ma'am, what?"

"Tell him, another angel in a dark place. He'll know what it means. Please, I can't give you my name in case he's in a meeting with someone."

"Okay, ma'am. Hold please." The hold music isn't bad, but I'm already twitching for a gun or knife when he finally picks up.

"Maya, is that you?" He sounds breathless.

"Yes, I didn't want to give my name in case you were with him. I don't want him to know I called you. Is it too late?" I hope he understands what I'm asking.

"Never! He'll never see another woman as he sees you, Maya. It's just you. What can I do for you?"

"I want a job. I want my man back. I want your help."

"That's a lot of wants. Should I help you after you hurt him like this?"

"Joshua, I was scared and I deal with a lot of guilt from my parents' deaths. I got that threat and knew he couldn't outrun another sniper. I won't be responsible for his death."

"I know about guilt, Maya. I also know about being scared. We found the note. We've been doing our own surveillance." He pauses as I've gotten used to him doing; Joshua waits for you to admit something. I'm about to when he says, "Okay, what do you want?"

"How about a partnership?"

"You got enough money to do that?" He knows I do.

"Yes, I do and you know it. I can bring you a lot of American businesses, including the military. First, I need to know how it's going with Ana's case. She hasn't really talked to me much. You never responded to my text message last month."

"Ana seems to be up to something, she's at your Grandmother's place working on it. She appears to feel the tails on her, but Jonathon has also put a tail on her. My gut says something is up. We've doubled the surveillance on her and I'm personally keeping an eye on both of them for you."

"Mine too. How is he?"

"Like hell, please call him soon. He's taking a couple days to do some research he said would take him some time."

"I need to get this all figured out. I'm talking to both of my bosses today. I'll have my solicitor get into contact with you so that we can start drawing up the papers. Please keep this between us."

"Only for a little bit, Maya. I can't lie to him."

"Okay, goodbye, Joshua." I hang up and head out to the office to start my resignations. I'll tell Derek tonight, I hope he doesn't get upset with me. Maybe he'll come with me. I don't know how Greg will take it.

"DEREK, WE NEED TO TALK."

My day went as I thought it would. Both my bosses tried to stop me, but with everything going on, they expected it.

"What's up, sexy?"

"I'm moving to London. I can't be away from him anymore. He is my life. If being with him puts him in danger, I'll be there to get between him and that bullet."

"Then I guess it's time for me to leave too."

"What?"

"After this December, I decided I'm tired of living in the past. I will put myself in front of any bullet you try to jump in front of. I'm going with you."

"You know I love you right?"

"Yeah I know, sexy. I love you too."

The rest of the evening we make plans for hopefully a bright future.

I still haven't been able to talk to Greg because he's in Europe on an assignment. I head to bed, finally feeling like this pain will end and my life will start again. The attack showed me that no matter if I'm with him or not, he'll be in danger. At least with me at his side, we have a chance. I want to call Ana in the morning, instead, as I start to fall asleep, I receive an email from her.

***To: marron_krav***

***From: Analovesmaya_preston***

***Maya,***

***Please pick me up at BA2329 in City of Brotherly Love, March 4. Don't tell anyone?***

***Love you,***

***A***

***PS he misses you!***

Okay, this is seriously cryptic. Oh well, she's my best friend and I told her I'd be there. She hasn't used the cell phone ever.

The next morning I call out sick for work. I grab a go bag from my closet, along with two burner phones. I open my gun safe and pull out two different calibers of Sigs, my two service weapons, and several knives. Out of the closet, I pull my SR-25 and plenty of ammo for them all. Yep, I'm that paranoid girl.

After the shooting at Duncan and Joshua's building, and both of the attacks, I made sure I always carried a piece on me, but today I feel the tension in the air around me. I'm fully decked out in tactical pants with my shit-kicking steel-toe boots, a body hugging sports bra, Henley t-shirt, and a hoodie. I slip my knife into the holster on my boot. I put on my belt with the double sheath for two of my throwing knives. I load it up. I clip on my holster for the twin punch knives and look at myself in the mirror. Yep, I'm almost ready. I braid my hair and twist that into a bun at the back of my neck. Now, I'm ready.

I take the elevator to the garage and throw the go bag in my toolbox. I check to see if my competition rifle and bigger gun are in their compartment, pull my sidearm out, and put it in the box under my seat. I check that I have two bulletproof jackets in the back and check my other gear. The body armor vest Duncan bought me for Christmas is in the back seat. I pull up the seat and place my SR-25 in its compartment. Of course, I always over pack, but you never know what you're going to run into.

Lack of sleep is seriously making me paranoid. I put one of the Sigs into my calf holster over my other boot, and a couple knives hidden in various areas on my body. I'm ready to kick some ass. I could use the fight.

I jump in my truck and head to Philadelphia. Only Ana would call it that, as non-American as she is, but if someone who doesn't know American slang was reading her email maybe they don't know. Maybe they'd have to look it up, it would give her, and I, more time.

As I get on the freeway, I notice a black sedan a couple cars behind me. Great time for a backup plan. Wish I could have ridden my bike, I could out run them with that for sure. I pull off the freeway into a truck stop, lock and set the alarm for my truck. I have one of my side arms under my hoodie in my back holster over my knives. I know walking into this truck stop armed is going to cause a few glances but I could care less right now. The sedan pulled into the McDonald's across the street. Yep, real obvious, assholes.

Truckers and other drivers look me up and down. I know I have the don't fuck with me look on my face but really, I brushed my hair and all today. When I walk into the back of the truck stop, I head for the coffee first, need some after my lack of sleep, and second, I need a distraction. I find it in the trucker checking me out.

"Hey, mister, can you help me?" I pull my badge and flash it to him. "Can you park your semi in front of that black truck to block the view from McDonald's?"

"Yes, ma'am." He walks out to do as I ask.

I pull out the burner phone and send the text that will get me all the help I need.

***Unknown #: 911 Rudolph has a red nose.***

***Duncan: Who's this?***

***Unknown #: Need your help, heading to Philly for sister. Being tailed. Forgive me. I miss you.***

***Duncan: I'm in D.C., pulling up to your flat. I decided to chase you.***

***Unknown #: Meet me at Philly airport at 1525 hours.***

***Duncan: I still love you.***

***Unknown #: I know. I never stopped loving you. I'll explain later.***

I do love him, it's true. I realized it at his condo and about an hour into my flight home. I was just too stubborn and couldn't figure out a way to make it work.

I was going to call Joshua today, but plans have changed, I needed to tell him how it went with my superiors. I hope that Duncan can make it. I hope he remembers my reference to Rudolph from lunch with Joshua. He's coming for me. God, I love that man. My heart lightens, but I need to stay focused. I hated confessing my love through text, but I wanted him to know just in case.

It's only a two and a half hour drive but it wasn't long enough for me to lose my tail. It's as if they know where I'm going. My diversion with the semi only helped for about thirty minutes. I can't figure out a way of losing them without showing my hand that I know they're there. I pull into the airport parking lot, take my second gun from my safe in the center console and put it next to my seat just in case. I pull my backup from my ankle and check it. I drop it on the floorboard, as I know I'll not be able to carry it in the airport. I want to take it but know that will draw too much attention.

I remove my hoodie and Henley, leaving me in my sports bra, and put on my standard issue vest, making sure my knives aren't visible because they'll be the only protection other than myself. I'm glad Abba made me take all those Israeli knife-fighting courses, I'm even happier David has kept me in practice. I know my heavy-duty body armor vest is stronger, but that's for Ana. I place it on the passenger seat.

I put my Henley and hoodie back on and check my appearance and the time. I'm glad I put my hair up, I'm going to need to be able to move without it in my way. I leave the third vest on the back seat. I leave my purse in the truck but pull my badges, and place them both in the hoodie pocket. My ID goes in my back pocket.

I run for the British Airways arrival area and begin my wait. It's at this point I figure out a way to get rid of my tail. I pull my Secret Service badge from the pocket and clip it to my jeans, leaving my D.C. Metro one in the pocket. Federal officers get more attention.

I'd tucked my Henley in so my vest doesn't show, plus I'm a strong believer in clothing helping with bullets. It's something that the older cops tell the younger ones, but I'll try anything. I know my standard issue vest won't work for point blank shots or even a high caliber sniper bullet.

Security was watching me carefully until they saw my badge. I'm now identified as a law enforcement officer, allowing me to walk around armed with the visible boot knife.

If only I had packed my guns instead.

## DUNCAN

My heart is about to beat out of my chest. Both of them are in danger. I call Joshua and clue him in. He's immediately cussing and getting the guys to run as much current information on Jonathon as they can. He hints that he has talked to Maya recently. He and I will be discussing his conversations with my girl.

He also helps get me some pull with the local police departments as I know when I catch up to my girl I'm going to have to rough someone up. He says they'll be heading out as soon as possible to help me. I pray I get to my girl before she does something stupid. She is so talented and smart, but she never thinks about that person that doesn't go by the rules.

I've spent the last three months working around the London area, trying to figure out my next move. I've missed her so much. This short time apart, with no contact, was far worse than the previous six months. I knew I was not going to be able to stay away from her much longer. She's my air and my very life.

I'm pulling into the Philadelphia airport and it's 1600 hours. I'm late. Please Lord, let them both be okay, I pray. My phone pings in my pocket.

# CHAPTER THIRTY-NINE

## MAYA

Ana steps out of the secure area, she has on dark sunglasses and a wig. How did TSA let her travel like that? Oh well, who knows. It's then that I see the swollen cheek and lip. I'm going to kill that son of a bitch. I notice two goons round the corner at the other end of the hall. I jump up, run to her, and pull her down another concourse.

"Hey, gorgeous, looks like I need to kill a fucktard," I say as I take her arm.

"I'm pregnant, Maya," she replies breathlessly.

"Fuck it all. Come on, we have company." I see a third guy come out of the same hall Ana did, damn she was followed from London. That's how they knew where I was heading.

"Ana, can you run?" I ask her, looking around for my next step.

"If I must."

"Sorry, sister, you must." We take off at a run. I pull my badge off my belt and flash it to security as we pass by. "Stop them. I'm Secret Service ERT, they're after my high value." I point to the goons following us.

The guards jump up to stop goon three, but one and two are gone. We make it to my truck when goons one and two walk up to us. I toss my burner phone to Ana. "Text the person I did earlier these exact words: 911 ERT. Parking lot two. Now."

"What does that mean?" she asks. I don't have time to explain entirely.

"Means I need you in my truck and drive off if they beat me. Put the vest on. My side arm is next to the seat and another on the floorboard. I love you, sister, tell him I love him too." I toss her my keys and walk up to the goons. Give me strength. I've been itching for a real fight for months. My internal fight song plays in my head as I walk up to them.

"Hello, boys, I need for you to back off. I'm a D.C. cop with a secondary badge with Secret Service, I don't think you're being paid enough for the check you're about to write with your asses," I say as I flash my Secret Service badge at them. I peek at my watch. It's two to four and he isn't here. I've trained for years to protect the ones I love, as I couldn't before.

I get in my stance as they walk up. I can tell who'll be the aggressor. He doesn't disappoint when he walks up, leaving the second guy to fall back and see what happens. Goon one throws a right cross, I redirect his punch and bend to go for the body. I give him several gut punches, then finish him with my knee to his chest and pull him back down to put his face into my knee. He falls to the ground, he's down but not out.

Goon two pulls his gun and points it at me and fires. I rush him, pull my knife from the back of my belt, and drop him with it landing in his throat. He never saw the knife even as it went into his throat. The blade is buried to the hilt. I'm not getting that one back. The bullet hits me in the upper left of my vest. I pull back to try to inhale from the shock of the pain.

Goon one is starting to rise and he pulls a gun too. Come on, damn motherfuckers, I'm not letting them have Ana. I grab one of my punch knives in my left hand as I take my second knife from the other side of my back.

"Girly, we didn't want to have to kill you, but you killed my friend, now you need to die." I pause at him calling me that. It reminds me of the attack at the gym. The bullet hits him between the eyes, swishing past me. I swing around, ready for another attack, as the second bullet hits him. All I see is Duncan rushing up to me. My breath catches as I lower my knives and he takes me into his arms.

"Oh bloody hell, baby, did he hit you?" I look down and see the blood from Goon one's broken nose on me.

"Nope, all his blood." Duncan wraps me tighter in his arms and kisses me like there's no tomorrow. I hear the sirens and the people, but I don't care. I don't tell him about the shot to the vest, I only feel the kiss I've waited three months for.

I hear Ana yelling and it pulls me from my fog. She stayed in the truck, she's frantically pointing to Goon three, whose gun is pointed at Duncan. I jump in front, feeling the bullet hit me in the chest as I throw my knife at him. Fuck that shit hurts. My left arm drops, my grip loosening on the punch knife. I hear it clang to the ground.

Both Duncan and Ana scream as I start to fall, and Duncan's gun goes off two more times. Oh hell, I can't believe I've been shot. Dammit! What a way to fuck up a good welcome to America kiss. I know my brain is flashing some crazy shit right now, but what the hell is wrong with me? I feel my body go cold and I'm out. Is death really this cold and quiet?

## DUNCAN

I couldn't believe my eyes when I saw her beat up the first guy. She was so smooth. I've seen Raul do Krav Maga for years, but I've never seen someone use it so well or make it look like a dance. The fact it was my girl made me proud and scared at the same time, making my gut twist.

When the second guy pulled his gun, I thought she'd stop. No, not my girl, she killed him with a knife she pulled so fast I barely saw her pull it from her back. Damn, that's my girl...my baby. Then the first guy came at her again, with a gun, I was finally close enough that I dropped him with one to the chest and one to the head. Not happening, bloody arsehole.

I couldn't get to my girl fast enough. The fact she's prepared to take me down shows her dedication in protecting my sister. I saw her body recoil after the first guy pulled his gun, so I expected the blood to be hers. Then what does the woman do after kissing me, she throws herself in front of a bullet meant for me and throws another knife. I drop him with another double tap, and her knife embeds in his chest.

My girl is in my arms and falling to the ground. Please let this be a nightmare. My mind flashes back to Christopher, I need to focus on checking on her. The two bullets I put in that arse aren't enough, I want to get up and unload my mag into him, but my girl is struggling. We fall to the ground, her in my arms, me on my knees.

I see her struggling for breath, that's when I see the first hit to her upper left shoulder area. The second shot was direct to her heart. The shots are too close, the vest probably failed. My mind is screaming no repeatedly. I won't lose her now.

My mind flashes back again to losing Christopher, how close this is to that. I shake my head and struggle with the fog. I love this woman. I'll die before I lose her. I reach down, check her airways, and pull the Velcro on the shoulders of her vest through her sweatshirt.

"Baby. Honey, I love you. Come on! NO! I can't live without you. I love you. Say something, baby, please," I scream, my sister is on her knees crying and screaming for help.

Maya lost consciousness as soon as we hit the ground. I'm hoping it's just from the air being knocked from her. I can feel the vest under her clothes is still mostly intact. The only problem I notice is the body armor vest I bought her for Christmas is on my sister, not her. That was a point blank shot from a .45 caliber revolver to an already compromised vest.

"Oh God, Duncan, all the blood. Help her, she's dying. Don't let her die, Duncan, we need her." I start to look for the source of all the blood. I pull a knife from my boot, slip it down the front of the sweatshirt, and thank the God above. I cut the shirt underneath until I get to her vest. It's destroyed by both hits.

"Come on, baby, it's the shock. Open your eyes. I know it hurts, but open your eyes so I know there's not any internal damage. Please, baby!" I beg and the smells hit me.

I lock down my emotions and the memories before I go back there. The blood, the air, the screaming, the pain of another loss. Please God, not my girl.

"I'll have you know this motherfucking shit hurts." She gasps and I know exactly what she means. I've taken a couple to my vest too, it hurts. I feel my heart calm.

"I know, baby, be careful, you could have some bruised or broken ribs. You took two to the vest." I make her stay down until the paramedics can check her.

"Bruised ribs, Duncan, she's shot in the chest. She's bleeding! She's dying! She can't die. I need her, I'm pregnant." My sister is yelling.

"What?" I look at Ana like she's got two heads.

"Ana, you need to calm down, the blood isn't all mine. I have a vest on, it knocked the wind out of me, that's all, sister." I see Maya's look of concern though, and know there's more damage than what she's saying.

"Oh thank God, Maya!" Ana gasps out.

"Did my sister just say she's pregnant? And did you really throw yourself in front of a bullet for me?" I try to change the subject from the fact my girl is lying to me about how much pain she's in.

"Yeah about that...I'm sorry, you were right. I'm sure I want you. I'll live in London or wherever you want to live. I love you, Duncan," she says as she still struggles for breath.

My own breath stops, my heart slows. "Baby, are you sure?"

"I'm sure, I've already spoken to my superiors at both jobs, and Joshua and I spoke yesterday."

"Jobs? You got the job with Secret Service?"

"I'll explain later. Help me up."

"No, stay here until the paramedics check you out."

"Reach into my hoodie pocket, both my badges are there, pull them out." She looks down to see her exposed vest. "Okay, check the ground and see where they fell." I find them, the first is her Metro PD ID with a badge, and the second makes my breath stop again.

"Baby, Secret Service ERT?"

"I told you I interviewed with them, but I'm not a close protection agent, I'm a sniper with them." She struggles to laugh.

"We will discuss this, baby."

"Hands up." The officers yell from around us.

"Metro PD and Secret Service," Maya says breathlessly.

I'm worried that she's got broken ribs, she's having trouble taking a full breath. I can see a small amount of blood trickling down to her hip where she's lying on the ground.

"We got a call from Securities International Incorporated in London, but they failed to tell us about the dead bodies," One officer says.

"We had no choice. I'm not carrying and he'll give you his sidearm," she answers, while looking in my eyes. She's trying to project she needs to follow the rules by me giving up my weapon, but I can see she's concerned about me being unarmed.

I lean down and kiss her forehead and whisper, "I got a couple backups, baby."

"Thank God," she whispers back as she again struggles for breath. I reach her right shoulder to remove the Velcro more on her vest, giving her some room.

"I need to check her. Can you step back?" A female paramedic is trying to move me away from Maya.

"You're going to have to check her with her on my lap right where she is. I'm not letting her go, ma'am. Plus we don't want to jostle her too much."

"Okay, but with all this blood—"

"Not mine!"

"Not hers." We both say at the same time, and I smile down at her.

"Can you tell me what's going on, please?"

"Double GSW to the vest, pain with a deep breath. Pain in the left side of my chest and shoulder. I also feel a little trickle of blood going down my side," Maya says very clinically. She whispers the last part so

Ana doesn't hear and panic again. It's what I thought, she either has broken or very bruised ribs. The blood bothers me, though.

I look at the bullet implanted in her vest, right over her heart. I could have lost her. The bullet mushroomed, but still looks like it partially broke through the vest.

"Ma'am, she lost consciousness for about two minutes after the hit."

"Okay, I need to check your vitals, officer, and remove your vest if we can."

"I'll help." I carefully pull the sleeves of her sweatshirt off her arms. With my knife, I finish cutting the front of her shirt and the sleeves so it falls off her.

I see the knife in a side pocket of her vest. I also see two more in her boots. The paramedic pulls them to hand to Ana, along with the side long Bowie under her right arm and the punch knife from the ground. The paramedic starts to pull the Velcro straps on her left side and I watch as she flinches and the blood begins to flow more.

"Ana, take her knives to the truck, okay." I want Ana away when they pull the vest off.

"Hold up, I only have a sports bra on. I also have another knife in my buckle, another punch on my belt, and one hidden deeper in my clothing. Honey, put my hoodie over me."

"It's okay, Officer Aaron. I'll be gentle, and after I confirm there isn't anything serious, we'll get you on a board and gurney then in the ambulance." The paramedic offers.

"I don't want to go to the hospital," Maya says full of determination.

"Sweetheart, please, for me. I'll get Ana in your truck and we'll follow you. Please!" I beg, I need to make sure she's okay before we go any further with helping Ana.

"Okay, but only cause you asked nicely." She groans as the paramedic pulls the vest from her chest carefully. My eyes zone in on the indent in her vest and down at her chest, the bullet hit with enough force she's already bruising. But the problem is the Kevlar started to fail with the second shot and there was a partial intrusion into her body. I see the small fragment of bullet and Kevlar that broke off and impacted into her skin. The paramedic rubs across her ribs, watching Maya's face carefully. She places gauze over the fragments so they can be removed at the hospital. She continues to rub along Maya's side.

"Ow, right there!" The paramedic rubbed right under Maya's left breast. I can't see much except the look of pain on her face. The paramedic continues with her assessment, when she presses on Maya's left shoulder, she groans again.

"Okay, sit tight, I'll be right back," she says as she stands to leave. The paramedic talks to another at the ambulance and I see them pull the backboard off the gurney. I look at Ana as she walks back up to us. She's as concerned as I am.

"Why is Ana wearing your body armor vest and you the regular one?" I ask, knowing that the vest I bought her is the strongest body armor made.

"Maya told me to put it on," Ana says defensively. It's then I realize why my girl gave my sister her heavy-duty vest and wore her standard issue one.

"Bugger! Maya, I love you, but we will be discussing your severe lack of self-preservation."

"What?" she says innocently, she knows I figured it out. Just then, two cops walk over to her truck to start opening the doors to search it.

"Ana, can you give me my keys?" She pushes the key fob to lock the vehicle.

"Hey, what's the big idea?" one of the cops says.

"Can't have you going through my truck without a warrant, gentleman," she tells them.

"What about the tool box?"

"Same." I look at her curiously.

"I'll tell you later," she murmurs.

The paramedic walks over with two more. They ask me to move again. This time I comply because I know what's going to happen now. They proceed to put Maya on the backboard and then lift her onto a gurney. She groans when they lift her. I really hope it's only bruised ribs, but I think they're broken or cracked. She's loaded into the ambulance. While they're assessing her again, I walk to my rental and get out my go bag and pack. I then walk back to check the progress, they decide she needs to be seen in the ER, as her breath sounds aren't where they should be. They believe she has a broken rib too. Plus they need to remove the projectiles from her chest.

Ana and I walk to the truck and proceed to follow them to the nearest hospital. I look back at the bodies and carnage we left. I feel like there will be more of this before this ends. I'll protect her with my own life. She wants to be with me now and I'll keep her there. I know that this was what Christopher meant when he said it's worth it. I also know I'll not live in fear of the life she's chosen, it's what we both want and need.

I send a quick text to Joshua, knowing he's in the air and on his way here. I explain the attack and us being on our way to the hospital. I need her in my arms again. I need to know she's okay.

# CHAPTER FORTY

## MAYA

I've just been discharged from the hospital. Two fractured ribs, several small shallow punctures from the fragments, and more bruises, including my shoulder. Philly PD wants us to stay, but I use my last favor with the Secret Service and my new Securities International partnership to go home. Greg helped pull strings to get me home too. He's worried and upset, he knows I put myself in danger.

Ana and Duncan have stayed by my side. I refused pain meds for now so I can drive and help Duncan protect Ana. What's Jonathon involved in? My stalker and Jonathon have got to be connected because they were after Ana, but what they said still haunts me. They called me girly just like the last two attacks. My mind is spinning with scenarios.

My captain has suspended me, pending an investigation. Guess I'll be getting up early to meet with him. The best part is security footage shows me identifying myself as police and Secret Service. I notified every guard we passed with my badge.

The problem is my captain knows me and I walked into a situation

I thought could go sideways with no backup and without notifying local PD. Good thing they never searched my truck, they don't know how bad it could have gotten. They made me strip down because of the goon's blood all over me. That's when they found the knife in my bra.

The x-ray tech had me confirm I was completely unarmed before they did the x-rays. I laugh to think about it. Duncan didn't find it amusing, although, he knows me well enough to know I'm going to thoroughly arm myself if I can.

First time being shot sucks. Because the guy was carrying a .45 revolver is why I got hurt so bad. The lighter vest and the two shots also contributed to my injuries. I wouldn't change anything, I love Duncan, and I can't lose him. I feel calm with that thought.

"Come on, baby, just let me help you into the scrubs so we can get you home. Why won't you take the pain meds? I can drive."

"Big Guy, I love you, but not enough to trust your English driving with my truck." They let me keep my sports bra and thong, they didn't have any blood on them.

"Ha, thanks, baby. Love you too and I'll remember this when we get to London. I seem to remember someone liking my DBS."

"Oh, low blow, babe. I won't be able to go to London for a while. I have to meet with my captain and the ERT division chief. Then I'll have to meet with my superiors at the Secret Service. I think if Greg could ground me right now, he would. I'm going to lose part of my ass, hope you won't miss it."

"It will be all right. Joshua is flying in tonight to help you and he hired you an attorney."

"Really? That's very nice of him, but I'll have a union rep there too." I haven't told Duncan the extent of my involvement with Securities International. I'm waiting until I sit him down, I'll be his boss now.

"Baby, we got your back. Where's your sidearm hidden? That was crazy going in with only knives."

"I didn't want to keep flashing my badge or go through the extra security procedures to carry it through the airport. I hoped that they'd try something at the terminal. Plus, I didn't expect Goon Three to get off the plane with Ana. Besides, I did pretty damn good myself. I did hit two with my knives."

"Where's it at? I found two in your truck on the way here, but I know enough about you that they're not your actual sidearm."

"Well, to be honest, I have two sidearms, one issued by MPD and the other from Secret Service. However, you're right, the two in my truck are both my backups. My actual sidearms are in the safe in my truck. My rifle is also in it, in another safe."

"Okay, baby, let's get you ready to get out of here." He grabs the scrubs the nurse left me and comes to help me get dressed.

"Duncan, get out of here. I'll help her dress," Ana says.

"Sis, I've seen enough, I can help her."

"Both of you can help if you're going to fight about it." I laugh, and groan from the pain of laughing.

After finally getting dressed, I assure the Philly detectives we weren't leaving the country. We head out to the parking lot. As I come to my truck, I do a full walk around and check everything. My proximity alarm never went off, so I know that no one has put a tracker on my truck. I disengage the alarm and check my exterior boxes.

"Baby, you're making me think you don't trust my driving."

"Hilarious, I'm checking for trackers and to make sure no one has messed with my equipment."

"Baby, your proximity alarm was on."

"I know, but I'm worried. I feel like all we're doing is responding to Jonathon's threats. We need to be getting ahead of him. I feel like we're being watched."

I pull my go bag out, pull out another burner phone, and check my regular phone for messages. Derek has called, but I'm going to wait until we get closer to the condo before I call him. I have several missed calls from Greg too.

"Don't call your dad yet," I tell Ana.

I try to pull myself up into the driver's seat but can't without making the pain worse. Duncan walks up behind me and lifts me up. Before he sets me into position, he turns me and kisses me.

"I thought I lost you today. I wouldn't be able to survive that. Since you left me, I've learned how hard my life would be without you. Baby, I don't want to ever lose you," he tells me as he looks into my eyes.

"I know. Seeing that gun pointed at you, all I could think was if you die they better kill me too," I confess. He hugs me to him, being gentle with my ribs and arm.

"Come on." He turns me into the truck. He helps Ana into the backseat and then climbs into the passenger seat.

"Duncan, do me a favor."

"What?"

"Open that center console and make sure my lock box is secured." I know I'm paranoid, but really feel like not only am I being watched but that this isn't done.

"Okay. Why is your rifle in the boot instead of in here?"

"The boot? I love how you call the bed of my truck a boot. Isn't a boot a trunk?"

"Yes, the trunk is the boot. Answer my question why is your rifle in the boot?"

"Oh, that's just my competition rifle and my .50 Cal. My SR-25 is in a custom compartment in the back, under where Ana is sitting."

"Oh, baby, you talking firearms turns me on. You have a .50 Cal. Bugger me, baby, we're going to a range and playing one of these days."

"Yuck, I'm back here." We all laugh at Ana's statement.

"Okay, little momma, do I need to get you anything special to eat?"

"No, just food." We head to the closest fast food joint to feed her. We do the drive-thru so we don't have to get out.

# CHAPTER FORTY ONE

## MAYA

We head south, back to D.C. We have about an hour left of our drive when my cell goes off. I look at the screen on the dash. Damn it, I wish this motherfucker would go away. I pick up the phone and bypass the Bluetooth so Ana can't hear him.

"Well, you survived I see."

"Ya, dickhead! What do you want?"

"I want my wife, now, you cunt!"

"Now. Now. No name-calling. I put her on a plane heading west."

"Liar, I know she's in the backseat of that fancy truck. Put her on the phone now, Maya. I'll kill Duncan if you don't. He'd be dead if you didn't jump in front of the bullet. Such self-sacrifice, what a joke."

"No! So was it you that sent the guy to my gym to try to beat me up?" I signal Duncan to push Ana down in the seat.

I put my finger to my lips so they both stay quiet and activate the Bluetooth. I've started to slow down and merge off the freeway, watching my mirrors. Duncan bristled when I mentioned the attack at the gym. Joshua must not have told him.

"You listen up, you fucking bitch, if you didn't have a vest on both you and that meathead would be dead. As for the gym, that was a friend sending you a message. The guy wasn't supposed to rough you up so much. He just hated losing to a woman. I don't care what my boss wants, I'll kill you if I get the chance. You're more trouble than you're worth. I agree with our friend you need to be taught a lesson." I look at Duncan to make sure he stays quiet and to see how he reacts to the "boss" revelation. Someone is pulling Jonathon's strings, but my other stalker is a part of this too.

"Well, I'm hearing what you're saying, but again I sent Ana away. If I can keep her from you, I will. You don't scare me. Come and get me, asshole."

"Put my fucking wife on!" he yells. I see Ana flinch from the backseat.

"I can't." I see the tail get off with us. Damn this is bad. I accelerate back onto the freeway, taking the median in an attempt to lose the tail.

"YOU CUNT! I'll get my wife back. She has something of mine and I want it now."

"Hey Jonathon, be careful, your American is showing. I know you're not English; I know a little about you. You will leave Ana alone or I'll kill you."

"Fucking bitch, I won't say it again! I'll kill James if I don't get my wife back. Is that clear enough? Ana, do you want to lose another parent? How about that friend of yours, Greg, is it? One phone call from me and a friend who has been trying to teach you a lesson will kill anyone I want." I look over to see Duncan furiously texting and Ana is trying to sit up. I reach through the seats and push her back down. I bite my tongue to bleeding to avoid the groan of pain that could be a sign of weakness coming out.

"Okay, fucktard, you've done pissed me off. Goodbye." I hang up and focus on getting ahead of the tail by some distance.

We're still a good way from my service area. I know I could get assistance from the Baltimore PD. I'm driving at excessive speeds in hopes of attracting some police, but it doesn't work. I get to just outside of District 5 and open the center console and pull my radio off the top of the gun safe.

"Officer needs assistance," I say into the radio.

"Officer, what's your location? Please identify."

"This is Officer Aaron, badge number 365492 of the Metro ERT. I'm in a black Ford Raptor Crew Cab on US50, New York Avenue, and getting ready to cross the Anacostia. Need assistance with an aggressive driver following me, a four-door sedan, dark colored. Appears to be two individuals in it."

"Officer Aaron, a patrol car is diverting from South Dakota en route to your location. Don't engage if you can."

"I'm currently driving eighty-five, I'll be exiting at North Capitol Street Northeast."

"Officer Aaron, this is patrol Three-William-Ten, we've just gotten on the 50."

"Patrol Three-William-Ten, I'm passing you now. The vehicle is about three behind me."

"Officer Aaron, is that you?" Another responder cuts in.

"Ya man, where are you at?" Thank God he's listening in.

"Waiting at our exit, I'll call." My cell rings and I pick up the call through the Bluetooth.

"Hey, sexy, what's this with you getting your cherry popped without me? You know the rules. Besides Dad is pissed." He jokes, Duncan growls. "Whoa, what was that? Did they give you that male hormone shit to heal your wounds?"

"That was her boyfriend, wanker. Who the bloody hell is this?" Duncan growls.

"Ah, Duncan stop, that's Derek, he's joking."

"I know enough about what popping a cherry means, Maya."

"Ah...he's talking about me being shot."

"Hey, Duncan, do we need to have this talk again?" Derek's voice comes over the speaker. "I'm not interested in your girl, she can kick my ass. And it's about time you got on a plane to chase her down, she's driving me crazy. I can't keep taking her to bars and keep her from boarding a plane to London. Plus, no one will spar with her anymore, they're afraid of her kicking their ass."

"Derek, shut up!" I yell. "I'll see you at the condo." I hang up, now I have to explain Derek.

"Duncan, you know Derek is my partner, spotter, my best friend, and my roommate."

"I know, but that doesn't mean I have to like it. Why does he always have to pick you up?" Duncan growls and Ana sighs. She knows about Derek's and my relationship.

"He's like a big brother to me. Duncan, I explained to you in London about Derek's and my friendship. He has been anxious about me sinking again. Please, Duncan, don't be jealous of him. I love you! However, he's a crucial part of my life, too! These last few months, I wouldn't have survived without Derek or Greg. Please, Duncan, understand he's the only friend other than Ana I have. I swear that you're the only man I think of that way, but he's a part of my life that I won't give up."

"Okay, baby, I'll put up with him until we move to London."

"Thank you, Duncan, but he's moving with us. Ana, sit up and put the vest on the floor back on. Also, lift the large part of the seat next to you and use your thumb to open the gun locker under it."

"My thumb?" she questions as she lifts the seat and it locks into position.

"Yeah, it's a fingerprint scanner. Only yours, mine, and Derek's are programmed. Before you freak, Duncan, I'll add you tonight."

"Okay," she says as we pull into the underground parking garage, Derek hot on our tail in his Charger. I pull in next to our bikes and throw the truck into park. I open the center console and unlock the case, then remove both my Sigs and the shoulder holster. I groan as I try to put it on.

"Baby, stop, you're going to hurt yourself more." Duncan grabs both of my Sigs and shoves them into my go bag, then pulls his Sig and starts to get out.

I turn around to Ana. "Hand me my rifle." She does. She then gives me a couple mags and I load one and chamber a round. I put the extras into my cleavage and the pockets of the scrubs.

"That's fucking hot, baby." I giggle at Duncan as he closes his door. I turn to see Derek is suited up and at my back door.

"Hey, sexy, who's the hottie? Wait, you're Ana. Your picture is all over Maya's condo. We finally meet, gorgeous." He bows and smiles at her.

Duncan walks around to help me out. He helps me strap my SR-25 to my back, cinching the harness without it hurting me too much. I reach into the go bag and pull out my Secret Service issued Sig .9mm, clear it and cock it for ready.

Derek reaches into the toolbox, unlocks the special chamber, and removes the .50 Cal, along with a couple of mags for it. He pulls it over his body and lets it rest down his back. He has the strap of his M4 wrapped around his right arm and the gun in his hand. If we need the .50 Cal, some serious shit's hitting the fan.

Derek has been with me for so long I forget how much he has gone through. He looks like an avenging angel right now with all his weapons. He's lethal and will fiercely protect Ana and me. He jokes that I kick his ass, but he's a black belt in Brazilian jiu-jitsu. Between him and his father, I never lack for learning new fighting techniques.

"Let's do this." I set the alarm on my truck as we walk away. My radio chirps, letting us know that the two guys in the tail were taken into custody, finally a small break. My cell goes off in my pocket but I can't take the time to answer it. I'll call him back later. After a few seconds, Derek's starts to go off. He looks at me and rolls his eyes.

"He isn't going to wait long, let's get this parade started," he says with a smile and nods at Duncan and me.

"Duncan, is Daddy safe?" Ana asks, causing me to stop and look at her.

"Yes, Joshua sent two guards and is moving him to a safe house."

"Thank God!"

I see Duncan has my go bag in his hand. I can't let my other service pistol out of my sight.

We make it to the elevators—me leading, with Ana in the middle, and the guys in the back. As the elevator door closes, I see someone step into the garage.

"Well damn, there are a lot of people at his beck and call."

"Saw him too. Let me off here," Duncan says, pressing the button for the next floor.

"What? You can't stop him by yourself?"

"Baby, I've got this. Get Ana into your flat, I know which one." Before he hands Derek my go bag, he pulls out my Sig MCX semi-auto rifle. "Baby, we really need to talk about your choice of toys." He smiles at me and leans down to kiss me.

"How do you know which condo is mine?"

"Baby, you might not have seen me for three months, but I saw you. I've been keeping an eye on you from a distance by the cameras; Timothy patched me into them. You're all I've needed. I'll see you shortly. You won't even miss me." He kisses my forehead and looks into my eyes.

I feel something inside me crumble. Oh God, please, don't take him too. He looks to Derek and nods.

"I love you, Duncan, come back to me."

"Well, it's about damn time you admitted that, sexy," Derek pipes in. I stick my tongue out at him.

Duncan jumps off on the main floor, while we continue up to my twelfth-floor condominium. As we're climbing, I hand my gun to Ana so I can put my go bag across my body. I pull out my MPD service weapon and put it into the back of the scrubs, thank goodness they're tied tight. I take the gun back and get ready. I feel the pull on my shoulder and ribs from the extra weight, but I want Derek to be able to maneuver easier.

When the elevator opens, Derek takes the lead and sweeps his side. I step out and sweep mine as best as I can. We start down the hall toward my condo with me in the rear. My door appears fine, so I unlock while Derek keeps a lookout. I'm worried about Duncan but try to focus on my task. I enter my condo, disengage the alarm, and proceed to the windows.

"Ana, stay in the hall with Derek until I shut down the blinds."

I grab the controller for the blinds and start closing them. I walk to all the rooms and close up the blinds in each room. My bedroom, the dining room, and living room are all on the most exposed side with the most windows. I love my view, but I can't have another sniper or dumbass taking a shot at me. I'd do it, so I know how to stop them.

At Derek's room, I hit the switches on the light switch to shut his blinds too. Derek stays at the door, waiting to engage the alarm until Duncan comes up. He turns to Ana.

"Okay, I sleep on the left on my side with my leg bent as so, you can spoon up to me," Derek says to her.

"Are you using cheesy movie lines on my best friend, Derek?" I ask

"I was trying." At Ana's confusion, Derek shakes his head. "Ghost-busters 2."

There's a knock on the door, Derek checks the security feed and unlocks the door, letting Duncan in. I breathe a sigh of relief, and then remember I have fractured ribs. Ow!

Duncan walks to his sister and hugs her, then comes to me. He lifts my go bag off me and disengages the cinch on my SR to put it on the coffee table. He gives me a look of confusion, wondering why I have it now.

"Why do you have this bag again?"

"It had my other service weapon in it, plus, I wanted Derek to be able to move freely."

"Okay, baby, time for you to get something to eat and relax. Joshua and three of my mates will arrive shortly to help."

"I don't have enough room for everyone."

"Maya, Ana can have my room, but first, give me the deets," Derek says.

"The what?" Duncan asks

"Derek is funny, well he thinks he is. He wants to know what's going on. You tell him, honey, while Ana and I get food."

"Maya, let me put something together. You look like you're about to topple over," Ana says.

"I won't lie, this shit hurts, but I can't just sit still."

I look at my phone and notice the multiple texts. I send Greg a quick note that I'm fine and will call as soon as I can. I hope that keeps him satisfied until we get settled.

"It's perfectly fine, besides, I love your flat," Ana says, pulling me from my phone.

"Thanks, I'm going to miss it." We walk into my kitchen. My condo is mostly open with a large gourmet kitchen.

"Maya, I'm so happy you want to move to London. I also love that you and Duncan are happy, but I know you. Are you okay? Are you ready for this? Have you told my brother everything?"

"Are you worried I'm going to hurt Duncan? I really care about him. I love him. These last three months have been a living hell for me. I'd rather be with him and deal with my fears than be without him again. I've told him a lot but not everything. I'll tell him."

"He's not leaving you. He isn't with you for the money either."

"I know, but it's the unknown I worry about. Now enough about me, how are you?"

"I need to eat, my little bean is hungry."

"I can't believe you're pregnant, but I'm here for you, always. You, Duncan, and your father are my family now. Derek and Greg have also become a part if you'll accept them. Now we have little bean. How far along are you?"

"Three months, I'm just about done with the first trimester. Jonathon doesn't know. After I found out, I started getting everything I needed to get away. I can't have my baby in that situation."

The security phone from the lobby rings, interrupting our conversation. Who could possibly be stopping by at this hour? I know it's not Greg yet.

"Hello, George." I say into the receiver. I wish they'd fired him after all the crap he pulled with Carl and Lawrence, but I understand why the association only reprimanded him. We never figured out who on the force was on the take.

"Yes, Ms. Aaron, there are four gentlemen here in the lobby. The only name I can get is a Mr. Donovan and his associates. He won't give me the names of the other three gentlemen."

"Let them up, George. Put Mr. Donovan on my visitor log, also add

Duncan Preston too, please." I'd add Ana, but I don't want further confirmation for Jonathon.

"Yes, ma'am. Are you sure you don't want me to add these other gentlemen?" I know he's fishing for names.

"No, just Mr. Donovan and Mr. Preston."

A few minutes later the doorbell rings. I look at Duncan and Derek, they're ready just in case. I pull the gun from the back of my scrubs.

"Open up, mate, it's your drinking buddies. Get off the wee lassie." I laugh and Duncan winks at me. I open the door and put my gun back into my waistband and greet our guests.

"Well hello, aren't you a bonnie lass. Wait a minute...I saw her first, Duncan." A tall blond, muscular guy says as he waggles his eyebrows.

"Hello, come in. We will introduce ourselves once everyone is in."

"As long as I get your number, lassie, I don't care what your name is," the blond says and Duncan growls at him.

"Well, that's a good sign. Pulled your willy out and stepped up I see," the blond says to Duncan.

The guys all file in with Joshua coming in last. I recognize them all, even the blond with the mouth. He was the guy trying to pick me up in front of the hotel after the Israeli gala. Joshua's eyes search the room and when he sees Ana's back in the kitchen, he visibly relaxes. He takes me in his arms and gently kisses my cheek.

"Glad to see you and the Big Guy patched up your relationship. I was getting tired of picking his arse up at the pubs." He chuckles. "Heard about the shooting, how are the ribs?" He leans closer and whispers, "The solicitors got all the paperwork arranged today and filed. It's official. Also, I never mentioned the other attack to Duncan." I sigh in relief.

"I fractured a couple, have a couple lacerations that didn't need stitches, and have a very bruised shoulder from the residual shock. Other than that, pretty good. Thanks for taking care of him. He heard but hasn't questioned me yet about it."

"What, Big Guy, you beating on your girl already? S&M is consensual, not you taking the lead without her permission," the blond man says. The gasp and crash get everyone's attention.

"Shut it, Ian, you bloody bastard." Duncan hollers as he beats me to the kitchen.

"Ana, it's okay, it was a joke in bad form. They don't know." As all the new guys look in the kitchen, the cuss words start to fly.

"Bugger me, I'll kill the bloke that laid a hand on her," the blond says.

"He's dead," Joshua exclaims. I know he only saw her back, but now her face confirms his worst fears.

"Damn, that motherfucking maggot is dead," Raul says in Spanish.

"I'll bury his money and make it hard for him to ever get money again," Timothy says.

"Duncan, we're on this," Joshua says again. I push past them all, holding my ribs to keep from jostling them.

"Come on, Ana, let's get you off center stage." I walk her to the sofa and direct her to sit. Duncan and the others follow.

"Okay, introductions, this here is my sister, Ana; Maya, my girlfriend; and Derek, her partner. These guys are my team. Joshua, my boss, Raul, Timothy or Tim, and finally Ian." Duncan says as he points to each. I know the introductions are for Derek and Ana's benefit.

"Welcome to my home and thank you for coming," I say. I pick my rifle up from the coffee table and start for my room with it.

"Oh, lassie, let us big guys handle the firearms." I hear the snicker from Derek and watch as Duncan and Joshua bump each other. Okay, they're letting me take care of this in my way. I plant a cute smile on my face.

"Okay, big guy, Ian is it?" I look over at Duncan and wink at him. "The proper American term for this situation is, 'you can have MY gun when you pry it from MY cold, dead fingers.' Also, if I hadn't fractured a couple of my ribs earlier today, I'd show you what happens to most men that underestimate me. Today alone I made one goon cry like a girl after I used his ass to wipe up his own blood and I killed a second with a throwing knife. Now if you want, I'm pretty sure if you ask my partner over there, he'll confirm that I don't sweat 600-meter shots. If you don't mind, I'm going to put this away while you pick up your jaw, then I'm going to order some food for us. Again, as I told Joshua when we first met, we can whip them out, I'll still kick your ass, but my honey over there gets very jealous. He doesn't like me to see another guy's junk, plus as a second-degree black belt in Krav Maga, I don't want to kill you."

"Bloody hell, Big Guy, your lassie just gave me a stiffy."

"Sod off, you tosser. She needs to eat and take some pain meds. Furthermore, don't make me kick your arse right here," Duncan exclaims.

"How'd she fracture her ribs?" Raul asks Duncan.

"Barking lass took two bullets to the vest, one meant for me," he growls.

"What?" the guys all say.

"Time to talk about this. Timothy, unpack your gear, start the searches, and set up the feeds," Joshua says and then looks at each of us with orders.

"Maya, you and Ana take a seat, Derek, order food. Duncan, stop being an alpha."

"So, I'm taking orders from him now, sexy?" Derek asks me.

"Please, Derek, for now. I'll explain in a few." I only partly explained our now involvement with Securities International.

"Okay. Anything for you."

I take a seat and wait. Duncan took my gun to my room. It's Ana's turn to tell us all why we're gathered here. I'll do whatever it takes to protect her. I think I already proved it, but I'll do much more for her if asked.

# CHAPTER FORTY-TWO

## MAYA

I sit back and watch Ana look around uncomfortably. I've never asked her about Joshua but from the looks of it, they are going to play like they don't know each other.

Everyone turns to look at her. Her shoulders hunch, her posture caving in on itself. She is going to close up and not talk, but I need her to tell us. It will be a step toward her healing, she needs to do this. She looks at me and I reach out to take her hand. I hope she knows I'm offering her strength and support.

"What do you want to know, Mr. Donovan?" she asks shyly.

"Mrs. Davidson, how about you tell me a little about your husband?" he asks.

"My husband, Jonathon, works for a consulting firm. He works with foreign diplomats. Mostly, he met them through my father's connections to the British Consulate in Tel Aviv. I know he has worked with some Pakistani, Ukrainians, some Palestinians, and I believe some men from the Philippines and even here in the States. His job is highly stressful and he can get angry. I decided several weeks ago that I needed to get out. Last evening I got on a plane to come to Maya. I guess he's not happy, as Maya says." She presses her other hand gently to her face.

"Mrs. Davidson, can I call you Anabel?"

"No, but you can call me Ana."

"Ana, what did Jonathon mean he 'wants it back'?" I ask her. She shakes her head.

"Can you ask me another question? I'm not ready to answer that question."

"Ana, we need to know what we're up against to protect you," Joshua says

"I'll not go back to him. If you don't help me, Maya gave me enough money to disappear, and I will."

"Ana, we aren't asking you to go back. We won't judge. I'll not judge. I want to protect you," he says as he kneels in front of her and he takes her hand in his.

"I met Jonathon at university. He was such a gentleman when we met. I tried to tell him I wasn't interested. I was seeing someone else at the time, but he'd always be waiting for me. When that relationship ended, we saw more of each other. I began to suspect he wasn't truthful with me. I never met any of his family. He'd say he was raised in London but didn't know his way around it. He'd say words like Maya does. The first time he hurt me I can't talk about right now. After our engagement, he beat me so severely, I had a hard time hiding the bruises from Daddy. In December, the beatings got worse. I had to stay home to hide the damage. Finally, in January, I found out I was pregnant. I won't raise my baby around him. I need to make sure he doesn't take my baby from me or hurts my family." She pauses and takes a deep breath. "He has meetings at the flat sometimes, so I recorded a few of them. Also, I copied his emails, paperwork, and some videos. They're all hidden somewhere safe and he wants them back."

"You took the documents?"

"No, I copied them, then gave some of them to a friend who works for the Post."

"What!" Duncan and I exclaim. Joshua grabs her hand again to focus her on him.

"What's the name of the firm Jonathon works for? Do you know anyone's names? Also, where's the information hidden?"

"It's called Consulting Incorporated, I think. I wasn't allowed to go to work functions. The only names I know are Lawrence Andrews and Stephan Landers, they'd come to the flat for meetings sometimes. Lawrence is my Uncle Marcus's nephew. Something happened in December that made Jonathon mad at Lawrence. There's another man that calls Jonathon a lot but I don't know his name, he calls him Sir. Another American, an angry one started calling too. I don't know any more than that couple. The documents and emails have some names attached. I've overheard him talking to a couple of different men that scare him. The evidence is hidden back in London, I can't tell you where yet. It's the only collateral I have to protect myself and my baby."

The phone for downstairs rings, everyone except Ana and I jumps up. Derek answers, and grants access to the deliveryman. Joshua hands him some cash to cover for his men. After the deliveryman leaves, Duncan brings a plate to both Ana and me.

"Ana, does Jonathon know you're pregnant?" Joshua asks.

"No."

"Your father is safe for now and we need to keep you safe."

"My friend at the Post was killed last week. Jonathon threatened to kill Daddy and Duncan if I ever left him. He'd tell me that he'd make sure that Maya was hurt real bad, but he needed her alive. He also knew about Derek and Greg, he threatened them too."

"I won't let anything happen to you. I promise!" His eyes search hers and Ana drops her gaze so he can't read her feelings. He still cares for her, but she is so broken now I don't know if she can care for him too.

"Hey, Bossman, she's right about the reporter for the Post, although, the reports are he died in a car crash," Timothy says, interrupting the quiet of everyone eating.

"Okay. Maya, tomorrow I'm going with you as a representative of our solicitor and the company. We have an attorney on retainer here also if necessary. Mr. Flemish has arranged everything for you." Joshua starts giving orders.

"I won't need you. I'll have a union rep. Hiring Mr. Flemish to handle all my legal matters, plus the company, was a good idea, he's earning his money now." I laugh.

"You're a partner in my firm. I will not have them smearing your name. In fact, how about we say you were acting on the company's behalf when you went to go get Ana? Plus, after the other attack, they're going to be watching you closer."

"I already told them I was just picking up a friend. I identified myself as a police officer and Secret Service agent. They'll probably have a problem with conflict of interest. I do know the previous attack is connected to today's attack, Jonathon all but admitted he knows who did it. I'll take whatever help you offer though, something isn't right with what went down."

"Okay."

"Wait, Joshua, did you just say Maya is a partner with the company?" Duncan asks, and all eyes focus on Joshua and me.

"Yes. She bought into the company with equal shares today." The whole room hushes. His men won't question him, although Duncan might be upset because I didn't tell him myself.

"Maya, is this right?" Yep, saw this coming.

"Yes, when we talked yesterday I offered to buy in. You wanted me to work with you, right?"

"Yes, I do want you to work for us, baby. Can you afford to buy into the partnership though?"

"It's done. Don't worry, Big Guy." I smile at him and watch him calm instantly.

I look over at Ana. She doesn't know how strong she really is. I watch Joshua watching her. Him professing to protect her with his very life should've signaled Duncan, but he's so focused on me right now.

"Timothy, get a hold of James, ask him who he introduced Jonathon to. Also, run a more in-depth check into Jonathon's latest meetings." Timothy nods and starts working on his laptops. Joshua turns to me after giving that order. "Maya, what can you tell me about the attackers?"

Work mode, I've got this. I sit up straighter, feeling the pull in my ribs. I push my watch into my wrist, Derek steps up, knowing what I'm doing.

"East coast accents, trying to cover them by pretending they were southern, they carried .45 revolvers. The one that got off the plane with Ana was supposed to be detained by TSA but was able to get away. All had no IDs on them according to Philly PD. The first shooter Duncan shot called me girly, just like the guy that attacked me at the gym did, and the guy from Duncan's condo."

"Good. Anything, Duncan?"

"No formal military training, although, they appeared to have some formal training with the guns. The bloke that shot Maya did a center mass shot. Other than what Maya said, I didn't talk, I just killed. The one that shot Maya was not wearing a vest. She buried a knife in his chest before I dropped him. Now tell me about this other attack?"

"Wait, can I interrupt?" Ian asks. "Did you say she buried a knife in a git's chest? After she buried one in another's throat? Bossman, she sounds as good as you with knives." I smile at him.

"Not right now, Ian," Joshua gruffly replies. He's all business now too.

"Duncan, a guy was sent to my gym to challenge me to a fight. I thought we were just training, but he attacked the gym owner and me. When I finally took him down and handcuffed him, the cops took him away. He was killed that night in a gang fight in the jail. I never got to question him. He told me he'd kill you if I didn't stay away from you, and Ana would be hurt unless I stopped my investigation into Jonathon. After the note I received at your flat, I knew you weren't safe, even with me away from you. They're going to use you against me, just like with Ana. I won't let that happen. When I got home that same night, my second knife that was stolen was stuck in my door with a note about killing someone and hurting another for me. We found out that David's shooting was about me not him."

"Anything else, Maya, I see you chewing on something," Joshua asks as he lowers his brows and gives a hard look to Ian to keep him quiet.

"I've been doing my own checking on Jonathon. He has many American mannerisms and I'd almost say Midwest slang. He moved to London about seven years ago, before that there isn't any record of him. I used my Secret Service credentials to do a more in-depth look. Jonathon Davidson didn't exist before he moved to London. I can't find out anything else about him, yet. He lost all his British when he was yelling at me on the phone. I'd like to put him in my crosshairs. When Jonathon called me earlier, he suggested that his boss didn't want me dead. I'm a part of this in a way too. I want to know why and to what ends. The best man at the wedding, Stephen, a loser that I ended up relocating his junk for him, has since called me and hinted he knows where I live and where I've been. I've been under surveillance. Also, this crap with Lawrence calling and stalking me is getting out of hand. We found out the attacker at the gym was an ex-cop from the Philadelphia area. I wonder if the detectives investigating my shooting knew him or are dirty too. There were two occupants of the vehicle that followed us from Philly and a third showed up here. Where's Jonathon getting all these men? There's someone bigger up the food chain yanking chains and paying bills. Plus, this second stalker has hinted he knows about the other."

"The one we saw in the garage ran off when I tried to confront him. Went through the lobby, never got eyes on him again," Duncan says.

"Babe, did you growl? You're supposed to use your words." I joke with Duncan.

"Hysterical, baby."

"Also, my stalker goes by the name Sir."

"Maya, can Timothy keep his set up in your dining room? Raul and Ian, start your exterior surveillance. Ana, why don't you go lie down. You too, Maya, take some pain meds and relax."

"Tim, the dining room is yours. If you guys need any weapons, there's a gun safe in my room if you need anything. If you can ride bikes, you can use mine."

"Mine is off limits, sorry, I don't share my girl." Derek jokes.

"No, we flew over in the private jet. No TSA searches. I think they should just ground pound, no bikes. Besides, what I saw of yours, it's too flashy for what we need tonight."

"Hey, I like my toys." I groan as I try to get up off the sofa. Duncan reaches out and gently lifts me.

"Okay. Come on, Ana, let's change the sheets in Derek's room and get you settled."

"I'll help her, you can barely move that arm," Joshua adds in.

"Well, let me show you where the sheets are. Duncan, can you help me get out of these scrubs and get into the shower?" I smile at him slyly.

"Okay, baby." His smile is just as sly; he wants what I'm offering just as much as I want it.

After I give Joshua clean sheets for the spare room, I pull out extra pillows and blankets for the others. I also show them where the sleeping bags are. Tomorrow they might have to get a hotel room. Duncan follows me into my room.

"Baby, come here." I walk into his arms.

"Duncan, you know I'm sorry, right? I was just so scared after that attack at your flat. The note said I had twenty-four hours. I'm also afraid of you not being there, not you leaving by choice, but by one of these many assholes. I've been alone for such a long time. After Carl told me I couldn't do relationships, I believed him, thinking I was the fucked up one. Plus my parents' deaths have me so scared, they went to dinner that night to reconcile from a fight over me. My mother wanted me to go to college and study what I wanted and Father wanted me to prep for law school. My mom tried so hard to give me a childhood, my dad only ever wanted to make me stronger and like him. I miss them both every day and worry they wouldn't be proud of me. I'm not a lawyer, but I work in the legal system. I was so happy with you and I know my mom would have loved that. She wouldn't have wanted me to hide, but I don't know how to. I thought I killed them. I know now that it was a tragic accident, but it will take me a long time to stop those thoughts. I also know that you'll be in danger no matter if I'm in your life or not. It's our jobs."

"Slow down, baby. Take a breath. Baby, I'll do everything I can to come home to you. If you want to stay here, we will. Secret Service isn't a job to walk away from. Your parents, both of them, would be proud of you. As for Carl, he's a wanker. You do relationships very well. I didn't mean to push you."

"Duncan, honey, I'm not walking away from the Secret Service. I'll work out of their London office part-time with a new task force Greg is starting there. He asked me to consider working with him as a consultant for Securities International. Derek wants to stay my spotter and go with me. Joshua is making me an offer I can't refuse; I get to work with this amazing man that I love. Being a partner with the company is a sound investment. Plus, I can keep you from the model and beautiful girl details."

"Baby, there's only been you for me since I first saw you in full tactical gear. Today, I could have lost you. I don't ever want to go through that. I just want you forever. I love you too."

"Okay, babe, let's take a shower."

"Now that I can do." He pulls his knife from his boot and cuts the scrub top off me, then he unhooks my bra and lets it fall. "No lifting your arm." He strips my scrub pants and thong, followed by his clothes. He lifts me into his arms and carries me into the master bathroom. He places a waterproof bandage over the gauze on my chest, and bends to kiss me after it's on.

"Baby, I want to make love to you so bad but you're hurt, so I'm going to wash you up for now."

"Sure, whatever you say, honey." I smile because I'll get him to change his mind, I need him.

"Don't give me attitude."

"Oh, I'm not." I bat my eyelashes as we climb into the shower. I turn and rub my ass against his cock. He groans and holds onto my hips.

"Baby, please play fair. You're hurt."

"Duncan, please." I know he gets off on me saying that. He doesn't make me wait long.

"Lean back into me."

He trails his hands up my body and rubs my breasts, then one hand glides down my belly to my pubic area. I groan as his fingers slide over my folds. He pushes his thumb against my clit.

"I've missed touching you, feeling your skin against mine." His other hand leaves my breast, where he's pinching my nipple. He inserts a finger into me, his thumb rubs my clit and his other hand holds my hips against him.

"Duncan, please." I try to turn, but his hand holds me firm.

"This is how you're getting off for now."

"No. Duncan, it's been so long. I need your cock in me." His fingers and thumb are bringing me so close. "Duncan, Please!" I shout. He groans and turns me, then lifts me as he sits on the shower seat. I straddle him and rise up as he pushes his cock into me.

"Mmmm." We both groan.

"Baby, this is heaven. Tell me if you start to hurt, keep your arm wrapped around you. I'll do all the work."

I begin to use my knees to lift off him slowly and he starts moving slowly too.

We're staring into each other's eyes as we bring ourselves to completion. His eyes are shining with love and I hope mine are too. I love this man so much. When that gun was pointed at him, I thought I was going to lose him. All I want right now is to show him how much I love him. The slow pace and the intense looks are building us both so high.

"Let go, baby," he says, and that's all it takes.

My body starts spasming with one of the strongest orgasms I've ever felt. He groans and empties his seed so far into me. He holds me gently until we both relax. He stands and helps me stand next to him. We proceed to wash each other carefully. I hurt, but I know the pain would have been worse if I lost him.

Tears run down my cheeks as he holds me close. Between everything that happened today, my lack of sleep, and the pain, I'm emotional. I took the pain meds and know I'll sleep soon. I hope I'll be up to form soon.

"I love you, Duncan. I promise to always be with you and to be faithful to you. I want to be a part of your life." I choke out through my sobs.

"Maya, baby, I love you so much too. I don't ever want to live without you. You're my worth it." He holds me a little tighter.

# CHAPTER FORTY THREE

## DUNCAN

We're lying in bed, her in my arms. I'm glad that Joshua finally talked her into taking a pain pill. Her breakdown in the bathroom ripped me to the core. I never want to see my girl cry like that again. She's so slight against me, soft to my hard, her strength astounds me every day.

I keep replaying the fight in my head. I can hardly breathe she's got me so tied up. When she left me after New Year's, I thought I'd die, but today was even worse. I remember the first time I saw her in that tactical gear, I wanted to get to know her. Then the first time I saw her get off that motorcycle I knew I wanted to spend the rest of my life between her beautiful thighs. I thanked God above I was going to get to know her.

I feel the blood coagulate in my body thinking of living without her. I need to get Jonathon away from her and Ana. I'm going to be an uncle. I think of Joshua kneeling in front of Ana, vowing to protect her. I've known him for many years, he never makes promises about safety. Maybe he's finally forgotten his Angel.

Watching my baby spank down Ian will be a memory of my life. What a day. My phone beeps on the nightstand.

***Jonathon: Hold her close, cause I'm going to take her away from you just like you took my wife. They'll both be ours before the sun rises.***

"Bloody motherfucker." I groan. Maya bolts awake and cries out as she pulls her ribs. Damn I need to calm myself.

***Me: You will die, you bloody wanker.***

***Jonathon: You and those men can't protect them. Ask your sister what I'm capable of.***

***Me: Come get them, wanker. I've plenty of bullets and my friends are better than yours.***

"He's taunting you now? He threatened to kill you before too." She murmurs next to me.

We both get up and dress. I help her get into a bra and t-shirt and yoga pants. She looks so tired and in pain. We head to the dining room where Timothy is doing work, and I hand him both of our phones. How does he know she and I were in bed together? There's some way he's getting information.

"The fucktard is texting me. Run those feeds of the cameras in the area and see if anyone else is piggybacking our feed."

Just then Maya's phone rings. It's the fucktard.

"Answer it, Maya," Timothy says as Joshua walks in.

MAYA

I slide my finger across the display and put it on speakerphone.

"Hey, fucker, you're up early."

"So are you, cunt. Where's my wife?"

"Not sure. Maybe dancing with a singing Elvis in Vegas."

"You have six hours to give me my wife, and make sure she brings those files with her, or someone will die."

"Dude, I don't know what you mean."

"Maya, Ana told me enough about you. I know you feel responsible for your parents' deaths. You don't want Ana and Duncan to feel that pain. You'll bring her to the Washington Memorial in six hours or I won't be responsible for what happens."

"Look, dickhead, you go right ahead and threaten because that's all you got. I'm not afraid of you."

"How about that partner of yours, want to lose him? Or maybe his father?"

"Nope, keep guessing."

"How about Duncan? Don't you snipers say that people die before they know you're there?"

Just then, there's a crash and glass breaking in the living room. I look over as Duncan pushes me down and lies on top of me. I look to where Derek was sleeping on the sofa. Please, not him.

"I'm okay, don't worry," Derek calls from the living room.

"That would be a friend leaving a calling card, goodbye, Maya. Oh and the same to whoever else is listening in, maybe Joshua. Josh, maybe you should ask Ana about the last time I caught you near her." He hangs up and we all turn to Joshua, who's fuming.

Duncan rises and pulls me up to him. We step into the living room and find Derek already looking for evidence.

"I was asleep on the couch when the window blew out."

"That's it! You have a private jet?" I look at Joshua and he nods. "Get them out of here. I'll take care of what I can from here."

"No, Maya, I'm not leaving you," Duncan says from behind me.

"Duncan, I need you to get on that plane. You heard him, he won't hurt me. Take Derek and go. I can do this by myself. Get Ana and James to safety, he won't hurt me. I can finish this now. I'll meet him at the Washington Memorial but not how he expects."

"I'll not leave you again, Maya. You're my life. We do this together as a team." He pulls me into his arms and holds me to him.

"Listen here, Maya, I won't leave you either. You're my family and my partner. Dad would never forgive me if I allowed something to happen to you too. Besides, you don't put someone in your cross hairs without me, remember. You're not alone anymore, all of these people are here for you too," Derek says as he walks up to Duncan and me. I reach out and take his hand too.

"Okay, then I spent some money on a piece of property and made sure my name wasn't on it or could be linked to me. I bought it through a different solicitor. I'll explain more when we figure out how he knew you were here." I point to Joshua. "I'll resign tomorrow, Joshua. Then we're going somewhere safe for Ana and her baby. What do you say, partner?"

"I say stop talking so cryptically. What do you mean by all that?"

"Maya, are you sure about this?" Duncan asks as he turns me into his arms.

"I purchased a vacation residence. Duncan, I'm very sure of this."

"Give me the address of your purchase and we will run it," Joshua says.

I turn to him and look around the room. The commotion woke up Ana, who's standing next to Duncan and me. Trust is hard but these men would die for Ana and Duncan, who's the snitch?

"Not until you tell me how he knew you were here. Plus, what was that crap about Ana being around you." Ana gasps beside me and starts fidgeting with her hair.

"Timothy's been running a sweep on everyone for surveillance equipment. Ana is the only one left. Although he'd have heard her say she's pregnant. Do you trust everyone in this room? How about the doorman?"

"All good questions. I do trust you all, and Derek has already proved himself to me. He and I are a family, so there's no doubt I trust him. George, the doorman, now that's an excellent question. I've been wondering about him for a while. I've had visitors allowed up here without me giving permission. He's also peeved off that you didn't identify all the guys. Furthermore, he just started driving a real nice car. I turned him into the condo association back in December. Plus we've never figured out how my security codes were bypassed until you installed a new system. He has to be the snitch."

"He also said he didn't see the guy from the garage when I knew he'd passed right by him," Duncan says.

"Duncan was right. Someone was piggybacking our feeds on the cameras in the area. Maya's place is under surveillance. Ana has a tracker on her shoe, but no sound equipment. We need to get out of here, we're sitting ducks," Timothy interrupts.

"First things first, let me take care of Jonathon's sniper. Then have the guys take care of George."

"Are you sure the sniper is still there?" Joshua asks.

"I'd be, plus Jonathon wouldn't have threatened if he were just playing around. Although, I don't think this sniper is a rock solid professional. I'd have never shown my hand regardless of what Jonathon thinks. I can find him now and he'll die. Honey, I need my gun. Derek, we'll use infrared and night vision. If this is the guy from London, I can take him. I let Carl think he's the better shot in college and on the team. If this is him, he'll see the error of his ways. Text Dad and let him know we're playing. Let's go dark, brother."

"Wait, you can't do this, baby. Your shoulder and ribs."

"I have no choice and I'll be as careful as I can. This is a game of patience and I'm usually the best at it. Derek, get the .50 cal ready also for you to shoot if we need it."

"On it, sexy, going dark. Let's play kids." He always gets into a mood when we do this.

# CHAPTER FORTY-FOUR

## MAYA

Derek and Duncan get the apartment ready. I'm getting down on the floor by the kitchen entrance, across the condo from the windows, when Duncan walks up with a sleeping bag and the pillows from my bed. He also has the tactical vest he bought me for Christmas. He helps me into it, cinching it up as carefully as he can.

Based on where the bullet hit, and even though my windows are almost to the floor, I need to put some distance between me and the windows to get a better aim. My condo being on the twelfth floor gives me the height advantage. I also have access to a private roof, but I don't want to expose us that much. I lie on the sleeping bag and Duncan puts the pillows around me. I've changed into all black under my tactical vest, even though it killed me to do it. The pain meds have worn off, so I'm at full functionality.

Joshua and Ana are by the entrance to Derek's room. Tim is in the dining room to my left. I had the guys flip my heavy table so he can barricade behind it. Ian and Raul are on the street. Timothy has all our coms linked.

Derek and Duncan lie on each side of me and are going to help with spotting. They're also in black with tactical body armor on. Derek has my .50 cal ready if we need it. He likes to shoot it, and in my condition, I won't be able to handle the recoil of it. Tim has the remote for the blinds and the guys on the ground are all ears.

"Joshua, should we contact the authorities to let them know what's going on? Derek let Greg know, but should we also call the police." I need to know because I'm technically the authorities and the private company here.

"I've contacted all the attorneys. I'll contact the authorities after you do this. Our first priority is protecting Ana." I see him pull her into the shadows more.

We open all the blinds, the one that took the bullet functions slower. It's delaying our search. I start doing the calculations in my head and have a good idea where the shooter is. Sure enough, I find him. Motherfucker!

"Son of a bitch! Derek, Duncan, back off into the kitchen, behind the counter. We won't need the .50 cal, I can take him with my gun." I know this shooter isn't going to shoot me, but he'll kill any man near me. "Tim unblock the blocked number for Carl from my phone, dial it, and put it on the speaker. Everyone else, stay back."

"Maya, I'm not leaving your side." Duncan is angry, he thinks the sniper spotted me.

"Duncan, honey, he hasn't spotted me yet and he won't hurt me. You, on the other hand, he'll try to kill. Please do as I say, don't disturb anything, because if he has infrared, he'll have us all in about 30 seconds." The call connects to the speaker.

Very carefully, I lie further down, flattening myself out more. I've got him and I know I can't kill him, but I'll make him sorry for doing this. After four rings, he picks up. I watch him in my scope as he answers. He still hasn't spotted me. He's scoping the room looking for the others.

"My love, I knew you'd call me. I don't want to hurt your friends or you again, but I will if you don't come back to me. You took my job and life away from me. I want it back, and if I have to kill them or you, I will."

"Carl, I'm not your love. I'll never go back to you. Don't do this, I don't want to kill you, but I will. You lost your job because you're a loose cannon. Did you kill your partner?"

"He was going to tell you everything. I had to stop him. As for your sugar daddy, I would have killed him if he hadn't turned. I'm not going to kill you quickly; I'm going to make you suffer. Here is an example of my anger right now. I think I could take care of that English guy that flew in on the private jet." I can't look over or take my eyes from him. He just sealed his fate.

"Don't threaten my family again, Carl."

"Love, I want that fucking money and I want what you took from me. If you'd listened to me after Jonathon had that idiot deliver those flowers in London, we wouldn't be here. Jonathon says the money is his and he says there's way more than what you actually have."

"That money isn't yours, it was my family's. If something happens to me you won't be able to touch it. As of right now, I gave it to someone else. Last warning, Carl, stand down."

"Maya, you're good, but you don't even know where to look for me. Why did you open the blinds? Trying to make it easy for me? You never were as good as me, girly. I've been watching you in my shadow for years. I was never really interested in you, but Sir wanted me to control you."

"Girly? Carl, did you hire the guys that have attacked me? Were you the one in London? You were never in my league. Again, last warning. I don't want to kill you, but I will." I ignore the part about him being put in my life. I'm going to make him miserable.

"If you hadn't distracted Duncan, I'd have had him. As for the men that attacked you, I was one of them. I wish I had hit you harder. Maybe I should've used that knife of yours on you instead of your door. I've been in that condo of yours. Do you know how easy it would've been for me to rape you that night?"

"Okay, that's all I needed to know. Nice knowing you, Carl." I nod to Tim to end the call.

"Joshua, you and Ana step back further into the hall."

"Baby, please talk to me," Duncan says from behind me. Derek pulled him back behind the counter. Derek knows Carl will kill.

"Get back, Duncan. I'll tell you what's going on in a second, must shoot someone now. He'll spot me in about ten seconds."

"No, baby, please." My gun fires, I groan from the light recoil, and the room explodes with movement.

The glass didn't blow this time, as I went through the same pane as Carl had earlier. Duncan is jumping to my side and Derek is in motion to cover me also. Both of them are over me, but I keep Carl in my sights until my team is safe.

"Ian, a block over, there's a parking garage, you'll find a guy with a broken gun. He also has a bullet in his shoulder. His name is Carl Nelson, he needs to be taken into custody; he killed a police officer."

"What?" Both Ana and Duncan exclaim at the same time.

"Duncan, you heard him, he's the one that shot at us in London, he shot David, killed an ERT officer, and threatened to rape me. He also helped hire the men that attacked us today and the guy from the gym. He tried to beat me up at your flat. I knew there was something about that girly comment. Carl used to call me girly and say, 'a girly can't out shoot him.' Ana, you know why he wants me. He confirmed that all these men are connected."

"Baby, you didn't kill him?" Duncan exclaims.

"No, he isn't worth it. Plus, he's only doing this because he wants my money. That's the only reason he dated me in college. He was focusing on the back, trying to shoot Joshua. He was getting ready to take the shot, so I took out his shoulder and gun. It was the best shot I had other than a head shot."

"What did he mean by your money?" I knew this question was going to come soon enough.

"We can't stay here any longer. Joshua, let's get this group into a hotel until our meetings later today." Joshua has his arm around Ana. Duncan knows I changed the subject.

"Baby, are you okay?" I lower my head now that I see Ian and Raul take Carl into custody. I'm so confused by all this. How did he know about the amount of money? Why does he think there's more? I'm rich, but the way he's talking makes it sound like Donald Trump wealthy.

"Duncan, he knew about you. He'd have killed you because he sees you as a threat to what he felt was his money. I'll explain more in a second. Close the blinds, Tim." Duncan helps me off the floor and secures my gun. I can do this, I look at Ana, and she walks to me, taking my hand.

"You can do this, Maya. He'll not react as others have in the past." She knows me so well.

"What's going on, Maya? I know about your money, but you're acting like there's something more with this money." Duncan is starting to get angry. Joshua walks up to him and nods too.

"Big Guy, just listen to her."

"First, we need to arrange a secure hotel for tonight. Second, we need to arrange for flying into Scotland. I bought an estate there with barns and cottages, plus a large manor house. I have workers there already doing construction on it and remodeling what needs to be done. We can secure it and I'll be able to see anyone coming. Joshua, as for the partnership, we're opening a second location in Scotland. I can finance everything now. Greg helped me bury the ownership."

Joshua nods again and looks to Duncan. The waves of anger coming off Duncan are similar to the waves of indecision coming from me. Can he handle this? I told him I was rich but not how rich.

"How can you finance this?" Duncan asks

"Duncan, I have to tell you something. This is the last secret, the rest of you can hear it. Ana already knows. Derek, I haven't told you or your father completely either. I'm wealthy, not like I won't have to worry about working for a year or two, but more like our great-grandchildren will never have to worry. Duncan, I wanted to tell you, but I didn't know how after Carl. I didn't know how to trust someone with it. It was blood money to me for so long, I only got it after everyone I loved died. Your father helped invest it and it just kept increasing. Savta was so worried about the Nazis that she just kept amassing property, art, and money. She was never going back to a concentration camp if she could help it. Do you understand? A few months ago, I walked away from an amazing man because I was scared. No matter how much money I have and if I spend it or not, I was alone. I don't want to be alone anymore. I live in the dark and I'm tired of it. I'm sick of being a monster. This money will take care of all of us, that's what my parents and Savta would want. The solicitor I visited in December said it would take him years to find all of Savta's properties throughout the world. You're it for me and I don't want to stop saying that. Ana's baby, Ana, James, Derek, Greg, Joshua, and the guys even, they're all my family now. I was looking through that scope and realized who was on the other end of that gun. I realized I don't want to hide my heart or my life anymore. I want you, Duncan. I want our great-grandchildren to have my money if you'll still have me."

"Oh God, baby, there hasn't been a day in nine months and there will never be a day I don't want you. I don't care about the money except that it would help us. That's hard to top though, so here goes..."

He lowers to his knee in front of me and pulls a ring from his pocket. "I bought this in December when I bought your bracelet. I knew you were my forever girl back then. You know me like no one else. You know about the nightmares I fight and jealousy I can't hide. That's why I kept pushing you. This was burning a hole in my pocket. I needed to claim you and all you wanted to do was run. I'll always follow you. No more running. I love you and would give my life for you, please marry me, baby."

"Really? Already? It's so soon, isn't it?"

"Maya, baby, I don't care, I just want you. It doesn't have to be tomorrow or next month, just when you're ready."

"Okay...yes!" He puts the ring on my finger, stands and kisses me.

The ring is a beautiful platinum band that divides with a large solitaire diamond over the narrow space the bands made. More diamonds are lining both of the separate groups. It's not too large and it's something I love.

The room erupts in applause as Ian and Raul walk in. They turned

Carl over to the authorities, just another problem I'll have to answer for tomorrow. Ian has a strange look on his face but then smiles. The authorities also took care of George.

"Way to go, mate. Bought time you claimed this lassie." Everyone walks over to hug us and congratulate us.

# CHAPTER FORTY-FIVE

## MAYA

Tim interrupts the congratulations, "Okay I got us a couple suites at a nearby hotel. With both Maya's truck and Derek's car, we should all fit. Maya, I have a moving service set up to come pack your home tonight. They'll ship your stuff to Ireland via Paris to throw off anyone. I have a second aircraft set up in Paris while our jet heads to Australia. As for your vehicles, they'll take a little longer, but I'll put them in storage for a while. Anything else?"

"What about our motorcycles?" Derek asks. Of course he'd worry about his girl.

"They'll go into storage with the cars." Tim smiles at him.

"Okay, works for me. That was fast, let's get out of here." I walk into my room and start packing a quick bag.

I check my guns and pack them to go with me now. I'll let the movers pack the rest of my stuff. My guns though are necessary. I'm trying to reach the box in my closet with the ornaments from my mom when Duncan walks in.

"Baby, let me get that, what's in it?"

"Some personal stuff I need to have with me," I say quietly.

"What, baby?"

"It's the ornaments. Can you also grab that second box? It's my mother and father's belongings I kept."

"Speaking of..." He walks to his bag and pulls out the angel he got me for Christmas. I smile and put it in the box with the rest. "She's been with me most of the time the last three months. I had to steal her from Joshua's office."

"What? Why?"

"He thought removing everything that reminded me of you would help me wait you out. It would also throw off your stalker that I gave up."

"Did it work?"

"Not a day went by that I didn't think of you. Your stalker also still threatened me."

"Same here, I'd run on my treadmill and see you when I looked out my windows. You went with me everywhere."

"I love you, baby."

"I love you too."

We load up in the vehicles to head to the hotel. Joshua, Ana, Duncan, and Ian ride with me. I drive again as Duncan doesn't know D.C. that well. Derek has the rest of the team with him in his Charger.

We avoid the new doorman so he can't tell anyone where we're going. Just in case. Derek and I decided to take two different directions to the hotel in hope that if we have a tail they'd not know who to follow. We left all our cell phones and the bug that was attached to Ana at the condo.

When we arrive at the hotel, Greg is waiting for us. I knew he wouldn't be able to wait until our meeting. He'll try to go with us now, but because of his job, he won't be able to.

Greg helped us get adjoining suites and even had a bag with him to stay with us. He used his Secret Service badge to get our rooms under an alias and I was able to pay cash. The first suite will have Duncan and me in the king bed with Ana in the queen and Joshua on the pullout. The second is for all the guys and they get to determine sleeping arrangements.

Derek, Greg, and I sit down and talk calmly about the future. They'll go with Joshua and me in the morning. I stand and hug both of them, they've become so much to me. Without Derek, I don't know where I'd be, we've been through so much.

"Sexy, it was nice to see you finally show Carl up. All those times you let him win and tonight you actually showed him what you could do. I'm proud of you. You're family and have been for many years, I'm not worried about tomorrow or the next days. Okay?"

"Derek, I'm taking you away from everything you know. Are you sure you want to do this?"

"Yes, I can't let my sister go off with a group and not want to protect her too."

"I'll go along for as long as I can. I'm due a vacation off the grid. Besides, I need to get to know this man who intends to marry you." Greg says as he smiles at me. I kiss his cheek.

"Thank you both, I love you."

"Derek, Greg, I'll protect her with my life," Duncan says from behind me. They look over my shoulder to him.

"I know, Big Guy. I want to get away from everything here. I need it. I can't live my life every day to remember them. They'll always have a piece of my heart, but I need to learn to live again. Tomorrow, after our meeting, I'll go say goodbye and finally start a new life like they'd have wanted. They'll always be with me here"—Derek taps his heart —"but I need to get on with my life finally. Watching Maya has helped me see how much I don't live." I love him so much. I hug him close to me again.

"I'm moving to London to take over the new task force there. I need to get away from here too. Thank you, Maya, for showing Derek how to live. Duncan, thank you for teaching her how to live." Greg says as he takes both Derek and me in his arms.

"Tomorrow, I'll go with you," I say to Derek. He looks at me surprised, in all our years together I've never gone to their graveside. I only blow kisses to my parents when I'm in Tel Aviv. I don't do cemeteries, but for him, I'll try. He's my brother. We both look at Greg and he shakes his head. He won't go with us, but he's happy that I'm going with Derek.

Our meeting with the superiors is at 10:00 a.m. so we decide to take a nap while the others relax until the meeting.

Duncan and I disagreed about him coming to the station with me. Finally, Joshua talked him into staying with Ana while he came with me. I see that Duncan is afraid to let me out of his sight, but I just can't let him hold me too tight. Even though I'll marry him and I love him, I need to be me. I'm strong, independent, and not afraid to love him anymore.

"You know that he's going to be climbing the walls before we get back, don't you?" Joshua asks.

"Yep, he'll be, but he needs to let me have some space once in a while."

"It's not about space, Maya, it's about him almost losing you yesterday. It's going to take him a while to not feel protective of you."

"How do you know?"

"Experience. Someday we'll discuss my past. Not today though, let's get this over with." I know he's partially talking about his Angel, but the rest I don't know.

We pull up in front of the station and I straighten my clothes. I wore a simple double-breasted pants suit in black, with my gun in its holster on my hip. All the guys are wearing different suits. Joshua is wearing a dark suit with a tie, Derek is in a suit with a vest and tie, and Greg is in his standard black suit. We all look very striking and sure of ourselves.

Joshua assured Derek and I this was what we needed to project so this would be easier for us. I turn to see Derek sitting behind me looking like I feel. I remember the day we signed up, our graduation, and the day we finally became partners. I know this will be the last time I walk through those doors.

"Officer Aaron, Officer Williams, your union rep is waiting for you in Conference Room One with the chief. Officer Aaron, a delivery was left for you, I put it in the meeting room too." I nod to the officer at the door.

Joshua, Derek, and I walk down the hall to the conference room. Greg stays back because of the conflict of interest with Derek. Joshua looks at me, knowing that the delivery isn't going to be good. We walk into the conference room and I see the bouquet of yellow carnations and the card. I walk over and lift the card carefully, using the sleeve of my jacket so I don't leave prints.

*Yellow carnations for the disappointment I feel toward you. No man but me will have you. I couldn't have your mother, but I will have you.*

*Love always,*

*Sir*

Before I can react to the card, my chief and the union rep walk into the conference room. The chief knows what's been going on, so he calls for a tech to come in and take the offensive note and bouquet from the room. I feel rattled and worried I won't be able to go through with this. I love Duncan and want to be with him, but I worry about the danger we're all in now.

"Officer Aaron, Officer Williams, please have a seat. Who's this?" My chief asks after the tech leaves.

"This is Joshua Donovan, he's one of the owners of Securities International." Derek and I sit across from them with Joshua standing behind us. I feel like we're in trouble, although I know we didn't do anything wrong.

"Officer Aaron, can I ask why Mr. Donovan is here?"

"I'm here to represent my business partner and to support her in this situation. Furthermore, Mr. Williams works for both of us too." Joshua states.

"Officer Aaron, was acting on your behalf yesterday?"

"Yes. I believe she spoke to you already about resigning to take a more permanent position with our company. By my investigation, Maya represented all parties fully and only acted with deadly force when was necessary. Derek did nothing wrong but support his partner and boss."

"After speaking with Mr. Nelson and searching his apartment, we have determined he's been following you for a while. With the confession you turned over and the evidence of his behavior, he confirmed that he was hired to shoot Duncan Preston and Officer Williams, but not who hired him. We're confident that he will tell us. He also confirmed that he was working with a Jonathon Davidson. We have also found out that Mr. Nelson hired the men that were killed and taken into custody yesterday. Interpol along with the London authorities have been contacted. The Philly police have cleared you and Duncan Preston, although they're still trying to identify the perps that attacked you and Mrs. Davidson. Officer Aaron, you're clear of any charges. Are you sure you want to leave? You and Officer Williams have been an asset to the Secret Service and us."

"Well Chief, I really appreciate you clearing my name and I thank you for everything you've done for me, but this is my next step. I know that working with Joshua will allow me to protect my family and myself from this stalker, and help with stopping terrorism." I shake their hands and unclip my badge, then I pull my sidearm, drop the mag, and clear the chamber. I set them all down on the table and nod my head at them. "Thank you. Here is my resignation letter, effective immediately." I set it down.

"Here is my letter too," Derek says as he stands and does the same. We both walk out with Joshua and Greg flanking me.

*Okay, Mom, Abba, here I go, help me!* I whisper the prayer to myself and take a deep breath.

"Welcome, partner! Welcome to the family!" Joshua puts his arm around my shoulder and we walk from the precinct. I look over and take Derek's hand as Greg steps back so we can share this moment. This was just as hard on him if not even more so.

"Are you sure about this, Derek?"

"Yeah, sexy. I'm tired of feeling like I'm in a losing battle."

"I agree with him too," Greg says.

As we're walking to my truck, I see a commotion to the left of the precinct. They're moving Carl to a van and he looks my way. All of the sudden I see him drop, the side of his head gone and hear the report of the gun echoing around the building. Joshua is pushing me down and on top of me before I can do anything.

Derek has pulled his backup and is looking around, lying next to us on the ground too. Greg has pulled his cell and gun, he calls for support as he covers me too. Carl was just taken out by a sniper. What the hell?

Joshua grabs my keys, jumps up, and pushes me into the truck. Derek and Greg jump into the back. Both are still on watch, looking for the shooter.

"These are bullet proof windows, right?" Joshua asks as he points to my windows.

"Yes, what the hell just happened?" I know I'm in shock. I stop and take a deep breath and start doing the process. "Shooter is about three blocks away or more from the fact the sound was delayed. I'd say this is a true professional, unlike Carl. Any ideas?"

"I think Jonathon's boss is cleaning up, what do you say?"

"Same. We better get out of here before they come asking us questions. Know how to get back to the hotel?" He nods and heads us back to the hotel.

From the back seat I see Derek pulling a scope from the seat pocket and looking around. We can't stay in the open, but we want to know more. That's when I realize.

"Joshua, we missed Jonathon's deadline."

"Yes we did, time to get out of here. You and Duncan take Derek where he needs to go, and we'll get to the airport."

We head back to the hotel and sure enough, I walk into Duncan pacing the area. I walk right into his arms. I need the assurance of his love now and he needs to know I don't regret my decision.

"I was cleared. The Philly police are dropping all charges against us too. Carl was shot by a sniper as we were leaving the precinct," I say into his chest.

"What? Are you okay, baby?"

"My shoulder and ribs are hurting from where Joshua pushed me to the pavement, but other than that I'm fine. A little confused. There was also a delivery to the precinct, they took the card."

"He was shot right in front of you?"

"They were moving him just as we were walking out."

"What're your thoughts, Joshua?" Duncan says over my head, still holding me to him.

"Like I told her, I think Jonathon's boss is cleaning up."

"I agree. Maya, are you sure about resigning?"

"I've never been more sure of anything. I want you, and besides your father's been trying to get me to move to London for years now." I smile at him. "Secret Service wants me to help in situations in London, so I didn't fully resign from them. Right, Greg?"

"That's right, sweetheart. I'm going to get some final details taken care of with the house. I'll fly over with you all and I'll start my job next month as planned. Is that okay with all of you?"

"Yes, you're welcome to come with us. I'd love to try to beat you at poker finally," Joshua replies, and we all laugh.

"I love you, baby," Duncan says as he gently picks me up and carries me into our room. As he lays me on the bed, I start to remove my clothes.

"Please, Duncan." I smile at him.

"Baby, I'm still afraid of hurting you. I want to hold you right now. Please?"

"Okay, for now." I pull my shirt back on. We lie in bed, our arms and legs entwined. "My stalker threatened you again. Are you sure you want to be a part of this? According to 'Sir', because he couldn't have my mother, he wants me. I don't understand any of this."

"Baby, I want you—stalker, defiance and all," he whispers against the top of my head.

DUNCAN

Maya, Derek, and I are at Rock Creek Cemetery. Derek is standing by a gravestone with an Angel bowed down kneeling over it. I see his last name with two more names below it. Maya and I walk up behind him when his head bows and his shoulders shake. She pulls from my grasp and walks to him, hugging him to her.

"Derek, it's okay if you want to stay, I'll understand, they've been with you for so long."

"No, Maya, it's time. I love them and will never stop, but I can't get over them if I'm here with them or they're this close."

"Only if you're okay. We can fly you back here if you need to come back."

"I already set up for the groundskeeper to take care of everything. Her mother will bring flowers for me. It's time."

"Yes, it's time." She pulls away and I see how devastated he is.

I know I'd be this way if I lost Maya. I look at the stone and see the names: Lisa and Baby Boy Williams. She was only twenty and the baby never made it. My gut twists when I realize what this man carries with him every day. I pat him on the shoulder.

"Listen, brother, I'll make sure that every month flowers are delivered and Joshua will fly you back on Christmas Eve if you need too."

"Thank you, Duncan. Thank you for giving my girl here a chance to live and giving me a reason to start over."

"Anything, you're family now."

"Okay, time to go." He bends down, kisses his fingers and places them on the stone. "Goodbye my love, you'll always be in my heart, but it's time for me to try to live." He turns and grabs Maya's right hand, I have my arm around her, and we walk back to her truck.

We pull up to the private airstrip just as an SUV rental pulls up. Joshua and Ana get out with the rest of the team and Greg. I'm glad he's coming with us. Maybe we can talk him into staying so he's not in danger. I know that Maya would never forgive herself if something happened to him too.

"Time to cross the pond, kiddies," Ian says with a smile.

We board the plane and head for our future. I know that Maya's stalker won't stop and I know that I need to protect my sister now more than ever. I look forward to my future with my family, always remembering Christopher's dying words.

*It was worth it.*

Maya, Ana, Father, and my team are worth it. I look down at the beautiful woman next to me and know I'll always protect her, but she's strong enough to protect herself too.

# EPILOGUE

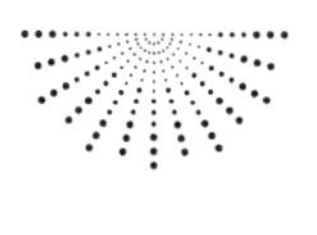

## MAYA

TWO MONTHS LATER

DUNDEE, SCOTLAND

It's May in the Highlands; I love it here in Scotland. The rolling green hills, fields, and lochs are something I think I've needed for a long time. They soothe my soul. My nightmares still come but not as often. I have Duncan to help me through them, just like I help him with his.

The main house is finished with its reconstruction. I took an extended leave from the Secret Service to protect Ana. Greg headed back to London last month to start his new job. We've decided to wait until after Ana's baby is born to get married.

My condo sold, my belongings are here, and our vehicles arrived today. Derek was so excited to see his girl, he took off for a long ride. My life feels complete except for the crap with Jonathon and my stalker. A week after we left D.C., a note with a bouquet of white Myrtle flowers showed up at Greg's Secret Service Division office in

D.C. I knew this was from someone that knew my mother very well, as they were the only flowers my father gave her every year on their anniversary.

*Maya, I'd guess that you're sick of flowers, but I needed to get your attention. I'll protect you with my very life if I must. Carl was an easy kill for me, he would've eventually come after you. Stay away and stay safe. I miss your mother every day.*

*Always,*

*Your protector*

I have no clue who it could be or what they mean, but I'll take their advice. I'll protect my family, and if a stranger wants to help me, I'll let them.

None of the charges from the U.S. incident has stuck yet on Jonathon or anyone else for that matter. We weren't followed to Scotland, but no one from London could go get his or her belongings.

Carl's murder is still under investigation with no leads. Joshua and I have become partners and are working on making a full-service security company. He and I regularly practice our knife skills, and the other guys are afraid of Duncan, so they don't fight me.

Derek is settling in with the team. I see him walking around a lot and worry he misses D.C., but he assures me he's fine. I hope someday for him to find what I have with Duncan. I know that love can never be replaced, but hope he'll learn to love again. He and Raul have become fast friends and ride dirt bikes around the property a lot. He's also formed a bond with Ana. I still watch Joshua around Ana, one day they'll figure out the other knows who they are and that they still care. I knock on Ana's door now. She's been acting strange for a while now.

"Ana, let me in."

"Come in, Maya," she says with a sigh.

"The crews are working on your cottage now. You'll have your own place soon. Please talk to me, what's going on?"

"Maya, do you believe in fate?"

"Yes, I wouldn't have Duncan if I didn't. Without knowing you, our moms started this, it was fate."

"Maya, please don't freak out."

"Okay."

"Joshua is Lieutenant."

"I know, I figured it out in December. You're his Angel."

"Yes."

"What happened in December that changed everything?"

"I realized I was still in love with him. I don't think he remembers me from all those years ago. That day we had lunch was the first time I'd seen him since our day. I missed him so much."

"He does remember you, he's giving you space and time, Ana. I'm pretty sure he still loves you too."

"You've talked to him?"

"No, not really, just call it intuition."

"What should I do?"

"Relax and cook that baby. If it's meant to be, it will happen."

"Okay."

Guess they're going to figure it out sooner rather than later. I know I shouldn't meddle, but I want Ana to learn to love and trust again too. I think I'm becoming a hopeless romantic.

I head to my room where Duncan is getting ready to step into the shower after a run.

"Want to join me, baby?" He's still so cautious with me.

"Hell, yes!" I strip down and climb in with him. I've barely cleared the lip of the shower when he picks me up and presses me against the wall. I wrap my legs around him.

"I love you, Maya, but this isn't going to be something sweet, I need you real bad."

"Good, no more kid gloves. Please, Duncan." He reaches between us to feel my wetness and kisses me.

"Baby are you always so wet?"

"Only for you, Duncan, my love." He presses into me as I push down onto his cock.

My head falls back against the wall and I'm already ready to climax. He leans into me, kissing my throat and dragging his teeth along it. He then bends down to suck a nipple into his mouth. He's pushing in and out of me, the dual points drive me closer.

"Duncan, honey, I'm going to come. Duncan, please."

"That's all I wanted to hear." He starts pushing me down harder onto him and bites onto my nipple. I explode around him, I hear him groan and feel him coming inside me.

"Duncan, I love you."

"Maya, I love you too. Have you thought about our conversation from last night?"

"No, Duncan, I have not." I know it's a little white lie, but I can't think about bringing a baby into this situation. He wants us to start trying after the wedding, but I fear bringing another child into our group could be dangerous. I still have my fears and insecurities, but I'm learning.

"Maya, just think about it. We don't have to try right away. Next time, just please tell me the truth."

"What?"

"I can tell when you're lying to me. I love you. I can wait to have children."

"I love you too. I promise I'll think about it. I'm just afraid of us leaving a child behind."

"I'll protect you and any of our kids to my dying breath."

"See, that's what I mean." I laugh at him.

He pulls out of me and we finish showering, washing each other off. We head to the bedroom where we again practice making a baby without trying. I'll die for this man and any child we have together, just as I'll die for Ana's baby.

I curl up to him and think about how wonderful my life is and how much I want to give him a child. A son. For the first time in years, I dream of a happy future with a dark haired little boy running through the fields.

"It has been said, 'time heals all wounds'. I do not agree. The wounds remain. In time, the mind, protecting its sanity, covers them with scar tissue and the pain lessons. But it is never gone."
Rose Kennedy

# ABOUT THE AUTHOR

E.M. Shue took her passion for reading and turned it into a story. This series was started with a dream, she woke up one morning and knew that she needed to explore the idea. After lots of hounding from her husband, she put to paper her thoughts. Maya and Duncan came from that dream, but a story that is still guiding her continues.

E.M. has an extensive history of different jobs and careers which she brings to her writing giving it a more authentic feel from medical, fire and rescue to travel and sales. The research has become one of her favorite parts of the preparation of writing. She wants her readers to feel immersed in the world around them and to understand every piece of equipment used.

E.M. has lived in Alaska most of her life and counts it as her home even though she was born in South West Michigan. She's a Red Wings fan and adores all things hockey. Her house is always full of activity from either her fun-loving truck driver husband, her two daughters that still live at home, her oldest daughter and husband, her three wild dogs and all the extra add-ons that come to hang out or just stop by. Her table is always opened to the stray kids that call her mom, and her middle daughter has usually cooked up something yummy. The family loves to just jump in the car and take the six-hour drive to Fairbanks to visit friends and relatives or the journey south to explore the coastal communities. Currently, E.M. works part-time and writes full time. Trying to spend time with her youngest who is still in high school and wants to be a writer too or her middle daughter that struggles with many medical conditions. She is working on more Securities International stories.

Friends become family in this crazy world of the Shue's.

Go sign up for E.M.'s readers to keep up to date on all things Securities International. Head over to www.authoremshue.com for details.

Other reads by E.M. Shue

**SECURITIES INTERNATIONAL SERIES**

**Sniper's Kiss | Angel's Kiss | Love's First Kiss**

Check out www.authoremshue.com/signed-paperbacks/

# ACKNOWLEDGMENTS

To my wonderful family, without you, I wouldn't have realized my dreams finally.
My daughters Paige, Kelsey, and Daniele for all your help with edits, music, and scenes.
Thank you, Paige, for making me touch and feel the guns and knives.
To Kelsey for showing me, strength comes from within. The fights you fight every day just to get up and move astound me.
Dani, I love how you are becoming a little writer too. Plus all the music ideas were fantastic.
Anthony, my son-in-law, thank you for all the fighting advice. I know Maya wouldn't be the fighter she is without it.
To my extended family thank you for all you did for me. I can't name you all but you know who you are. You are the family I've chosen to be in my life and the ones that God has blessed me with thank you all.
To Wendy and Louie Oliva, how can someone say thank you to the people who kept believing in me when I couldn't believe in myself. You didn't need to but you did. I will always cherish our friendship. I love you both so very much.
To the Isley-Hall Family thank you for talking guns with me guys.

Kimberly thank you for having drinks with me when I needed it. Love you all!

To my mom thank you for introducing me to romance novels when I was a teenager. I love you.

Finally, the love of my life, every day you show me what true love is. You are the hardest working man I know and a wonderful example to our children. I love you more today than the day I married you. Thank you for putting up with my crazy ideas and all the support. Thank you for asking me out when the weather was bad all those years ago.